*an*
# UNLIKELY HERO

## TIERNEY JAMES

Copyright © 2013 Tierney James
All rights reserved.

ISBN: 1480276030
ISBN-13: 9781480276031

Library of Congress Control Number: 2012921450
CreateSpace Independent Publishing Platform
North Charleston, South Carolina

Dedicated to the men and women who work in the shadows so that we can remain safe from those that would do us harm.

# *Acknowledgements*

Finally I get to thank those who have pushed me to fulfill a dream that begun when I was a little girl discovering the magic of words. First I need to say thank you to Meghan Fanning for making me promise that I would not let another day go by without putting the stories in my head to paper. She became my editor and cheerleader along this bumpy road. Then there's Susie Knust, an author and a new friend, who I timidly gave a few pages of what I thought were random scribbles. Her encouragement through this process made me believe that dreams can come true. Then there's that wonderful teacher in elementary school that gave me the tools to think, dream and write. Thank you, Ms. Bonnet.

# *Chapter 1*

Sticky from the late summer night air, Jamaal meticulously continued to work on the bomb lying on the workbench. His dark hand slipped only once, causing the Libyan to suck in his breath and step back. For weeks he'd practiced in the desert of his home with others just like him learning how to make these kinds of bombs. A quick student, Jamaal had gotten the attention of one man who decided his skills needed to be put to the ultimate test. A promise of money only slightly overshadowed the reward of hurting the Americans. As his heartbeat returned to normal he once more fingered what he hoped would be a weapon of distraction. Finally Jamaal slowly removed his hands and smiled at the completion of the toy-like monster. It hadn't taken any more work than a conventional bomb, he decided.

Dynamite had been ridiculously easy to obtain from a mining company north of Nevada City which was in the process of closing. The difficult part had been securing the radioactive material. But a disgruntled hospital employee willingly provided access for Jamaal's boss to obtain the final component for the weapon before him. Various online markets sold military toys that were so life-like Jamaal wondered why Homeland Security hadn't shut them down. The secure radioactive container easily slipped inside the missile. His boss had convinced him it would be enough. Adapting his army green missile with explosives, although tricky, had not been beyond his ability. The connection to the launcher was another matter.

# AN UNLIKELY HERO

Would it adapt to carrying this small attachment now that it was heavier? For the last several hours Jamaal had trouble with the launcher turning on prematurely with the added weight. By accident he discovered if he propped it upright as if it were being held the lights failed to flash a warning of launch.

No longer would he be the butt of jokes calling him a stupid fool.

His associates would be pleased.

His reward and recognition would be great.

Only one more thing to do. Launch. Tomorrow. The first of many tomorrows.

It would be simple. Near dawn he would load the readapted toy which had been fitted with his attachment into the trunk of his car. Sacramento was less than an hour away so he wanted to leave early enough to find a good parking spot along the way. He had been monitoring traffic helicopters for weeks. He knew exactly which one would be the target. Bringing it down over a populated area where several highways merged would be child's play. The authorities would realize later something more heinous had occurred than a helicopter crashing into rush hour traffic. By then what little radioactive poison survived would throw authorities into a panic. His boss could move forward with bigger plans while the country kept eyes on Sacramento.

Jamaal yawned, realizing he'd been working since early morning without much of a break. After making sure the weapon was secure, he gently let his hands hover over the finished project and smiled once more, knowing his glory would soon be visible to the world. Backing toward the shed door he reached behind him to twist the doorknob. Even now Jamaal struggled to tear his eyes away from his creation. As the door creaked open Jamaal unwittingly paused long enough for the neighbor's cat to slip quietly into the shadows of the stacked lumber in the corner.

The light extinguished, Jamaal stepped into the night, closing the door behind him. The smell of the neighbor's freshly cut grass made him decide that would be what he missed about California. There wasn't much grass in Libya. A breeze touched his serious face as he tucked his head and made for his back door. Nearby someone had fired up a grill for a late night's dinner. He paused, hearing a dog bark and the distant laughter of men sharing something he would never understand. This country was too friendly, too trusting. He wondered in that moment if he would be able to sleep? The others had already gone to bed. Softly he called the cat that had been coming around at night. A saucer of milk each visit kept the creature returning.

The excited cry of the cat inside the shed forced Jamaal's feet to trip, sprawling him onto the damp grass. Pushing up in desperation he stumbled toward the shed hearing the clatter of obstacles the cat moved as it raced toward what he guessed was a mouse.

Something close to lightning speed touched the mouse and it was running for its life, but not before the tabby cried out and pounded on the very spot in which the small creature had tried to disappear. A roar, flashing red lights and a hissing sound imploded the room when the cat landed on the man's machine. With agile reflexes the feline leaped once more onto the floor and escaped into the corner, not noticing that the rodent was right next to him. The workbench began to vibrate and in the next instant the machine expelled a tail of fire and crashed through the windows into the night sky.

The cries of anguish from the man startled the cat into making a quick escape as the door flung open. Dogs began to bark throughout the neighborhood. Porch lights flickered on and then off as houses began to stir at the wails of a desperate man running into his backyard before collapsing to his knees.

\* \* \*

"A client, Robert! How could you?" Tessa Scott doubled her fists as they landed angrily on her hips, a stance she often took when ready to do battle. She fell wearily onto the bed, staring up at the ceiling. The day had been one mishap after another. The bleach spilled on her favorite pair of shorts. It took three hours to get the oil changed at Wal-Mart. Her two older sons got into a fistfight in front of Reverend Phillips. When she tried to break them up, her precious little girl had laughed, saying "Oh shit!" The boys had frozen at that point, looking very sheepish and innocent. To the credit of Daniel, the middle child, he switched the attention from his little sister to her. "Mom, Dad told you if you didn't stop saying that word one of us would pick it up." The good reverend could hardly contain his smile of embarrassment and graciously left them in the tire and lube waiting room of Wal-Mart.

To make matters worse the dryer was acting so sluggish that she ended up hanging their clothes that were to be packed for vacation, outside on a clothesline, only to be called by Mr. Crawley from next door who reminded her that there was a covenant in the subdivision about public displays of laundry. He emphasized a hillbilly could do that in Tennessee where she grew up, but it was unacceptable in northern California. Of course the clothes, although fresh smelling now, all needed to be ironed. She hadn't even had a shower today or looked in a mirror since 8 a.m. After heading the children off to bathtubs, Tessa had longed to crumple onto the bed to breathe. That's when Robert had come home, bounded up the stairs and jumped into the room like a twelve year old.

He held his finger to his lips and gently pulled her up as her body tried to slide back down to the bed. "I know. I know. I should have called first." Robert kissed her cheek and rubbed her back gently. "It's just dinner, sweetheart." Robert tried to disarm her with his boyish charm as he began pushing her toward the bathroom.

Tessa pushed him at arm's length. "We're leaving early tomorrow morning for Tahoe. You should've taken him out."

"He likes the domestic scene, honey, impresses him when the people around him are into family."

Tessa rolled her eyes upward then leveled a hard gaze at her husband. "Since when are you into family? You missed all but two of Sean Patrick's ballgames, the spring concert at school and Heather's third birthday party! We haven't had a night out in six months! Daniel is so glued to the computer he's beginning to think you're a virtual reality game show host!"

Robert chuckled weakly and followed her into the bathroom. "I'll fire up the grill and take a few steaks out of the cooler already packed for Tahoe. All you have to do is toss a salad, nuke a couple of potatoes and presto!" he said happily.

"Oh Robert, I'm tired," she moaned, knowing she'd lost as he pulled her into his arms tenderly.

Robert wrinkled his brow. "For Heaven sakes why? You're home all day. You just play with the kids and stuff." He released her suddenly and fled into the bedroom. "Fix yourself up a bit, will ya? You look like you've been on combat maneuvers." Robert removed his tie and eagerly left the room, whistling *You Ain't Nothin' but a Hound Dog.*"

Tessa turned to look at herself in the mirror and was shocked at how old she looked. The day, no, the years were taking their toll on her. She felt used up. Drained of energy and of life, the thirty five year old housewife wondered where her dreams had gone, her beauty, and her drive? Had she sacrificed them all for Robert's career? Did the well-being of her children crowd out any room for her own desires? The answer was simple. Yes. Tessa had become invisible as a person of distinction.

Mindlessly, Tessa turned on the shower and stripped off her grimy, bleach spotted clothes. As she stepped into the shower and let the hot water vaporize her sadness, Tessa began to form a decision. Somewhere between the peach smelling shampoo and the quickly shaved legs, Tessa turned a corner into a new life, one she had not exactly expected, but one she embraced nonetheless.

Robert swung Heather up into his tan arms and hugged her, careful never to take his eyes off Mr. Feldspar, who was rattling on and on about his son that was a quarterback for Texas A & M. He felt Heather's warm kisses on his cheek and quickly put her down so he could concentrate, regretting that once again he'd put the job first. There was nothing as important as little girl kisses and he could see in Heather's pouty mouth that she didn't understand.

As Heather skipped out of the room in her pink pajamas, Tessa strolled in as if the act had been the height of her day. Robert suddenly found himself not listening to Mr. Feldspar. He marveled at how beautiful his wife looked tonight and vowed to tell her later, if he didn't fall asleep first. Even though she'd put on a few pounds since Heather was born, Tessa still looked good in a pair of black slacks and that ivory tunic she sometimes wore. He saw the same pouty mouth that she'd given to Heather and forced himself to tear his eyes away as he interrupted the client.

"Mr. Feldspar, this is Tessa, my better half." Robert slightly brushed against her elbow as she outstretched her slim fingers to entwine with Mr. Feldspar's hand. The smell of peaches in her blond hair made Robert feel a little dizzy. They continued to hold hands as Mr. Feldspar remarked on how charming her little girl was and that now he could see why. Tessa laughed lightly followed by a comment about how nice to have him come for dinner. Good old Tessa! She was always there in a pinch. Robert could tell that the client was devouring Tessa's attention like French chocolate cheesecake.

"Mom, Daniel hid my binoculars!" Ten-year-old Sean Patrick entered the room in camouflage cotton pajamas. His young body already showed signs of maturing into a rugged teenager that would probably grow into a taller man than his nearly six foot father. His dark brown hair had been streaked by the exposure of the summer sun. There was a way he narrowed his round brown eyes that made everyone sit up and take notice immediately. This child would be a commander someday, Tessa realized with pleasure. Having wanted to enter the army herself after high school, Tessa had always encouraged her son's interest in military toys, games and movies. Envisioning him at West Point or the Naval Academy was a faraway dream right now. Although her parents had forbidden her to even think about joining, Tessa promised herself if her child chose that direction no one would stand in his way. Her eyes momentarily flicked to her husband. *Not even you, Robert,* she vowed.

She smiled patiently at her oldest child. "I packed them for you, sweetheart. I knew you would want to be spying on unsuspecting tourists at the lake. Daniel is just doing another mind game on you." Gently, Tessa pulled Sean Patrick closer to her side and faced him toward Mr. Feldspar. "Sean, this is a friend of Daddy's. Mr. Feldspar's son plays football for Texas A & M."

Sean Patrick pulled back his shoulders and stuck out his hand. "Nice to meet you, sir."

"Back at ya, son." Mr. Feldspar glanced over at Robert. "Manners. Not much of that these days."

"I'll be going now, sir. Dad. Mom." Sean Patrick pivoted on his heels like he was marching to war and exited the room in a timely manner.

Tessa sighed. "Children. They make life wonderful." She turned back toward the kitchen after refilling Mr. Feldspar's tea class. After making the salad she placed three baking potatoes in the microwave. By the time she'd carried the sides to the porch where the men sat laughing a commotion broke out upstairs. The sound of a door slamming rushed through the open kitchen window followed by yells and pounding fists against some wooden surface.

"Tessa, you'd better see to the boys," Robert said nervously as he waved a hand toward the upstairs' windows.

"I think you're right. Oh, I think the steaks are ready. The grill is smoking."

As Robert retrieved the steaks from the patio grill, Tessa headed upstairs to find Sean Patrick sitting cross-legged outside the bathroom door with his arms folded. A scowl on his lips and a clenched jaw told Tessa that Daniel was now either a POW or had been forced into one of Tessa's old dresses and tied up with a pair of pantyhose.

"Sean Patrick! Report!"

"Daniel needs to pay for tricking me. He needs to learn some respect for his elders. I simply tied him up then used some of your makeup on him, then took his picture." At this he grinned. "Mission accomplished."

"Well done, major. Now release the prisoner." Tessa watched him open the door and bit her lip as her eyes fell upon her middle child. It was all she could do to keep from bursting into gales of laughter at seeing her son all rosy cheeked and ruby lipped. "Sean, untie him."

"He'll attack."

"I'll take my chances. Now move!" Tessa folded her arms as eight year old Daniel was released. Sean Patrick quickly retreated behind his mother as Daniel leveled a murderous look at his brother. "I think you boys should go to bed."

"Mom!" Daniel wailed in protest. He pointed a finger at his brother. "He…" Daniel grabbed a hand towel hanging lopsided on the sink.

"Took revenge. I know. What have we learned from this?"

Sean Patrick might be the military, but Daniel was Commander in Chief. "Always have a way out."

"Sean?"

"Run silent, run deep or you'll have to listen to your mom's psychology crap for the millionth time," he smirked.

Tessa swatted him hard on his bottom, which caused both boys to laugh and grab her tightly so she couldn't move. "I give up!" she giggled. "You better go to bed. Your father is not happy with your behavior."

"So what's new?" Sean Patrick frowned.

"He loves you very much, boys. He works very hard for us."

Daniel gave his mother one more hug. "Night, Mom. I love you."

Sean Patrick put his hands on his hips and mocked his brother in a girlish voice. "Night, Mommy, I love you." Daniel stuck out his tongue and disappeared out the door of the bathroom, wiping his face on one of Tessa's new towels. Down the hall he scampered into the room he shared with his brother.

Sean Patrick relaxed and looked up at his mother. "You look pretty, Mom." He then reached up and slipped his hand behind her neck, tugging her gently down to eye level. Whispering he said, "I love you too!" He stole a kiss then ran down the hall to his room.

Picking a towel up off the floor, Tessa caught a glimpse of herself in the mirror. Not bad, she thought. Her shoulder length blond hair had curled up enough to give it body and even in this light she could tell it was shiny. Although applied lightly, her makeup was flawless, giving her complexion a healthy glow. Maybe she wasn't so old after all. Most people didn't guess she was on the upside of thirty-five. The youthfulness in her appearance kept people imagining that she must have been a young bride and started on a family rather early. Tessa never bothered to tell them otherwise. Forty was beginning to loom on the horizon. Blessed with a cosmetic edge, Tessa wasn't about to surrender without a fight.

Pulling back her shoulders, Tessa sucked in her stomach as long as she could, hoping the extra pounds would melt away. When the air gushed out of her mouth, the stomach reappeared.

"Mommy! Mommy!" Heather's hysterical bird-like voice rose above the patter of her little sock feet in the hall. Tessa stepped out of the bathroom just in time for Heather to collide into her legs. She encircled her mother's legs and held tightly. "A long star just fell into the back-yard! I promise!" Her little curly head looked up at Tessa, eyes wide with wonder and fear. "I amn't telling' a story either, Mommy!" Heather squeezed her mother again and laid her soft cheek firmly against Tessa. Tessa couldn't help but smile at the invented word "amn't". She and Robert never allowed the word "ain't" so Heather had invented a word to replace "am not" by using "amn't". It was too adorable to correct. Then there were the imaginative stories she liked to create like a star falling in their backyard.

Tessa gently touched her precious baby on the head and paused long enough to feel the softness of Heather's long reddish brown hair. None of her children looked like her. She thought all her children would be blond and blue eyed, but they had taken the dark good looks of their father. "Did you make a wish? When you see a falling star you can."

The little girl's body relaxed as she grabbed Tessa's hand and pulled her toward her bedroom. "I get a wish? Come help me!" She began to hop and twist to the point that Tessa could hardly keep from tripping.

"Everything alright, Tessa?" Robert and Mr. Feldspar had come inside to sit at the kitchen table to escape buzzing mosquitoes. They were already making progress on their T-bone steaks and adding butter with ranch dressing to their potatoes.

"I had to help Heather make a wish on a falling star. Saw one fall in the backyard, she said." Tessa couldn't help but smile at Heather's insistence. "I don't guess you saw anything before attacking those steaks."

The men chuckled and the meal progressed leisurely without any more interruptions. The children were soon asleep and Mr. Feldspar didn't stay long after dinner, saying he still had some work to do back at the hotel before turning in for the night. He thanked the Scotts for their hospitality and took his leave.

Robert helped Tessa clear the table while chatting about the account that Mr. Feldspar would be bringing to the law firm where he'd been made a partner. It was obvious from Tessa's quiet, cool demeanor that she was going to sulk until he apologized again and focused on how special she was to him.

"I love you, Tessa." Robert tried to slip an arm around his wife but she dodged him and began wiping off the table.

"You love what I can do for you, Robert. When you love someone you see them for what they are all the time. To you I'm a playmate for the kids, and someone to cook your meals and entertain your clients, and of course, have sex with you when you want!" Tessa said sadly.

"That's not true," Robert snapped, offended that maybe she'd been partially correct and thrown it in his face. "I'm taking you on a vacation aren't I?"

Tessa stopped wiping the table and glared up at her husband of twelve years. "Some vacation. You rent a cabin. I still cook and clean and watch the kids while you fish."

"If you feel that way just stay home. I'll take the kids. How hard can it be?" he said throwing up his hands. "I'll teach them a whole lot more responsibility than you do, that's for sure. You stay home and decorate, have tea with the girls and talk about how rough you have it!" Robert wasn't aware that his voice had grown louder or that his left eye had begun to twitch with irritation.

For an instant Tessa froze, thinking of Robert taking care of the kids for two weeks without her. That was terrifying! She nearly started to apologize, then remembered the "how hard can it be" comment and decided to swallow her fear. In the calmest voice she could muster Tessa spoke. "Alright." The word sounded as if it had gone on forever; like when you call out into a canyon and you hear the echo for an eternity. "If you're sure, Robert."

Robert straightened up his hunched frame so fast it looked as if someone had slid a rod down the back of his shirt. Something like panic flashed in his eyes and he quickly tried to cover his lack of confidence, but not before Tessa saw the truth. Slowly she smiled, as she stepped toward her husband who now decided to back away from her. "I'll just lay around the house in my pjs." Her voice had taken on that southern drawl from childhood and her head slightly tilted so that the light sparked her pale blue eyes. "I'll take long baths, eat junk food all day, and call my momma twice a day."

"Humph! Just like every day!"

"That's right, Robert. I'm just another lazy housewife who doesn't have a lick of sense!"

Robert knew when her voice got deeper into that southern thing, he'd cooked his goose. The thought occurred to him that maybe he'd bitten off more than he could chew. If only he hadn't offered to let her stay home. He almost begged her to come along but thought better of it when he jerked up his chin in defiance. "It'll be great to get to be mom and dad to the kids. They'll probably remember this vacation forever!" he bragged nervously.

Tessa chuckled wickedly as she threw her towel in the sink and brushed past him. "I think truer words were never spoken, Robert."

"Where are you going?" Robert began flipping off light switches.

"To bed. I plan to have an exciting day tomorrow."

# *Chapter 2*

Sommersview was a quiet street in a gated subdivision that spoke of up and coming new money. Each lot was at least an acre and every unique house made of brick or stucco boasted a minimum of twenty five hundred square feet of living space. All the houses had fashionable, well-manicured lawns, sprinkler systems, and some even an in ground swimming pool. The exception was the two story Victorian house that appeared to be out of sync with the neighboring trend of California chic. Old-fashioned roses bloomed profusely. Marigolds, so thick they looked like a yellow carpet, grew alongside the circular driveway. Black-eyed Susans, zinnias, periwinkles, all clustered together formed the beginnings of an English cottage garden. This home had no brick or stucco, just the timeless beauty of a bygone era. Although the house was obviously new, care had been taken to make the exterior speak of maturity.

Chase Hunter caught himself remembering his grandmother's house in Edwardsville, Illinois and the times he'd played on her big front porch as a boy. But the moment faded as quickly as it had come when Chase saw the Scott family fill the yard with excited children, suitcases and fishing poles.

"Looks like we're in luck, Tony! They're leaving on a trip." Chase watched the monitor in the rear of the nondescript, white van. "What's with the kisses and hugs, folks? Get going!" he moaned. "The mom doesn't appear to be going." He clenched his fist and banged it down on the metal shelf protruding out over his legs.

"Take it easy, Chase!" Tony peered closer at the monitor and smiled. "Kind of a looker, don't you think?"

"There may be a bomb over there, remember? Get your brains out of your pants for once." Chase glanced over at the smirking agent and frowned. "Seriously."

Tony only shrugged as he leaned back and checked his gun strapped under his arm. "Good thing the police got that tip last night about some kind of fireworks going off in the neighborhood or we could be in deep…"

"Why the hell isn't she going with them?" Chase was a people watcher. It didn't take him long to know something was amiss with the "Cleavers." Their body language spoke volumes. The little girl clung to her mother with one arm while wiping at a tear with the other as the mother kissed and spoke lovingly to her. The man patted his daughter, and then took her to her car seat where she was snuggly fastened in. He then turned and kissed his wife shortly on the lips, said something, then quickly jumped in the SUV and backed out of the driveway where he disappeared down the street and out of the subdivision.

Tony looked more closely at the monitor. "I know one thing for sure-if that sweet thing was my wife, I wouldn't be just givin' her a peck on the mouth."

Chase watched the woman stand rigidly as her family faded from sight when he realized she was staring at the van. A bewildered look caused her brow to crease as she shaded her eyes to block the glare of the warm California sun. But in a moment she'd come to terms with whatever tumbled in her imagination and retreated into the house.

"Whoops! We've been made, Chase. Mrs. Scott is phoning the police!" Tony grinned and patched into her phone line. "Grass Valley police. Yes. Not a problem. We'll send a car around right away." Tony disconnected. "She could be trouble."

"Move the van down the street. Have Thomas bring the truck around and I'll get in after I have a look around. Police reports say something shot into the sky and disappeared in this area. This place would be on the right trajectory for it to land."

Tony started the van. "Too bad we didn't get the report until this morning. Whoever shot that thing off was long gone by the time Enigma raided the house. If we hadn't got a lucky break about that missing radioactive material in L.A. we'd never even give this a second look. Finger prints are being run but the boss doesn't expect they were that sloppy."

"Probably burned their prints off before they started the job." Chase frowned. "Looked like whoever it was left in a hurry. Neighbors didn't seem to know much about them but why would they? That section is made up of blue collar workers. This area," Chase lifted his chin as he stared at the Scott house, "smells of money, nannies and once a week gardeners. Our little Grass Valley housewife over there can smell trouble a mile away. She's probably president of the neighborhood watch committee."

Satisfied that the police would take care of the suspicious van across the street, Tessa eyed the swaying flowerbeds in the backyard with pride. Hard work and a green thumb had transformed a lifeless space into a calming retreat that her family cherished and friends admired. The explosion of reds, yellows and purples breathed life into every corner of the acre she called home. White vinca and snow-on-the-mountain outlined every mulched bed and walkway. The tall white picket fence separated the Scotts from a grouchy neighbor, but even he could often be spotted admiring the beautiful, almost wistful atmosphere that Tessa had created. It was during this moment's pause that something caught her eye in the flowerbed. Whatever it was, the sun bounced off its metallic finish and caused Tessa to squint.

Walking to the object sticking out from one of her prized tea roses, Tessa began to imagine that this must be another one of Daniel's new inventions. Roughly, she fished it out and held the two-foot missile-like structure in her hand. If it had been Sean Patrick's, the toy would have been a gun, G.I. Joe or some futuristic weapon. Daniel on the other hand would insist his creation have lights, a whistle, and obnoxious noises and would most likely have a computer adapter. His argument would be that this toy would eventually have a higher purpose for the good of mankind. At least that's what he tried to tell her every time they went to Toys R Us or a computer store.

Tessa turned it over, examining it closer. Definitely Daniel's. The lights were flashing and a ticking sound made the projectile vibrate in her hand. She couldn't remember buying this toy or a kit to make such a thing. There didn't seem to be an off switch and the humming was getting a little too high pitched for her liking. Nonchalantly, Tessa hit it with the heel of her palm. The ticking and humming stopped but a slight vibration continued.

"Great! I broke it," she moaned. Once more she hit the toy with her fingertips. This time it shut down with a hiss.

"You need to control those boys of yours," fussed the neighbor, Mr. Crawley. "They make too much noise!"

"Yes, Mr. Crawley." Tessa could hardly contain the giggle that threatened to escape her lips as she eyed the grouchy neighbor leaning over the fence so that the sun glistened off his partially baldhead. He began a litany of complaints so that Tessa finally rolled her eyes in exasperation and sighed. She was sure that he must complain that Santa Claus possessed too great a giving spirit. "Sorry, Mr. Crawley." Tessa continued to tolerate the daily borage of complaints because the old man lived alone and was a Korean War veteran. Her grandfather, had he been alive, would have approved. Deep down, she knew it was Mr. Crawley's way of getting her attention. His next comment however, took her by surprise. "You should've gone with your husband!" He shook his finger angrily at her. "A woman shouldn't stay home alone."

Tessa made some excuse to escape and headed back to the house carrying the toy only to drop it clumsily onto the floor as she entered the mudroom. She wiped her feet, picked up the toy and carried it into the family room where she tossed it into the toy basket near the fireplace. Just as she placed her cup of morning coffee into the microwave the doorbell chimed.

"Yes?" Tessa eyed the man as she tried to see where the missing white van had gone. But her eyes landed on the brown pickup in her driveway with the logo "CIA Plumbing."

As Chase gazed into Mrs. Scott's tranquil blue eyes he seemed to lose his voice. She reminded him of a painting he'd once seen in the Art Institute of Chicago. His thoughts jumbled and his heart began to pound. The unexpected sensation made him feel awkward. His eyes drifted up to her windblown blonde hair that hinted at unruly curls, and then slid down to her small nose and moist lips that looked too perfect for a housewife with three kids and a mortgage. His eyes continued to travel down her body noticing the curves a man could get lost in. Mrs. Scott certainly didn't subscribe to *thinner is better.*

"Yes?" she repeated impatiently.

"You called for a plumber?" Chase's good old boy voice was a little overdone.

"Three weeks ago." She guarded the door as if it were Fort Knox. "And I didn't call CIA Plumbing."

"I know. The service you called is sumped," he laughed at his bad joke, especially after she didn't seem amused. "Plumbers have to hand out some of their load. You got me."

Tessa eyed him cautiously. He was too handsome to be a plumber and she was sure his faded jeans weren't going to slide down over the crack of his butt when he crawled under a sink. "What does CIA stand for?"

Again the good old boy laugh. "Central Intelligence Agency. Thought it'd make people trust me." His grin was disarming.

"Clearly you're a little out of touch with what is trustworthy. Do you have a card?"

As Chase fumbled for a business card the voice in his ear remote spoke, "Jeeze! Are you sure she doesn't work for us?" Tony sounded concerned his buddy wasn't going to get inside the house. What was Chase doing? He didn't usually stall for time. "The bomb is definitely in or around the house, Chase. Be careful. Thomas and I got your back if she spanks you." Chase frowned at hearing both men chuckle.

"Here ya go. Look lady, I got lots to do. If ya don't need me now, fine! He took out a work order from his pocket. "You Mrs. Scott?"

"Yes."

"What'll it be?"

Tessa read the card and stepped aside for the cocky plumber to enter.

"Upstairs bathroom. There's a leak under the sink and I think there's another one in the powder room," she pointed down the hall, "down there. I hear this drip in the wall too."

He held up a tough looking hand for her to be silent. "Enough. One thing at a time." Chase started up the spiral staircase and disappeared from Tessa's sight.

She frowned as a sigh escaped her lips. A fleeting thought occurred to her about calling the number to check on the plumber but then her eyes fell on the gallons of paint Robert had brought in for her. Stacked on the dining room floor, along with brushes, drop cloth and edging tape, it gave Tessa a sense of dread. This didn't look like much fun and she certainly wasn't in the mood to get started. Today would be a free day. No kids. No husband. No counting calories. No problems.

Tessa could hear the brown-eyed plumber in the kids' bathroom as she retrieved her cup of coffee from the microwave and leaned against the counter. Her mind drifted to her family and she wondered what they were doing. Already she doubted her decision to stay home. Her soul was empty without her precious family.

"Dad, she's going to hurl!" shouted Daniel as he tried to edge away from his sister in the backseat.

Robert heard a disgusting liquid sound hit the back of his seat. The smell of vomit filled the car instantly along with the soft cry of his daughter and the moans of his sons. Fortunately he'd reached the overlook at Donner Pass. A sarcastic thought of the Donner Party turning their noses up at wanting to eat his family crossed his mind as he jumped out of the car and opened the door to inspect the mess his daughter had created.

"I'm gonna be sick too!" Daniel flung open his door and gagged over the edge of the rock wall lining the overlook. Sean Patrick was soon beside him gagging as well.

Robert stared at the pink, lumpy explosion on the back of his seat, Heather's lap and her clothes. She reached out to him and he froze. His first thoughts were, "Yuk! I'm not touching that." But then he carefully reached in and released her from the small car seat, lifting her carefully to the ground. "There, there, sweetie. Daddy will get you some water and some clean clothes." As he began damage control he heard Tessa's words of warning. "Don't feed them greasy fast-food for breakfast. It sometimes makes them sick."

"We'll keep this our little secret from your mother, huh kids?" Robert coaxed as they began on their way once more.

Sean Patrick, sitting in the front with his father, crossed his arms as if in protest. "We'll see how the rest of the trip goes. Sure wish Mom was here."

"So do I," thought Robert in dreaded anticipation of the next two weeks.

Chase searched through the bedrooms and the baths upstairs with no luck of finding the weapon. The Enigma Agency hadn't wanted to alarm the neighborhood or the town. The news media could make any dangerous situation into a circus. Whatever happened at the garage that caught on fire a street over the night before was still a bit of a mystery. Evidence indicated a possible bomb had been launched. This place appeared not to have suffered any recent trauma other than a floor littered with toys and ballet slippers. He listened carefully for a ticking sound but only heard the soft humming of Mrs. Scott downstairs stirring happily in the kitchen. Was that the smell of cookies baking? He tapped the earpiece roughly. "Nothing, Tony. Any signals?"

"Sensors say it's inside. Try downstairs. Better fess up and get her the hell out."

Stealth-like, Chase slipped down the stairs and into the front parlor to get his bearings. He could see into the dining room easily and beyond into the kitchen. The family room appeared to be off the kitchen. Quickly, he changed positions in order to get a better view of the far room. Nothing unusual.

"You're close, Chase. Really close. What'a ya see?"

"Nothing!" he growled deep in his throat.

Tessa felt another presence in the house. Maybe she should have called to check out the plumber. He could be an ax murderer for all she knew. The aroma of baking cookies permeated the warm country kitchen. She stopped stirring the remaining cookie mixture and slowly turned to look at something that caught her attention from the corner of her eye. Gasping, Tessa put her hand to her throat as a short, thin man stepped out of the mudroom into her kitchen. His ruddy complexion was dark and uneven. Bushy eyebrows nearly grew together over small jet black eyes that glared dangerously at her. There was no lust, just anger and contempt. His narrow lips were nearly hidden by a thick black moustache. Tessa froze momentarily with fear. All the CSI and Law and Order television shows she had ever seen flashed through her mind. She would be the next victim soon to be the plot around the hit series that aired every night of the week. The man crouched forward, taking one slow, unsure step as his ebony eyes narrowed then searched the room and those beyond like a mine sweeper bent on avoiding disaster.

"Honey," Tessa called out in a loud shaky voice. "We have company!"

Chase stiffened. He could see the Middle Eastern man clearly from his half hidden position in the dining room. Whispering warily, Chase reached out to his partners in the van. "Tony, guess who's here?" No response.

"Tony?" An uneasy realization washed over Chase, knowing he may very well be on his own. His partners had been neutralized.

Tessa could feel her legs dissolving into liquid Jell-O as her hands reached back to steady herself against the counter. "Get out or I'll..."

"Shut up! Where is the bomb?" The man growled in a heavy accent she recognized only as Middle Eastern. "Quick or I'll kill you here!"

Tessa glanced at the door and could see the plumber creeping closer. He held his finger to his lips and motioned for her to edge closer so the invader would follow. She realized he planned to jump the mad man before her. "Look, I don't know what you want! But..." Slowly, dangerously, Tessa moved toward the brown-eyed plumber waiting to save her.

"Enough! The bomb, woman! The bomb!"

Tessa tried to steady her quivering voice. "No. I'll never give it to you."

The dark man stopped his approach.

Chase froze as well. She knew. Who was this woman?

"That's right," she tried to keep the wobble out of her voice to stall as her eyes tried to watch Chase without being obvious. "Who are you?"

He clenched his fist and threw his head back with a frustrated yell. Slowly he lowered his beady, insane eyes on her as if any moment he would explode. "I am Jamaal! Now tell me where it is or I'll slice you in a million pieces. You are alone. There is no one to help you. The bomb, woman!"

The memory of two airliners crashing into the Twin Towers jolted Tessa into an uncommon courage she didn't know she possessed. "Jamaal, you're too late. Someone was already here."

Jamaal leapt across the kitchen floor, grabbing Tessa by the throat. From the fold of his ragged shirt he produced a long knife. Tessa's eyes bulged at the sight of the weapon with a fleeting question of whether it was just rusty or stained with dried blood. "American whore, tell me who it was before I..." Jamaal's nose was but inches from Tessa's, but her wide, terrified eyes were focused on something behind him. Just then Jamaal felt a tap on his shoulder. Even with his body rigid with shock, he managed to slowly turn his head to see the brown eyed plumber, smiling a toothy grin, with a M9 Beretta pointed at his ear.

"We meet again, Jamaal." Chase's voice was level and cool. "Essid must have you on a short leash these days. What did you screw up this time? Oh wait a minute! You lost a bomb."

"You know this man!" Tessa said hoarsely. "What kind of a plumber are you?"

Both men looked at her in bewilderment.

Jamaal, enraged, cried out as he swung the knife toward Tessa's throat. Before the knife could meet its mark, Tessa felt her fingers touch the still hot cup of coffee. With one quick move she threw the hot liquid in Jamaal's face. His surprised cry caused him to drop the knife and take a step backwards. Tessa escaped past the two men into the family room, staggering with fear and relief.

The intruder recovered quickly and with cat-like swiftness, picked up one of her rolling pins from the collection Tessa had acquired over years. She remembered Robert complaining that one day her collections of anything old would be the death of him. With a powerful lunge, and a swing of the rolling pin, Jamaal came at Chase knocking the gun from his hand. The Beretta went sprawling across her clean, slick wood floors.

The two men struggled as Tessa remembered her son's toy found in the garden. Quickly, she darted to the toy box and jerked the missile-like object from among the Lego's, G.I. Joes and soccer balls, fumbling with it in the air recklessly, only to catch it again before it hit the floor. The weight of it was heavy and unexpected. Why hadn't she noticed this before?

The sound of breaking glass, thuds and groans startled Tessa into lifting her eyes to see the two bloody combatants in the kitchen. The surreal smell of burning cookies reached her nose at the moment the two men fell to the floor reaching for Chase's gun. Without a second thought, Tessa clumsily placed the missile under her arm and pressed it firmly to her body. Just as Jamaal crawled toward the Beretta, Tessa entered the now smoky room and grabbed the bag of flour off the counter, only to dump it on the floor, before Jamaal.

Jamaal tried to scamper up on one hand but hit the flour and went sprawling again, dropping the gun on Chase's chest. Chase pushed himself up on one knee. His eyes widened at the site of the bomb under Tessa's arm, just as she snatched another rolling pin from the counter. With one haphazard swing, Tessa slugged Jamaal across the back of the head.

He collapsed with a groan and a heavy sigh. Tessa's breath, ragged and labored, prevented her from speaking clearly. "Get up!" she panted. Chase did so slowly, wondering if he'd not stumbled onto another terrorist cell.

"Who are you and what is this thing?" She dropped the missile from under her arm, but caught the tip of it with her hand.

Chase felt his heart in his throat as he tried to catch it himself. "Lady, that is a bomb. I want you to hand it over nice and slow." He lowered his gun slightly and reached out his other hand.

"I think I'll just make another call to the police. They should already be in the area," she warned drawing the bomb nearer to her heaving breasts.

A hard, sinister look flashed in Chase's eyes as he jerked the gun back up and aimed. Tessa's mouth opened for a scream just as he began shooting and grabbing for her shoulder. "Down!"

The gunfire was deafening. She felt the plumber push her into the dining room as his hand pressed her head downwards. The realization that the Beretta was not the only gun firing caused Tessa to tilt her head sideways to see three more Middle Eastern men dressed in some sort of gray jumpsuits invading her house, unloading their semiautomatic rifles in her home. The sounds of exploding China and splintering cabinet doors ricocheted in the Scott home. Tessa's heart pounded so hard that she could barely breathe.

"Out the door, lady and get in the truck!" Chase panted as the gunfire ceased. He could see the other men circling, looking for a way to rush them as Jamaal staggered to his feet. Replacing the magazine in his gun, Chase found himself pressing Tessa up against the wall where she couldn't move. "They're about to charge. Go!"

Tessa tried to turn the door knob to no avail. Locked. Placing the bomb back under her arm once more, Tessa heard the plumber yell. "Here they come! Now, lady!"

Bullets began to clip all around their heads as Tessa felt a scream escape from down deep in her lungs.

Robert handed the last of the supplies to his sons as he felt a little tug on his pant leg. It was Heather, frowning and squinting from the warm Tahoe sun. "I miss Mommy" she said in a small, helpless voice. "Why didn't my Mommy come?" she demanded as Robert lifted her up into his strong arms.

"Mommy wanted a little rest and relaxation, Cupcake."

"What will she do without us, Daddy?" She liked being carried by her father.

"Shop, talk on the phone, have tea with her girlfriends, basically, nothing at all," he grumbled.

"That sounds boring."

Robert spotted the boys throwing rocks in the lake. "Yeah, she'll probably be so bored she'll come up here tomorrow."

At least then he could really have a vacation.

## *Chapter 3*

Tires squealed as the CIA Plumbing truck raced backwards down the driveway. Bullets began bouncing off trees and the hood of the vehicle. Tessa ducked down, still clinging to what moments ago she thought was a toy. Just as she tried to sit up Chase banged his fist on her back, balancing his weapon across her half raised shoulders. He fired rapidly. Tessa tried to cover her ears as she somehow sandwiched the bomb between her lap and breasts. A frightened cry escaped her mouth as the rear window shattered, raining glass in her hair and down her back.

"Hold on! They're following!"

Tessa rose to look back and saw four men jumping in a weathered van with a crumpled bumper. "Dear Lord!" she quaked. The CIA truck accelerated beyond neighborhood rules. "I am so in trouble," she mumbled. Just then Chase sped through the subdivision gates into the path of an oncoming delivery truck. When Tessa screamed Chase swerved, landing the tires on her side of the truck onto the curb. The jolt threw her into Chase's lap. Quickly, she tried to push away and realized her hand had landed between his legs. Jerking her head up to look at the brown eyed devil beside her, Tessa was shocked to see him grinning like a wicked schoolboy.

"Not now, Mrs. Scott. I'm a little busy." His voice was so cool and nonchalant that Tessa almost forgot the danger she'd plunged into. Awkwardly, she shoved herself back to the passenger side.

# AN UNLIKELY HERO

The truck dropped back down on the road and began taking the curves at top speed.

Tessa began searching the seat with her hands. "Oh no!"

"What!" Chase demanded, as he looked sideways at her for a split second. "Something wrong with the bomb?"

"No! There's no seatbelts in here!" Tessa didn't realize how utterly absurd her fears were until Chase began to laugh.

"I guess we're breaking the law then!" he yelled catching a glimpse of the approaching terrorists in the rearview mirror. He tapped on the radio then his ear piece as he noticed that Tessa clung to the bomb like a newborn child about to slip from her grip. "Anybody! Officers down at Sommersview. Repeat, officers down."

A male voice sounded from some hidden speaker causing Tessa to jump with fright. "Copy that. Where are you?"

"Highway 10, headed west toward the Yuba River. We've got company too." Chase pulled out around a slow moving minivan, accelerated and managed to whip in front of an eighteen wheeler that began blowing his horn in anger at the near miss.

"You're going to kill us!" Tessa screeched. "Let me out!"

"Who is that?" the hidden voice demanded.

"Mrs. Scott. She has the bomb. I couldn't leave her there to get cremated with the rest of the house."

"My house is on fire?" Tessa yelled in horror.

"Is the bomb activated?" the voice was level but concerned.

"Mrs. Scott?" Chase looked over at Tessa as she unfolded the bomb from her arms. A hum had begun with the several small flashing lights. "Yeah, Enigma, I'd say it's activated." Chase eyed Tessa and realized she was seeing it in its real form for the first time. "Essid's friends are still coming at us. Give that trucker behind me a call will ya? License plate ERZ7773." Chase reached over and gently touched Tessa's shoulder. "We'll be okay, Mrs. Scott. Maybe you better hand me the bomb."

"I can't" she whimpered.

"Sure you can. It's a bomb. It'll be okay."

"No," Tessa nervously shook her head. "I really can't." Tessa leaned back and let the bomb move slightly forward. Her index finger had somehow gotten shoved into an opening. The swelling had already begun and there was no removing it. Tears welled up in her terrified blue eyes. "What kind of bomb is this?" Swallowing hard, Tessa lifted her chin up in a raw courage that until now had been unknown to her. She imagined her family at Lake Tahoe, fishing and nibbling on peanut butter and jelly sandwiches that she'd packed for them. The sounds of their questions, laughter and playful pranks swirled in her head. Robert would be smiling at the perfect little family they'd created together, even if he wasn't sure what he was doing. Deep inside her Tessa knew he would be thinking of her.

Chase looked back at the eighteen-wheeler and saw him pick up his cell phone. "Come on, buddy. Help me out here." Just then he saw the terrorists start around the huge truck behind him. Suddenly, the trucker dropped his phone, laid on the horn until Chase raised his eyes up at the rearview mirror. The trucker was making the thumbs up sign. He poured on the gas and managed to push the truck to 95 miles per hour.

"The bomb." Tessa spoke so softly that it startled Chase. "What kind is it?"

Chase glanced back at the oncoming terrorists. They were nearly in the middle of the eighteen-wheeler. "Could be radioactive, Mrs. Scott." He watched her closely. She opened her mouth but nothing came out. Licking her lips, Tessa tried again.

"We probably don't have much time then. This was ticking earlier when I found it."

Chase nodded. "That's right."

"Up ahead there's a steep ravine. This time of year it's still flooded. The water makes its way into the Yuba River but there's a series of small earthen dams on this end that will help contain any contamination and maybe the explosion won't hurt anyone. The government owns twenty miles on either side of the ravine."

"What are you saying, Mrs. Scott?" Chase took his eyes off the road to examine Tessa's terrified profile as she stared out the windshield.

"If we make it that far, get out and I'll drive over the cliff." Tears spilled down her cheek as she slowly turned her face toward the mysterious man. "I don't want another 9/11."

Chase tore his eyes away from the pretty face of his unsolicited heroine and began speaking loudly to some invisible presence. "This thing is counting down!"

"Okay, Hunter! We have your location. Leave that puppy in the vehicle and send it over the cliff into the Yuba."

"Negative! Mrs. Scott has got her finger stuck in it. She's volunteering to do the deed!"

Silence dropped like a hammer on the connection then static roared it back to life.

"You heard them, Mr. Hunter! Stop this car now! Save yourself! I promise I'll have God send angels to protect you from now on. Please. Stop!" Tessa gripped the dashboard with her one free hand. She realized those words didn't make any sense to her either. "Do it before I lose my nerve."

In the rearview mirror Chase watched the trucker swerve his powerful machine into the passing terrorists as they sped up alongside him. With startling impact the eighteen-wheeler slammed the rusty van off into the gravel causing it to wobble then roll awkwardly down a steep slope. He could hear the screech of rubber against pavement as the eighteen-wheeler tried to stop. One problem solved.

The Yuba River stretched out lazily meeting the horizon. In that moment he knew Mrs. Scott had been right in choosing the location for possible detonation. Quickly Chase slammed on the brakes as he slid into a roadside park. A cloud of dust surrounded them and slowly pushed into the broken window, making Mrs. Scott cough. She fanned the brown air away in an irritated fashion as if she were on a Sunday afternoon picnic and had just discovered a mosquito buzzing her head. Chase reached across and tried unsuccessfully to remove her finger. There wouldn't be time to cut off Tessa's finger to save her life.

"Mrs. Scott," Chase left the truck idling as he put in park. He'd driven to an area where the ground slopped down nearly twenty five feet before dropping another one hundred feet into the ravine. "I don't know who you are but you're the angel in my book!" Chase could see that the time left on the digital read out was three minutes. "When you're ready touch the brake with your foot. Can you reach it?" She nodded bravely. "Good. At the same time pull this down," he pointed to the gear shift, "into drive. Got it?"

"Yes!" she nodded anxiously like a little child being told what to do.

Chase didn't know why he suddenly reached over and pulled Mrs. Scott to him. Something in her eyes made his chest hurt. The blond curl falling over one cheek made him wish he'd met this woman earlier. Before he could stop himself he pressed his mouth against her trembling lips. The taste of dust and fear mingled with his own sweat and regret. Her eyes grew wide with surprise as he pushed away and out the door. "Tell the big guy I want you as my angel, Mrs. Scott."

He shut the door and hurried to the passenger side to reassure her if needed. But the time of reckoning had captured Tessa. She no longer saw him as she looked down at the bomb once again seeing the time had moved to one remaining minute. With a deep breath, Tessa's foot stretched to reach the brake. The shift was moved into drive. Strangely, she felt no fear, only sadness as the truck slowly inched forward. Sadness that she'd not see her children grow into accomplished adults; sadness that she'd never hold another baby in her arms or know the love of her husband's body against her own. But her faith in God gave her peace, knowing that someday she would be reunited with all those she loved.

The ravine was coming closer.

The cell phone in Chase's pants pocket vibrated. With annoyance, Chase retrieved it as he began walking faster alongside the truck. He knew he should stop. The explosion might still kill him. Some kind of regret pushed him along as he watched Mrs. Scott snuggle the bomb to her breast.

"Thank God, Hunter! We lost contact in the truck!" Chase said nothing. "Good news! Mrs. Scott doesn't have the bomb. Whatever she's got her finger stuck in isn't the bomb."

Chase Hunter threw down the phone as he began to run toward the truck.

# *Chapter 4*

Lake Tahoe shimmered in the early summer sun. The wind blowing gently across the crystal clear water sent shivers across the bare arms of the Scott children as their father finished unloading luggage and supplies from the SUV. He paused a few seconds to look at his children staring at the lake and noticed them hugging their arms. A smile came to his lips as he saw his oldest, Sean Patrick, put an arm around his baby sister to keep her warm. She leaned into his side then circled his waist with her cubby arms, hugging him tightly. Daniel tosseled Heather's curly hair playfully as he bent down and whispered something in her ear. Both boys were very tender and loving toward their little sister. Something about Heather made others want to comfort her.

She was missing her mother, Robert knew. Those two were tight. Heather was Tessa's shadow. She would cry sometimes when Tessa would go out to lunch with friends or to the grocery store without her. Robert often heard Heather tell her mom, "You're my best friend, Mommy! I really love you." He sometimes wished Heather felt the same about him. It was obvious she preferred Tessa over him. Even the boys would ask Tessa's advice before approaching him. But then again, he knew he'd caused that ugly reality by being obsessed with work and making a future for his family. Being an interactive father was difficult after working twelve hour days several times a week. All he wanted to do was watch Monday night football sometimes or relax with a good book. What was wrong with that?

The children turned slightly to look at their father. Robert gulped at seeing their distrusting expressions. All he'd ever really done with them on his own could be counted as chores. Unless Tessa took charge, there rarely had been much fun involved. He just didn't know how to let go.

Tessa now had given him a chance to change all that. If she'd come along there would already be activities, hotdogs on the grill and wildflowers on the table. There would be laughter and teasing with the promise of an afternoon nap for him. But now he would have to make the magic happen. It would be his biggest accomplishment. Today Robert would acquaint himself with those beautiful children Tessa had given him. How hard could being the hero parent be?

Timidly Robert sat down the heavy, blue cooler packed with delicious meals his wife had so lovingly prepared for their trip. He sucked up his courage then exhaled just before pushing himself into a casual stroll toward the kids. They seemed to move closer together, expecting some kind of reprimand. How had he ever let this thorny crevice separate his life from those he loved? Could he win them back?

"Wow! That's some view, huh kids?"

They nodded then turned their eyes back toward the lake.

"What'd ya say we carry the gear into the cabin? Then we'll make a fire by the lake and cook some dogs!"

Sean Patrick sighed. "There's no open fire, Dad. Fire season is starting."

Robert bit his lip. This was going to be harder than he thought. "Okay! We'll eat those peanut butter and jelly sandwiches your mom made for us when we go out in the boat. I think I saw some chocolate chip cookies too."

All eyes looked up with hope. "Boat?" they said in surprise.

"Yep!" Robert found a magic word apparently. "I'm renting a boat and we'll have a picnic on the lake! Sound fun?"

"Yeah!" they cheered. Little Heather smiled and moved to her father without any hesitation. He lifted her up into his arms. Her little arms circled his neck just as he felt a wet kiss on his cheek. He could feel his heart warm at her little touch. The boys patted their father's arm and began talking excitedly. Maybe this would work after all. If only Tessa could see him now!

\* \* \*

Chase Hunter scrambled after the truck like a madman. He caught hold of the door handle only to feel his feet start to slip out from under him. The acceleration made opening the door impossible. "Open the door, Mrs. Scott!" He yelled waving one arm wildly.

Tessa turned her head to stare in bewilderment at the handsome stranger who had dragged her into this mess. She glanced at the fast approaching cliff to the ravine then quickly back at Chase. Something had gone terribly wrong! But what? With her free hand Tessa grabbed the door handle only to have it come off and clank to the floor.

Chase's eyes widened in horror at seeing the dilemma. He felt the door rattle beneath his hand as it slipped away. "Kick it open, Mrs. Scott!" He shouted as he stumbled nearly to the ground.

Tessa, confused at what she may have done wrong, but hearing the new instructions, leaned away from the door and kicked three times with a force that surprised her. As the door flew open Tessa raised up just in time to see a large hand reach in and grab her shirt. She could feel it begin to ripe away as her body became airborne through the open door.

The ground flew up at her as the sound of crunching metal and falling rocks reached her ears just seconds before the impact of Chase's truck hit the rocks below them. At the same time Tessa felt the wind burst from her lungs when Chase landed with all his weight on top of her. The momentum of the landing and the steep grade of the hill spun them into a roll toward the edge. Tessa could feel Chase digging his heels in to stop their plunge and she instinctively began grabbing at vines growing along the ground. Just as her body began to slip over the edge a scream tried to escape but there was no wind to expedite the terror. Suddenly Tessa felt her legs dangling in thin air and strong arms pulling her back to safety. She could hear heavy breathing and grunting as her movement continued upward.

"Are you alright, Mrs. Scott?" Chase panted as he removed vines from her hair and a dirt clod from her face. When she opened her mouth to speak and grabbed her chest he realized that he'd knocked the wind out of her during the extraction from the truck. "You're alright, Mrs. Scott. There's no bomb. Just try to breathe. Relax." He rubbed her arms gently as she fought to a sitting position.

A gasp of dusty air filled Tessa's empty lungs. Waves of coughs spasmed her body as she felt the stranger thump her on the back. Collecting her confused wits, Tessa pushed his hands away and tried to stand up only to be assisted by Chase. Strangely, his firm touch made her feel uncomfortable. "What is going on!" she demanded with a choke stepping away on wobbly legs. "The bomb!" Tessa looked down at her hand that no longer contained the mini nuke. "I've lost it! Dear Lord!" She began to look around the area. "It must have come off when you pulled me from the truck!" she choked, now on the verge of tears. "You saved my life!"

Chase's stern eyes searched the perimeter as he casually pushed Tessa aside. He walked with a quick determination toward a flashing object tangled in some brush nearby. Bending down he jerked the once menacing object into the air. Moments before it had been stuck on Tessa Scott's finger. "This is a child's toy." He examined it after reading the toy manufacture's name on the side.

"Looks like a bomb," Tessa said covering her mouth with a scratched and bleeding hand. The loose dust mingled roughly with her tears, turned Tessa's face into a patchwork of thin, muddy streaks. The realization dawned on that her life had nearly been sacrificed for nothing.

"The bad news is the real one is still out there." He threw the toy against a tree in anger. The shattering caused Tessa to flinch and step back from this suddenly menacing man.

Chase's attention turned to the eighteen-wheeler stopped on the main road. The large man exiting from the cab now carried a sawed off shotgun. As he came around the front of the truck he pulled up his sagging jeans with one hand and lifted the gun to his shoulder with the other. When he saw Chase running toward him with the scarecrow of a woman close behind, he nodded a greeting like a four star general. He was proud of the work he'd just done, although he really wasn't sure just what it was he'd saved. All he knew was some dispatcher had commanded him to intervene for this athletic looking daredevil who nearly ran over the cliff.

"Where are they?" Chase never stopped as he ran past the trucker to the edge of road.

The trucker pointed with his gun then returned it to his shoulder.

Tessa hurried to Chase's side in time to see him slide down the hillside toward the upside down van that appeared to be smoldering. "Get over here and help him!" she snapped at the truck driver.

He complied with a snarl as he opened the cab door and carefully placed the shotgun back inside. This time it took both his hands to pull up his sagging jeans just before he cautiously edged down the hillside to join Chase. The scent of sweat and greasy onion rings clung to his clothes as he lumbered down toward the van. With relief, the trucker halted when Chase raised a hand for him to turn around.

Tessa pushed pass the trucker and awkwardly side stepped down the embankment.

Chase circled the crushed van cautiously. Unaware of her presence, he pulled out a Beretta from the back waistband of his jeans. Quickly, he knelt down to look through the shattered windows. One arm dangled out through the windshield.

Visible, as Tessa drew near, was the driver pinned underneath the front of the van. The sight of so much blood and exposed bone caused Tessa to suddenly wretch. As she slid her ripped shirt sleeve across her mouth, Tessa watched the captain check for a pulse on each man, all the while keeping his weapon pointed with intent. Even from where she stood, the moan of yet another person came from the rear of the van.

Chase quickly ran to the back of the van with gun aimed for deadly contact if necessary. The rear door had been ripped off during the crash. The back end, although badly damaged, tilted upward having landed on a large flat rock. Just inside the twisted van lay the fourth terrorist that had invaded the Scott home. He reached toward Chase with pleading eyes. Blood streaked his face where glass had torn at his brown skin. A gash above his right eye gushed over an already bruised cheekbone. Half of one ear lay open and bleeding down his neck.

"Help me," he cried weakly. Tessa noticed the Middle Eastern accent. It was Jamaal, the man who had threatened her in her own home.

Chase did not lower his weapon. "Who are you with? Essid?"

"Please," he moaned.

"Where's the bomb?" Chase growled the demand.

"I donno," he coughed a blood splatter that landed back on his face. "Please!" he cried. "Help me."

Chase reached inside the van. Grabbing the man's collar he roughly dragged him out across broken glass and twisted metal. The scream of pain punctured the silence around them.

Tessa gasped at the cruelty in which the captain threw the injured man on the ground. The man screamed again when Chase jerked him to his feet like a rag doll. He shoved him forward where his friends lay trapped in the van.

"I need answers," Chase yelled in the man's ear.

The man cowered as he felt the butt of the pistol hit him upside the head. "Now."

Tessa tried to turn her legs around but was frozen at the scene before her. Never had she witnessed such brute force.

Chase stepped away from the injured man and lowered his gun to inside the van. "Where's the bomb?"

Nothing.

Chase fired three rounds into the man inside the van. With callousness, Chase shoved his prisoner against the van. "Your buddy on the hood isn't going to make it without medical help. Give me what I want or …"

"I do not know!" he wept.

"Fine!" Without looking, Chase extended his arm and unloaded his gun into the man on the hood. "Their blood is on your hands! You're next unless you start talking!"

"Yes! Yes! Whatever you want!" Tears burst from his eyes like a punctured dam. "I-I need medical help."

Chase jerked him around then shoved him toward the embankment. Suddenly his eyes fell on Tessa. The horror in those pretty blue eyes troubled him. The overpowering urge to comfort her unsettled him more than wrestling with terrorists bent on killing thousands of Americans.

"What the hell!" Chase snarled, disgusted at himself for such a feeling of tenderness. "Get up there!" he commanded.

Tessa tried to scramble up the hillside only to slip and fall to one knee. She felt the rock bruise her bone but quickly regained her footing as Chase continued to push the injured man upward with the gun.

They reached the top at the same time. The trucker had witnessed the scene below. He quickly backed away from the oncoming injured man who gasped for air while Chase's breath seemed almost normal.

Chase extended his hand to the trucker and told him he'd single handedly saved the state of California from a very dangerous terrorist cell. The chest of the trucker puffed out like a proud peacock. He tilted his greasy

John Deere hat back with a finger that resembled a large sausage. The toothy smile followed by a loud obnoxious laugh grated against Tessa's nerves. The obvious patronization of this man was meant to buy his patriotic silence. Even she could spot an oncoming cover-up.

"There will be a cleanup crew in ten minutes, my friend," Chase informed him. "They will, I'm sure, have further orders for you. Because of your assistance I wouldn't be surprised if they didn't hire you in some capacity."

"Who are 'they'? CIA? FBI?" The man's voice had nearly dropped to a whisper as if someone might be listening.

Chase leaned his head in closer as he noticed Tessa Scott raise a skeptical eyebrow and fold her arms with great irritation across her chest. "I'm not at liberty to say. But we are connected to Home Land Security. Tell them you assisted Captain Chase Hunter."

The trucker grabbed his cap and slammed it against his large thigh. "I knew it!" he laughed. "Ain't that somethin'? Me. Helpin' Home Land Security."

Chase extended his hand. "It's men like you who are our first line of defense. Thank you!" Chase made a point of a vice-like grip that made the trucker whence for a second.

The thump, thump of helicopter rotary blades reached their ears and in seconds the Sikorsky helicopter landed. Chase never got tired of hearing the Black Hawk swoop in for retrieval. This particular UH-60 had become an integral part of his organization's every day operations due to its versatility. Chase reached for Tessa's hand and jerked in the direction of the waiting helicopter. He felt the resistance building in her rigid body. With another tug Tessa began to follow.

After shoving his gun into the back of his waistband, Chase propelled the injured man forward by slapping him on the back of the head. With an anguished moan the terrorist once again moved with unsteady steps. A team of four men dressed in gray clothing exited the unmarked helicopter and swarmed the scene. With a nod to Chase they sat about the task of making the mayhem invisible.

Tessa nervously approached the helicopter. Her senses were on overload. Fear gripped her as another man, dressed in black hopped down from the helicopter to take the prisoner. His menacing appearance halted her steps only to be grabbed and lifted up in Chase's arms. Carelessly Chase tossed Tessa into the helicopter where she landed on a now sore hip received during the extraction from the truck. As Chase and the other two men entered the door, she felt another set of hands pushing her into a seat then buckling her seatbelt. She guessed him to be the pilot.

"Don't you ever touch me like that again!" Tessa screamed above the rising roar of the helicopter.

Chase shook his head as he pushed in beside her. "Can't hear you! Hang on!" He could read lips. He realized his rough treatment had aggravated an already frightened civilian.

The helicopter lifted and swung around toward Sacramento. Tessa's stomach lurched suddenly. The terrorist and the man in black sat facing her. Blood oozed from the terrorist's wounds along his face and arms. With bowed head, his lips moved in some unknown prayer. The man in black, however, glared openly at her. His crooked smile and narrow eyes feasted on her from head to toe. When Chase gave him a swift kick in the boot, the man in black laughed out loud and winked at her. From that moment on he gazed casually out the window as if they were on a sightseeing tour of California.

Tessa's head began to throb as panic flooded her imagination. Where were they headed? How was she going to reach Robert? A heavy realization washed over her that something had transformed her pastoral life into a nightmare.

## Chapter 5

Tessa sat bewildered and frightened in a room that smelled of mold and bleach. Windowless, the only light in the small room softly glowed from a loose hanging light bulb that barely broke the darkness in her dingy concrete surroundings. The metal table before her was cool to the touch. She couldn't tell if the room was air conditioned or just cold from being below grade level. Her wooden chair wobbled with the slightest movement. At first she'd tried opening the door only to find it locked as she knew it would be. Wasn't that how all the crime shows went? They were surely watching her, although Tessa had not detected a two way mirror or video feed. She just knew. So she sat quietly. Planning. Scheming really. How was she going to get out of this mess?

What about her family? Were they missing her? Could she get a message to them? Why hadn't she caved in to Robert and gone to Tahoe? At least she'd be safe in the loving arms of her family. Tessa shook the dead weight of regret from her plan. Thoughts of those she loved would confuse what she needed to do to escape.

Why had she been blindfolded a few minutes into the flight? Tessa could still remember the reassuring words of the man who saved her life as the helicopter had landed. "You'll be okay, Mrs. Scott. I won't let anything happen to you. You're in a safe place. We have to secure the prisoner before we discuss your involvement."

She remembered reaching for the blindfold as she tried to push those strong hands away from her arms. Suddenly he'd grabbed both her hands in just one of his. His voice, calm and frosty, whispered in her ear. "Don't make me tie you up, Mrs. Scott." Tessa had stiffened with fear but nodded in defeat. "That's a good girl. You've been through hell today. I promise I'll make this all go away as soon as I can."

Should she trust him? Not likely. But hadn't he saved her life just a few hours ago? Then the image of him unloading his gun into those injured men flooded fear into her reasoning process. She'd witnessed two murders. How could he be with Homeland Security? She wondered if that trucker survived the "cleanup crew" as the man named Chase had called them.

The sound of a dead bolt retracting echoed in the room. Slowly, Tessa stood and backed against the wall. Were they coming to make the final clean up?

In walked the larger than life, her protector, with a slight smile on his wide expressive mouth. His clothes were still dirty and torn from the earlier conflict. He had managed to remove the grime from his high cheekbones. His nose looked like it may have been broken at some time and a small faded scar lay above his right eyebrow. Tessa couldn't decide if his short hair was black or just dark brown. But when he stepped into the light she saw that it was a little of both. Those wide set eyes were dark chocolate and took her in like a thirsty man in the desert. She felt exposed under that gaze as if he were reading her mind. He was over six foot. She'd compared him with her husband's height earlier. There wasn't a soft spot on him. It wasn't hard to remember feeling him on top of her when they'd crashed onto the ground. The memory of the power in his arms as he'd pulled her to safety made Tessa blush now as her eyes examined him.

"I'm Chase Hunter, Mrs. Scott." He stood with his feet slightly apart as if inspecting the troops. His hands locked in front of him. "I apologize for keeping you here for so long." He took a step forward but stopped when Tessa slid away from him. "I'm afraid we still have some unfinished business." His smile, although meant to be disarming, only made Tessa shiver with fear.

"What kind of business?" Tessa pulled back her shoulders as if that might look brave. "I want to go home!"

"I'm afraid that's not possible." Chase dropped his locked hands and placed them on his hips. "We need some information."

Tessa nodded and moved toward him. "Okay." Her voice soft and forgiving made Chase smile revealing straight white teeth.

"Shall we?" He nodded toward the door.

"Oh no!" Tessa moaned as she batted her eyes quickly.

"What's wrong?"

"My contact lens! It fell out."

Chase dropped his hands from his hips and looked down at the concrete floor. With both hands Tessa grabbed his shirt and pulled him to her chest. The look of surprise in his eyes was followed by excruciating pain as Tessa rammed her knee into Chase's groin. When he staggered to stay on his feet, she lifted the rickety chair and swung it into his arched back. With the sound of splintering wood came a curse as Chase fell to the floor. Quickly, Tessa darted out of the room and slammed the door shut, making sure it locked before turning to run up the now visible stairs. Grabbing a broken broom handle propped against the wall, Tessa clenched it tightly like a samurai's sword.

Cautiously, Tessa made her way up the dimly lit stairs. She heard the static of a walkie talkie then a man's voice. Someone waited at the top of the stairs out of sight. Tessa laid down her broom stick on the landing that led up the next flight of stairs. She eased back behind a stack of boxes that created a dark corner.

"Help! Chase has been hurt! Please, someone!" she screamed, then crouched a little lower behind the boxes. A second later a camouflage dressed man barreled down the steps to the rescue only to step on the broom stick handle sending his feet into the air and his head crashing against the concrete step. Tessa could see he was unconscious as she slipped out from her hideout. Retrieving the stick, Tessa rushed up the stairs only to stop and press her ear to the door. Nothing.

Cracking open the steel door revealed light. Blessed light! Tessa pushed harder on the door and slipped her bruised and aching body into a hallway lined with windows. Distracted by the normal passage of traffic on the nearby street, she failed to notice the man coming through the doors at the end of the hall until his familiar East European voice startled her back to reality.

"Well, what do we have here?" It was the man dressed in black from the helicopter. He didn't try to approach her as he folded his arms across his chest. His eyes darted toward the basement doors looking for Chase. "Alone at last." His voice sounded matter of fact.

Tessa panicked. Turning her eyes toward the ground level windows, Tessa knew she had but one option. With all the strength she could gather, Tessa backed up and ran toward the windows, using the broom handle as a javelin. Upon impact the javelin propelled her backwards like a rubber ball. She hit the wall so hard the broom stick flew out of her hands only to be caught in midair by the man in black as he calmly approached.

"Bullet proof," he said looking down at her crude weapon, "and broomstick proof." He smiled wickedly. "And what have you done with Captain Hunter?"

\* \* \*

Robert looked bewildered at his Blackberry, as if doing so would suddenly explain why Tessa wasn't answering her phone. He wanted to let her know they had arrived safely at the lake and that the kids were just fine. Robert had looked forward to rubbing salt into Tessa's *super mom* wounds all day. The kids wanted to tell her all about the boat and picnic and what a great time they were having even though she wasn't there to weave her spell of magical bliss.

Part of him wanted to say he was sorry too. Sorry for being such a jerk and insinuating her duties at home aligned with watching the grass grow. He felt exhaustion settling into his body and desperately wanted a nap. But the kids needed supervision down by the lake even if they were just skipping rocks. And what was he going to do for supper? Geeze! Why had he ticked Tessa off? This was all his fault but if he gave in now Tessa would gloat for the rest of his life.

At that he decided he missed that beautiful smile and longed to hold her in his arms as she laughed and teased him. His heart thickened with regret as his eyes looked out at the lake. They could've sat out tonight and counted the stars. That always got her in the mood. The thought of her soft naked skin next to his started to make his clothes feel tight and uncomfortable.

He opened the Blackberry one more time. Maybe he would just leave her a message saying the kids missed her.

\* \* \*

Agent Nicholas Zoric, former Serbian Nationalist, sat on the edge of an empty desk, cleaning his nails with a switchblade knife. He watched with one eye toward the wall of windows that enclosed Director Benjamin Clark's temporary office. Dressed in a suit and tie, the director paced his generous office before Nicholas Zoric's friend Chase Hunter. Chase sat in a chair looking up at his boss seemingly unconcerned at the verbal abuse being hurled at him. Nicholas carefully closed his knife and smiled over at Tessa Scott who was handcuffed to a well cushioned office chair. For the last ten minutes she had been eyeing her surroundings, looking for another means of escape, he guessed with great amusement.

"What's gotten into the boss?" Vernon Kemp stopped next to Nicholas and stared nervously into the office where Benjamin continued to berate the team leader at Enigma. "I've never seen him in such a rage, especially at Hunter."

It was true. Chase Hunter was the golden boy at Enigma, the secretive operational force under the protection of Home Land Security. Cloaked in mystery, only the president and Secretary Tobias Stewart, head of Home Land Security, knew the full extent of their operations. They filled a gap of missing intelligence desperately needed after 911.

Teetering on misuse of the law, Enigma had been able to gather vital intelligence from not only within the U.S. but the world. Having the uncanny ability to fit almost any profile and assimilate into any population, Chase was the poster child of Enigma. The president's complete trust in Chase's operational force never wavered and gave him free reign when it came to national security. Only Tobias Stewart kept Chase from turning the law and intelligence gathering into a legal nightmare. The way to keep Chase in check was to put Benjamin Clark as his superior, the one man that Chase respected as much as the president.

Vernon shoved his hands deep into the pockets of his ragged jeans. Although some said Vernon Kemp was probably the smartest man in the world when it came to computer technology and artificial intelligence, his appearance implied he was an over aged skateboarder who had dropped by to bum a few bucks from his friends. His hair, red and unruly, fell past his ears. Boyish freckles were evident across his small nose and rosy cheeks. His lopsided smile revealed a bottom row of crooked teeth. Although well into his twenties, Vernon looked like he just graduated from high school. The black glasses he occasionally pushed up on his nose gave Vernon a somewhat geeky look. It wasn't until you looked into his hazel colored eyes that evidence of a shrewd, almost devilish manipulator materialized. The innocent gamer transformed into a storm trooper with a keyboard.

With a Ph.D. from MIT in computer analysis and design at the age of twenty one, Vernon quickly came to the attention of the defense department. They hired him immediately to further their work in artificial intelligence. After developing software which would revolutionize the computer industry, Vernon's work mysteriously disappeared at the Pentagon. Vernon quit his job and became an underground conspiracy theorist. Some of the power moguls were so angry at his leaving the Pentagon that a picture of Vernon in the crosshairs of one of their AK47s materialized on one of the conspiracy networks that Vernon liked to frequent.

Just after President Buck Austin took office he instructed Benjamin Clark to recruit Vernon Kemp for his new secret agency, Enigma. A man like that needed to channel his talent toward helping the good guys especially if he had the Pentagon big shots in a stew. Vernon only came on board after meeting Chase Hunter and being told he could do whatever he wanted as long as it didn't interfere with national security.

"What's the problem?" Vernon glanced down at the grim faced Serbian. The man in black, as usual, made him a little uneasy.

When a rare smile broke across his thin, narrow face, Vernon's eyebrows arched. "Chase got bested by a girl!" Nicholas Zoric chuckled.

Vernon's eyes widened. "By who?" The Serbian nodded toward the pitiful, ragged woman handcuffed to the chair across the room. Vernon saw the puny figure slouched in the chair with ripped clothing and dirty hair. Her face smudged with blood and sweat, she looked more like a discarded kitten than a saber toothed tiger that could best the great Captain Hunter. He looked around but saw no one else. "Her?"

Nicholas Zoric nodded as he stood and continued to smile. "She's my hero."

Vernon snickered his usual weasel laugh drawing Tessa's angry glare. "Introduce me!" Usually Vernon became tongue tied around women. His shyness was legendary. His smooth operator persona evaporated into an awkward stutter when females tried to approach.

Nicholas pushed Vernon toward the subdued prisoner. "Watch yourself. Her bark is definitely not as bad as her bite."

Benjamin Clark paced before Chase Hunter, livid at the day's events. Two men down at the scene, a house shot up by unknown terrorists, a nuclear device at large, a cleanup near the Yuba River, and now a seemingly innocent woman involved.

Chase started to stand. His back ached from the earlier attack by Tessa Scott.

"Sit down!" Benjamin demanded with the tone of a base drum. Benjamin rarely raised his voice. His hawk-like eyes, narrow nose and stern expression commanded attention whenever he spoke. His soft, firm voice drew more respect than shouting. Chase eased himself back down into his wooded armchair, surprised at the anger his boss displayed. It wasn't often that Benjamin could be read so easily.

"Can you explain to me how a soccer mom came into possession of a nuclear device created by some obscure terrorist outfit, then managed to knock one unconscious so the two of you could escape?" Chase started to open his mouth when Benjamin held up a large leathery hand for silence. "Then there's the little, tiny fact," he held up his index finger and thumb measuring about an inch, "that she managed to trick, and overcome you so she could escape our holding cell!" Chase flinched at the pain he'd felt when Tessa had rammed her knee into his groin. "And dare I forget" he growled, "that she nearly killed one of your men with no more than a broomstick!"

"How is he?" Chase interrupted with genuine concern.

Benjamin stopped his pacing and leaned against his desk as he loosened his paisley tie. "Has a concussion. If he hadn't been wearing his helmet the doctor said he'd be dead!" Benjamin crossed his arms and glared up at the ceiling as if searching for words. "Secretary Stewart wants some answers and fast!"

Chase let the steam escape from Benjamin's anger. He knew a cool head would prevail after the shock of the day's events began to be absorbed. The rise and fall of Benjamin's chest slowed to a steady rhythm as the silence of the room began to smother the fire of his temper. When Benjamin sighed, Chase knew it was safe to speak.

"The doc fixed Jamaal up. He's waiting downstairs to be interrogated." Grasping the arm of the chair, Chase pushed himself up. A stiffness began to attack his bones. It had been a hell of a morning. The adrenalin rush prevented pain earlier, but now that order had returned to his world, Chase felt his age. "I'll take Zoric with me."

Zoric and Chase shared a history neither talked about to others. Each knew the other had their back. Chase regretted that the men helping earlier in the day nearly lost their lives at the hands of the terrorists, but was grateful that Zoric had not been available for the job. Few got Chase's respect and trust. Nicholas Zoric was one of them.

Taking Zoric into an interrogation situation usually proved successful. His dark hollow looks made him seem more like a vampire than an American agent with Enigma. His cold bloodshot eyes showed no emotion. The scars across his cheek and neck hinted at a dangerous past. A thick, black mustache peppered with gray spoke of middle age unlike his straight black hair he pulled back into a ponytail that rested on his lean neck. Zoric wasn't a big man, only five foot eleven compared to Chase's six foot one frame.

He had been an accomplished artist in Sarajevo before the war. Young, optimistic and talented, Nicholas Zoric married his childhood sweetheart and quickly started a family. The war took everything; his family, his talent, his reason to live. He became a cold blooded killer in the name of justice. Zoric became one of the walking dead of Serbia. Now, when he wasn't on mission, he taught art classes at the university. His ability to inflict pain on the deserving proved a great asset to Enigma and they took advantage of that talent whenever it suited them.

Nicholas Zoric marveled at how Vernon Kemp had suddenly emerged from his shy, awkward self into a babbling idiot as the pretty lady handcuffed to the chair drew him into a normal conversation. He'd never seen Vernon so relaxed around a woman. Zoric admitted even though Mrs. Scott was disheveled, the bruises, smudges and ripped clothing failed to hide a pretty woman. Those blue eyes swallowed a man's common sense. Their intense attention to Vernon's voice swayed even him, a lost soul.

Zoric nudged Vernon's shoulder with a fist. "Boss waitin'. Better come," he said moving toward the glass wall where Benjamin and Chase watched with sour looks. "Now, Vernon."

Vernon said one more thing to Mrs. Scott. It sounded like some kind of promise. He passed Zoric as he shoved his hands back into his jean pockets. His whistling drowned out Zoric's warning, but Vernon ambled into the glass office carefree and smiling.

"What the hell were you doing?" Chase's low controlled voice sent a disgruntled message.

"Nothin'." Vernon suddenly looked confused. Chase gave a side long glance at Mrs. Scott then back to him. "Oh. Tessa and I were just..."

"Tessa?" Benjamin Clark interrupted as his strange grey eyes focused on Vernon with a kind of liquid fire consistency. "Tessa! Who gave you permission to fraternize with the prisoner?"

Vernon blinked rapidly. "You're right. I shouldn't let people who humiliate us know we're human." Vernon's habit of trivializing a reprimand annoyed Benjamin Clark's 'total control' attitude. Just as Benjamin straightened to his full height and pulled back his shoulders, Chase stepped in front of Vernon.

"Until we get this straightened out its best not to talk to Mrs. Scott."

Vernon shoved his hands deeper into his pockets and rolled his eyes disrespectfully. "Whatever, dude." The pleasure he got from irritating Benjamin Clark would be put on hold. The thought of angering Chase was another matter entirely.

The discussion quickly moved to strategy for extracting more information from Jamaal, the remaining terrorist. The four men had showed up at the Scott house to retrieve a bomb. Clearly they were not aware the vessel found in the backyard was a decoy. How had they known to look there? If that wasn't the bomb where was it? Why had their equipment failed and given a false positive for radioactive matter?

"The equipment didn't fail. Just came from the lab. The readout rang true." Vernon took out his glasses from his shirt pocket and began twirling them in his left hand. "Which means...?"

"The bomb is still at her house." Benjamin groaned as he ran his hand through his short grey hair. He had never looked more like an angry American eagle than at this moment. "Maybe Mrs. Scott can recap the last twenty four hours for us."

"I doubt it," Zoric said in his gravelly voice he'd acquired from years of smoking.

Benjamin straightened as if being challenged. He didn't really trust Nicholas Zoric. Too dark. Too everything suspicious and creepy. "And why not?" he snapped.

Zoric nodded to the spot where he'd left the innocent housewife. "Because she's gone."

All eyes turned to the outside office where an empty chair sat with only a pair of handcuffs dangling down one side.

# Chapter 6

The park ranger moved with stealthy silence through the trees until she reached the crystal blue lake. One hundred yards to the north she could see a large cabin bustling with activity. Kids skipped rocks across the waters that gently ebbed to shore. A rather good looking man in a red baseball cap sat nearby in a lawn chair with his hands locked behind his head. Sunglasses blocked the direction of where his eyes rested but the ranger guessed it focused on the children. From time to time he would smile and appeared to make a comment about their rock skips.

The little girl began to cry when the oldest boy let loose his rock too quickly and it flew back, hitting her. The man jumped from his chair and quickly scooped up the child as if he'd just saved her from stepping on a landmine. Dads could be so dramatic when it came to their little girls.

"There, there, Heather. Let Daddy see," Robert coaxed as he tried to remove her chubby hands from the large red spot above her right eye. His pulse quickened at seeing the trickle of blood.

"Dad, I'm sorry!" Sean Patrick looked horrified and gently patted his sister's leg. "Sorry, Pookie!" He often called his sister silly names that made her smile. She angrily pushed his hand away. "Let Daddy see, Heather. Please," Sean Patrick begged.

Daniel joined them, concern showing on his young face. "Better get something on that, Dad."

Robert frowned down at his sons. "You need to be more careful around your sister. She's little!"

"Am not!" Heather protested as she pushed against Robert's chest with both hands. "I'm a big girl!" she insisted.

"She sure is," came an unknown feminine voice a few feet away.

Robert slightly flinched at the surprise intrusion. A park ranger dressed in a green uniform carried a faded camouflaged backpack which she slung down to rest on a tree stump. Her wide brimmed hat shaded her oval face, revealing only a hint of soft tan features. Light brown hair, the color of a baby fawn, strayed from her ponytail and framed her cheeks. Robert couldn't help but notice in that instant that the top two buttons on her snug fitting shirt had been undone. The ranger nonchalantly wiped perspiration from her neck with a man's handkerchief, and then stuffed it in her pants pocket.

"Let's have a look, shall we?" The ranger squatted as Robert lowered Heather to the ground.

Heather pushed out her lower lip and wiped the last of the tears away before jerking up her chin in a show of bravery. She looked like her mother in that moment, Robert thought warmly. Tessa always put on a brave show when she became worried, frightened or confused. The world thought she was a rock. Robert knew, however, his Tessa was the best con artist in the west. Just now Heather showed signs of that determination to overcome the situation with bravery and strength. He was glad Tessa had passed that trait on to his precious daughter.

"Us girls are a lot tougher than men realize." The voice of the ranger carried a slight Irish accent adding to her comforting appeal. "Can I see your injury?"

Heather cocked her head slightly. "What's injury?" She said batting her eyes and unconsciously lifting her fingers to the spot where the rock had connected.

The ranger smiled, revealing teeth that had been whitened. She pointed to the spot on Heather's forehead. A small round bump had begun to rise. "There. Can I see? Looks like these guys don't have a clue on how we girls need to be treated."

Heather took a hesitant step toward the ranger. "Okay," she said softly.

The ranger noticed a tiny cut. She stood and went to her backpack where she retrieved a first aid kit. "This might sting just a bit but at least you won't get an infection and have to go to the doctor. I think if I do this you won't have to get a shot." Heather's eyes widened at the word "shot" and nodded enthusiastically. The ranger gently cleaned the area and applied some antibiotic cream. "It just so happens I have some pretty cool bandages too. Would you like one to wear? That will remind your brothers to be more careful." Heather nodded again, this time with a wide smile. The bandages had Disney princesses on them.

"That didn't hurt a bit!"

"You see! Us girls are tough!" the ranger laughed as she stood. Her hazel eyes went to Robert. "She'll be fine."

Robert removed his hat and wiped his brow as if by doing so would remove the fright he'd suffered in the last ten minutes. "Thanks." He stuck out his hand. "I'm Robert Scott. This is our first day of vacation. Wouldn't you know there'd be an accident right off the bat?"

His smile, the ranger noticed, was a little flirtatious. She didn't mind. After all, Robert Scott was a very good looking man. Nearly six foot, Robert's lean body looked like a tennis player. Although not muscular, he was in great shape. Neatly shaven, Robert's skin looked tan and healthy. The narrow nose where his sunglasses rested gave his face an angular shape that spoke of masculinity. The hand that gripped hers was strong, accustomed to physical work. Her father had always said you could tell a lot about a man by his handshake. If this were true, Robert Scott might just turn out to be an interesting visitor to Lake Tahoe.

"I'm Ranger Lynch. Honey Lynch." she said holding onto his hand a little longer than considered proper. "No Mrs. Scott?" she inquired looking back at the cabin.

Robert suddenly felt a little nervous. "No Mrs. Scott." He smiled again looking down into the pretty face of the ranger. "I mean my wife may come later," he stammered a little too quickly. "I insisted she take a few days for herself. You know, let me take care of the kids. I thought she'd appreciate the time off. She certainly deserves it," he laughed as he glanced toward the kids watching with curiosity at the scene unfolding.

"Mom is eating lunch with friends and getting her nails done," Daniel offered up the information with sarcasm.

"Really," Honey said smiling down at the little boy then back at Robert.

"This is a test to see how Dad does with us," Sean Patrick interjected.

"How's he doing?" Honey asked with amused interest.

The kids looked at each other as if to confer. They all nodded. "So far so good," Sean Patrick offered offhandedly as if his father wasn't standing there.

"Go play, guys. Get some ice out of the cooler for Heather's bump too! And watch out this time!" Robert warned as they ran back to the water's edge.

Robert turned his eyes back to the pretty ranger. She looked like a no nonsense kind of person. Although petite her grip a moment ago revealed Honey could handle herself. She wore no makeup, only a little clear lip gloss. The natural, wholesome features of her face made her look like an ad for ski equipment.

"On foot?" Robert was still unclear about how the ranger had materialized. His radar was up and something made him sense caution.

Honey put her small hands on her hips. She wore a gun, Robert noticed. "No. My truck is parked just on the other side of that stand of trees. There's an old logging road."

"Looking for something?" Robert still didn't understand why she was here.

Honey's smile faded as she took out sunglasses from her shirt pocket and placed them on her delicate nose. "Actually, Mr. Scott," Honey lowered her voice. "There has been a jail break in Carson City. The fugitives are on foot."

"Geeze!" Robert sighed taking another look at his children. "Are they up here?"

Honey shrugged. "This is a good place to get lost if you don't want to be found." She followed his gaze toward the laughing children. "Don't wander too far off the beaten path. There is plenty of law enforcement out looking for these guys. I'll swing back by tonight to check on you. I'll let others know you're here. Got a phone?"

Robert removed his Blackberry from his hip pocket. "Can't get very good service up here."

Honey casually took his phone and pretended to inspect it.

"Daddy! I caught a fishy!" Heather screamed with delight. "Help me! Help me!"

Robert ran to her side to help reel in the four inch small mouth bass. The wiggling fish slopped water in Heather's eyes. She squealed with delight as Robert removed the hook from its mouth.

"Why is it breathing like that, Daddy?" Heather's look of concern made her reach out and stroke the little creature.

"It can't breathe out of the water, sweetheart."

"Oh no!" Heather sighed sympathetically. "It's so little. Does it have a mommy?"

"Well, probably. Should we put it back in the water and send it home?"

Heather stuck out her lip in disappointment. "I guess so. I want to name it first."

Robert nodded in agreement. His sons were now looking on, watching the ultimate release of the fish. "Swimmer. I name her Swimmer."

"How do you know it's a her?" Sean Patrick asked with a frown. Releasing a perfectly good fish was just ridiculous.

Heather squinted against the afternoon sun as she looked up at her brother. "How do you know it's not? Besides it's pretty so it has to be a girl."

Sean Patrick threw up his hands in defeat as he turned back toward the ranger. He saw her close up his father's phone. She smiled at him innocently. He eyed her with reserve as he watched her approach. The ranger wasn't sure of his age but realized this one probably had watched enough American television to suspect anyone examining someone else's phone.

"How's the fishing this year?" She looked out over the tranquil blue waters and distant snowcapped peaks. Was there any place more beautiful than Tahoe?

"Are you really a ranger?" Sean Patrick inquired.

"Sure!" she laughed. "Do you think because I'm a girl I can't be a ranger?"

Sean shook his head and picked up another rock only to skip it four times across the water. "Because you don't know how the fishing is."

"Well it changes from day to day. Any fisherman will tell you that."

"You don't look like a ranger either." Sean Patrick looked up at Honey one eye closed against the bright sunlight.

"Really? What does a ranger look like?" Honey expected him to tell her how pretty she was or that most rangers looked like Smokey the Bear. She never tired of being complimented.

"They dress different than you." Sean Patrick said matter of fact.

Honey could feel tightness in the back of her shoulders. Her fingers twitched nervously as she removed her hat and wiped her forehead against her sleeve. She didn't respond to Sean Patrick's observation.

"My friend Jose's father is a ranger and his uniform is different than yours."

"This is Nevada, you live in California. Our uniforms could be different."

"How'd ya know I live in California?" Sean Patrick eyed her with increased suspicion.

Honey smiled and reached down to ruffle his dark hair. He looked like his handsome father. The eyes were a little sharper and his demeanor a little less trusting, but the resemblance was there. "Your license plates." She nodded toward their car.

Sean Patrick looked back at the car then up at the ranger. "Oh." he said simply. He then moved closer to the water seemingly forgetting about his concerns.

Kids! Honey thought. Why would anyone want them? They smell, eat you out of house and home, and can make you have the pediatrician on speed dial instead of your favorite restaurant. They wrecked your bank account, not to mention your figure.

Honey watched Robert stand up after releasing the fish. "Bravo! A job well done, Mr. Scott."

"Please call me Robert."

Honey handed back his phone. "Robert, I need to go. Look, I have a string of fish in my truck. They're filleted, iced down and ready to go. I think this particular cabin has an outdoor gas grill. Why don't I fix them for you guys tonight? If these felons aren't caught I'll have to look around this area again anyway."

Robert shrugged. "That would be great. I have some potato salad and baked beans my wife fixed. We'll have a feast!" his boyish smile made Honey offer her hand again and gave it an extra squeeze that seemed to make Robert withdraw his hand a little quickly. She waved to the kids and headed toward the stand of trees where she soon disappeared.

He watched her until she disappeared among the towering trees. Her sensuous walk must drive those boys at the ranger station crazy, Robert thought, remembering the suggestive farewell handshake. He smiled proudly. "Still got it," he mumbled to himself, delighted that a sweet young thing like Honey had noticed him.

\* \* \*

Honey picked up speed as she pushed through the low hanging branches. She nearly lost her hat but grabbed it just as it slipped onto the back of her neck. A breeze moaned softly through the top of the trees making them creak. Pine needles crunched beneath her boots. The warm afternoon smell of summer engulfed her suddenly. She began walking slowly, enjoying the sounds of branches moving in the wind and the solitude she rarely experienced. When the forest opened back up Honey saw that her government issued park truck had a low front tire on the passenger side. She'd need to take care of that before coming back up here tonight.

The road was already dusty from the lack of rain. Another lazy breeze picked up a cloud of red dust and swirled it up and over her head as she reached for the door handle of the truck. She quickly slid into the passenger seat and opened the glove box, looking for a map.

"So? Did you talk to him?" An unconcerned masculine voice broke the peaceful rhythm of the rustling trees and bird songs.

Honey looked at the driver. Short and stocky, her partner reminded her of Jabba the Hut from Star Wars. Unlike Jabba, this man was olive skinned with dark circles under his eyes. His nose was long and too big for his chubby face. The thick fingers that gripped the stirring wheel looked like burnt sausages. Several days of not shaving left a dark shadow encircling his face from ear to ear. His greasy black hair had been dampened and combed straight back. Honey could smell body odor. He repulsed her.

"Yeah. I'm going back tonight to cook dinner."

The driver turned narrowed eyes to examine her beautiful body. He chuckled. "Keep him busy while I look around."

"He's married. There's kids," she snapped knowing he expected her to seduce Robert Scott.

"Fine. Make sure he has a little too much wine so he'll sleep soundly."

Honey frowned. "Let's go, Mansur. By the way," she said looking down at her map of California and Nevada. "What does Mansur mean?"

Mansur turned his emotionless eyes back to the road and started the engine. "Divinely led," he said through a forced smile.

# Chapter 7

Tessa knew how to pick the lock on a pair of handcuffs after reading the biography of Harry Houdini to a sixth grade class she'd volunteered in several years earlier. She offered the challenge for students to read three more biographies and promised to escape from a pair of handcuffs like Harry Houdini as a reward. Her research online and practice with a friend of the family who had been a Grass Valley policeman helped her learn the art of escape. It was simple really. All you needed was a bobby pin. If her hands had been cuffed behind her back the trick wouldn't have worked. Then there was the advantage of having only one hand cuffed to the chair. She didn't have a bobby pin but had managed to lift a paper clip from the desk next to her when the man in black's eyes had looked away momentarily. When her captors left her alone Tessa got to work on the cuffs keeping one eye on the inner office where a heated conversation kept the attention off her.

Since the sparsely furnished office space where she had been forced to sit was dimly lit, Tessa felt confident she could slip out undetected. Unoccupied empty desks in the space, maybe ten or eleven showed no evidence of ever having been used. All were clean and unused. Chairs sat neatly against the lip of each desk like a display scene at Office Max. No trash. No waste baskets for that matter. No office supplies or computers. Empty gray walls, nondescript carpet and low ceiling tiles made the room seem less expansive than it really was. More importantly there were no other people except for her captors. If these people were Homeland Security why wasn't this place bustling with nervous activity considering a dirty bomb was somewhere in the city?

Tessa knew these men were dangerous. Even that seemingly nice kid, Vernon, had a quirky look in his eye. Too eager to please, she thought. That scary man in black must have been a demon in another life. The icy stare he dropped on her had sent shivers up her spine. Then there was Chase Hunter. She wasn't sure what to think of him. Obviously he commanded this group. But who was the suited man that reined them in? She gave him only a passing thought as she slowly rose from her chair and gave one final glance around the room that seemed to be a work in progress.

She'd stayed close to the wall rather than run across the room which would have drawn attention. Even though it took longer to reach the double doors, Tessa knew her chances of escape lay with a cool head and patience. At first the doors seemed to be stuck. Tessa pushed her hip into it and the door squeaked open. She held her breath at the sound, glancing back at the men deep in discussion. Just as she started through the door, her eyes fell on an discarded fountain pen with the engraved letters B.C. lying on a nearby desk. The sharp point might just be a needed tool or weapon to continue her escape from this building. With eyes on the inner office and one foot propping open the door, Tessa strained to reach the pen. She slipped gently through the doorway and turned to find herself in a short hall that ended with an elevator.

She ran to the metal doors, and quickly pushed the down button four times hoping that would bring escape sooner. Looking down at her weapon, she read the inscription, "Benjamin Clark." Tessa turned it around with her fingers. What if someone else was on the elevator? Where were the stairs? She looked for an exit sign as the elevator dinged its arrival. The doors slowly opened as Tessa's eyes turned back to her attempted route to freedom.

Tessa's heart skipped a beat when a tall woman dressed in high heeled shoes, a designer jacket and dress glared out at her. Her beauty took Tessa's breath away. A long, black braided ponytail fell to the middle of her back. Wide full lips painted red made her look like she was pouting. High cheekbones on a perfectly heart shaped face with flawless olive skin made Tessa a little green with envy. Tessa noticed the same hard look in those beautiful exotic eyes that she'd observed in her captors. This one took everything in as if ownership of the world was hers for the asking. Her slim, firm body moved with the agility of a tigress as she slowly moved off the elevator making bewildered eye contact with Tessa.

"Hi!" Tessa smiled, forcing a pleasant voice. "They're waiting inside for you. The powwow has already started. Chase is mad as hell too."

The woman continued past her without acknowledgment or emotion.

Tessa casually slipped into the elevator and poked the close button several times. Before she could move to the rear of the elevator she watched in horror as the exotic beauty froze in place and appeared to straighten to what seemed to be an inch taller. Slowly she turned her head to look over her shoulder at Tessa who lifted her hand in a friendly salute.

Before Tessa knew what was happening the woman turned and plowed toward her like a launched torpedo. The doors began to close as a slender hand with well-manicured nails pushed the doors back with a determined grunt. Tessa raised the ink pen and rammed it into the hand that blocked her escape to freedom.

Only a small gasp escaped the woman as she forced her hip against the door which opened. Slowly, as if removing lent from a cashmere sweater, the beauty pulled the leaking ink pen from her hand. When the pen connected, ink had sprayed over her red and white dress. She turned killer hazel green eyes toward Tessa as she cocked her head in surprise. With her long firm arms, the woman reached in and grabbed Tessa by the front of her shirt and yanked her from the elevator. The strength in the woman's arm caused Tessa to stumble back down the hall toward the office where she had been a prisoner moments before.

"I think..." Tessa stammered, hoping a woman would be more sympathetic.

"Shut up!" the woman hissed as she shoved Tessa again into the closed double doors. With one hand flinging the doors open and the other pushing Tessa through, the dangerous beauty caught sight of her team exiting the office with great concern and speed.

Tessa's body made contact with one of the desks with such force that it screeched, echoing across the half empty office space. She cringed as she became encircled by the mysterious people who had tossed her into a whirlpool of conspiracy and treachery. Her breath, ragged and short, whispered a prayer of protection for herself and her family. They were all looking a little shocked and irritated at her. Tessa guessed they weren't used to dealing with civilians. She backed away from them along the edge of the desk until a chair on wheels was shoved toward her blocking any further thought of retreat.

"Betty Crocker here was on her way to the elevator!" the beauty snapped, pointing a finger toward her as if it were a loaded gun. "Look what she did to my dress!" The blood on her hand didn't disturb her as much as the ruined clothing.

Chase eyed her body with appreciation. "How did that happen?" He nodded toward the ink and blood trailing down her generous bosom.

Everyone seemed to hold their breath except Benjamin Clark. His focus remained on Tessa.

"She stabbed me with a fountain pen!" How could such a beautiful woman growl like a pit bull, Tessa wondered?

Tessa straightened as if by doing so she'd gain some composure. "I'm so sorry!" Tessa tried to sound apologetic. "If you'll send me the cleaning bill, I'll..."

"You idiot! This cost $800! It's ruined!"

Tessa bristled at her angry, rude manner. "Really? I bought one just like it off the rack at Target," she said off handedly.

The woman started to take a step toward Tessa with a doubled fist, but stopped as Chase burst out laughing. Tessa didn't know quite what to think about the scene before her since everyone now stared at Chase in astonishment. He laughed so hard a tear squeezed from his left eye. Slowly, the other men began to chuckle. Tessa thought the laughter must be contagious but she wasn't getting the joke. Only the woman didn't laugh. Her breathing matched Tessa's. Then without warning the woman lunged toward her with two doubled fists.

Tessa gasped or screamed, she wasn't sure which, when Chase slid in front of the beauty and grabbed her around the arms tightly.

"Let me go!" she demanded still glaring at Tessa. "I'll teach the little bitch to..."

Chase shoved her back into Zoric. "Lay a hand on Mrs. Scott and you're off my team," Chase warned firmly. "You can well afford another dress, Sam."

So the Amazon had a name: Sam. Samantha?

Sam appeared to be startled by Chase's rescue. The others tried to hide their amusement by turning from her. "Why is she still here?" She toned down her anger and looked to Benjamin Clark. Sam knew better than to speak disrespectfully to him.

Tessa cleared her throat but her voice still cracked when she spoke. "Are you going to kill me?"

Benjamin smiled patiently and offered his hand as part of the introduction. "I'm Benjamin." He withdrew his hand after she took it hesitantly for a moment. "Now why would you think we were going to kill you, Mrs. Scott? We're the good guys."

Something in his eyes reassured Tessa. His voice, calm and even led her to believe this man could be trusted. She took a step closer to him for what she hoped would be security. Chase's large presence loomed too close, unnerving her beyond anything she'd ever experienced. His penetrating gaze unsettled her even more. She'd witnessed those pools of chocolate brown eyes go from control to a black murderous rage just hours earlier. "I watched him," she nodded toward Chase with a shaky finger, "kill two injured men this morning. Same as murder," she choked. Her knees were shaking so she reached back to steady herself against the empty desk.

"Mrs. Scott," Ben's voice lulled her into a safe place, "those men were already dead. Captain Hunter is no murderer. He had to convince the remaining one that he had everything to lose."

Tessa glanced back at the other men who still looked amused and nodded some kind of assurance to her so she would believe. When her eyes shifted to Chase she had the uncomfortable absurd sensation he could probe her brain. She felt naked and exposed on a level she'd never known before. Remembering his sudden kiss in the truck burned her cheeks with embarrassment. He must have thought of it as well because his eyes darted recklessly to her lips. A slight grin toyed with the edges of his mouth. He had saved her life. Why would a killer do that? But ultimately it was Sam that convinced her Benjamin Clark was telling the truth. The rolling of her eyes and the obvious jealousy that sprang into her body language showed irritation at the gentle treatment another woman was being offered.

"I want to go home," she pleaded.

"And you will, Mrs. Scott. Tessa," Benjamin Clark was a little disarming with his coy smile. "May I call you Tessa?" She nodded keeping a skeptical eye on the remaining team. "There's just this one thing."

Tessa straightened. "What thing?"

Chase dropped his hands from his hips and folded his arms across his chest. "We need you to help us one more time."

Tessa reluctantly met his eyes with hers trying desperately not to be intimidated by their dark depths. It felt like drowning, looking into those dangerously hypnotic eyes. "And if I refuse?" Tessa jerked her chin up in defiance even though only she knew it was a ridiculous attempt at standing strong.

Chase narrowed his eyes as he cut them toward Zoric. The man in black stepped forward as if hearing a silent command. "I think you've met Nicholas Zoric."

Tessa feared the choice set before her. The implication now appeared to be: refuse their request and deal with the man called Zoric or cooperate in order to be returned home.

\* \* \*

Jamaal lay on his simple army issue cot trying to get comfortable with the cuts and bruises he'd sustained in the accident. A doctor had seen to his wounds but his whole body ached from being tossed around in the rolling van when it had plunged off the embankment, thanks to that reckless truck driver. He needed a hospital, not some doctor who clearly patched him up only to be broken apart again when these people chose to interrogate him. With no blanket to cover his bare chest, the chill of this place made his anxiety grow. At least they had not taken his pants. The cold cement floor added to his discomfort against his bare feet. The silence grew deafening. Concrete and silence. Cold steel bars and dim light coming from outside his cell. Nothing to remember. No sounds or sights to give him direction. This place was a void for prisoners who weren't supposed to know where they had been taken. Even his sense of smell betrayed him. It was too antiseptic.

There were two other cells in this abyss of nothing. His cell sandwiched between the two. The one to his left, the last cell, had become some kind of storage unit for a table and two chairs stacked neatly against the far wall.

Something reddish brown stained one of the legs of the table. He guessed it to be blood. The first cell, to his right, mirrored his own. Nondescript. Empty. Clean.

A faraway sound reached Jamaal's ears. They must be coming for him. Would he be strong or cave with the interrogation Americans had become so proficient at? Jamaal wasn't good with pain. He didn't pretend to be brave. Antagonizing his keepers with lowered eyes and defiant silence would be almost impossible for him. Just the thought of that dark man dressed in black made his skin crawl. Then there was the big man who had pulled him from the wrecked van; no hesitation at emptying his gun into his fellow martyrs. His cold, dark eyes held no emotion or fear. Men like that were not so different than the people who had recruited him months ago.

The sound of a heavy door closing and echoing footsteps began to filter down to his hell. More than one voice now. A woman? Angry voices grew louder as did the sound of resistance. The sound of dragging, then grunts, and more dragging suddenly filled the small room as a woman was shoved violently against the first cell. She sobbed as the man in black appeared. He reached down carelessly and jerked her to a standing position by the collar of her shirt.

"Please! I don't understand! Just let me go home. I won't tell anyone!"

Jamaal pushed himself into the far dark corner of his cell as if by doing so he might just become invisible. Let the woman suffer the brutality of the man in black. After all what could he do to protect her?

Then he recognized the woman. It had been her home he'd invaded. An innocent? No such thing in America. Jamaal remembered how roughly the big man had treated her at the helicopter. She had been blind folded before him then told to be quiet and she wouldn't get hurt. Perhaps they had changed their minds. Maybe she wasn't so innocent after all.

He watched as she grabbed the dark man's arm that held her while he unlocked the spring-loaded bolt to the cell with his key. The man pulled her body so close to his that Jamaal could see his breath move the hair that fell in her eyes. "Maybe I'll come back later when everyone is gone, sweetheart." The woman tried to push away but was yanked back and crushed against his chest with both arms. "I like a fighter. Rest up. You'll need your strength, I'm thinking," he laughed with sinister satisfaction.

He pushed her hair back with his bony hand and lowered his mouth to hers. Just before contact the woman rammed her knee into the dark man's groin. Stumbling backwards with an anguished moan, Nicholas Zoric managed to hold on to Tessa's shirt. It ripped where the sleeve met the shoulder as she tried to twist free. Tessa tried to shove her way free but Zoric's fingers lost none of their vice-like grip as he recovered from her attack.

Zoric took a deep breath and jerked her after him as he limped into the cell. He shoved her to the floor onto her sore hip. With a satanic smirk, Zoric removed a piece of cord from his back pocket and began to twist it around both his hands. "I think now is as good a time as any to get better acquainted."

Tessa crawled to the corner of the cell nearest Jamaal's. Tears began to flow once more as she held her hands up in defense. "Please!" she begged sniffing and shaking her head in denial of the impending attack.

"I like the begging. It's a nice touch," Zoric chuckled.

Just then a slight movement in the cell next to Tessa's drew Zoric's attention. His head jerked up and squinted into the dimly lit space until he made out a man cowering in the farthest corner. Zoric looked back down at Tessa and appeared to reverse his decision of an attack. Slowly he unwound the cord and replaced it in his pocket. Backing out of the cell he cut his dangerous eyes back toward Jamaal. Without looking back at Tessa he reached for the cell door and slammed it shut. Only when he heard Tessa's gasp of fright did he look back at the sobbing creature on the floor. A padlock hung precariously from the once spring loaded bolt that no longer worked. He snapped it shut then moved toward Jamaal's cell, glaring inside at a shadowy figure plastered against the far row of bars. Zoric smiled again at the intended victim and chuckled as he jerked on Jamaal's padlock to make sure it was secure.

"Could be a good night."

Zoric turned casually and made his way out of the containment area.

When the bang of a steel door echoed down to the cells, a flood of anguished sobs racked Tessa's body. She bowed her head over her drawn up knees and cried for several minutes before lifting her closed eyes upward. "Please, God! Get me out of here. I know you can deliver me. You always have. Please don't let me die here alone and without my family. Please save me!"

"He will be back," Jamaal spoke softly, disturbed only slightly by the brutal treatment of this woman.

Tessa scrambled to the cot on the far wall at the sound of a man's voice. "Who are you?" She tried to wipe tears quickly and appear composed.

Jamaal stepped closer where a ribbon of light from a dangling light bulb outside his cell fell across his face. "Don't you remember? My name is Jamaal."

Tessa edged off the cot and took a step closer. "You're the man from the van." Her voice still held an element of fear.

"Yes."

"You broke into my house." she said with despair. "Why? You tried to kill me!" she nearly choked on the words.

"No! No! Not me! I would not do such a thing. I did not know what would happen." His voice was quick and unsure. "Believe me! I would never hurt an innocent woman like you. I only meant to scare you!"

"Liar!" Tessa remembered the Twin Towers in New York City and how thousands of people had lost their lives because of hate in the name of Allah. "You called me a whore. You had a knife." She made an attempt to wipe her tears away with what was left of her shirt sleeve near the shoulder.

Jamaal took hold of the bars. "I was only frightened like you, Mrs. Scott, but…"

"How do you know my name?" Tessa ask in shock. "Who are you? Why were you at my house? I heard them say something about a bomb. Did you plant a bomb at my house?" she said in panic.

"Shh! Keep your voice down. They may be listening. We are both in a lot of trouble."

"They aren't listening! That mad man doesn't want any evidence that he…" tears began to flow again. "I heard him talking to the man who killed your friends. This place is only a holding facility. We'll be moved soon."

Jamaal began to pace nervously. "Not good." He continued to pace. "I knew this was a bad idea. I should not have listened to them!"

"Who? And who are you," she sniffed as she stepped closer.

"They are Lion's Breath."

"Lion's Breath. I don't understand."

Quietly, he stared at something beyond and invisible to her. A disheartened sigh slowly escaped his cracked lips that had been split open by the accident, she noticed or by the brutal Captain Hunter's calloused fists. "Many years ago, a hundred or more, I think, the lions roamed the deserts of our grandfathers and great grandfathers. Now they are gone, destroyed by European and North American hunters seeking trophies. Our lands from Morocco to Saudi Arabia and beyond were purged of the brave beast because the people not of us feared their power. The sound of their roars will soon be heard again," he said with a half-smile as his eyes darted to the woman. He liked her eyes, the color of a desert sky. "Your people will once again fear the roar of the lion. But by the time you realize his approach, you will already feel the lion's breath. His teeth will have begun to devour your godless nation."

Tessa, bewildered and confused, frowned at the ramblings of the man who destroyed her home. "How long until Lion's Breath begins?"

"A month ago I learned of the plan."

"What plan?" Tessa grabbed the bars. "Maybe we can help each other. Will someone come to save you?"

"No." Jamaal's voice fell in disappointment. "But if I escape I can help you too."

Tessa felt uneasy, knowing she shouldn't trust anything a man with everything to lose was saying. "How can I help?"

Jamaal moved toward the bars. "You can give me the key you took from the man in black."

"What?" Tessa's eyes widened in confusion as she started to step away from the bars. Before she could move further from the man, Jamaal reached through and grabbed her by the hair, jerking her against the cold hard surface. He ran his hand down her back until his hand rested on her back pants pocket. Tessa squirmed at his invasive touch. She pushed at his bare chest as his hand slipped inside the pocket and withdrew the key she'd stolen from Zoric when she'd jammed her knee into his groin. That split second had been long enough to slip her fingers into his shirt pocket. It had practically fallen into her hand as he'd bent over with pain. She'd watched him put it there just before he'd led her to her cell.

Jamaal released her and backed away from the bars. "I am sorry, Mrs. Scott. I need this more than you, although I appreciate the effort you made on my behalf."

Tessa watched as Jamaal reached through the bars. Lifting the pad lock with one hand he inserted the key with the other. "You can't leave me here for that monster! Please!"

The sound of the lock opening echoed softly in the room of cells. Jamaal moved to Tessa's cell and lifted the lock. Tessa hurried to the door. He looked at her sadly and smiled. "You are an American whore. You deserve the treatment waiting for you, Mrs. Scott." He turned and started to run.

"No! Wait! Please!" Tessa screamed. "Don't leave me here! I beg you!" She waited to hear the slamming of the steel door but Jamaal had carefully closed it behind him. Tessa knew his escape would be easy from that point. There were no guards because no hope of escape had been possible.

Tessa sat down on the cot resigned to waiting for what would come next. How had she gotten herself into this mess? Nothing had ever prepared her for such a scenario. Yet here she was on the doorstep of disaster, her family so far away, her home in ruins most likely, and a dirty bomb set to go off in Sacramento.

A silent prayer for strength was offered just as the sound of a steel door opening and hurried footsteps reached her ears. Tessa remained on the cot, hands folded patiently in her lap. Closer. More than one person. Who would it be? Zoric? Captain Hunter?

"Mrs. Scott?" Tessa looked up to see Zoric unlocking the door for Captain Chase Hunter. He rushed in and towered over her. Her eyes darted between the two men before settling on Zoric. Slowly she stood, pulled back her shoulders and jerked her chin up in pride. Chase lifted his hand up in a high-five gesture. Tessa smiled and slapped his palm with her own high-five. "You did it!" he smiled proudly. "Good job!"

"I pushed the tracking device into his chest when he took the key. He never suspected."

"And he won't. It molds against the skin, thinner than a band aid." Chase turned to Zoric and continued to smile. "She's a little spit fire don't you think?"

Zoric stepped forward and saw the sudden smile vanish from Tessa's face. He hated he'd frightened her. "Mrs. Scott," he lowered his eyes for just a split second. Those beautiful blue eyes of hers, although blood shot from crying, unsettled him. The innocent should never have to go through the fear he'd forced on her. "I beg your forgiveness, Mrs. Scott. I am sorry that I had to mistreat you." He dared to take another step toward her. "I promise if anyone ever, from this moment on, tries to harm you or your family they will deal with me."

Tessa eyed him carefully. She closed the distance between them and stuck out her hand. "Forgiven." Zoric slipped his large bony hand around hers and they shook. As he started to release her hand Tessa tightened her grip. "But we're not even," she warned. Zoric raised his eyebrows in bewilderment as she withdrew her hand.

"Understood," he said cautiously.

Chase flashed a disarming smile at Tessa and laid his hand on her elbow. "Ready to go home?"

Just as she started out the cell Tessa caught a glance between Zoric and Chase that made her think life wasn't going to go back to normal just yet.

## *Chapter 8*

The kitchen in the Scott house still smoldered from the small fire caused by over baked cookies. Water pooled on the granite counter tops and on the recently installed wood floors. They were ruined now, Tessa realized as she took in her once beautiful home. Water pinged softly as it dripped from the upper cabinets into the stainless steel sink where her rolling pins rested like burnt matchsticks. Holding back the tears, Tessa wandered into the other rooms of her life as a firefighter nearly the size of the Captain Hunter brushed past her to engage him in a quiet conversation. His eyes darted toward Tessa then turned back to the firefighter and nodded knowingly before taking his leave.

Her grandmother's dishes shot to pieces inside the once beautiful antique china cabinet she'd bought on eBay for an insanely cheap price, looked like pieces of Swiss cheese. Toppled chairs, damaged walls, and years of memories shattered throughout the main floor of the Scott home avalanched an emotional wall of helplessness onto Tessa so suddenly that she didn't realize her body trembled violently. A dam of tears burst from her eyes as she covered her mouth to keep from screaming.

"Mrs. Scott?" It was Chase Hunter. He handed her a bottle of water. It was doubtful there had been any whole glasses left in the house so he'd sent someone out to his Hummer to retrieve this slight distraction. "We'll make this right, Mrs. Scott. I promise."

Tessa looked up at Chase as she sipped the water bottle she held with one hand and brushed silent tears aside with the other. She nodded and glanced around the room again. She lifted a Pottery Barn catalog from the floor and chuckled through an escaped sob. "I was going to make all this," she waved the book around the room slowly, "into something right out of Pottery Barn before Robert and the kids got back." After taking one more sip of water, she capped the bottle and smiled bravely up at Captain Hunter. "Kinda has that lived in look now, don't ya think?"

"Shabby chic maybe." Chase Hunter returned the smile, drinking in the fluid blue eyes that fought back further tears. When she laughed at his comment he found himself laughing as well. He didn't know why. The sound of her voice just seemed to demand it.

Out of the corner of his eye he noticed several Enigma personnel staring at him. His look quickly went fiercely dark as he nodded for them to return to work.

One stood firm, her thin black eyebrows raised in disbelief. Like the others, she'd never heard Chase laugh. His threatening pinched brow and narrowed eyes failed to intimidate her. She moved her dark brown fingers across a hand held computer screen about the size of a notepad. Taking a step forward, a piece of glass crunched beneath her small black patent heels.

"I'm not nearly finished, Captain Hunter. My crew needs a few more hours." Her light brown eyes stayed focused on the computer screen.

"Hello," Tessa said softly. "I'm Tessa Scott."

The short woman raised her eyes to Chase then Tessa as if asking permission to speak. With one hand she pulled on the black jacket of her suit then tucked part of her white blouse a little more securely into the waistband of her skirt. Her black hair, tightly bound into a bun, glistened with hair gel. She reached up and touched her bare earlobes before answering. "Mrs. Scott..."

"Please call me Tessa."

"Very well. Tessa, I'm Claudia."

She offered nothing more. There appeared to be something off about her. The African American woman's eyes turned back to her screen where she punched something in quickly, then leveled her gaze on Captain Hunter.

Chase nodded toward Claudia and smiled politely at Tessa. "Claudia is our librarian. I'm afraid we couldn't get along without her." His tone sounded gentle and caring, something Tessa realized he could turn on and off like a faucet. The charm he exuded worked on the truck driver earlier in the day. Tessa couldn't tell if the compliment affected Claudia or not. "Take as long as you need, Claudia. I'm sure your team will be as efficient as ever."

"What is she doing, Captain Hunter?" Tessa felt the soldier's hand on her arm gently push her away from the librarian. "Is this for insurance purposes? I think I have the name of our agent..." Tessa walked to the kitchen in search of her little phone book she kept with important numbers. His hand guided her carefully toward the stairs.

"That won't be necessary, Mrs. Scott. We'll take care of everything."

"Oh." Tessa turned to face the unnerving Captain Hunter. "I would like to change clothes and pack a bag for a few days before I get started on this mess. I'll stay in town at a motel."

"Do I have your word that you'll not try and escape, send girlfriends a message or call Robert?" His voice and expression clearly sent a warning. "Because my patience is wearing a little thin." The tight smile on his lips spoke volumes.

Tessa held up two fingers. "Scouts honor!" Before he could comment Tessa bounded up the stairs. Suddenly she stopped and turned back to look down at the captain who surprisingly had been admiring her backside. "Do I have water?"

Chase looked over at the librarian for confirmation. He then nodded up at Tessa without expression. "Be quick about it, Mrs. Scott."

"Tessa. Call me Tessa."

Once again he nodded and turned away to speak quietly with the librarian.

Captain Chase Hunter moved from room to room looking for clues as to why the terrorists thought the bomb would be here. Distracted by toys, mementos, a photo of Tessa and her husband in a loving embrace at a Chinese restaurant, forced Chase to tug at his own ghosts that remained buried most of the time. Concentration wavered as he shook off the feeling of regret that threatened his focus. He closed his eyes and took a deep breath, remembering his missionary parents helping others, his older sister singing like an angel in the church choir. Another breath. His grandfather on the

Qualla Reservation teaching him to hunt and fish entered his thoughts, followed by the memories of his first kiss, his first love, his first....

"Captain?" It was the librarian. His eyes narrowed angrily as they landed on the small black woman who still stared at her computer screen. She wasn't very good at visual clues to people's mood. Being diagnosed with a mild form of autism, Claudia carefully compartmentalized every scrap of information discovered on a wide range of topics and persons of interest. She managed to win a special place on the Enigma team with this gift. Due to her inability to interrupt Chase's moods, Claudia usually acquired the job of bringing news he might not want to hear. "You better look at this." She turned the screen around and lifted it up so he could clearly read the information.

He did so without touching the computer. Claudia didn't appreciate anyone touching her baby. His eyes scanned the information as his arms folded across his broad chest. When he finished he looked sharply at the librarian. "I'll download everything to your hand held, Captain. There's more. She's been busy. I've never heard you laugh before," she added as a look of confusion met Chase's hard glare at his phone.

"Thank you, Claudia. Continue." Ignoring the comment he turned to leave, then stopped. "Gather up all the computers, games, etc. before..."

"Already packed, Captain." Claudia tried to smile. She wasn't very good at chit chat. "I'll be sure Vernon has a look at everything."

"Well done!" he snapped, knowing she would appreciate the praise in her own way. He left her and started up the stairs. Tessa was taking too long. Taking the stairs two at a time, Chase quickly moved toward the master bedroom. He'd been in there earlier in the day when he'd pretended to be a plumber. The image of the white and ivory décor jogged his memory as he remembered the tranquil, uncluttered room that Tessa shared with her lawyer husband. Just as he grasped the doorknob, the door flung open and Tessa barreled into his chest, causing her to stumble backwards. Chase did not offer to catch her as he drank in the site before him.

Tessa had transformed herself into the image of the girl next door. Her still wet hair pulled up into a ponytail, made her soft pale features look much younger than he'd noticed earlier. Dressed in a plain white blouse and blue jeans, that was rolled up into a cuff above the ankle made Tessa look anything but dangerous as her bio had suggested.

Catching her breath, Tessa smiled innocently at the frowning captain. "Think I'd run off?" When he didn't respond Tessa realized his eyes were slowly taking in the room, evaluating some obscure information he must think relevant to the day's activities. Or maybe he was trying to figure her out. That thought amused her. What was to figure out? Her life paralleled paint drying. "I was able to get a message off after all," she teased.

Chase's eyes quickly returned to Tessa like a laser. His forehead furrowed with anger. "How did you do that?"

Tessa sat down on the edge of the bed and began putting on the tennis shoes she'd held in her hand. They were new so the bright white seemed to glow. She finished tying the strings and looked up to see that Chase had moved closer, this time with a menacing glare aimed at her. "I keep carrier pigeons in the bathroom. Your team hadn't been up here to find them so I took advantage of my one opportunity to reach my contacts at CNN. You're in trouble now." Tessa sighed and bounced up with a teasing smile.

"Funny." Chase grumbled as he moved toward the window and moved back the sheer white curtains to view the backyard full of flowers, swings and bicycles. A home. A home he'd never have. "Get your bag," he said flatly. "I'll take you to a safe house."

Tessa's smile faded. "Why? I did what you ask. I'm not going anywhere with you," she complained as she lifted her small leopard overnight bag and a wallet from the bed. She moved toward the door with determination and head held high.

"Why did you go to Morocco four years ago?" Chase said folding his arms across his chest. Watching her stop suddenly and turn to face him gave Chase suspicions that he was about to hear a lie coming from the mouth of an angel.

This time Tessa didn't offer a teasing smile. She looked tired and confused at the whole day's experience. "Why don't you ask Claudia? I'm sure she can tell you. That's what she really does isn't it? She's a cyber-cop who spies on innocent people's lives, assumes the worst, transfers the benign to fit some kind of conspiracy to cover your mistakes at Enigma?"

Chase eyed her from head to toe. How could someone with angelic looks be this clever and quick? Was she fooling him with this innocent routine? "Why?" He had a way of demanding quietly.

"Robert took me there because my favorite Bogart movie is Casablanca. If Claudia will dig a little deeper she'll see that's where we went on our anniversary!" she said in a low, condescending voice. "And if you'll check hospital records you'll see my daughter was born nine months later." Tessa pulled back her shoulders and readjusted her grip on the overnight bag. "It was a surprise. Robert saved for two years to take me there. Trust me as tight as Robert is with money that was a real treat for me."

She didn't think it was important to include that Robert had an international conference in Rabat on the future of disputed territories and lands of the 21$^{st}$ century. His taking her meant that he only had to pay for half of the trip. Mostly she had sat by the pool and read a book. The trip to Casablanca had been a side trip offered to the attendees to make their trip to Morocco a memorial one. Nine months later Tessa gave birth to a seven pound baby girl. She'd wanted to name her Ingrid after the actress that starred in Casablanca but Robert had thought that was too boring for his beautiful little girl.

"All in my file," she said flippantly. "Or it will be when Claudia finishes. Pretty boring stuff. However, I'm sure you guys will do a good job embellishing it so it can fit a specific need or target. Am I in trouble?" Tessa kept her voice steady. She missed her family.

Chase stormed past her as he relieved her of the faux leopard bag. "You are trouble, Tessa Scott."

At the foot of the stairs Chase observed Claudia and two other Enigma personnel watching a computer screen they'd collected from the family room. The small lap top sat precariously atop a broken vase on the dining room table. A desperate voice asking for help reached his ears as he pushed aside the men. The screen had been a video email sent earlier in the day.

"Mrs. Scott!" the old man pleaded. He held up his hands to show they'd been tied at the wrist with clothesline cord. A ripped, brown grocery bag partially covered his head. Somehow he'd managed to contact Tessa Scott. "Please you've got to get out of town. There are men here," he looked behind him as if listening carefully, then back at the screen. "Middle Eastern, radicals. They want me to activate a bomb. They have plans to…" There were voices in the background. Anxious. Rapid. "I think it's a dirty bomb. They think I …" Several men burst into the room where the old man spoke, shouting and waving handguns. One stood in the background, observing. He moved forward and looked into the computer screen smiling next to Mr. Crawley. Suddenly the old man landed a shoulder into the man, spun around and hit send. The screen went dark. Silence ensued as all eyes turned to Tessa Scott, standing wide eyed on the bottom stair, her hands covering her mouth in horror.

"Mr. Crawley! My neighbor!"

\* \* \*

Within minutes of Tessa's identification of the man on the computer screen twenty Enigma personnel had invaded the home of Mr. Jericho Crawley. The reason the terrorists had decided to invade the Scott home now had clearly been defined. If the old man had not tried to warn Tessa, none of this would have occurred. Claudia left her team to finish up at the Scott house so she could get started on the neighbor's. Ordered to follow, Tessa stayed with Chase as he entered the Crawley home. A wealth of fingerprints revealed four men, two of which were now dead in a ravine near the Yuba River, a third escaped from an Enigma jail and then this fourth man who turned off the computer. Essid.

Chase recognized him instantly. Their first encounter in Afghanistan revealed the cold, calculating terrorist Essid would become. Essid wanted information on why the American soldiers had come to the village. Refusing to accept the Americans had only brought food and medicine to their starving people, Essid decided to send a message to other villages who accepted help from the Americans. He ordered his men to slaughter every man woman and child. When Delta Force entered two days later, only small smoldering fires of death remained. Another village after hearing about the murders refused any help from the Americans but offered a name of the butcher. Essid, a Libyan who enjoyed killing. The calm voice and face of the man turning off the computer was Essid. Chase knew him, of course, from working in Delta Force and his own experience. His men searched for days to find the Libyan.

In those days Chase lived in a mountain village among Afghan freedom fighters who opposed the Taliban. When several young girls went missing Chase led the men out on a search. After two days they were found beaten and raped by Taliban insurgents. Weeks later a Taliban informant pointed the finger at a Libyan named Essid who'd been in the area spreading a little cheer with his deep pockets. His reward had been the two young girls. After tiring of them he'd freely given them to the ruthless Taliban. Chase made it his mission to hunt Essid down so the village could seek their own form of revenge. After six months Essid found himself in a jail in Kandahar, along with several of his followers. After being transferred to Pakistan, where Chase planned to interrogate him, Essid escaped with the help of a Pakistani soldier. Apparently the promise of a bribe bought his freedom. The little justice that survived came when Essid shot the Pakistani for not being true to his job.

"Mr. Crawley must have told them it was in my yard," Tessa realized. "Last night my little girl said she saw a falling star. It must have been the bomb." Tessa shivered at the thought of what might have happened if it had exploded.

"Did she say it fell in the yard?" Chase inquired as he moved toward the backyard. He entered Mr. Crawley's backyard through French doors onto a covered patio. Two lawn chairs, a small charcoal grill and a TV tray was all that occupied the large concrete space. No flowers, little grass, several live oaks that had seen better days, gave the yard an abandoned feel.

Tessa followed quickly after Chase like an anxious puppy. "I donno. Maybe. I thought she'd seen a meteor so I had her make a wish." She walked to the tall white picket fence where Mr. Crawley had bombarded her with another list of complaints only this morning. She looked over into her beautiful yard full of flowers and felt her heart lurch, remembering her children playing tag and whiffle ball. Silently she said a prayer of thanks that her family was safely in the mountains away from the unfolding nightmare. Just to hold the children and kiss their sweaty little heads would seem like paradise. The touch of Robert's hand holding hers as they'd strolled into church last Sunday now felt like the most romantic experience of a life time. In her heart she whispered, "I love you, Robert. I'm sorry."

"Something?" Chase broke through her reverie as he came up close enough to slightly brush against her arm. He quickly stepped aside as if he'd been stung by one of the honeybees floating about the white butterfly bush in the Scott yard. His voice, serious and direct, held little emotion or concern. This appeared to be just another day to him.

Startled, Tessa cleared her throat to explain how Mr. Crawley had seemed crankier than usual when he'd found out she'd not left with her family. There was the list of complaints and finger pointing, but Tessa had, as always, smiled, nodded and promised to do better. "But look," she pointed down at the ground. "My sprinklers go off around three in the morning. That way by the time the children come out to play they don't track mud into the house. I never noticed earlier but there are muddy footprints going away from the fence. Someone came over the fence into my yard, tracked in the flower beds then came back. See," she pointed behind her, "there are several more steps before the grass managed to take it off. I bet you'll find traces of it on the rug in his mudroom."

Both turned and traced the footsteps back into the mudroom. "Get a man in here, Claudia to see if there's any trace of radiation," ordered Chase. "I bet our little nuisance is buried in Mrs. Scott's flower garden."

The captain continued through the house looking for a clue as to why Mr. Crawley had been a target. "There are no pictures of him or a family."

Tessa nodded and sadly looked out the family room window where Mr. Crawley had a perfect view of her backyard. He must have watched them daily. Maybe he even enjoyed all their noise, baseball games and bar-b-ques. Tessa found some news clippings lying on the coffee table. Respectfully, one by one, she lifted them up to read.

*Sean Patrick Scott scores the winning run for Little Tigers!*
*Three area teachers receive award for excellence in teaching.*
*Local family volunteers at homeless shelter for Thanksgiving.*

There were others: all about the Scotts. They had been lovingly clipped and preserved in plastic covers. They were the only family he had. His only way to interact with the Scotts had been to complain. The feeling of regret swelled inside her. All this time she'd thought him a cranky, disgruntled neighbor.

"Looks like you've got a stalker," came the dispassionate voice of Claudia.

Tessa frowned defensively as Claudia lifted, and then tossed one of the articles recklessly on the couch. Quickly, Tessa retrieved it and replaced it back with the others. "Don't touch these," she warned. "They have nothing to do with this mess or your little secret covert group of thugs!"

Claudia's eyebrows arched in confusion hearing a voice tone change. She cut her eyes toward Chase to receive a nod. With a shrug, the librarian moved on, quietly giving directions to others throughout the house.

As he made a call, Chase checked his watch then motioned for Tessa to follow him outside the house. Surprised at the sun on the horizon, she guessed the captain wanted her to get settled so he could get back to work. He had been relatively quiet since she'd insulted his organization and Claudia. The thought occurred to her that Enigma probably didn't have many witnesses to their operation. Tessa imagined nothing good would come of this encounter with Enigma even after she'd placed herself in harm's way several times over the last ten hours.

"Now what?" Tessa asked, sticking her hands in her jean pockets. The evening air was growing cool. She'd forgotten to throw a sweater in her bag. A slight shiver forced her hands out of her pockets so she could hug her elbows up against her chest.

"There are no photos of Mr. Crawley. I suspect he worked for a government agency that helped erase his identity."

"CIA?" Tessa just couldn't imagine Mr. Crawley working for the CIA.

Chase smothered a chuckled. "Civilians always think of the CIA as erasing identities. There are other government groups that are pretty fond of that too."

"Like Enigma? By the way, is Chase Hunter your real name?"

The sudden appearance of tiny lines at the corners of his brown eyes indicated Chase fought back narrowing them in frustration. "Let's focus on Mr. Crawley. Obviously he has some attachment to you and your family." Tessa wasn't very good at hiding her feelings or emotions in those pretty blue eyes. He saw the worry and distress replace her obstinate attitude toward him. "Ride with me back to Sacramento and tell me everything you know about your neighbor. In the meantime, I'll have Vernon try to locate what he's been up to."

Tessa nodded in surrender. "Okay." She saw the surprise in Chase's eyes. He'd expected another confrontation. "If I can help find Mr. Crawley then I'm in. He tried to warn me. I'm afraid he might die alone. Those men are trying to destroy my way of life."

Tessa climbed into the black Hummer when Chase opened the door for her. "I want to talk to my family."

"Soon." Chase said as he got behind the wheel and started the engine. "He's been trying to reach you all day."

Tessa's eyes widened with optimism. "Really! How…"

"All your calls have been forwarded to my phone for security purposes. You can't inform him of any of today's events. Understand?" His voice left no room for misunderstanding.

"Understood, Captain Hunter." She gave a mocking salute.

Deep inside her, Tessa smiled, knowing a friendly voice who loved her would go a long way to brighten her mood. Even though the air conditioning roared to life, Tessa lowered her window to feel the night air free her of the fear that threatened to drown her.

Again she prayed silently. *"Please watch over my family, God and the people of California. And keep this man"* her eyes cut to Chase, *"safe and clear headed because I'm terrified."*

\* \* \*

Robert tucked his daughter into her feather bed and kissed her forehead. "Love you, sweetie! Sleep tight!"

"Don't let the bed bugs bite!" she giggled. Then a frown came across her cherub face as her lips pushed out into a pout. "I miss Mommy, Daddy. Call her again. I wanna say good night."

Robert smiled weakly. He hadn't been able to reach her all day or any of her girlfriends. He'd left messages on the land line and her cell. Where could she be? Was Tessa so angry with him that she couldn't even check to see how her children made it through the day?

He dialed again as he stroked Heather's curly hair and realized it was the same texture as Tessa's. She looked so much like her mother, the way she pouted, smiled, laughed. Everything. In that moment his heart filled with love for his wife and all that she did for them every day without ever hearing a thank you from him. His three kids were amazing because of her. Lord knows, he hadn't been there to aid in the raising. Today had been an eye opener. There hadn't been much time to relax as he'd single handedly become activities director for the family. Would he be able to last two weeks?

Robert stood suddenly as he realized he had a connection on his phone. "Tessa?"

"I wanna talk to Mommy!" Heather said throwing back the covers.

"Tessa?" he said again.

Chase Hunter held out the phone to Tessa just as they'd pulled into an underground parking garage near the Sacramento capital. As she grabbed for it, Chase pulled it back in warning. "Remember what we discussed, Mrs. Scott."

She nodded quickly like a small anxious child as she took the phone. "Hello! Robert!" Tessa wasn't sure she'd be able to contain the flood of tears.

"Tessa! Where have you been?" The worry in his voice was evident. Before he could say another word Heather stole the phone.

"Mommy! Mommy!"

Tessa laughed. The speaker remained on so Chase could hear every word. "Yes, sweetie! I love you. Have you had a good day?"

"Oh yes! Daddy has been so fun!"

Tessa almost regretted hearing that little bit of praise. "Really? What have you been doing?" Heather began talking so fast that Tessa couldn't begin to translate. All she could do was laugh. Seconds later the boys were on, talking about the boat, hiking and the puke in the backseat just before a squabble broke out over who caught the biggest fish.

"Love you!"

"You too, Mom!"

She heard Robert shoo them off to bed. When the sound of a screen door slammed, Tessa knew he must be on the front porch of their little rented cabin. How peaceful it must be there so near the lake. No dirty bombs to worry about. No missing neighbors or terrorists. No secret government organization holding you hostage. Her eyes went to Chase who stared at nothing through the windshield, but listened to every word she spoke. "Robert?" she said softly.

"I've been worried. Why didn't you answer your phone all day?"

"Sorry. I've been busy."

"Did you get started on the painting? Oh and I forgot to pay the electric bill. Could you take care of that?"

Tessa frowned. "No. I didn't get started on the painting."

Robert sighed as he sat down in one of the rockers. "Did you play around with your girlfriends?" He regretted sounding flippant as soon as he'd opened his mouth.

"Well if you must know, I've been chasing down terrorists," she retorted lightly as Chase turned his narrowed brown eyes on her. "Yes. They tried to take me hostage but the plumber saved me by shooting up the house. Thankfully, old Mr. Crawley intervened and they took him instead."

"Good. Maybe now you can get some work done," he chuckled nervously. "You always had a cute flare for the dramatic." Robert cleared his throat. "The kids miss you, honey. I'm sorry I hurt your feelings."

Tessa smiled and pressed the phone closer as if caressing Robert's cheek. "Oh, Robert. I'm sorry too."

Robert chuckled. "Maybe you could come up after you're finished painting the house!" he said cheerfully.

Tessa pulled the phone away from her ear and looked at it as if some mysterious information had just entered the universe. "Are you kidding me!" she said lowly, hoping that Chase Hunter couldn't tell her anger had risen to new heights.

Again a nervous chuckle. "Of course I'm kidding, honey!" Robert's rocker squeaked as he began to rock. He had no way of knowing a formidable Enigma captain was guiding his wife through a maze of secret tunnels below the streets of Sacramento. It wasn't until Robert heard a strangely familiar ding that he inquired. "Was that an elevator?" He stopped rocking. What could Tessa be doing?

Tessa watched the stern faced captain breathe on an identification pad to enter through the clear doors of a busy control room filled with people, all monitoring computer screens or overhead flat screens you would normally see at a convention. "Elevator? Oh, that's right; you've been gone so long you no longer recognize the sound of a microwave." Tessa sounded almost light hearted as she teased her husband. She wasn't going to straight out lie to him. "Guess you really do need me!"

Robert sighed. "Yes, more than anything."

"Call me tomorrow, Robert. Kiss the kids for me. I'm beat. Love you!" Tessa clicked off before her husband could brow beat her into joining them at Lake Tahoe. Raising her chin in defiance once more at the suspicious captain, Tessa nonchalantly handed back his phone. "Happy?"

Taking the phone he looked down into her manipulating blue eyes that made him more than a little uneasy. "Charming!" he snapped.

Together they pushed through another set of doors. Tessa burst into laughter. The sound of Chase Hunter's sarcastic response caused a release of the day's terrifying tension. As they neared the inner offices, he blew his breath on another security pad before placing his hand on some kind of sensor. A green ribbon of light appeared and scanned his entire body. "Charming?" She choked back the laughter as steel doors slowly opened. He pulled her in after him.

"Why is that so funny?"

She looked around her small enclosure, all shiny, sterile and nondescript. Chase put his hands on his hips, a gesture Tessa began to recognize as Chase's way of evaluating a situation. "You're a big strong guy with killer brown eyes." Again she chuckled, trying to figure out where they were. "You look like someone who eats nails and barbwire for breakfast. And then you say something like 'charming'."

This time when she started to laugh, Chase found himself intoxicated by the sound and joined in just as the opposite side of the tiny room opened into the inner office of Benjamin Clark. Tessa found his deep, warm laugh somehow comforting as they turned to face the Enigma team that Captain Chase Hunter commanded. Some of them stood, others sat at a desk, but all of them froze and looked at the two when the sound of their laughter filled the room.

Benjamin Clark frowned as he eyed his team leader with one thick eyebrow arched in confusion and aggravation. Chase quickly soured as he met the hawk like eyes of his boss. "Having a good time, Captain Hunter?"

"No sir."

"I should hope not." His eyes went to Tessa Scott, standing like a high school beauty queen next to the warrior who had been to hell and back. He realized by her wandering gaze she struggled to make sense of her surroundings. Earlier in the day she'd been in, as yet, an unused part of the Enigma headquarters. Tessa had now been exposed to the hub of their work. He wasn't sure what he ultimately would need to do about that problem.

Benjamin could count the times he'd heard Captain Chase Hunter laugh out loud and this was the second time today. He watched Tessa wither under his fierce gaze as she stepped a little back and behind the captain. Benjamin didn't like surprises. Mrs. Scott was proving to be an interesting encounter. He turned his stocky body to stand before the entire team. The wall behind him transformed into a computer screen.

A map appeared of Grass Valley. Points were marked as to the location of Tessa and Mr. Crawley's house. The site of the unexpected launch was marked in red. Tessa realized how close she'd lived to the terrorist. Although her neighborhood was a gated community, the one behind her was not. The house in question had not been that far away. Why would someone living in such a beautiful place want to destroy it? How could a life be so filled with hate and hopelessness that the only option was destruction?

"Mrs. Scott?" Benjamin Clark singled her out. She straightened, leery of what she may have done wrong again. "You were right. There were traces of radioactivity in the mud." He saw the anxiety in her eyes. "Fortunately the levels were very small. And," he nodded toward her as he turned his back on them once more, "thanks to Mrs. Scott, we did find a small dirty bomb in her flower bed."

All eyes turned her way. Zoric, the villainous looking man she'd encountered earlier in the day, smirked a satisfied "well done." Vernon, the computer genius gave her a wink and thumbs up. Sam, the stunningly beautiful woman she'd been captured by at the elevator, only eyed her with contempt before turning her large cat like eyes back to their boss.

But it was Chase Hunter she timidly looked at for approval. His acknowledgement failed to come. She turned her eyes back to Benjamin. He went on to say the bomb appeared to have landed in Mr. Crawley's yard near the fence. "It appears Mr. Crawley buried it in your yard, Mrs. Scott. Given that he made comments about you not leaving on vacation with your family indicates he thought it would be safe there." Benjamin moved to the edge of his mahogany desk and leaned on the edge. "We think Mr. Crawley knew what it was and used one of your son's toys to trick the terrorists. We suspect he'd had contact with these men before, maybe wanting advice. Why he didn't call authorities is a little suspect." He took a deep breath then ran his hand across his face as if wiping away cobwebs. "It's on the way to the lab for further evaluation. At this point we don't know for sure if there is another bomb."

Timidly, Tessa took a step forward. "And Mr. Crawley? What about him?"

Ben nodded. "None of the agencies claim him but both the FBI and the CIA dodged our inquiries. No work history, no family, no previous address, no nothing as far as we've found which adds more evidence that Mr. Crawley was someone important who knew about such weapons."

Tessa took another step. "But," she looked up at Chase. His hard eyes fell on her like hammers at her interruption. "He moved here from Oak Ridge, Tennessee. We used to talk about it since I worked there too when I was in college." The team exchanged serious glances. "And..." Tessa felt a tingling sensation, knowing this little bit of information meant something or the Enigma team wouldn't be staring at her.

"Out with it, Betty Crocker!" snapped Sam with a growl. "We don't have all day. Maybe if you'd given us this information earlier we wouldn't be playing catch up!"

Tessa withered at her reprimand. Her mouth went dry and her words came out a stutter. "I, I'm so sorry. I, I..."

Chase reached out and touched her arm. "Take your time, Mrs. Scott." He leveled his dark eyes at Sam causing her to take a step back and frown. "And what?"

"Before that," Tessa swallowed hard, "Mr. Crawley lived in Santa Fe."

"New Mexico?" Chase asked. She nodded. "That's thirty minutes from Los Alamos," he said pointing to Vernon who sat down at a computer and began tapping keys so fast it sounded like one continuous tone. "Did he say why he moved to Tennessee, Mrs. Scott?" She seemed frozen except for the large blue eyes that looked up at him in terror.

"Yes! He worked at a lab until he retired."

"A lab?" Chase said looking over at Vernon who nodded and began tapping even faster on the computer. "Did he ever tell you..?"

Tessa gasped. "It was Oak Ridge National Laboratory!"

"You're sure?" Chase said as his hand remained on her arm.

"Yes. I remember thinking how close that was to my parent's house in Nashville." Tessa gulped. "Who was Mr. Crawley really?"

"Got him!" Vernon yelled out with pride. He turned the laptop around for everyone to see. There was a picture of a young man around thirty five and another of a man in his late fifties. "Mr. Crawley retired ten years ago and left for parts unknown, much to the FBI's disappointment!" Vernon laughed knowing he'd bested them. "He apparently wrote a paper that was never published about the safety measures both at Los Alamos and Oak Ridge concerning isotope production."

"Isotopes?" Tessa shook her head. "Why would isotopes be so important?"

Sam came up behind Vernon and reached over his shoulder to pull the lap top back around. Her body rested against the young Vernon's back. Slowly she pulled back to view the screen, pretending not to notice Vernon was paralyzed at her touch. A hint of perspiration showed just under his wild red hair that fell over his forehead...

Sam casually informed Tessa of the importance. "Isotopes are used in nuclear medicine. It aids in the medical and diagnosis of disease. Some isotopes are used in the study of environmental science such as understanding acid rain, flow paths for geochemical and hydrologic modeling."

"You're over my head now," Tessa said lightly not wanting to be the victim of Sam's disgusted opinion of her.

"No kidding," Sam said sarcastically as she folded her arms across her breasts. "In other words isotopes are used in everything from defense programs to food irradiation which makes our food safer to eat and have a longer shelf life. The U.S. now has to import nearly 90% of our isotopes because our facilities cannot produce enough."

"The Department of Energy is trying to convince congress to build some new facilities so our dependence on Russia and other foreign powers will not put our national security in jeopardy," Benjamin Clark added.

Tessa nodded in understanding, visualizing the big picture. "So without isotopes people go undiagnosed, and salmonella poisons our food."

"Some 40% of all raw poultry has traces of salmonella." Sam continued. "Then there's E Coli which affects 7,000 to 20,000 Americans a year. The cost of this can reach a half a billion dollars. Irradiation is widely used on food items grown in or near the ground such as spices and vegetables that are dehydrated. All these items are exposed to bacteria and mold."

"Not to mention insects and rodents that frequent growing centers," Vernon chimed in with a shiver. "I hate rodents!"

"And," a new voice entered the room. "Isotopes may be a possible alternative power source for longer-life space missions. If we produce enough isotopes for use in fundamental science projects it may just simulate electronic devices when exposed to cosmic radiation." Former astronaut Carter Johnson smiled mischievously as he entered the room "Great stuff isotopes!" His eyes fell on Tessa who had now recognized him and couldn't seem to speak. "And you must be the new girl," Carter said with the charm of a political candidate running for president. "I'm Carter." He stepped toward Tessa and stuck out his hand.

Tessa swallowed hard, afraid her admiration for the former astronaut would be evident. She'd followed Carter Johnson's work at NASA over the years. Having been a co-pilot on six shuttle missions and a pilot on two, Carter had flown into space more than any other astronaut. His expertise was in aerospace and mechanical engineering.

She remembered reading an article about him in *Time* magazine after he'd suddenly left NASA to take a job in the private sector. The reporter implied he had been asked to leave because of his reckless behavior and tendency to be a thrill seeker. NASA invested a lot of money in their astronauts and didn't need them taking unnecessary risks. His biggest mistake, the article reported, was getting involved with two women astronauts who both claimed to be his lover. Unfortunately one of those astronauts had been Russian and planned to write a book about her six months aboard the International Space Station with Carter Johnson. Both space agencies were furious. The Russians took care of their problem as only they can. It wasn't until the second female astronaut hired a contract killer for the Russian that NASA decided to let Carter go his own way. He was a public relations nightmare.

Tessa took his hand and felt it close around hers. He gave a sensual squeeze and continued to hold her hand as he smiled flirtatiously. "So you're the sweet thing that took our glorious captain to his knees." His laughter sounded like a high school quarterback used to having everyone enjoy the joke. Carter lifted his eyes to Chase who seemed to be frowning more than usual. Tessa tried to remove her hand but Carter continued to hold it. "Tessa, better watch this guy," Carter spoke to her but his eyes were clearly on Chase. "He's a smoother talker than me. You'll never know when this guy is lying to you."

Tessa's eyes darted to Chase in alarm, wondering if she'd let her guard down too much. She managed to free her hand. "Nice to meet you, Carter. I've followed your career for ten years. I admire all you managed to accomplish at NASA." She hoped her voice didn't sound like hero worship.

Chase pushed between Tessa and Carter moving her toward Vernon's computer screen. "You obviously don't know about everything he accomplished at NASA."

Instead of being put off by Chase's condescending tone, Carter laughed good naturedly and slapped Chase on the shoulder. "Don't worry, buddy. I won't spoil your fun with the little housewife."

Tessa whirled around in anger. "You know I'm getting pretty sick and tired of people treating me as if I'm not in the room. I'm not a total air head! Maybe I don't have all the degrees behind my name like all of you but I seriously doubt all of you combined have as much common sense as I do in my little finger!" Tessa reached down and turned Vernon's computer screen around and folded her arms. "And if you think you've found Jericho Crawley, you're sadly mistaken! Because," Tessa pointed at the screen, "that's not him!"

## *Chapter 9*

Holding a cup of steaming coffee, Robert stood on the front porch, drinking in the beauty of Lake Tahoe. He and Tessa often wondered if there was any place on earth as beautiful as this mountain hideaway they shared each year for two weeks. The smell of pines and fresh air could be intoxicating.

He rubbed his eyes. Sleep had eluded him for a long time but dozed off only to be awakened by something around four in the morning. After checking all the doors and windows, Robert made rounds, looking out each window into the darkness for over an hour. The story about those escaped convicts forced an uncomfortable uneasiness on him. Soon he felt wide awake and pulled out a novel to read. He thought the western involving gunslingers and Indians would invite sleep. The book, lame in plot, was laid aside as he rested his head back against the rocker he had brought inside the living room from the porch the previous evening.

Honey Lynch, wholesome and sexy that one. Strange how she popped up yesterday. Her company last evening had been welcomed but a little uncomfortable. Entertaining attractive women without Tessa around made him feel guilty. He wasn't sure why. It had been obvious that Honey was interested in his company. The trout had been delicious. The kids had eaten every bite. She had finally said goodnight when it looked like Robert wasn't going to send the kids off to bed. Once again she'd disappeared into the woods like a phantom. He'd ask about her vehicle and shouldn't he and kids drive her to her car. But Honey had only smiled teasingly and said she could take care of herself. After all she carried a gun. That part unnerved him more than the escaped convicts. Maybe she was a psychotic killer looking for unarmed campers. Robert smiled as he took another sip of coffee. Nothing that looked that good could be a killer. He was sure of that.

*  *  *

"Mrs. Scott?" Captain Chase Hunter spoke in a quiet voice as he sat down next to Tessa. She'd fallen asleep shortly after takeoff at two in the morning. Her head rested against the window with a blanket pulled up to her neck. The small pillow had fallen down on her shoulder. Even though the overstuffed leather seats were the best money could buy for this type of luxury jet, there was no substitute for a good bed. She'd turned down the offer of the one bedroom, saying she didn't want any special treatment.

Sam, Carter and Vernon had gotten off the plane at Los Alamos. Unloading their equipment had taken only thirty minutes. Zoric continued on with Chase and Tessa to Knoxville, Tennessee. Tessa never knew they'd landed and taken off again. Chase covered her with a blanket after the second takeoff. He sat across the aisle from her facing the opposite direction so he could keep an eye on her. It wasn't until Zoric flopped down across from him that he realized he'd been staring at the new lady in his life.

"So what do you think?" Zoric said in his raspy voice.

"Ben said that Jamaal was intercepted by three men outside Sacramento. We lost track of him after he was taken to a carwash and scrubbed down by hot jets of water." Chase's demonic smile showed no sympathy. "Even though we lost him after that I'd have given anything to watch that creep get his just desserts."

Zoric laid his head back and grinned sadistically. "No, man," he nodded toward Tessa Scott. "I mean the woman. What do you think?"

Chase glanced over at Tessa and turned back to a folded map he quickly opened. He shrugged. "Interesting."

"Interesting hell! She's amazing!" Zoric chuckled quietly so as not to wake her. "How can someone who looks like that get into so much trouble?" He leaned forward and smiled, revealing a chipped tooth. "She's gotten to you, old friend."

Chase scowled. "Got that right. That's why I've developed this twitch," he said pointing to his left eye.

"Naaah! It is something else I think," he said leaning back in his seat. Zoric closed his eyes and remembered his wife and daughters one more time before he slept. It had been a ritual for many years now. "I think you have found the one person who can make you face the past and finally see the future."

"Shut up, Zoric," he said offhandedly. "You artist types are all alike."

"Romantic," he said quietly as sleep approached.

"I was thinking weird."

With a soft chuckle Zoric let his sleepy smile fade. "Yes. Weird and romantic."

That had been several hours ago. The sun was brilliant above the clouds but the weather report indicated showers all day. The pilots had flown around some turbulence in New Orleans, going northeast through St. Louis. Although Benjamin Clark's newest toy, the Aerion SBJ, could out fly anything in the sky, going to Mach 1.8 easily, the pilots felt like they needed to break her in before pushing the limit. The plane gave Chase and his team a time advantage even though they weren't maximizing the advantage of the 80 million dollar aircraft.

He'd searched the computer for Lion's Breath after Zoric faded into sleep. The number of articles on the extinction of North African lions filled more cyberspace than Chase desired to read. A few chosen summaries convinced Chase that the symbol of lions killing and eating the infidels deemed the possibility of an imminent terrorist attack a viable risk. He rubbed his eyes with thumb and forefinger and decided he'd leave them closed for only a few minutes to ponder the information he'd read.

The sun's piercing rays opened them again as he realized he'd taken a nap. A sideways glance at Tessa revealed she slept soundly. It was time to wake her although looking at the angelic expression of innocence and peace on her face forced him to acknowledge Zoric was correct. Tessa Scott got to him. He wasn't sure how, but she'd affected him in a way no one ever had before. As he stretched lazily his eyes fell on Zoric who sat across from him with his legs extended across two seats. He sat with his back against the window, sketch pad in hand, looking at Tessa as his hand quickly captured her essence.

Zoric shifted his eyes to meet Chase's. "Don't you wish we could sleep like that?" he grinned.

"What do you think you're doing?' Chase stood and grabbed the sketch pad. "I didn't know you were drawing again." He handed the pad back carelessly.

"I want you to have something to remember when we are finished with her."

"I'll make some coffee," he said frowning as he moved away.

Tessa Scott stirred lazily as she smelled coffee. "Hmm. Is that coffee I smell?" She pushed the blanket away trying to remember when she'd gotten it. Sitting up, Tessa stretched her arms out in front of her before rubbing her face with cool hands. A shiver ran across her as she realized the air conditioner was set lower than considered "green" at her house.

"Here," Chase said handing her a mug of steaming coffee. "It's an African blend. Ben is partial to that. I added cream and sugar."

Tessa took the mug with both hands, caressing it, as the warmth spread through her fingers and palms. Just before she took the first sip she tilted her head and met the captain's wide brown eyes with her own. Most of the day before he'd had them narrowed or hooded, deep in thought. Now they were relaxed, wide and handsome. "How did you know I took cream and sugar? Surely Claudia didn't know that too."

"You had vanilla creamer in your frig. That's not a guy thing. There was a sugar bowl full of sweetener too." Tessa nodded in acceptance of his answer. "But," Chase smiled warmly, "I saw you add cream and sugar last night around midnight when Vernon brought you coffee." He was rewarded with a smile.

Sleep had made her blonde hair curl out of the ponytail holder. One wayward curl fell across her forehead and Chase resisted the urge to move it away from her bright blue eyes. He'd never seen eyes that shade of blue. Although her lipstick had long faded and the thick lashes lacked mascara, Chase found the woman lovely. A slight tightness came into his chest and he instinctively put a hand on his heart.

"Are you alright, Captain Hunter?" Tessa saw the creases around his eyes appear as he'd touched his chest.

Chase stood and backed into the aisle, smiling. "Not enough sleep and too much caffeine. We'll be landing in ten minutes. Buckled?"

Tessa took another sip of her coffee. "Buckled. And thanks for the coffee, Captain Hunter."

He nodded and turned away and moved to the front of the plane where he spoke briefly to the pilot. He then sat down in a seat near the front, buckled himself in and waited for the sound of rubber meeting runway.

\* \* \*

Benjamin Clark squeezed the phone as if his hand were wrapped around the Secretary of Homeland Security's neck. "No! You're not on speaker phone! I've got people on the scene without this intel." Ben switched the phone to his shoulder where he could sandwich it there with his tilted gray head.

He picked up the secure phone developed by an Enigma sponsor. All his team members carried one. The size made it look like all the others on the market, but this one could do anything just short of launching a nuclear strike. Vernon had snickered at that restriction, commenting that he'd already had a look around in that department. At the time Benjamin decided to put Vernon on probation from field work for the serious misuse of Enigma property in hopes of teaching him a lesson. Benjamin quickly realized his mistake when Vernon spent the time snooping in other areas that didn't concern him. The phone blinked to life as Benjamin slipped it onto the back of his handset.

"What the hell was that sound?" Tobias fumed. Even the Secretary of Homeland Security remained in the dark about some of the fancy toys Enigma possessed. Benjamin intended to keep it that way.

"Dropped the phone. Continue, Tobias. We don't have all day. You put my people in danger without this information."

"Those misfits are like junkyard dogs, Ben. They wrote the book on surviving unlikely scenarios and you know it."

"Those junkyard dogs are going to bite you in the ass one of these days. Now what do you have?"

"Secretary Jackson,"

"Of the Department of Energy?"

"The same. He phones me at 2a.m. and wants a meeting. Turns out Essid worked for the DOE for the last two years." Tobias heard a disgusted exhale on the other end of the phone. He could almost see the usually calm leader of Enigma start to redden with anger. "The FBI missed this during the interview process. He has a pretty good background profile. No problems with the lie detector test. He'd lightened his skin, dyed his hair and even wore blue contact lenses. He looked more American that you!"

People in high places-the White House, FBI, CIA, NSA and Homeland Security knew that Benjamin Clark was the half-brother of the Prime Minister of Israel. His hawkish good looks and no nonsense disposition made him a favorite of the spy business. When the president needed to meet or talk to Ben's brother off the record, it was handled through Enigma without the other agencies ever knowing about it. The hint that Benjamin Clark wasn't a full fledge card carrying American had come up before. Several CIA agents still limped from that misconception.

"Sorry, Ben. You know what I mean," Tobias cleared his throat. "Anyway, Jackson shows up at my place looking like a scared rabbit. Thinks he's being watched. Always was a little paranoid if you ask me. Anyway Essid left Washington last week but not before he tried to hack into the Oak Ridge National Laboratory schematics and security system. We think whoever is assisting him may have the information needed to bring down the lab."

"So why is he so skittish? What are you not telling me, Tobias?"

"One night the two of them ended up at the same party. You know Jackson," Tobias hesitated, "doesn't like the ladies, if you know what I mean."

"I don't like where this is going, Tobias!"

"Apparently Essid goes home with Jackson, gets him drunk followed by a little rough slap and tickle. When Jackson wakes up the next day he's tied to a toilet, buck naked. Fortunately, his cleaning lady shows up in the afternoon. Not only was he embarrassed but his place had been ransacked top to bottom. He refused to let the cleaning lady call the police, thank God, and sent her home. Like the idiot that he is, he'd given Essid his protected password that enabled him to have a look around in both Oak Ridge and Los Alamos. He tried to contain the mess by changing all the security codes and alert both labs of a possible breach. But the damage had already been done."

"And he waited to tell Homeland Security until this morning!" Ben barked with exasperation.

"He's in the oval office even as we speak with his letter of resignation. We have a clean-up crew standing by in case of blood spatter."

Benjamin grinned knowing how cowboy the president could be. "I thought you took all the president's guns away from him."

"Hell! You know how the president is. He might cut Jackson's heart out with a letter opener."

"Hope it's a dull one so it takes longer." Benjamin looked at the large clock hanging on the wall with Eastern Time written below it. He had clocks all around the room that told the time in any given time zone around the world. "What else you got for me?"

"You aren't going to like it."

\* \* \*

Essid calmly turned on the television, muting the sound immediately. He activated the button for hearing impaired so that only the words would scroll across the bottom of the screen. He tried twice before finding CNN. Nothing about the bomb made it into the news. Essid frowned then hurled the television remote at its screen. Another obstacle. He turned around to check on his prisoner who still slept on the cot near the warehouse window. There was no movement.

Essid hoped Jericho Crawley hadn't died during the night. He needed him a little longer. He wasn't confident that the information extracted last night could be counted on as credible. The old man had fought them at first, refusing to give any hint about where the isotopes were kept. Jericho Crawley knew not only where they were kept but where they were manufactured and shipped. Some things never changed, not even after 9/11. The old man had warned them, but too many gaps in security plagued the nation at the time. No one listened to a crazy old scientist. Fortunately for Essid he'd uncovered the letter of warning from Crawley during his two year stint at Oak Ridge National Laboratory. The weaknesses noted and possibilities realized directed Essid's path to California where he'd been observing Jericho Crawley for six months. He knew Jamaal to be a bumbling idiot. He just didn't realized what a total failure he would turn out to be. It had been the plan to take Crawley after chaos ensued in Sacramento. Had it been the will of Allah for the bomb to land in Crawley's yard? His men believed this to be true. Essid wasn't convinced.

It wasn't difficult to predict the trajectory of the wayward missile carrying the small bomb. If Crawley hadn't been out in the middle of the night moving around in his yard their sensors would never have known for certain which house to invade. Essid smiled with satisfaction knowing his plan still could be salvaged.

The old man took a beating pretty good, Essid had to admit. He even spit on one of the interrogators, Jamaal, at one point. It wasn't until Essid opened his laptop and sat it in front of Jericho Crawley, that he saw pain and fear in his eyes.

"Yes, Mr. Crawley, take a good look. It's a live feed." Essid waited patiently. Jericho's half closed eye tried to focus on the screen. "What do you see?"

Jericho batted his eyes for clarity. "No!" he moaned.

Essid smiled as he bent down and looked at the figures moving on the screen. "So you recognize them. Good. I believe that one is Sean Patrick, and oh look! There's Heather hugging her daddy's neck. I wonder where Daniel could be. Let's scan a bit out," Essid said kindly as he touched a button. "There he is! And with a fetching park ranger, I see." Essid straightened and folded his arms across his chest. "Honey is not as sweet as her name, I'm afraid." The screen was pulled away by another captor. "Now, I need to know where you created the super vault that stores the isotopes. It's not on the schematics. I want those isotopes before I level the lab. So be a good boy and tell me." He grabbed the computer again and turned it around carefully. The sound of children laughing as they played flashlight tag reduced Jericho Crawley to tears.

"Don't hurt them. Please."

"I have no wish to harm children, Mr. Crawley. Just give me the information and I'll make sure they continue with their vacation."

The old man had nodded in surrender. It took him only minutes to fill in the missing pieces of information Essid needed to complete his work. Afterwards, Crawley was given food and water before tying him to his cot.

"What now?" Jamaal ask timidly as he handed Essid a cup of hot tea. The interrogation the night before had frightened him. He had blundered the bomb and gotten men killed. Jamaal now walked a thin line of life and death.

Essid turned his now brown eyes on the failure before him. To make matters worse Jamaal managed to end up in Captain Chase Hunter's possession. If the captain had wanted Jamaal to remain captured there would not have been a successful escape. Experience taught him the captain could be devious. The contempt brewing inside him remained hidden behind a veil of calm. "You have made quite a mess in the last twenty four hours, Jamaal. What have you to say for yourself?"

Jamaal rubbed his hands together nervously. "It wasn't my fault, Essid! I..."

Essid impatiently held up his hand in protest. "Stop," he whispered. After picking up Jamaal the day before, it was assumed that he'd been bugged. Taken to a carwash, Jamaal was forced to strip naked and lie on the hood of their rental while he suffered the beating of twenty jets of hot water. Essid was well aware of skin absorbing trackers. Although bruised and burned by the jets of hot water, Jamaal survived to face a much more frightening fate: Essid.

"I have a little job for you."

"Anything, Essid," Jamaal said a little too quickly. "How can I make this right?"

"Help Honey when she kills the Scott family."

# *Chapter 10*

Los Alamos National Laboratory (LANL), located in northern New Mexico, had become one of the largest science and technology institutions in the world since 1943. Its research in renewable energy, medicine, nanotechnology and supercomputing competed for a $2.2 billion budget along with the departments that conducted program research in national security, outer space, and renewable energy. Most Americans had no idea that isotopes used in medicine were created here along with the design of nuclear weapons.

Carter Johnson stood impatiently with Vernon and Sam in the conference room of the Biosafety-Level 3 facility waiting for Alan Yates, the chief security officer, to join them. Carter had worked here many times and felt comfortable navigating the numerous ins and outs of LANL's sprawling complex. NASA had sent Carter here to do research on projects that correlated with the military base at White Sands.

He once had made an emergency landing here in the space shuttle, Endeavor, after the pilot suffered a heart attack halfway through the fifteen day mission. A hurricane brewed in Florida and fog blanketed the west coast. White Sands had been the only other choice. NASA wanted to wait due to the expensive cost of flying in equipment to retrieve the shuttle after landing. That had been the beginning of the end for Carter Johnson when he'd refused to follow orders to save a fellow astronaut's life.

# AN UNLIKELY HERO

Afterwards, Carter found himself assigned to training other astronauts, lab experiments at Los Alamos and Cap Com during other flights into space. Although other astronauts worshiped Carter's gutsy antics both in and out of the space program, the last president used him as an excuse to cut funding for the Mars programs. Carter's romantic exploits in space with female astronauts, especially the Russian astrophysicist, had been the final straw. Out of frustration, Carter resigned under increasing pressure from NASA.

When President Buck Austin took office he made sure NASA shored up its budget, put the Mars projects back on track, fired the current administrator and hired the man Carter Johnson suggested. Being a fellow Texan, Carter had been the president's first choice. After listening to the president's concerns on national security one weekend at Camp David, Carter met Benjamin Clark. While the president grilled some steaks, much to the chef's protest, to a crispy well done, Benjamin explained about the new secret agency, Enigma. Being more of a thrill seeker than a nose to the grind stone kind of genius, Carter joined Enigma.

"Did you hear that?" It was Benjamin on speaker phone.

"Yes, sir," Carter growled. "That changes our plans. We need to intercept those isotopes before Essid gets his hands on them. The outer perimeter has been secured. There's no way of knowing if the nuclear reactor has been compromised for another 45 minutes when the computer does an automatic sweep." Carter nodded to Vernon. "Vernon is on it now. He'll find a way in."

"Get the remaining personnel out of there! If that place blows..."

"Science research will be set back twenty years. Got it."

Carter signed off just as the chief security officer rushed through the door. "No one in or out in the last three hours since you joined us. However," Alan Yates said shaking his head, "four men came in yesterday afternoon with Homeland Security clearance that is nowhere to be found."

Sam put her hands on her hips and rolled her eyes up to the ceiling. "Let me guess. You just found the real HLS agents dead."

Alan nodded. "A guy found them off trail when he took his dogs for a run this morning. The police are just now getting around to contacting us to see if we were missing any employees. They were stripped of ID and clothes."

\* \* \*

Mansur watched Honey Lynch appear out of the woods that stood near the Scott cabin. The frown on her face meant something didn't go as she'd planned. Long strides with those tanned legs gave evidence of an athlete. As she reached up to tie her light brown hair in a knot, Mansur let his eyes slide hungrily across her breasts. Small wet circles had formed under her arms from being in the sun. She spied him ogling at her and jerked her arms down in anger.

"Careful, Mansur." Honey pushed past him to pick up the secure phone lying on the truck seat. She slid in with one leg dangling outside the door. Honey narrowed her eyes at Mansur after quickly dialing. "Wouldn't want Essid to know that you..." just then the other end of the line connected. Honey kept her eyes on Mansur as he began to move road gravel around nervously with the toe of his boot. "They're leaving." Honey sighed. "I don't know! I suppose to town. Those kids are nonstop motion. Mr. Scott looks worn out. He was up moving around pretty early this morning, checking windows and doors. After that he read until daylight then dosed off in his chair. Guess he's spooked about the escaped convicts." She switched the phone to the other ear. "Good. Who are you sending?" Honey's face darkened. "And then can I shoot him?" The line disconnected.

\* \* \*

Never had Tessa imagined that a helicopter could be so loud when she'd boarded at the airport. Taking the Black Hawk would enable them to land at the lab. She covered her ears at first until Zoric gently placed a set of headphones on her head. He'd smiled, almost fatherly at her, and then changed the mood when he buckled her into the seat. His touch had been a little too personal. Jerking back into the seat to avoid his long boney fingers only drew a satanic smile from his narrow lips.

Relieved at seeing the captain jump into the front seat, Tessa watched him turn his eyes back to her then to Zoric. He patted the ghoul on the shoulder then mouthed *Knock it off!* Zoric fastened himself in next to Tessa. Reaching over he patted her hand in reassurance then withdrew.

Tessa felt her stomach lurch as the helicopter lifted. This time no blindfold was needed. No threats to be quiet. The urgency had escalated to where everyone focused on something other than herself.

Once more her family swam into her mind: laughing, singing, catching butterflies and dipping toes into the cool waters of Lake Tahoe. Picnics, fishing poles and star gazing were all a part of the paradise Tessa had sacrificed for her anger and pride. Never again would she be so careless with the gift God had given her. Did they miss her? Could Robert take good care of her babies? *Please, God! Let them be safe. Send them an angel.*

Tessa had never viewed the Smokey Mountains from the air. Having traveled more than most, Tessa always compared the faraway places she visited to east Tennessee. Nothing came close to the beauty of the land or the hospitality of the people. "A slice of Heaven," her father had said every summer when they'd made their annual vacation trip to Gatlinburg.

"Daddy, I'm going to live here someday!" Tessa would proclaim.

"I hope so, baby girl," her father would laugh. "Then I can come see you all the time."

Growing up just outside Nashville in Franklin, Tennessee had given Tessa a normal childhood with all the trappings of living in a small, quaint town. Her parents had been childhood sweethearts, married, had three children, worked hard and gone to church every Sunday morning, evening and Wednesday night potluck for her entire life. Going off to college at the University of Tennessee in Knoxville had seemed like another world. Tessa knew she'd be close to her beloved Smokey Mountains and accepted the scholarship before even discussing it with her parents.

Had that been when Tessa began down that road of independence? Hadn't her father wanted her to go to Vanderbilt so she could come home at night? Her father allowed her to attend the Knoxville school as long as she didn't let her grades drop below a B+. If they did she'd have to come home. Only twice did her grades drop: once because her brother had been in a car accident and she'd rushed home, missing a test, and when her grandmother passed away just before finals. By that time Tessa's father had become a Tennessee Volunteer fan and never hinted she needed to return to Franklin. To think she was so close to home and couldn't go visit her parents added another layer of guilt and regret.

Tessa watched the lips of the three men moving. They had her earpiece turned off. Why? And why did they need her to come along on this clandestine folly? It wasn't like she had any special black ops training. Oak Ridge National Laboratory was synonymous with brilliant men and women. The mere thought of the periodic table gave Tessa a headache. Afraid of heights, rodents, earthquakes and unwashed hands before dinner padded her profile as the most unlikely of heroes. Yet here she was, strapped in a Black Hawk helicopter, surrounded by shadowy men carrying guns that looked like something from a science fiction movie.

A fleeting thought concerning her new ability on how to trick a Middle Eastern terrorist entered her already confused state. Wouldn't having her house shot up and being forced into a secretive government agency in the middle of Sacramento be included on her updated resume? Inwardly she smiled at the thought. The other soccer moms were going to love this story.

Tessa caught her breath when she realized the captain was staring at her through his aviator sunglasses. Her earpiece came to life. "The reason you're coming along…" Tessa squirmed. Could he read minds too? "You once worked for a Dr. Carl Haskin when you attended U.T., am I correct?"

Tessa tried not to look surprised that the captain knew that information. After all, Enigma appeared to have made her life an open book for these nondescript men who had imprisoned her. With a quick nod, Tessa squeezed her eyes shut feelings the helicopter descend suddenly. Her hand went to her stomach before opening her eyes. The captain still remained focused on her.

"Alright?" Again she nodded. "Other than being a nanny for his children, how did you assist Dr. Haskin?"

"Is that why you dragged me here!" she sounded a little more contentious than intended. Swallowing hard, Tessa licked her dry lips. She thought she was going to be sick. "Yes, I was a nanny for his children. When I needed a graduate assistant position to continue with my masters, Dr. Haskin recommended me."

"But your masters were in cultural and environmental geography, why were you working with Dr. Haskin at Oak Ridge?

"He needed an assistant." Tessa realized her involvement now had a deeper meaning. "Dr. Haskin had me grade papers, assist with experiments he deemed too sensitive for the general population of students and faculty. He trusted me, mostly because I didn't know what the heck he was talking about most of the time. There was never any hidden agenda with us. He and his wife even took me with them on vacation. Mrs. Haskin was a doctor of internal medicine. I made their life a little easier. I wanted a free education and I got one. My assistant job paid $1500 a month and my tuition was free."

Wiping the perspiration from her forehead, Tessa watched the ground swim up to meet them. When the door slid back, Tessa didn't wait for assistance in unbuckling her restraints. The rotor blades whipped her hair into her eyes as a hand pushed her head down and forced her forward.

Two men in military type uniforms waited in the shadows of the main building. They motioned for the three to join them. They carried the carbine Black Diamond Specter XLs. Tessa thought the weapons alone looked menacing enough to get the situation under control. Bullet proof vests lay on the ground behind them and were immediately snatched up. She watched how quickly the captain and Zoric slipped into them. Abruptly Tessa found herself under the capable hands of Captain Hunter as he fastened her into the third vest.

Chase secured the vest and let his hands linger a little longer than intended on Tessa's arms. "You'll be alright, Mrs. Scott. However," he drank in the wide pools of blue in her terrified eyes. "I need your promise you'll follow my orders." The pilot joined them carrying gas masks. The captain handed her one as the others took theirs. "We have reason to believe there's been a breach here. A mayday call went out at 0600. Said they were under attack. Enigma has secured the perimeter, but…"

Tessa turned nervous eyes to her surroundings and began to spot other heavily armed men in shadowy corners. "But what?" she whispered in trepidation.

The captain pulled down her gas mask before answering. "Our video feed has people face down in some of the corridors. Gas sensors are on the inside. We won't know the threat until we enter." Zoric handed Chase some kind of electronic device that he checked quickly. When lights began to blink he turned his attention back to Tessa. He didn't like a civilian getting involved in this. He could see that Tessa had begun to hyperventilate. Pulling up her mask so she could take a gulp of air, Chase couldn't stop himself from reaching out to move an unruly curl that had fallen onto her forehead. Suddenly, Chase realized Tessa was watching his forefinger trail down her cheek with narrowed, angry eyes.

Slapping at his hand, Tessa squared her narrow shoulders. "I'm asking you for the last time, why am I here? Either tell me or I'm going to start screaming bloody murder." Chase straightened to his full height and frowned. He took out his phone, punched in a code and turned it for Tessa to see. "Dr. Haskins made the distressed call. He said there were men in gas masks." His look grew hard. "His instructions were to wire 100 million dollars to his off shore account by 1100 hours or the scientists he'd secured in a safe vault would die." Chase played the recording as he glanced at his watch. Time was running out. He watched Tessa's expression turn from resolve to uncertainty.

"Dr. Haskins would never do that!" Tessa protested and pushed Chase's hand away as he tried to pull down her mask. "He's a kind and a decent man. I once saw him rescue a cockroach from his garage and take it to the woods so his wife wouldn't stomp on it."

"That was then."

Just as Tessa reached up to touch her mask she poked a finger in the captain's hard chest. "Tell me what you want."

Zoric knew Chase would not take this civilian's obstinate manners much longer. His team followed orders blindly and without question. Even Benjamin Clark, head of Enigma, rarely second guessed Captain Chase Hunter's methods. The captain, for all his education and experience, found it difficult to communicate with civilians in this line of work.

"You're our eyes. The last schematics we have of this place," Zoric tried to nudge Chase aside to defuse his rising temper, "is fourteen years ago." Tessa's brow creased at the preposterous notion that Home Land Security hadn't reviewed this information after 9/11. "We've heard of a super vault. Do you know anything about that?"

"Yes! Dr. Haskins and another scientist I never met designed it. The vault could be used to store sensitive experiments, research and even people during a state of emergency." Tessa shrugged. "I thought it was for tornadoes or something. Then one day," Tessa's eyes grew large, "he said it was only a matter of time before someone started a war. Dr. Haskins said everything you'd need to live for six months would be there."

"Have you seen the vault?"

"Yes. He made me sign a document to never reveal its location because of its importance to national security. Dr. Haskins said there were only ten people who knew about the vault and only three who knew of its location. I was one of those."

"Why you?" Chase smelled a May December romance. He could just imagine what a looker Tessa Scott had been fourteen years ago. Take away the ten extra pounds from childbirth; add a healthy tan, a free spirit and you have all the makings of a goddess in the eyes of a nerdy scientist who has his head stuck under a microscope all day.

"He trusted me because we went to church together. I was his kids' Sunday School teacher."

"Perfect," Chase moaned as his eyes cut to Zoric who bore the faint smirk of a man who had been thinking the same scenario. "Well it appears your Dr. Haskins has made a deal with the devil himself. If he has allowed terrorists into Oak Ridge and murdered our scientists and done God knows what else, I'll personally make sure he burns in Hell!"

Tessa surrendered with a nod as she pulled down her gas mask. It certainly didn't look good for her friend. As plastic explosives were applied to the steel enforced door, she began to doubt her devotion to a man she'd known in college. A Christmas card with the family newsletter she received each year didn't mean all was well. The children she so lovingly cared for were grown now, attending college at Stanford. What would make such a decent man go so horribly astray? She felt Zoric and the captain push her against the concrete wall as a blast opened the door to the unknown.

"Stay close, Mrs. Scott!" Chase warned as he motioned for his men to enter the building. "I don't want any more civilians getting hurt. Follow my orders." Chase watched her nod furiously that she understood as he pulled down his mask.

Tessa bent low behind the captain as he entered the building with Zoric at his side, both carrying P-90 automatic weapons. Nothing could have prepared her for what lie ahead.

\* \* \*

"We're under fire! Where the hell are you, Carter!" Sam demanded as she forcibly escorted three scientists down a smoke filled corridor. Moments before she'd set off a smoke bomb to cover their escape. Two men had appeared carrying pistols and began shooting wildly as Sam pushed her charges into a safe room and returned fire. She'd hit one of them in the chest but the remaining terrorists had yelled for help. When she heard the gunman coughing, Sam ordered the frightened scientists out into the hall. "Take a deep breath, and then run down the hall as fast as you can!"

"But what if there are more of them at the other end?" the short man in glasses said as he practiced gulping air.

"If we don't get out of here, there won't be an 'other end'! Now move!" When they timidly stepped out into the corridor, Sam pushed them down low so as not to inhale too much smoke. They froze until her automatic weapon began blasting the silence. Sam later confessed she didn't know the pudgy guy with glasses would be able to run so fast. He easily sprinted pass the younger, more athletic woman as return gunfire began to echo down the once tranquil halls of Los Alamos National Laboratory. The woman screamed as indiscriminate bullets bounced off the walls.

"Go! Go! Go!" Sam yelled as she stopped to reload behind some kind of computer tower blocking the hall.

"Sam! They're safe! Now get the hell out of there," Carter said not far from her. "I'll cover you."

"Here they come!"

Carter stepped out into the smoky fog and began firing his Glock as Sam backed up also firing before turning and running. Together Sam and Carter took cover and waited for the terrorists to approach. Visibility started to improve enough for the terrorists to slip from their protection. "Aim for their arms, Sam. We need to interrogate them. Are we clear?" he said whispering into her ear.

Sam kept her eyes on the target. "You get that close to me again and I'll shoot you some place other than your arm." Sam turned her face to Carter who smiled with desire. "Are we clear?"

"Perfectly." Carter was but a breath from Sam's enticing mouth. "Shall we?"

Sam nodded as they both stood and charged down the hall, yelling at the top of their lungs. The two terrorists were so stunned they didn't get a round off before the Enigma duo slammed their weapons upside their faces, bringing them down to the floor with a loud grunt. The sound of their weapons hitting the floor drew a sigh of relief from Carter.

Sam's man tried to get up until she kicked him so hard in the side that he curled up into a quivering ball. Slowly, Sam squatted down next to the man and rammed her gun into his ear. In flawless Arabic, Sam growled, "I love my job you piece of crap. Give me a reason to unload this gun into your head."

Carter jerked the second man to his feet. When he tried to squirm free, Carter landed his pistol on his nose. Blood splattered on the both of them. "We have a few questions for you," Carter said calmly looking down at his uniform. He looked at Sam. "I just had this cleaned."

Sam stood. "So? Do you have a date or something?"

"Chicks dig this kind of thing. Now look at me!"

The man spit on Carter's boots. "I tell you nothing!"

Carter sighed and looked at Sam. Without hesitation she shot her man in the thigh. A scream pierced the hall which got him another kick in the side.

"I told you in the arm!" Carter frowned. A satanic smile spread across Sam's face as she began to reload her pistol and eye Carter's captive. "Now," his eyes turned back to the captive with the bleeding nose. "We were saying? Oh! We have a few questions we'd like to ask you if you have time." Carter had transformed into his charming self.

"That woman is crazy!" the terrorist shivered as he dragged a sleeve across his bleeding nose.

"Yes. She's also really hot," Carter said smiling over at the angry Sam who had begun gritting her teeth. Never a good sign. "So, buddy," Carter said slipping an arm around the terrorist's shoulder. "Either you can talk to me," he said before lifting a finger toward Sam, "or to her. She also really hates all that Taliban-control-the-women stuff. Unfortunately she doesn't quite get the whole end objective of interrogation," he laughed. "Am I right, Sam?"

Sam pulled the trigger and shot her captive in the arm. Another scream.

"Sam!" Carter shouted.

"You said shoot him in the arm!" Her wide, dangerous eyes went to Carter's man then smiled sweetly with a sadistic show of gritted teeth. "Just following orders."

Carter nodded. "I did tell you to do that didn't I?" He shrugged nonchalantly.

"I'll tell you anything! Just keep her away from me!"

"Can I kill this one?" Sam asked coldly as she looked down at the unconscious man on the floor.

Carter slapped the quivering captive on the back. "Well, let's see how this one does. We may need that one if…What's your name?'

"Jeremy."

Carter laughed. "Of course it is! If Jeremy doesn't work out we may need to ask yours a few questions."

"Better hurry," Sam said holstering her weapon. "Looks like this one may bleed out."

"Got it! Hurry it is."

Carter and Sam could play this kind of game all day. Fortunately for them, Jeremy was more than eager to answer all their questions.

\* \* \*

Ten armed soldiers, Tessa guessed they were black ops, not that she really knew anything about black ops, but it seemed a reasonable assessment, surrounded them as Captain Hunter led them down the corridor. The first causality was a man in his late forties, early fifties. Face down in his own blood, it was obvious his throat had been slit. The sight of such a horrific murder forced Tessa to wobble with nausea. To think that she watched all those crime dramas on television using science to solve cases disgusted her. This drama became surreal as she lowered herself behind two of the soldiers. Stepping over the dead man, Tessa cringed, but forced herself to not look back. Her legs quivered with uncertainty and fear.

The captain tested the air and shook his head at the others. Tessa wasn't sure if that meant there were no traces of gas or that they needed to proceed with extreme caution. Either way, Tessa reassured herself by touching the heavy mask again for the hundredth time.

The captain came to a halt and reached back for Tessa. Catching her by the hand he tugged forcibly forward. "Which way?" His voice was a bit muffled but Tessa understood. She pointed to the right. "How far?"

Tessa held up ten fingers for minutes. The captain nodded. Using her index finger, Tessa pointed down then used four fingers. Down four stories. Got it, the captain gave the okay sign and looked at his men who also made eye contact that they understood. Slowly the team began to fan out and room by room to look for intruders.

Eyeing the elevators at the first level, Captain Hunter had one of his men disable them. Visible blood splatter on the door leading to the stairs caught Tessa off guard. When she gasped, the captain followed her wide eyed stare. Motioning to one of his men, the soldier slipped through the door.

Zoric pushed up beside Captain Hunter and removed his mask. "Checked the gas sensors. None detected on this and the three levels below. Fourth level has been breached."

Everyone pushed their masks down around their neck. Several men entered the stairwell. Tessa learned later they were checking other floors for causalities.

Captain Hunter touched his ear. "What you got for me, Vernon?"

Vernon sounded worried. "All hell broke loose here. Carter and Sam have a prisoner. Interrogating now. Doesn't look good."

The captain frowned. "My men have secured the first and second sub levels. Where is everyone?" he demanded looking around for ORNL employees.

"Someone on the inside activated the emergency protocol drill. If everyone followed procedure, most will be tucked away in a safe hidey hole on each floor. Our Intel says they look like steel cabinets about the size of a meat locker. See anything like that?"

Captain Hunter scanned the sterile environment where he now stood. Spotting a path of overturned chairs and scattered papers, he located a door that appeared to be the entrance to a cabinet. "There!" he murmured to Zoric. The two moved forward cautiously reaching the white, ceramic-like door in seconds. Each stood to the side with guns leveled with deadly aim.

## *Chapter 11*

Tessa silently inched closer and lowered herself behind a work station. She rose up just enough to see Zoric fling the door open and the captain swing in with gun lowered. Several screams punctured the silence as Tessa watched Zoric turn into the locker, blocking Tessa's sight. Next she heard the captain's low words of encouragement and motioned to exit with his weapon. Hurriedly ten people filed out, pale and wide eyed.

"Take the nearest exit." Captain Hunter sounded matter of fact without any kind of urgency. "He," nodding to Zoric, "will show you where to go for cover. You did well today." The captain then spoke a language to Zoric that Tessa did not recognize. Tessa wondered again about the relationship between the two, but not enough to erase the picture of the murdered man near the exit they'd passed moments earlier.

Tessa stood up suddenly and took Zoric's arm as he passed. Startled and more than a little pleased he stopped, eyeing her with interest. "There's another exit, on the other side of those doors." She motioned behind him. "It's not another corridor. The only access is from inside." Zoric let a little confusion slip into his eyes. "The way we came in will be…" Zoric nodded in understanding. Scientists were not accustomed to their world being turned upside down. If Enigma planned to cover this up, like Tessa knew they would, exposure to the grim reality had to be kept to a minimum.

The scientists looked at her with fearful eyes. One woman clutched a man's arm while he patted her hand with nervous reassurance. Several others seem to be looking side to side while others appeared to want to rescue some work at their stations. "You must go now," Tessa spoke softly, offering a weak encouraging smile. "This will be over soon. I promise. Nothing will be disturbed. We are not here for your work."

"Why are you here," an overweight man with a pug face demanded? "I'm not going until I know why those mask men came barging in here an hour ago and told us to take cover or else."

Captain Hunter stood to his full height and rested his rifle on his other arm. "How many men?"

"Ten. Maybe twelve."

"Which is it? Ten? Twelve?"

"Twelve. Now what is this about? A drill? Or are we under attack?" The pug face man put his hands on his hips and his voice showed more irritation than fear. "I'm not going anywhere until I get some answers. I'll not be pushed around by some storm troopers."

Tessa gasped at the ungrateful man who blocked everyone's exit. Zoric smiled wickedly as his bloodshot eyes focused on the obstinate scientist. He pointed his weapon at the man's chest as he spoke through gritted teeth. "I knew I didn't like you the second I laid eyes on you."

Captain Hunter lowered his weapon suddenly and swiftly grabbed the man by his white lab coat and yanked him aside. "Okay folks, out those doors like she said." He nodded toward Tessa signaling that she now had that responsibility. "There'll be someone to lead you to cover once on the outside. Keep your heads down and not a word to anyone! Understood?" They all nodded eagerly and began moving toward the door that Tessa had quickly opened and motioned for them. Although the scientists knew of the exit, their adrenaline had impeded their reasoning to the point of needing someone to point the way.

As the door swooshed shut Tessa joined the men with trepidation. The two Enigma agents eyed the man left behind with contempt.

"I've changed my mind. I'll join the others." Pug face took a step toward the exit doors but was cut off by Zoric who raised his weapon a little higher toward the man's head.

"Sorry. We don't have time for that."

"But!" he started to protest but stopped when the captain held up his hand, looking angrily down at the floor. Beads of perspiration began to trickle down pug face's sideburns. "You can't…" he started again and decided to gulp a swallow when the captain leveled his narrowed eyes at him.

"We'll ask the lady." Captain cradled his weapon in his arms as a laser like stare bore into his captive. "She's in training. What should we do?"

Tessa knew he meant only for the scientist to be more respectful. However, she couldn't swallow how ungrateful he'd been at having been rescued. "I say tie him, gag him, and then throw his ungrateful butt back in the locker." All three men turned to look at her in astonishment. Tessa shrugged. "That's what the handbook says!" she said lifting her hands in mock exasperation. "Now get with the program boys! We've got work to do!" With that she marched boldly to the locker and pointed inside. "Let's go hotshot!"

"Please," he begged as Zoric ripped off a piece of duct tape from his pack. "I'll not make a sound. Just don't gag or tie me up."

The men looked to Tessa. "Don't even think about coming out. Our men have orders to shoot to kill anyone wandering the hall. Got that, sweet cheeks?" Tessa said as the scientist began bobbing his head in agreement. "We'll be back within the hour. Can you handle that?'

"Yes. Thank you, mam!"

"One more thing," Tessa said stopping Zoric from slamming the door shut. Pug face waited in anticipation. "You owe these men an apology for insulting their brave attempt to rescue you."

"Of course! I apologize with my whole heart. If there is anything I can ever do for you, please call on me." He wiped the sweat from his face and slouched onto a stool.

Tessa pushed the door shut with her foot and turned precariously to face the men who stared at her in surprise. With a shrug, Tessa adjusted her Kevlar vest, and then retied her ponytail with a sly smile. As she wrinkled her nose Tessa softly said, "I always wanted to do something like that."

"I think I'm in love," Zoric said calmly in his thick East European accent.

"Oh," Tessa said nervously.

"Fall in, G.I. Jane," Captain Hunter said as they moved out of the room into yet another lab. Two more safe lockers were discovered with some thirty people. Two of the captain's men joined them, escorting them out with Tessa's assistance.

Slipping into the stairwell five of the captain's men rejoined them. A cautious downward spiral began, their backs pressed close to the concrete walls painted a sterile white. The slightest step seemed to echo a deafening explosion to Tessa who feared the terrorists might locate them with a shower of bullets or deadly gas. More of the captain's men waited at sub level three. Body language shouted readiness to engage the enemy, but their steely eyed demeanor left Tessa somehow comforted that these men knew what they were doing. They had no intention of sacrificing one of their own for the sake of terror. Whatever it took to secure lives here at Oak Ridge would be accomplished one way or the other. It was the "other" that gave Tessa pause.

A young soldier held up three fingers then used his thumb to point inside sub level three. A series of sign language signals ensued between the men. From what Tessa could understand there were three armed men with hostages. One of the men held a wallet size computer and with a few typed instructions, suddenly the lights were extinguished.

Captain Hunter felt Tessa Scott grab his arm when the stairwell went black. Everyone but her had flipped their night vision apparatus to disperse the darkness. He reached across his weapon with his free hand and gently touched her shoulder. Leaning in, Chase could smell her hair as it touched his unshaven face. "Stay here," he whispered. "Will secure."

"Don't leave me!" Tessa begged as she turned to face him, not realizing how close her mouth was to his. "Please."

The others looked around at their captain in anticipation. "Here," he fished in his vest and removed a small key chain flashlight and a lipstick size canister. "If someone comes through that door besides us and you can't get out of the way use this."

Tessa slipped her hand into his, strangely aware of its warmth and strength. She shook her head in confusion.

"The flashlight and the red pepper spray I removed from your purse. I'm sure you know what to do." Chase felt her nod. He patted her cheek. "If I had a broomstick I'd gladly give it to you," he tried to sound reassuring as he moved his lips near her ear.

Suddenly Tessa brought her arms around his chest and gave Captain Chase Hunter a quick hug. "I'll say a prayer for you and your men," she breathed lightly. "Be safe!"

The sound of a heavy door being pulled open, the smell of sweat and the brush of deadly force, caused Tessa to shove herself into the wall, hoping in the worst case scenario she'd be invisible. Her unstable shaky knees longed to collapse to the floor as she found herself alone, but sheer will power forced them to lock and stand ready. She had a flashlight. Why not take this opportunity to make a run for it? Surrounded by darkness she imagined the sweet beam of light that could lead her upwards to safety, maybe even to escape. No one would know she wasn't one of the ORNL personnel if she grabbed a lab coat. After all there were some 22,000 people working at Oak Ridge. Blending in would be unbelievably simple.

Her mind began to click details of catching a ride to the airport when the flash of gunfire erupted inside sublevel three. The hope of escape evaporated as quickly as it had materialized. The rapid sounds of automatic fire mixed with loud voices of surprise forced Tessa to fumble her way into the corner behind the door, paralyzed with the fear that she would never see her family again.

"Oh God, please, please, don't let them die!" she whispered to herself. Silent tears began rolling down her cheek as her grip on the flashlight tightened and her thumb pushed the lip off the cap of her red pepper spray. Touching the small canister with her index finger, she managed to locate the spray nozzle. If the situation demanded it, Tessa didn't want to make the mistake of spraying herself in the face.

Loud voices began moving down the hall. The sound of return fire exploded in her ears. She knew instantly that the invaders were nearing her. The flash of several gunshots were too explosive to be the men of Captain Hunter. It had been obvious that their assault weapons carried silencers. Men like that make war silently.

Two men slammed into the door, firing precariously into the darkness from within. The gun flash lit their faces for only a split second, but it was long enough to see one of them take a hit in the head, splattering blood over the entire window of the door. Tessa watched in horror as the second man pushed his comrade aside. The door began to open as the remaining man fired. Tessa heard the sound of anguish then the clatter of a weapon hitting the floor. The terrorist had shot one of the captain's men. The soldier must have been close because the terrorist stepped away from the door cautiously, letting the door escape his grip. The dead terrorist's arm fell through the opening, propping it open.

Tessa inched forward and felt the hand of the dead man beneath her foot. Her inclination was to panic, but something caught her eye as she peeked through to the hall. An emergency exit light had not been extinguished, allowing Tessa to see the terrorist bend over and take the soldier's assault weapon. In the red glow of the exit sign, he looked like Satan as he smiled down at the wounded soldier.

# Chapter *12*

"You are going to die, infidel. Tell me how many others are here."

"Go to hell!" the soldier snarled slipping his left hand cautiously down the side of his leg where he'd been shot.

"You first!" the terrorist replied angrily.

"Excuse me," Tessa said as she tapped the invader on the shoulder.

Startled he whipped around just as Tessa let lose her pepper spray in his face. Tessa caught the falling weapon carelessly in her arms like a baby. Staggering backwards, the terrorist yelped in pain just before he fell over the downed soldier, landing haphazardly on the floor with a thud. The soldier pulled his ten inch bladed knife from his pants leg pocket and rammed it into the terrorist's heart.

"Oh, dear Lord!" she cried looking down at the dead man then to the soldier who was trying to stand.

"Lady," he said reaching out to her as he groaned with the pressure he put on his leg, "I don't know who you are but I'm sure glad you're on our side."

"I, I," Tessa didn't realize she was stuttering. Instinctively she offered him assistance to stand. She'd never seen someone killed. "I'm going to be sick!" Tessa turned and grabbed a trash can under the exit light. Since she hadn't eaten since the day before all that came out was dry heaves.

Just then more soldiers began rushing down the corridor, Captain Hunter in the lead with Zoric bringing up the rear. Everyone was accounted for, it seemed. "I see you took out the two that got away," the captain breathed a sigh of relief. His eyes then went to Tessa who had her head stuck in the trash can, coughing and gagging. "Did she see you do this?" The tone of concern sounded more like a growl.

"She saved my life, captain." He nodded down at the stabbed man. "If she hadn't come in here and pepper sprayed him I'd be dead. He had me cold. I owe my life to her." One of the other soldiers helped prop him up and retrieved his knife.

Captain Hunter moved to her side. "Are you alright?" His calm, unemotional voice caused Tessa to jerk her head up and fall back against the wall. There was nothing left in her so that she could speak. She couldn't nod, grunt or cry. Carefully Captain Hunter removed the carbine from her arms then handed it to Zoric. He snapped his fingers at one of the men and was brought something to wash her face. His touch was gentle. Next Chase carefully took her hands and cleaned them too. The cooling sensation helped her to swallow and look into the captain's dark eyes that were only visible because he'd lifted the night vision apparatus. The light of the exit side cast a peculiar glow over his face and neck. He never took his eyes from hers while he cleaned her hands. Later she realized he'd been showing her the blood spilled today was not on her hands.

Many years earlier Tessa had read a book about angels. It was a work of fiction but based on some rather interesting facts and experiences of people who had encountered angels. All of them had said they weren't cherub like creatures, but mighty warriors that were enormously strong and resolute about their objectives. Looking into the unflinching eyes of Captain Chase Hunter, Tessa began to wonder if he wasn't one of those warrior angels. Doesn't the Bible say that angels walk among us? A weak smile of relief toyed with the corner of her lips.

"Drink this, Mrs. Scott." Chase held a bottle of tepid water to her lips until she began to drink. "Better?"

"Is everyone," she looked down the wide corridor expecting someone to appear, "safe? Were they hurt?"

The captain informed her all were accounted for, locked securely in various locations on this sublevel. Several had cuts and bruises from their encounters with the gunmen but there were no deaths. Some would need medical attention but not so soon as to jeopardize the completion of the mission. The gunmen had open fired and were quickly subdued. Two were now locked in a room with several scientists who volunteered rather eagerly to watch over the intruders. The captain's men bound their wrists and ankles along with a rather uncomfortable gag before leaving. The scientists were not in danger of learning anything vital considering neither of the gunmen could speak English.

Taking one last sip of water, Tessa handed the bottle back to the captain. "Thank you." Her voice sounded like she'd been gargling thumb tacks.

"Ready?" Chase tried to offer an encouraging grin. "You're doing fine. This will soon be over, Mrs. Scott." Chase motioned everyone out into the stairwell with a slight motion of his thumb. Reaching out to Tessa, he took hold of her elbow and tugged her away from the wall. "I need you, Mrs. Scott."

Tessa found herself inches from the captain's body. A hard swallow sounded in her throat as Chase's steady, brown eyes bore into her. "You, you do?" Something about this man made her anxious, irritated and mesmerized all in the same instant. She knew her voice sounded like a love sick school girl looking into the eyes of a rock star.

The captain stepped back toward the door leading Tessa forward. The dead body had been removed. Tessa squinted to try and see the blood splattered glass. One of the captain's men nonchalantly slipped in her line of vision and pulled the door back so far that the darkness blocked out any hint of blood. She couldn't help but grab Chase's forearm as the darkness began to engulf them.

"We need to move to the fourth level where the super vault level is located, Mrs. Scott. What can you tell me about it?" He began gently leading her down the flight of stairs. "How many have access? Size? Purpose? Capabilities? Anything, Mrs. Scott." His men gathered at the bottom of the stairs in anticipation of the next assault. Bodies tense with fortitude, the men looked to the captain for instructions. Chase suddenly stopped, feeling the landing beneath his feet. He carefully assisted Tessa as his eyes went to the solid concrete wall.

There were no more stairs and no place to go. Had Tessa been mistaken? After all, it had been nearly twelve years. He waited patiently for Tessa's response, noting that she swallowed with a little difficulty as she cleared her throat. Tessa licked her lips nervously. Fear still revealed itself in her eyes that seemed to sparkle in night vision.

"Mrs. Scott?" Chase realized she was blind in so much darkness. He should have retrieved the night vision goggles from the wounded soldier at the top of the stairs who now guarded the stairwell. Tessa would have felt more confident. But then he wouldn't have been able to observe her so closely and freely as he did now.

Her eyes drank in the darkness, wide and blinded by the abyss of black. Shifting them at the sound of a restless soldier's feet caused Tessa to reach for Chase's arm with a feathered touch of her fingertips. The jolt of satisfaction he experienced both disturbed and pained him as tightness gripped his chest. Chase made a mental note to see the Enigma doctor upon completion of the mission. Heart attacks didn't happen to men his age and in his physical condition. After shouldering his weapon, Chase laid his hand on Tessa's to discover how cold her skin had become with the fear she must be experiencing.

"Mrs. Scott, there is nothing here." Chase motioned for one of the men to relinquish his goggles.

Tessa quickly donned the goggles and examined the wall before her. Chase watched her curiously as she reached out and touched the cement wall. "Yes. This is it, Captain Hunter."

"I see nothing, Tessa" Zoric commented as he stepped forward to stand beside her.

This time Tessa didn't shy away. The intense focus in her eyes gave both Zoric and Chase pause as they studied the woman who had become instrumental to this clandestine state of affairs. Both men looked from the woman to the wall. When she smiled Tessa turned to face the men.

"Yes!" Tessa's sudden enthusiasm made her a little breathless. "Yes! It's here! Look," she said waving at the entire wall. "It's not just cement blocks. You see here," she pointed to a row of blocks, "it's a grid. Twenty-six across, twenty six down, each block representing a letter of the alphabet." Tessa touched the wall. "They also represent numbers. The trick is to put in the correct numbers and letters to open it."

"We're screwed, captain," one of the men whispered. "How do we get in?"

Chase turned his eyes back to Tessa, knowing her assistance probably had come to an abrupt end. "How many people have this code is hard to say. It was still in the planning stages when I left. Dr. Haskins didn't plan to make it accessible to just anyone at the ORNL. He was definite about that. Although the vault was completed before I left, Dr. Haskins hadn't completed all aspects of the security."

Chase sighed in frustration. "These walls are too thick to blow with what we're carrying. We need someone with the code. Any ideas, Mrs. Scott?"

Tessa looked to the wall on her left, farthest away from the stairs. Walking awkwardly because of the night vision apparatus, Tessa reached the wall and touched one of the blocks without any reaction. After the third time a glowing computer screen appeared.

The shock of the light made Tessa step back, nearly falling. She felt familiar hands catch her and jerk the goggles from her face. Managing to look up into the deep brown eyes of Captain Chase Hunter gave Tessa energy to push away and straighten herself. He too, now stood goggle free. Others were lifting their goggles up onto their foreheads.

"Mrs. Scott, you have a lot of explaining to do when we get out of here," Chase said nodding at the blinking computer screen. "You know the code, don't you?"

"I'm not sure."

"What do you think it is?"

"$E=MC^2$."

"Brilliant. What lame brain thought of that one?"

"I did." Tessa said simply ignoring the insult. "No one would suspect a graduate student outside of Dr. Haskins department would be allowed to do such a thing. He'd just made me read Einstein's biography so $E=MC2$.

"Oh." Again Chase sighed with irritation. "Why didn't I guess that one? Do it," he motioned with his weapon that he removed from his shoulder.

"Computer?"

"Yes, Tessa. It's been a long time." The voice was male.

"The computer recognizes your voice. Priceless," Zoric chuckled.

"What do I need to do in order to access the super vault?"

"Hand and retinal scans must be successful before further directions will be initiated." A picture of a right and left hand appeared on the screen along with two eyes. Tessa placed the palms of her hands inside the drawing and leaned in to look into the life like blinking eyes. Within seconds the picture disappeared. "Thank you, Tessa. Do you still like ham and cheese sandwiches?"

"No. I like BLTs, hold the mayo."

"That's right. You may precede, Tessa."

"Now what?" Chase inquired as Tessa turned to face him.

"Just wait." Then in a bright flash, the smaller grid on the wall came to life with bright letters, going both horizontally and vertically creating a square. She began touching letters what seemed to be randomly after first counting spaces between the letters.

"That is incorrect, Tessa. Would you like to try again?"

Chase looked down at his charge and wondered if God was playing a cruel joke on him. "Try it," he ordered.

Tessa frowned up at him and shook her head. "I'm sure the doctor has a short cut now but I would never have been privy to that information.' She turned back to the computer. "No thank you, computer. Look back in your memory. This is correct."

"And if it isn't?" Chase inquired, bewildered at her knowledge of such sensitive government security systems.

"Then another inner wall will seal us off and only Dr. Haskins can release it. Explosives would be of little help. Computer?"

"Great!" Chase fumed, trying to think of another way inside the vault. Just as he was about to give the order to retreat up the stairs, the wall became opaque, like frosted glass, as it slowly began sliding back within itself, revealing a well-lit warehouse of monumental portions.

Stunned at the revelation, the men tensed and readied their weapons. All eyes searched the inside perimeter. "What the hell?" Chase whispered. "Remind me to thank you when this is over."

"I can't believe it! What is all this?" Tessa too, stood in awe of the enormous operations so far underground.

"This, my dear Tessa," Zoric grinned, "is your tax dollars at work." He nudged Chase with his elbow. "Can we keep her, Dad?" Zoric teased as his bloodshot eyes cut to Tessa who seemed mesmerized by the science fiction world that lay before her.

Chase frowned as he stepped forward, "Now what, Mrs. Scott?"

Tessa motioned toward a reception desk where a series of security computers exposed the various sections of the underground laboratory. "There should be some information there."

Chase motioned for two of his men to attend to the security system and quickly returned with directions and video feed. "Take a look at this, captain. Looks like our boy is helping them retrieve something out of a container."

The container, barrel round and yellow carried the international symbol for radioactive. Several more rested precariously on a table where men dressed in black examined a way to open them. Dr. Haskins chastised them anxiously, saying they risked radiation exposure if the containers were damaged. Someone interpreted the warning and the terrorists took several steps back for safety.

Enigma commandos began to fan out upon some silent command given by Chase. They were converging on an area some one hundred yards deep into the super vault. No one had time to speculate on the types of scientific discoveries and secret projects operated in this underground think tank. It apparently also had living areas set aside for long, uninterrupted stays. The independent power source had not been affected by Vernon's long distance computer wizardry as proof of the low hum of working machines and bright halogen lights.

As Chase approached silently, he motioned for Tessa to get down and behind several of the armed soldiers. She nodded and for once followed instructions. Voices began to reach his ears. Sounds of arguing, begging and even a female voice whimpering could be heard between the clips of destruction emptied into the room through a semiautomatic weapon. He didn't need a video feed to hear the desperation ahead.

"Stop! Stop!" came the cries of frustration and hopelessness. "You're destroying years of work!"

A strangled, hyena laugh ensued then more gunfire. "I need the isotopes now, doctor, or I'll start shooting the hostages, starting with the pregnant one whimpering like a spoiled child." He cut his dark eyes toward the young woman cowering in the corner, tears rolling down her puffy red face. "Then I'll have your family eliminated. You know your wife is quite attractive. Maybe my man will pleasure himself first." His mouth formed into a crocodile smile. "And when we find your sons, and make no mistake, we will find them, well let's just say they…"

"Enough! I'll do what you want. But, please, let Penny go. She knows nothing about this isotope project. She's a lab tech. That's all."

Chase neared the hostages in stealth style. He activated his camera on his ear piece. Are you getting this, Ben?"

"Roger that, Chase. His wife's terrorist has been taken down. She's on the way to the airport. Dr. Haskins has two sons attending Stanford. They're hiking near Tahoe. Extraction in progress." Chase waited until he could zoom in on the terrorist for further information. "No face recognition in our system. I'll have our people keep working on it. By the looks of it, five of the top U.S. scientists are in that room. Their death or capture could be devastating to national security. Do whatever is necessary to stabilize the situation."

"Only two others, captain. I don't have a clear shot. The pregnant woman is in my line of sight." A soldier whispered into his mike.

Zoric's even keeled voice interrupted. "Have Tessa go in for the woman. I don't think he'd shoot a woman."

"Negative. I'm not putting another civilian in danger."

"Too late for that my friend. She's in over her head anyway."

Chase looked back at Tessa Scott, crouched down, watching him like he held the keys to heaven and hell. Even from here he could see the fear in those beautiful blue eyes. Country or beautiful woman? Chase heard the pregnant woman begin to cry. If anything unnerved a terrorist bent on getting his way it was a terrified, sobbing female. He reluctantly motioned for Tessa to come closer. After reassuring her that Dr. Haskins had indeed been forced into this act of terrorism, he briefly explained the immediate problem and what he needed her to do. Watching her force a swallow, he nearly changed his mind. When she nodded, Tessa reached for a transparent clipboard atop a file cabinet with some random chart full of formulas and scribbles. The pair of black glasses that rested next to it were placed low on her nose with such care that she once again puzzled Chase as to who she really might be. Was this another one of God's humorous pranks? Would this woman be the one to finally put him out of his misery?

"Get the woman down and to the left. There's an office space. See it?" Tessa nodded quietly. "I won't let anything happen to you, Mrs. Scott."

"You keep saying that and things keep happening!" she quipped.

Chase grinned. "Don't be a hero."

"Never."

Tessa straightened up and quietly walked to the end of the clear partition, lined with tables and file cabinets. The voices seemed deafening now. Why had she agreed to this suicide stunt? Could she just not say no to the handsome captain or did she crave a reckless scenario so desperately that she was willing to put herself in harm's way for an adrenaline rush? The last two days had been just that. Never had she felt so alive in a surreal world.

The sound of uncontrollable tears reached her ears. A pregnant young woman; terrorized by armed men would not be good for the baby. She thought of her own sweet babies and how safe the experience had been. Stopping, Tessa said a prayer of thanks for her children being somewhere safe with their father. Turning her head to look over her shoulder she could see the captain's men follow him to be near her. Tessa squared her shoulders and began humming *The Ants Go Marching One by One.* Her eyes focused on the clipboard as she turned the corner into chaos.

# Chapter 13

Her humming continued until an angry voice shouted at her so loud that Tessa dropped her clipboard.

"Stop!" Tessa recognized the voice of the man who had been terrorizing.

Dr. Haskins and the other captives.

"Who are you?"

"What the..." Dr. Haskin's familiar and gentle voice sounded shocked.

"I'm sorry, Dr. Haskins! I took some cold medicine and fell asleep in my office!" Tessa eyed the frightened doctors. Her eyes came to rest on the woman Dr. Haskins had called Penny. She couldn't be more that twenty-five; probably a graduate assistant from the University of Tennessee.

Dr. Haskins opened his mouth to speak when the terrorist held up a hand in protest. The man eyed Tessa suspiciously noting her calm with rising alarm. The man's eyes began to dart around the area for changes. Had the underground vault been breached?

Tessa recognized the look of doubt in the man's narrowed eyes as his body tensed and his pistol outstretched toward her.

"Oh dear God!" she screamed. "What is going on? My God! My God!" she screamed trying to cover her mouth as she rushed toward Penny who now shook with uncontrollable fear.

As Tessa pushed Penny into the office the terrorist gun exploded through the glass wall, shattering glass over her back. Penny's scream echoed in Tessa's ears as she pushed her awkward body to the floor. Just as

Tessa turned her head to look back over her shoulder, she saw Captain Chase Hunter's profile in the doorway of the office. Raising his semiautomatic rifle, he fired off two rounds.

In that moment in time, when the captain turned his head to glance down at Tessa lying on the floor covering the pregnant woman, his eyes took on a dangerous glow that both frightened and thrilled her. He had saved her life yet again. God once again had heard Tessa's cries and sent this angel of death to protect her. Their eyes locked in some strange new bond of trust and something else that made Tessa's heart race with anticipation.

Moments before Chase had held his breath as Tessa Scott had disappeared around the file cabinet. His man on the other side of the hostages barely breathed the description of the situation unfolding before them. Zoric managed to slip into position for another shot of the third terrorist. When the captain heard Tessa's signal words "My God" he rushed forward with his men to take down the leader. The momentary sound of a gunshot breaking glass ignited a fire of revenge deep inside Chase so that when he rounded the corner of the file cabinet he reached the office doorway in two steps. In a split second he'd raised his weapon and put two shots into the leader forcing the weapon from his now bloody hand held against his chest. Later he remembered the sounds of crying, relief and his men taking out the other terrorists.

Just as Chase raised his weapon to fire he had for a split second been transfixed by Tessa Scott lying on the floor, covered in glass, protecting another with her body. His heart had stopped, thinking a bullet had found its mark when the glass shattered seconds before. When the blue eyed housewife of Grass Valley, California had turned to look hopefully at him an unfamiliar wave of relief had washed over him.

"Dr. Haskins," Chase said offering a hand to pull him up from the floor, "are there any other intruders down here?"

The doctor quickly began assisting the others, some struggling to stand. "No." He nodded toward the leader who began to moan. Chase had made his shots carefully so as to severely injure, not kill. "He said he would have my wife killed if his man didn't hear from him in the next ten minutes," Dr. Haskins said looking nervously at his watch.

Chase nodded. "Your wife is safe. She'll be waiting for you at the airport."

"Thank God!" he sighed in heavy relief.

There was God again; getting in Chase's way of grim reality.

Carelessly Chase rolled the leader over with his foot so he could look up at the man who shot him. "Who are you?" Chase growled as he pointed his weapon down at his heart.

"Help me," he whispered.

"Just as soon as you help me," Chase responded coldly.

"Go to hell, infidel," he groaned.

Chase kneeled down next to the bleeding terrorist. "Ben?" He touched his earpiece to access Benjamin Clark back at headquarters. Chase wanted an ID.

"Not in our data banks, Chase. I don't recognize him from any of our Intel. He's new. Not Middle Eastern by the looks of him."

"Go to hell," he whispered again.

"Yeah. That's probably inevitable, but you'll be there long before me if you don't start talkin'. And just so you know, my men and I all wipe our ammo with pig fat before loading up. So don't think you'll be spending eternity with a bunch of virgins."

The look of intimidation finally sprang to the wounded man's eyes. "Okay. I'll talk. Just don't let me die," he begged. Chase nodded at one of his men to take over as Zoric came to stand at his side.

"You better get in there, Chase." Zoric tilted his head toward the office where he'd left Tessa and the pregnant woman. "There's another situation."

Chase slung his weapon and hurried to find Dr. Haskins helping Tessa kick glass away from the center of the floor. His eyes fell on Penny breathing hard with her hand on her stomach, eyes wild with terror. She let out a cry as she doubled in pain. Penny was in labor. "We need an ambulance and medic team now!"

Tessa didn't know who the captain was talking to; someone in cyber space she guessed. All she knew was that help would not come in time. "Captain, her water broke. She's having the baby now!"

"What?" Dr. Haskins spoke as if in a fog as he straightened. He began backing out the door, for the first time truly afraid. He didn't like blood if it weren't on a lab slide under a microscope. Suddenly Dr. Haskins looked out at the downed leader being attended to and the cuts and bruises that were now evident among his colleagues.

"Get him out of here, Captain Hunter," Tessa ordered as she grabbed a lab coat hanging on a hook behind the desk. She watched the captain roughly grab the doctor by the front of the shirt and shove him backwards through the door without taking his laser like focus from her hurried activity. She spread the starched white coat on the floor before moving to help Penny.

"Captain, have you ever delivered a baby?" Tessa asked as she began stroking Penny's head.

Chase propped his weapon in the corner and kneeled down next to the frightened woman. "As a matter of fact, I have," he smiled with a kind of disarming charm. "Penny, we're going to have a baby, sweetheart." He patted her exposed leg, feeling the warm blood meet his fingers.

"My baby!" she cried.

"Your baby will be just fine, Penny."

Tessa found herself breathing calmly at the silky tone the captain now used with the terrified mother-to-be. He gently positioned her legs so they were bent at the knees and spread apart. Like magic, Zoric appeared with a first aid kit and handed Chase a pair of scissors. "I'm going to remove your panties, Penny," Chase smiled devilishly. "You can tell your husband about that any way you like when this is all over."

Penny smiled and began to breathe normally just as another contraction gripped her body.

"Breathe like this, Penny." Tessa imitated the breathing exercises she'd learned in her own birthing classes. Penny quickly followed and soon was at rest again.

"I think we're going to have a baby, sweetheart," Chase coaxed calmly.

"Oh!" she grunted.

"Nothing to worry about, dear. This ain't my first rodeo," he chuckled as he stroked her leg. "My parents were medical missionaries in China when I was growing up. I assisted on my first appendectomy when I was ten." His eyes drifted from Penny's face to Tessa who openly stared at him in disbelief. "Then I went on to be the medic when I joined the Rangers."

His comments were telling her something, Tessa knew. Sharing this information could be a clue to what kind of man Captain Chase Hunter really must be. He was a good man cloaked in a dangerous roll of ultimate hero. Those dark eyes reached out to her like a drowning soul. "You're lucky to have him, Penny."

"I don't even know your names," she said trying to lick her lips. She watched the scary man, who had brought in the first aid kit, come stand behind Tessa. He handed her something. In seconds Tessa had lifted Penny up enough to sip some water from a bottle. "Who are you?"

"I see the baby's head, Penny. You're going to have to be a good girl now, and really push." He watched her nod and she scrunched up her face to push. "Good! Breathe with my friend," he paused as he looked at Tessa. "Breathe with Agent Melanie. Now push!"

Another agonizing push, a breath and another push. "One more, Penny!" Chase encouraged. "Prettiest baby I ever saw. Come on! Push!"

# *Chapter 14*

Robert watched the children gobble down their burgers and fries followed by ice cream which he immediately regretted, having forgotten that Daniel was lactose intolerant. After his son let out a huge belch and his siblings started laughing with loud gusto, Robert quickly ushered them out of the restaurant under the glare of several sour faced customers.

"Your mother is going to have to work on your manners," he scolded crossly as he swung Heather up into his arms so they could cross the street to their parked SUV. "Look both ways, boys. Mom would kill me if anything happened to you."

Sean Patrick sniggered at the thought of his mom getting angry enough to swat a fly off her much less using deadly force on his father. He grabbed Daniel's arm to pull him along. "Daniel, come on!" Sean Patrick yanked Daniel forward just missing a tourist watching a pretty brunette walking along the sidewalk instead of the road. "Hey! There's Honey!" Sean Patrick said happily as he waved to the forest ranger dressed in blue jeans and a tight U2 tee shirt.

Robert followed his son's waving hand and saw the pretty young Honey smile and wave back at his son. Something inside him warned to stay clear of the flirtatious ranger, but before he could unlock the car, both boys ran to her side and started talking about their morning. Robert carried Heather far enough to set her feet on the sidewalk and she too ran to Honey.

"Hi, Robert. I see you've been entertaining the troops like the good dad you are," Honey smiled seductively and she cocked her head at him and winked playfully. "Your wife is a lucky girl. Most men wouldn't let their wives stay at home for a much needed break. I hope she appreciates you."

Robert thought there was some implication as to her interest level, but remained confused as to what he should do about it. It wasn't like he knew many single women. From what one of the attorneys at work had said, women today like to be the aggressor. Even though the attorney was married, he enjoyed straying and being "eaten alive" as he like to say, by anyone other than his wife whenever possible. Robert frowned at betraying a woman like Tessa.

He'd fallen head over heels in love with Tessa the first time he'd seen her in Knoxville, Tennessee. She was playing with two young boys in the park, instructing them on how to hit a baseball. At first he'd thought the children were hers. The next day he'd accidently on purpose ran into her again and offered to help her in the training of the boys. When he discovered she was their nanny, Robert's heart would not be appeased until he made Tessa fall in love with him.

Intelligent and beautiful, Robert had never thought such a woman could love him. But she did and with her whole heart and soul. Having just passed the bar in California, Robert had been offered a position with a prestigious law firm. When Tessa had accepted his marriage proposal, a wave of relief had washed over him. On the day of his wedding, before God, he'd promised to love and cherish her forever. Now, here he was looking at Honey Lynch like a little boy in a candy store wondering if he was still desirable to someone other than his wife.

Knowing that his job took a great deal of time from his family, Robert's justification was always that he needed to provide a good life for the ones he loved. The truth, he had begun to realize, was that he just liked his job more than being home for important events. That seemed like woman's work to him. And he just didn't know what to do with the kids most of the time. It seemed so easy for Tessa to be the hero with the kids. They thought of him as the strict disciplinarian. Sometimes they even seemed shy around him. Granted, he wanted and needed to be proud of the children, but taking the time to participate interfered with the ladder of success he chose to climb.

Why couldn't Tessa just continue to raise their kids like she'd always done? After all, she was good at it, loved it even.

His love for Tessa had never wavered, but her constant reminder of his lack of input to family construction grated on him at times. In his opinion the years she worked at school she had the entire summer off to decorate, play with the kids, chat with her lazy girlfriends and volunteer at the soup kitchen? He'd even given up going to church with them most of the time. "Have to work," he'd say but was back in time to watch the 49ers or the Chargers play football. At least the boys liked to watch the game with him. Tessa couldn't let the moment pass without mentioning the boys knew they would at least get to breathe the same air as their father for a few hours.

Tessa had returned to a part time teaching job when Heather had turned three. "A little spending money would be nice," she claimed. The lady across the street had volunteered to watch Heather for free since her daughter had been the same age. It actually had given the neighbor a few hours of freedom while the girls played dolls. In return, Tessa watched the girls if her neighbor had a date night with her husband or needed a day off in the summer. Heather would be four by summer's end so Tessa had decided to return to work full time. The preschool was a block from her teaching position and Heather had eagerly wanted to attend so she could be "big" like her brothers. Now the money would really be rolling in, Robert thought happily. More money to invest and plan for the future made him feel he could better protect his family.

A little guilt rolled over him as he smiled timidly at Honey Lynch. Tessa often accused him of being flirty or overly friendly to the ladies, but he hadn't meant anything by it. Mostly Robert was just working the crowd for clients. His Tessa was always the prettiest one in the room, the most thoughtful when someone was in need and the sexiest girl he'd ever known; at least when she wanted to be. Tessa could also be stubborn and horribly right at the most inopportune times. It would be just like her to pout if he'd set his foot down about the budget or her spending unnecessary money on the kids. Taking up for the kids when they were obviously out of line was another pet peeve of his. Of course, now, after spending just two days alone with his three little monsters, Robert was beginning to understand the dynamics of parenting.

"Can we, Dad?" the kids chorused loudly.

Robert snapped out of his reverie. "What?"

Honey laughed warmly and patted Robert's arm with her tan fingers. His muscle flexed instinctively at her fingertips. "I said I have some extra passes to the Ponderosa if you and the kids would like to join me. The old television set for Bonanza is still there with a Wild West town. You can dress up like gunfighters and get your picture taken. There's a chuck wagon that will take you out in the early morning, rustle up some breakfast and show you the beauty of Lake Tahoe." Honey looked back at the kids. "Two weeks ago a bear tried to join them."

The children gasped. "What happened? Did he eat the people?" Daniel shivered with hope.

Honey smiled. "Nope! Luckily I tagged along because there had been a few sightings."

"Wow," Heather cooed.

"What did you do?" Sean Patrick asked as his brow wrinkled in skepticism.

"I shot my gun in the air a few times and he ran off. We set a trap and caught him the next day."

"Cool!" Daniel nodded. "Where is he now?"

"We tagged him with a radio collar then released him far into the mountains. He'll be happier there, away from humans."

Robert ruffled Sean Patrick's hair. "I don't know," he said with hesitation.

Sean Patrick looked up at his father with pleading eyes. "Please, Dad! Mom would never let us do something like that if she knew a bear had been around. She's afraid of her own shadow."

Honey put her arms around Daniel and gave him a slight squeeze. "I wouldn't offer the passes if I thought you'd be in danger. Most of the time you'll be in the old west town. It will fill up your day," she promised sheepishly, seeming to notice Robert was struggling to keep the kids occupied.

Sean Patrick frowned. "But there might be danger, right?"

Honey met Robert's eyes and smiled in that seductive way she had when her words were only for him. "Danger indeed!" she promised mischievously.

"Why not?" His surrender carried a twinge of guilt, knowing that part of his decision came from knowing the lovely park ranger would be tagging along.

The kids jumped for joy and started talking all at once as they moved toward the car. Honey helped Heather into her car seat then came around the car to double check Sean Patrick's seatbelt in the front seat. "Can't be too careful, Sean Patrick." Her eyes met Robert's as he slid behind the wheel. She thought she detected a slight blush. "Your passes will be at the gate. I'll catch up with you."

They said their goodbyes as the SUV slowly pulled out into traffic. Honey waved and laughed as she heard them begin singing *The Ants Going Marching One by One*. Watching them disappear toward their road to the cabin, her cell phone began to buzz. The fake smile disappeared so quickly from her face that she squeezed her cheeks to make them loose again.

"Yeah. They just left. Geeze! I hate kids." Honey switched the phone to her other ear. "They're where?" she snapped. "I thought you said those boys were at Stanford," she said impatiently, realizing the voice at the other end expected something more of her special talent. "And when I find them?" she quizzed, but already knew the answer. "I'll be in touch. Don't worry. I'll take care of Dr. Haskin's boys."

Honey returned the phone to her pocket and looked up at the breathtakingly blue sky. Inhaling deeply, she placed her hands on her hips and smiled wickedly.

"What are you smiling at?" Mansur questioned when the truck door opened and Honey hopped in almost gleefully.

Without giving her partner a second glance she sighed. "This job is turning out to be more interesting than I thought."

\* \* \*

Benjamin Clark stood facing his expansive window, staring out over Sacramento. Pondering the unfolding scenarios of the last two days, he evaluated the possible solutions and outcomes, none of which gave him comfort. He would never understand the need to destroy innocent people for the sake of your beliefs, even if it were falsely claimed in the name of God. That included Allah, Buddha, Hari Krishna or any other known deity. It boiled down to power and control in Ben's mind.

He'd grown up in two worlds: North Carolina and Israel. His mother, a political science major in college, had earned an internship at the American

Embassy in Tel Aviv her senior year. During one of her weekend trips to explore Israel, she had been caught in a hostage situation in Jerusalem by a Palestinian group called Eternal Death. A young army captain came through the doors, guns blazing and killed three of the four terrorists. The fourth managed to hide until Ben's father secured the room. He'd just ushered a young American girl out of her hiding place when he saw the fourth Palestinian rise up and aim his gun. To protect the American, the captain jumped in front of her to take her bullet, but not before empting his gun into the final terrorist.

His father had nearly died. The young American girl never left his side during those dark days. When he began to recover, the warm smile of his saved hostage gave him encouragement. One day when he'd awaken, he saw that the girl he'd come to know as Bethany Clark, held his young son Gilad. They were playing patty-cake. His wife had died the year before; not by the hands of terrorists, but from a car accident. Authorities thought she'd fallen asleep at the wheel after working an extra shift for a sick friend. Ben's father buried his heart in his work the same time he'd buried his wife. Later he would tell Ben that his mother had healed him that day as he'd watched little Gilad fall asleep in her arms.

Bethany's family, never keen on their daughter's thirst for adventure, couldn't accept that she might some day stay in Israel. The romance between the genteel southern girl of North Carolina and the rugged, often times brash, Israeli army captain flourished even though the relationship continued in a long distance format. After eloping, Bethany quickly became pregnant with Ben. To reassure Bethany's family, Captain Benjamin Levy insisted his young wife and child remain in the U.S. as he continued his work in Israel. Every holiday, both Jewish and American, the Israeli captain tried to visit. He even let his oldest son remain with his wife's family six months out of the year. But the remaining six months both boys were to be with their father. Bethany often stayed in Israel too, loving the culture and excitement of the Middle East. Both boys attended American high school and college before taking their very different paths. Gilad chose Israel to serve and protect. Ben remained in the states to eventually serve in the military and two presidential administrations before becoming the head of Enigma.

While growing up, Ben had often quizzed his stern father about why he'd carried his mother's maiden name rather the Hebrew name of his ancestors. It wasn't until Ben entered college that now General Levy told his son that one day he would be called upon to serve both the United States and Israel. With a Hebrew name everyone would question the wisdom of his decisions. Now Ben's brother Gilad led Israel in the twenty first century and he ran the secret agency of the president of the United States. His father would have been proud of his sons had he lived.

Ben's thoughts turned to his team in the field. They were the brightest, most focused group that Enigma possessed. But they were not without their quirks that sometimes made Ben stare at the ceiling of his bedroom in the middle of the night. Since he'd taken over at Enigma sleep often eluded him. Living on strong coffee and vigorous exercise seemed to be enough to keep Ben sharp and equipped to handle their diverse personalities and abilities. Without Ben's gift to coordinate information, supply equipment and vital personnel to complete a mission, the teams' lives could be jeopardized.

Lately his team leader, Chase Hunter, had given him concern. Benjamin Clark had known Chase since the day he'd graduated from West Point. After visiting with his sister and grandfathers for a few days, Chase had welcomed entering the military. He quickly aspired to being an Army Ranger and found the physical and mental challenges fit his need to control situations. Benjamin had been a colonel back then and found that he admired the young, no holds barred soldier. Several years passed before Benjamin approached Chase about becoming a Delta Force elite fighter. Knowing that Chase had just buried his only sibling, he saw the fire of anger and revenge burning in his soul. Ben knew if he could take that passion and turn it into a Delta Force soldier, the world would be a safer place. It had not been easy molding Chase Hunter. In spite of the fact that he welcomed the physical and mental challenges the Delta Force presented, he didn't respect authority. After numerous confrontations, threats and punishment, Chase realized he'd found a home among the Delta Force and a friend in Benjamin Clark.

The years had taken their toll on Chase Hunter. He'd lost his parents in China at the hands of the Communists. A college romance gone badly left his sister dead of an overdose. Chase accused the questionable character of her lover of causing her untimely death but was unsuccessful bringing him to justice. He'd seen hideous slaughter of innocent people in Sudan and the Democratic Republic of Congo. In spite of the tragedies Chase had begun to live a normal life again, teaching night classes for fellow soldiers and serving under General Benjamin Clark at the Pentagon. Then on September 11, 2001, terrorists crashed into the Twin Towers, and the Pentagon, killing people senselessly that he cared about. Chase had saved Ben's life that day, carrying him through smoke and fire, and returning over and over again into the chaos to try and rescue others. It wasn't until that next day his fraternal grandfather informed him that his grandmother lost her life in the North Tower of the World Trade Center. After that day intensity swallowed the soldier, making him stronger and dangerously lethal. Ben cringed at the things he'd ask the Delta Force captain to do in order to make a safe America. Never once had Chase complained or suggested another way to accomplish the mission. He seemed to take satisfaction that he might be making a difference even after losing comrades in arms in Iraq and Afghanistan.

Ben had recruited Chase for Enigma, knowing Chase was the leader others would follow blindly. Promises provided time for Chase to do what he loved, teach Renaissance literature at the university level. The first year of joining Enigma had given Chase a false sense of normalcy. Without conviction, Ben suggested Chase, with a little effort, might try putting down roots, start a family, and live like most Americans. That normal part hadn't lasted. Enigma seemed to always be on the brink of a disaster, sending Chase into Afghanistan time and time again. Due to his gift of languages and skin color Enigma liked to drop him in a war torn hell hole for gathering intelligence to unravel conspiracies threatening his own country. The only thing that remained conventional was his teaching position at Sacramento Sciences and Technical University where he gained popularity with his students. However the last two years had even robbed him of the joy of teaching. He now taught on line classes that met once a month. No one knew if he missed a class for some clandestine outpost at the end of world. Someone could easily slip in and pretend to be an online professor.

The director wasn't sure when he began to observe a change in Chase Hunter. He'd become sullen, irritable, and short tempered. Normally, Chase was quiet and understanding of his students' needs, but a year ago he'd gotten wind of him over reacting to a student's lack of interest in his class and failed him. Although the student went through appropriate channels to rectify the problem, Chase would not budge. The English department sided with their professor but not without a severe warning. The chairman of the department notified Chase of the formal grievance with no penalty only to suffer a threatening confrontation resulting in security being called.

Although many men envied Chase when it came to the ladies, Ben worried that his behavior of *love them and leave them* might eventually be his undoing. There was never any joy in his love life; nothing ever lasted more than a month or two, and several hearts had been broken in the process, which Chase had given little thought or concern. "Time to move on," he'd say. "She was getting a little clingy."

But the overall attitude of the team leader eroded into a dismal, unsympathetic soldier that carried a very large chip on his shoulder. Chase didn't know how to cry or laugh, or so Ben thought until yesterday when he'd gotten off the elevator laughing at something Mrs. Tessa Scott had said. His face was bright with interest and humor, even under such tense circumstances. Ben noticed Chase watched her every move, when she was working with Vernon, and especially when Carter Johnson had strolled over to offer a comment. Chase had gotten in between Sam and Mrs. Scott, threatening to banish a valued team member if harm came to the woman. Even Chase's best friend, Zoric, had been nudged into line for staring too openly at the fresh faced housewife from Grass Valley. Ben witnessed the whole scene by audio at Oak Ridge National Laboratory. Chase remained in complete control, as always, but there was something different about him. Could it be that Mrs. Scott had touched a nerve in the mighty Chase Hunter? Would she turn him into someone more human, or enhance his already protective killer instinct?

His phone rang; the direct line to Carter and Sam at Los Alamos.

"Carter?" As always Ben's voice was the epitome of calm and reason.

"Not good news, Ben. This place is going to blow if we don't smoke out the two remaining guys impersonating Homeland Security agents. They've accessed the nuclear laboratory where all the experimental work on future deterrent capabilities is housed. The Complex Transformation system is well underway here."

"English, Carter!"

"This Complex Transformation system would enable us to take our nuclear weapons to a more responsive level during a national emergency. Although they don't seem to want anything, their goal appears to be to destroy as much of the work here as possible. The United States no longer has the nuclear capability as during the Cold War. This system can predict how best to use what we have and to create other nuclear deterrents quicker and more efficiently. The door would be open to see our shortcomings, Ben. It's an Achilles heel. Maybe not tomorrow or next year, but in the future our inability to respond to a nuclear threat will be a result of today."

Ben heard Carter talking to someone else. "Talk to me, Carter."

"Sam says one of the combatants we captured earlier says these guys have the ability to transfer our research to some overseas server. Vernon is going in the back door to stall them while LANL's people shore up security. He's pretty good at placing obstacles. He'll do it, Ben."

"No way to storm the lab where they're holed up?" Ben already knew if it could've been done, Sam and Carter would be in there now.

"The outer wall has been booby trapped with plastic explosives. If we go in the entire lab goes, research and all. What we can do is pipe gas through the duct work. Just have to figure out how. You'd think with this many brains in one place we'd be doing more than sucking up all the oxygen."

Ben half smiled at his man Carter. Leave it to him to see something humorous in a dangerous situation. "How long, Carter?"

Carter looked over at Vernon who rapped at top speed on the keyboard of his computer. Other computer gurus assisted, taking orders from time to time from Vernon on what maneuver to try next. When Vernon threw his hands in the air with a wild yelp, he gave Carter thumbs up.

"Most of the research has been transferred to a dummy account. Our not so smart hackers in there think they've sent all the files to someone in the Cape Verde Islands."

"You're sure?" Carter demanded, knowing how cocky the young genius could be with his computer brain and ego.

Vernon turned his head slightly as he pushed thick red locks of hair away from his face. His face flushed a bit at being questioned about something no one else knew more about than him. His lips puckered in a mock pout. "Pretty sure," he taunted.

Carter took a step toward Vernon, one fist doubled, the other raising his nine millimeter pistol enough to pose a threat. "You'd better be damn sure, Vern or so help me I'll shoot you along with the other terrorists."

"Dude," Vernon smiled nervously, knowing Carter was not in a read between the lines mood, "I'm sure. Chill out. These guys," he nodded toward four other computer analysts, "are almost as good as me! Right guys?" Vernon held up his hand to high five them. They did so reluctantly as they kept a skeptical eye on Carter Johnson.

Sam shouldered her weapon and ruffled Vernon's red locks then pulled playfully at his left ear. "Good job!" she smiled warmly. "If Vernon says he got the research then believe him," she said sliding a slim, silky hand down Vernon's face, which nearly paralyzed him with desire.

"Got it!" one of the computer scientists proclaimed.

Vernon smiled as he looked at the five screens before him. "We have visual, Carter. Pulling up their bios now." Carter came to stand behind Vernon with Sam. She purposely leaned into Vernon to view the screen with a keener eye. Laying her cheek gently against his drove him to type faster. His heart frozen with embarrassment, Vernon realized he'd not shaved that morning, not that he needed to every day, but still the thought of Sam's warm cheek touching his made him want this moment to be as perfect and memorable for her as it was for him. "These guys have no facial recognition profiles. I've sent them to the FBI for their files."

Sam straightened her tall, slim frame. "They're in somebody's file, Vernon. They couldn't have made it this far without some working knowledge of this place, computer technology and the importance of new age deterrent strategies. Check," Sam gave him a verbal list of ideas which he started imputing almost as fast as she spoke them. "Here it is! Samantha, you're a genius."

Sam touched Vernon's ear again causing him to fidget. "Yes, I know. Thanks for noticing, Vernon," she cooed. "Now, talk to me."

"Former students at the Missouri University of Science and Technology, majored in computer science and metallurgy, a strange combination, don't you think?"

"No physics?" Carter asked as Vernon began scrolling through the terrorists' college records. "There! Backup." Carter looked at the classes both men had taken the last year. "Doesn't look like they're going to be rocket scientists with those grades."

"True. But look at this class." Vernon pulled up the description. "Ever take any explosive classes, Carter?"

Carter eyed the suspicious courses. "Get the university on the phone for me and the professor who is doing the research."

One of the other men at the computer terminal began dialing to get an outside line.

Vernon laughed and pointed out other shortcomings. "See here. Several of these classes were dropped last semester. No scholarships to speak of. They appear to be related. Brothers I'm guessing. Let's see where they originate." Vernon explored the computer like a marksman on a big game hunt. Not even Sam could tease him off the scent now. "Yep. Went to school in Libya until their uncle sent them here to live with their... Are you ready for this?" Vernon turned his chair around to face his teammates. "They lived with Essid's family until they moved to Rolla, Missouri to attend the university." Vernon folded his arms across his chest. "How the hell did they get into that school? They're not that bright."

Carter smirked down at Vernon. "I don't care what Sam says about you, Vernon. You're the best asset this team has. Good job!"

Vernon shifted his eyes up at Sam who smiled down at him with amusement. "Don't listen to him, Vernon. He is jealous that I find you more attractive than a dare devil astronaut who can't pass by a mirror without admiring his reflection." Sam turned her large almond shaped eyes on Carter whose smile began to fade at her declaration. "You see, my little cupcake," Sam said ruffling Vernon's curly red hair, "he torments himself at the truth. Oh well," she sighed, walking past Carter, chin held high.

Carter joined her as they eyed the barricaded double doors before them. His cocky smirk had returned. "Better start tormenting yourself, Miss High and Mighty. It appears our straight arrow of a leader has a tiny crush on a certain housewife from Grass Valley. Notice how he..."

"Shut up!" Sam said as she checked her weapon. "You forget Chase's rule about married women? He's just trying to get as much mileage as possible out of a source."

"I guess that's one way to look at it." Carter said hearing a warning whistle from Vernon as he motioned for him to pick up the wall phone. He grinned as he watched Sam's smile fade into a tight lipped frown.

She wasn't subtle at letting Chase know she could be his anytime anyplace girl if desired. Everyone knew Chase had resisted the beautiful temptation offered him on numerous occasions. Any man that could still breathe would have been thrilled to explore the pleasures of the intriguing and beautiful Samantha.

Carter informed the professor on the phone the dilemma facing them at the Los Alamos National Laboratory. With a few questions, silence and a thank you, Carter disconnected the phone, nodding to Vernon. "Simple. Let's do this the easy way, shall we?"

Although the would be Homeland Security frauds disengaged the security software so their movements could not be observed, they were unaware that two weeks earlier Vernon had overseen the installation of new spyware he'd developed. The heat censored cameras in the ceiling were no bigger than a dime and were activated only when the old system failed in some way. In this case, the system had been illicitly compromised. Vernon could now watch their every, nervous movement about the lab in which they'd decided to make a stand.

While Sam and Carter soaked the exterior doors with liquid nitrogen to neutralize the plastic explosives, Vernon watched helplessly as the men in the lab gently applied more explosives in key areas. They knew it would only be a matter of time before the infidels found a way to crash through the doors. Their work, after all, had been completed. All the files had been transferred overseas; their place in paradise guaranteed.

Vernon grinned happily as he pushed a few buttons on his keyboard and watched the water pipes explode with cascades of water, just as he'd initiated the sprinkler system with a false positive of smoke. Moments before Carter had blasted the plastic explosives around the door to the lab with high powered jets of water, neutralizing the exterior for safety.

"You're good to go!" Vernon said as he accessed yet another key to open the doors to the lab held hostage by inept jihadists. "They're running around like a chicken with his head cut off!" he laughed so hard his sides hurt. "I'm right behind you," he said pushing away from his terminal and pulling out his nine milometer handgun. He looked down at the Los Alamos techs that had assisted him, nodding toward the door. "You probably should let your boss know we've secured their lab. Oh, and you're going to need an ambulance. Sam doesn't like getting her feet wet. Those boots she's wearing are new. She's really going to have to take it out on someone." As he moved toward his teammates he heard the others making the important calls that needed to be placed.

\* \* \*

Essid knew the downtown warehouse where he kept Jericho Crawley created a dangerous risk of being discovered. As soon as darkness fell he would take his hostage and move to a more secure location; provided the old man was still alive. Not hearing from his men at Oak Ridge gave him concern. The last call came from Dr. Haskin's home after they'd taken his wife. Their boys were luckily in California, attending Stanford University; another great bargaining chip for him. And now the news reports from FOX announced an evacuation had taken place at Los Alamos due to a water main break and a small fire.

"What is going on!" he screamed as he kicked the folding chair sitting at the small table where two men played cards.

The two men looked at each other nervously, not wanting to be on the receiving end of Essid's tantrum. Essid angrily knocked the cards off the small table. "Get the car ready. We're leaving soon." The men rose cautiously. "Hurry up, you idiots. Can you do nothing but sit and play cards? Must I tell you every little thing that must be done?" Essid ran his long fingers through his shiny black hair as he tried to compose himself. Anger would blind his normally rational behavior. Taking a deep breath, he slowly walked over to the windows that were caked with dust. The sun shone so brightly through the panes they appeared to be frosted. It didn't matter. He was looking beyond the view into his future.

What would become of him after all of this planning and scheming for so many years? Would the one who had blind sighted the United States draw praise from fellow Jihadists? It wasn't that he really cared that much about Islam. Too many frightened people followed the ways of the prophet for his liking. All this was for much more.

The thought of snatching a few hours' sleep toyed with his exhausted brain. He loved those times when his brain had been pushed to the limit and forced his body to shut down to reboot itself. The dreams would come during those deep dark times. Lions, once free and numerous across his land, returned to hunt and stalk its prey. Always the climax of his dreams came when the infidels meandered in the darkness, not feeling the lion's breath until the deadly moment when life became eternal darkness. Essid smiled. Yes. A few hours of dreams offered him clarity and assurance.

## *Chapter 15*

The steel doors swished opened to reveal Benjamin Clark's team: dirty, tired and anxiously exchanging information about their daily operations that had separated them. Dragging in last walked a quiet and pale, Tessa Scott. Her eyes darted back and forth between the team as they verbalized the various aspects of the challenges presented to them throughout the day. Clearly, Mrs. Scott stood on the perimeter of exhaustion and confusion considering the graphic events that had engulfed her over the last two days. Although the team members spoke calmly, even chuckled from time to time, about the details of the day, Tessa Scott looked on anxiously as if experiencing the information for the first time. Ben guessed reiterating what had actually transpired would give a normal civilian pause. Even so, Ben thought it remarkable that the unassuming housewife of Grass Valley hadn't been reduced into a blithering idiot.

"Prisoners?" Ben approached the Enigma team, folding his arms across his chest. All eyes went to Chase.

"FBI took ours at Oak Ridge. That's why we're late. Had to catch them up to speed. They were none too happy that we were on site without their help. Wanted to know who we were." Chase smirked just as Ben unfolded his arms and gave his team leader a hard stare. "Don't worry. I assured him he'd have to go to Homeland and discuss it with them. Let Tobias Stewart squirm out of it."

Ben cut his eyes to Carter Johnson who flopped down in a leather desk chair, propping his feet up on the desk. "Same here. FBI was there most of the day. I think some spooks from Langley were too. The feds kept arguing with some other guys who the DOE sent out. I stayed out of it. While they were screwin' round, we took care of the problem." He smiled over at Vernon and winked at Sam.

"And you, Mrs. Scott?" Ben leveled a laser like glare at her innocent expression. "How did you do?"

Tessa straightened up and looked around at Zoric and Chase who said nothing on her behalf. Clearing her throat not once but twice made the others grin in tolerance. "Okay," she whispered.

"Okay?" Ben growled a little rougher than he'd intended as she took a step back. "I understand you spoke at length to Dr. Haskins and his wife. Anything we should know about?"

Tessa looked over at the captain who offered nothing but an attentive gaze. "No. Nothing." She nodded to Chase and Zoric. "They heard…"

"Very well then," he said cutting her off. "The Haskin boys haven't been located yet. We have a recovery team on the way to Tahoe to…"

"Tahoe?" Tessa seemed to come alive. "That's where my family is staying. Are they in danger?" Tessa's heart began to beat faster. Her face became flushed.

Benjamin arched an eyebrow in restrained anger at her interruption. "Mrs. Scott…"

"Answer me!" she demanded with more backbone than Tessa realized she possessed.

All the others seemed to find something else to focus their eyes on, except Captain Chase Hunter. He looked unemotionally at his new addition to Enigma. Moments before he'd thought her to be finished for the day, maybe for the week, but with one mention of Tahoe she'd come alive. His eyes slid down to her chest which was rising and falling with anxiousness. The flushed face meant her heart beat at a terrified rate. A smile within fought to break loose knowing that Benjamin Clark had no idea what he was toying with in Mrs. Tessa Scott.

"There is no need to be alarmed, Mrs. Scott, unless you think the Haskin boys would try and contact your family. Will they?" Ben had straightened his thick frame to its full six foot and looked down his narrow eagle-like nose at her. His voice had been stern and accusing but remained calm.

"No. They have no idea that we would be there." Her eyes narrowed and landed on Chase with contempt, "or I should say, *they* would be there! I haven't seen the boys since they started Stanford. You know how kids are; anyone over twenty is boring and out of touch."

"Then your family is not likely to even know about the extraction process." Ben took his eyes off of the housewife and commanded the attention of his team. "Now for Mr. Crawley."

Zoric brought Tessa a black leather desk chair and pulled up another one next to her and smiled. This time she returned the smile and quickly darted her eyes away from his appreciative gaze. She had seen what this East European was capable of for two days. He was probably ten years older than her, but his hollow eyes and sunken cheekbones made him appear older. Something heavy weighed in those bloodshot eyes as well a cold and calculating element Tessa didn't wish to know about first hand. The man clearly did not hesitate to take a life. Putting the moves on her, even though she was a married woman clearly didn't affect him. Forcing herself to listen to Benjamin Clark made the close proximity of his darkly clad body seem less menacing. Besides, she caught a warning glance exchanged between Chase and Zoric that added a layer of safety to her raw feelings of helplessness.

"We know for sure that Essid has our former nuclear physicist, Jericho Crawley, hiding somewhere here in Sacramento. He sent several men on a private plane in order to distract us last evening. We caught up with them when they were forced to land in Boise. In the meantime our little songbird, Jamaal got rid of his tracker by going through a carwash. We managed to follow him until a car slammed into our tail, sending both our guys to the hospital."

"The causalities are adding up," Chase interjected as he ran his fingers back through his black hair. "Was the accident intentional?"

"We think so. Some college kid was given two hundred dollars to run a red light about the time we were going through. Unlikely the kid knew anything about the operation. He's been treated and released with a hefty fine awaiting him in court. He'll need more than two hundred dollars, I'm afraid." Benjamin rested his left hip on the edge of the desk where Carter had his feet propped. "We're still not sure why all of this has occurred now;

the mini nuke never would have exploded, according to the lab rats anyway, too many elements missing for it to do any damage. The Oak Ridge scenario would make sense by itself had they been successful at retrieving the isotopes and access to other work going on there. But why Los Alamos at the same time?"

"You'll have to admit it had all of us, FBI, CIA, NSA and every other acronym you can think of scurrying around like it was the second coming of Christ," Carter said nonchalantly. "I think the isotope angle is what we're after. Global Navigation is located on a ridge about an hour away from Auburn."

"I'm sorry. Global Navigation? I've never seen anything about it. I come through Auburn all the time." Tessa knew her ignorance showed like a glowing orb.

"Global Navigation has the potential to become a major provider of isotopes for North America. It's located off the beaten path; nondescript place considering the important work they do there." Carter removed his feet from the desk and leaned in toward Tessa, realizing he just might have a captive audience to impress. "Currently we depend heavily on the Chalk River reactor in Canada to supply us with isotopes used to diagnosis cancer and heart disease. The problem is the reactor is 53 years old and tends to have problems. In 2009 there was a heavy water leak which ended up shutting the whole thing down for 15 months. So the world suddenly faced a loss of about one third of all the isotopes available. The Department of Energy had already begun its own reactor project in 2002 unbeknownst to California tree huggers who would have done everything in their power to keep it from completion. People hear 'nuclear reactor' and think you're making bombs or energy. The Global Navigation website indicates they're on the cutting edge of medical research and disease resistant crops for third world countries."

"A lie?" Tessa questioned innocently.

Benjamin took his hand held computer and punched in a few commands casually. "Not a lie exactly. It's just not the whole truth," he said, turning his body slightly to view the pictures that appeared on the flat screen behind him. "I think you're right, Carter, but why here? Why now? What's the point?" He nodded toward the screen. "These are the players so far. All seem to be taking orders from Essid. Having people at Oak Ridge,

Los Alamos and here takes a chunk of change to orchestrate. Essid's financials show he's comfortable but not wealthy by any means."

Vernon moved to his own computer and began searching. "It will take a while to look around. If the FBI guys didn't find it…"

"The FBI didn't know enough to keep him from working for the Secretary of the DOE so I doubt they looked to see if he had a sugar daddy someplace!" Ben said hotly.

"Which one is Essid?" Tessa cleared her throat nervously, not wanting to stand out as an imbecile among these brilliant Enigma agents with supersized egos. She stood slowly as if by doing so would increase her attention to detail. Everyone looked at her incredulously as if she were kidding. "I mean, I know he was on my computer yesterday, but to be honest things were happening so fast I didn't really get a look at him." She was stammering like a sixteen old year school girl who'd just been ask to prom by the star quarterback. Tessa tried to retreat back into her chair, but felt Zoric's hand pat her hand that clutched the armrest.

"It's okay, Tessa Scott." Although his voice sounded gravelly, Tessa noted a tone of kindness.

Chase moved toward the screen and pointed to the picture of a man standing in front of a mosque, dressed in traditional clothing. The CIA had managed to find an old file photo which showed Essid when his beard had not been shaven or his hair cut in a western style, but the resemblance could not be mistaken in the photo. He noticed a recognition spring to Tessa's eyes mixed with a little fear. If Chase had not arrived as a plumber when he did, it would have been only a matter of minutes before Essid issued an order to kill her, if not worse. This was a man without a conscience.

"Is he from Russia or an old Soviet republic?" Tessa said joining Chase at the screen.

Ben joined the two. "No. Why do you ask?"

"Because he's standing in front of the Juma mosque in Baku, Azerbaijan." Finally, something Tessa knew about. All eyes fell on her like a ball ping hammer. Their expressions were a mixture of anger and disbelief at the absurd interjection concerning things beyond her comprehension. Noting the skepticism, Tessa quickly explained. "Last year I took a class at Nevada County Campus of Sierra College in Grass Valley. It was called Journeys to Religious Shrines of the World. I chose the countries in Central Asia that touched the Caspian Sea for my final project paper. One of those countries was Azerbaijan. According to Soviet history, the Russians liked to use Azerbaijan as an example of how they demonstrated religious tolerance. But the fact was that out of the hundreds and hundreds of mosques that once dotted the countryside by the 1980s, only twenty one large mosques were allowed to hold services in Baku. There were maybe eleven to fifteen others that remained in the country of any consequence. Out of that there were thousands of officially private houses of prayer and unfortunately, many secret Islamic sects as well." Tessa took a deep breath. Now that she'd rambled on with excitement about her project, she realized with disappointment that it really did sound a little self-serving.

"And how'd you do?" Captain Chase Hunter folded his muscled arms across his chest and smiled as he arched his eyebrows.

"Excuse me?" Tessa said, feeling that wave of shyness wash over her under his steady gaze.

"The project. How'd you do?"

Tessa raised her chin in pride and tried to stand tall. "I made an A."

Chase chuckled and used the back of his hand to slap Benjamin lightly across the chest who now stared with new eyes at the picture of Essid. "And why haven't any of you noticed that!" Ben barked as he cut his eyes to the others. "A civilian had to see something none of our government agencies noticed!" He turned his sharp eyes back at Tessa. For a second he felt swallowed up in their tranquil beauty. This woman had no idea what she'd done. "How do you explain all of this, Mrs. Scott?"

"All of what, Mr. Clark?" Tessa took a step back and tried to lean against the desk where Carter still sat.

"This! These men invade your house, take your neighbor that just so happens to be a nuclear scientist, and then you just happen to know Dr. Haskin who does the leading isotope research in the U.S. Then," Ben took a step toward her, keeping his voice low and calm, but losing none of the intimidation factor, "you save one of Captain Hunter's men from a terrorist, put yourself in danger for a pregnant woman and now you tell us you took a class that caused you to study Azerbaijan which has made you give us what is possibly the key to this whole mess." By now Ben towered over Tessa who had inched herself onto the desk, leaning back away from his physical presence. "How in the name of Heaven do you explain that, Mrs. Scott?"

"Divine intervention?" Tessa said with the sudden realization that everything she'd ever done and experienced had led up to this moment. Could God have set before her opportunities, gifts and encounters to arrive at this one place in time so that she could help save her country from those that would do it harm. An avalanche of warm courage began surging through her body as she looked around the room at the other Enigma team members. They looked skeptical but impressed with her retort to Benjamin Clark. "Divine intervention," she said again with confidence this time. "How else would you explain it?" A smile began to break lazily across her face.

Benjamin couldn't help himself and returned the smile. "If that is true, then may God help us all at Enigma." He looked at the others and pointed accusingly. "Don't let those Langley know-it-alls find out about her."

Tessa hopped off the desk. "Does that mean I'm part of the team?" she asked quickly.

"No!" Sam answered crossly. "You can't waltz in here and throw a tidbit of info out and expect us to think you're one of us," she said sarcastically.

Vernon brought his laptop around to the front of the room and hit a button so that more information appeared on the large screen. "Hold that thought, Sam."

Carter came around the desk and stared at the screen. "Now we're making more sense." He nodded for the others to gather closer. "Global Navigation is accepting their first large shipment of Molybdenum 99 this week to meet the demand of a reliable supply of medical isotopes. Anyone care to guess where it's coming from?" Carter smiled over at Tessa whose eyes were wide with interest. "That's right, girls and boys! Russia!" Carter moved to Tessa's side and slipped an arm around her shoulders. "And thanks to Tessa, we just might know why everyone's favorite terrorist, Essid, is involved."

Vernon highlighted a column of numbers. "It seems several countries around central Asia have been bankrolling Essid's project. He has an off shore account in the Caymans under another name. See?" The Enigma team looked at the name in astonishment. "None of these Caspian Sea countries have any love for Russia. If they thought they'd make Russia's credibility sink lower than it already is and hurt the U.S. in the process, it would be like killing two birds with one stone," Vernon said offhandedly.

Carter felt Tessa move out from under his arm as he spoke. "Russia needs this *let me help save mankind* image to take hold. Their disputes with the new oil fields in Turkmenistan, the ongoing turmoil in Chechnya and a gradual slide back toward communism have the whole world looking at them like European trailer trash."

Chase Hunter sighed. "He's right. But why is Essid so up in arms about Russia. It's gotta be more than destroying mosques in Azerbaijan. The Essid I know is not a very good Muslim. A full profile was compiled when we caught him in Afghanistan. He's been known to eat pork, drink until he couldn't hit the floor with his hat and go weeks without praying. He might be playing that Jihad game for the world to see, but trust me; he isn't religious unless it suits him." Chase turned to Tessa. "Any ideas?"

Tessa started to speak when Sam pushed up beside her and shifted her weight to one hip, causing every single man in the room to take notice, even the mighty Chase Hunter. "Does he have family there? Maybe the Russians killed them, or worse."

Tessa wondered what would be worse than killing your family, but before she gave it another thought she spoke. "A woman. I bet it's a woman."

Sam sniggered disrespectfully. "A man like Essid doesn't love a woman, he possesses them like property."

Tessa nodded in defeat. "Of course you're right. But what if it was and no one looked at the possibility because it's so out of character for him."

Chase realized Tessa had made eye contact with him. That sudden jolt of pain hit his chest again as he raised his hand to rub the spot over his heart. "Vernon?"

"On it, boss!" he said tapping away at his key board.

Chase tore his eyes away from the Grass Valley housewife to look at his watch. "Let's take a break and do dinner. We'll meet back here tomorrow. It's been a long couple of days."

Ben agreed. "I'll call Claudia and see how she's doing."

Tessa couldn't help but notice that Ben seemed to be giving some visual message to the captain. She sucked up her courage and ask: "When can I go home?"

"Soon," Ben replied as he turned his back on her. "You'll need a place to stay tonight. We'll find you something near here provided any of us get a chance to sleep." Ben casually waved a back hand at the Enigma team as he disappeared into his office. "Chase?"

"I'll take care of her."

Within minutes, Chase and Tessa were in his Hummer steering into the darkness, carefully obeying stoplights and pedestrian crosswalks. Tessa realized how close they'd been to Old Town, Sacramento at that point. She noticed a sign coming out of the underground parking lot that said, *Sacramento University of Science and Technological Research.* How many times had she'd seen that sign on the highway, watched promo commercials on television and even walked near there on her way to Old Town? People of Sacramento had no idea what lay just beyond the entrance to these halls of learning.

Casually, Tessa tried to steal a look at the stoic Captain Chase Hunter. Even in this semi darkness, his rugged good looks made her swallow a little harder than she wanted. His dark eyes indicated some ethnic heritage from a generation or so back. A scar just over his eye appeared more pronounced under the pale green lights of the dashboard. Several times in the last two days she'd experienced the strength in those strong arms that she now admired. Even though Chase smiled little, the few times he'd looked at her with that amused grin had given Tessa a kind of calm and warmth that she'd never experienced. Who was this man? What exactly was Enigma?

"You're staring at me," he said so suddenly that Tessa jumped.

"Sorry. I'm just a little tired. Where are we going?"

Captain Chase Hunter turned his dark eyes on her and smiled, revealing straight white teeth. Something about that smile reminded her of the wolf in Little Red Riding Hood. With indifference Chase said: "My apartment. You can stay with me tonight."

# Chapter 16

With a devilish smile, Essid moved toward the cot where Jericho Crawley now sat, drinking a cup of McDonalds coffee. The old man's left eye was swollen nearly shut and a large bruise, the size of a man's fist, covered the other cheek. A hint of dried blood around his nostrils gave Essid some satisfaction, knowing that his means of persuasion had been justified. After all, now the old man would help him with the Molybdenum 99 after it had been safely removed from Global Navigation. The containers would be rigged with explosives, rendering Global Navigation the biggest waste of American tax dollars the world had ever seen. Leading scientists of isotope recovery would cease to exist. And with any luck he'd be able to kill a few Russians for dessert.

Global Navigation planned a congratulatory dinner in two days after the delivery process had been completed. Production would begin the following day. The dinner would be held on location in the conference center followed by dancing and entertainment. It was a black tie affair and many in the medical research industry had been invited. Due to the possibility of increased security on such an occasion, procedures were now executed to cancel the event. Essid and his people planned to destroy the life-saving isotope material before it had a chance to be put to good use.

Essid closed his eyes with thoughts of the heavy water leak at Los Alamos where he'd sent his cousins. They weren't the brightest, but oh so gullible and loyal. The isotope reactor would be shut down for months because of their acts. That would slow down the isotope production even further. After hearing from the oldest cousin, Essid felt reassured of their success in transferring the research data he required. His call came just before the lab had been stormed by some security organization. The sound of gunshots and screams preceded the line going dead. Nothing to do about it now; their father would be told they died for the cause. Surely they would grasp some comfort from that ridiculous idea. The only cause he cared about for now was undoing the tedious negotiations between the Russian and American medical community. What did he care if thousands of cancers would go undiagnosed until it was too late, or that crop disease might leave millions of people starving in third world countries? Revenge was sweet medicine for the disease that had eaten his life away for so long.

\* \* \*

The wagon bumped along on a narrow dirt road among the pines surrounding Lake Tahoe. The cowboy rode a dark Appaloosa alongside the wagon as he led the group of tourists in a song of "Ole Suzanna". The air, crisp and clean, made the beauty of the mountains and meadows opening up before them appear surreal and tranquil. The smell of coffee and biscuits swirled upon the morning breeze that greeted the cowboy wannabes as they arrived for their breakfast at the Ponderosa Ranch. The ranch had been used for the wildly popular television series in the 1960s called *Bonanza*. Reruns on the Western Channel and other cable networks had continued its popularity. Everyone attending had tried to dress the part by wearing cowboy hats, vests, and boots. Some of the ladies wore fancy western style shirts with their overalls or jeans.

Besides the Scott family, there were only two other kids with their parents. Visiting from a small mining town in Missouri, the father sang robustly with the cowboy. Robert smiled to himself when he overheard the teenage girl say that no way was she going to eat a Hoss burger later in the day if they went back to the old west town of Virginia City. The boy laughed and teased his sister that she was in for a tough day with that kind of attitude. Robert wondered if his children would enjoy each other when they became teens. He really hoped so. Watching his children climb down from the wagon and surround him with excited chatter swelled his heart with love and pride. All this time, he'd been missing out on the symphony of laughter and love. He realized what a gift he'd been given, a wife who adored him and took care of them, children that were so amazingly smart and funny, that he shuttered to think he'd almost missed it. All this time, Tessa had not been complaining he never spent enough time with the family, but had been begging him to experience this miracle before it passed him by.

One thing for sure, Robert vowed when they returned home he would put his wife on a pedestal and make her life a lot easier. Although this trip had not been the relaxing vacation he'd desired, Robert acknowledged it certainly had been entertaining. For a brief moment Robert felt regret that he'd made such a mess of things at home. But then again, if he hadn't, he would never have gotten to know his rascals.

The kids helped themselves to seconds on the pancakes. They proclaimed them to be the best in the world and wanted a copy of the recipe to give their mom. Biscuits, gravy, bacon and scrambled eggs went along with the pancakes and warm maple syrup. A long table covered with a red checkered tablecloth seated twenty visitors. Everyone chatted between bites of food, sharing where they were from and why they chose the Ponderosa to visit.

"I hear you had a bear visitor a week or so back," Robert said thinking about Honey's story of shooting her gun in the air to protect the breakfast visitors. He couldn't help but wonder why she hadn't joined them.

The singing cowboy poured Robert more steaming coffee in his tin cup. "I'd remember if a bear had visited us," he said looking over at the cook. "Hey, Bill, hear anything about a bear being around here?"

The cook shook his head and flipped another pancake in his big iron skillet. "Nah. No bears around here. Incline Village had one about two months ago wandering around, getting in trashcans, but the rangers trapped him and hauled him off somewhere remote. I wouldn't worry about that if I were you."

A wave of unease washed over Robert as he recalled Honey's story she'd told the kids. Was she just trying to create an exciting adventure for the kids? He remembered the way her eyes had met his with that *come hither* look. "Did I hear some guys escaped a jail in Carson City a few days ago?" Robert asked offhandedly.

The cook shrugged as he poured the last of the batter into his skillet. "Donno. Maybe. Don't watch TV much. All bad news these days."

"Don't look at me," the singing cowboy smiled. "I don't even have a TV. Besides those cops in Carson City always get their man. If they got out they're back in by now."

Robert sat his cup down. Something wasn't right about Honey Lynch. Maybe she'd not join them later today as she'd promised. But if she did Robert began compiling a mental list of questions to cross examine her. After all, he was a lawyer.

Feeling a gentle tug at his elbow, Robert twisted his body on the picnic table bench to see his little daughter. He hadn't noticed her slip off her seat across from him. Swinging his legs over the bench he pulled her into his lap with a hug and a kiss. "Having a good time?" he said enthusiastically. She nodded happily and reached around him to take the last piece of his bacon. Robert then realized his boys were not next to him. "Where's your brothers, sweetie?" Robert said beginning that built in panic scan parents obtain with the birth of their children.

"Gone," she said softly.

*\*\*\**

Tessa Scott followed Chase into the building that held the Enigma organization as the sun was just coming up. It had not been a restful night. Anger still clouded her eyes, and her jaw muscles flexed over and over again in irritation at not being allowed to go home or call her family. After heating a couple of frozen meat and potato dinners in the microwave, Chase had eaten without saying a word to her as they sat at his black granite topped bar. He cleared away their disposable dishes and stuck their water glasses in the dishwasher which was nearly full. After telling her he was going to take a shower, Chase disappeared behind the closed door of his bedroom. Minutes later Tessa heard the shower start.

Sitting in a frozen-like state at the bar, Tessa surveyed the captain's eighth floor apartment. One whole wall was glass that overlooked the city of sparkling lights. Black leather furnishings and cherry stained bookcases on each side of the contemporary style fireplace filled the loft style living room. Open to the kitchen, done in the same cherry cabinetry with stainless steel appliances, the apartment was void of any personal touches. The look of a hired decorator existed with the few pieces of art hanging on the walls for a shot of color. Nothing too revealing about who Captain Chase Hunter might be outside of Enigma jumped out at her as she eased off the tufted, leather barstool to investigate further. The floors were stained dark with only an ivory shag rug in front of the couch to break up the monotony of the sterile room. A flat screen TV had been installed over the fireplace. *Boys and their toys,* thought Tessa without emotion.

Only the dozens of books gracing the shelves next to the fireplace indicated a new layer to the captain. Tessa, drawn to books of any kind, quickly crossed the room to read the titles. Shakespeare, Chaucer, Marlowe, Johnson and several books with "sir" before the author's name looked old and worn as Tessa ran her fingers across the binding. A violin case next to a music stand, rested precariously on angle in one corner. The case appeared to be worn and a little rough around the edges; like the captain, she thought in seriousness. She wondered about the possibility of his ability to play such a delicate instrument with such deadly hands.

Her eyes had then gone to the front door. Should she try and leave? Would the captain come after her? Did she owe it to Mr. Crawley to see this thing through? Hadn't she done enough already?

"Planning your escape?" Chase had entered the room without her knowing it. He'd caught her standing before the door, staring at the possibilities. Dressed now in sweats and a tee shirt, he looked like an ad for Ralph Lauren; instead of Soldier of Fortune.

"Love what you've done with the place," she said flippantly as she turned and moved back to the bar, which seemed like miles away from Chase. "My place is such a disaster. You'll have to give me the name of your decorator." She offered a condescending smile.

Chase approached Tessa slowly as if stalking prey, forcing her to retreat around the bar into the kitchen. "What makes you think I didn't decorate this place?" He brushed past her and opened the refrigerator, reaching in for two beers.

"Oh please," she chuckled nervously as she cautiously moved back to the other side of the bar. "Do you play the violin?" Her eyes darted to the violin case.

Locking eyes with his unwilling hero, Chase nodded. "My mother insisted I have a well-rounded education. It was one of the few things I managed to bring out of China when I left."

He popped one lid off a beer and offered it to Tessa. When she refused with a shake of her head, Chase smiled broadly then gulped down the cold liquid before speaking. "Afraid I'm going to get you drunk and take advantage of you?" When she didn't answer he waved the bottle gently at the room. "Claudia did all this for me." Tessa's nervousness was almost amusing. "And so you can put your mind at ease, I don't sleep with married women. I'm keeping you close because for some strange reason you've become a part of all this. I feel obligated to make sure nothing happens to you until this is over." Finishing off the beer, Chase sat the bottle on the bar and disappeared into the bedroom only to return with a pillow and blanket. "I'll sleep on the couch. The bed has clean sheets. Towels are in the linen closet. You'll find them I'm sure." He tossed the blanket and pillow on the couch.

Trying to back toward the bedroom door casually, she tripped over the edge of the rug and nearly fell. When she looked at Chase he looked amused as he worked on the second beer. "And for your information I don't drink alcohol," she said off handedly.

Chase took another sip of the cold liquid. "Let me guess. You're one of those holier-than-thou Evangelicals that doesn't drink, dance, swear or anything else that could be remotely fun. Since you have three kids I assume you're okay with sex."

Tessa jerked her head up as if he were trying to insult her beliefs. "Maybe. Is that a problem?"

His smile faded a bit. "My parents were Evangelicals."

"Are they really medical missionaries?"

The obvious interest Tessa showed made Chase eye her with a little regret. "Not anymore."

"Why?"

"The Chinese Red Guard killed them." With that he turned toward the couch. "There's a lock on the bedroom door if that makes you feel safer. See you in the morning."

When morning came Chase had knocked on her door saying they needed to get to Enigma. Tessa felt rushed and still half asleep when she'd joined him in the kitchen. Styrofoam cups filled with coffee, just like she took it, and a Little Debbie cake to eat on the way tasted wonderful. She frowned at such a breakfast but ended up wishing she had another as they'd driven down the street toward Enigma.

Anxiousness about the upcoming day made her feel on edge and exasperation toward the captain. He'd asked her a couple of civil questions of no particular importance; *how's the coffee, did you sleep well, did you pack all your things, how long have you been married.* That last question had nearly sent her over the edge. She snapped that if he needed to know any more personal information about her he should just ask Claudia. After that, the two had ridden in silence until they'd reached Enigma. Tessa had not budged when Chase exited the Hummer as she considered what her options might be to change her circumstances. Without resolution, Tessa soon found herself tagging along after Chase; two steps to his every one; another source of frustration.

Once in the elevator, Tessa felt the sensation of going down. Had she done this yesterday? Where was she being taken? Chase stood straight, almost at attention with his hands clasp in front of his body. Today he dressed casually, jeans, dark colored tee shirt and tennis shoes. He looked normal; although that seemed a little trite considering what the captain was capable of doing.

Moving forward when the door swished open, Chase stepped aside and held the door, waiting for Tessa to decide to join him. His eyes did not look inside the elevator to coax her to decide. Finally, Tessa sighed in surrender and stomped out and kept going forward, even though she had no idea where she was. It looked similar to where she'd try to escape the day before only to be stopped by that Amazon, Sam. She felt Chase behind her even though his steps were stealth-like. Chase reached for the doorknob to open the door for her when Tessa stopped and turned to face her captor. She looked up into his dark eyes and searched his tan face for something; she didn't know exactly what.

"Did you shoot those men in the van that first day?" Tessa ask accusingly.

Chase felt an urge to rub that painful spot again above his heart. He needed to make a doctor's appointment. "Yes." Her eyes widened a little revealing more of their blueness. "But they were already dead. If I had needed to kill them in order to get the information to stop whatever this is, make no mistake, Tessa, I would have killed them." He was aware that he had swallowed and held his breath.

A soft smile stretched her lips slightly; enough to give her face brightness. "Okay. I believe you." This time she smiled broadly. Confusion leaped to the captain's eyes and his hand tightened on the doorknob. "You called me 'Tessa'."

Chase nodded and felt his mouth turn up in his own smirk. "I apologize, Mrs. Scott. It's been a long couple of days."

His hand started to turn the knob when she reached out and laid her palm over the back of his large, rough hand. She felt him flex slightly as if wanting to pull away. "Please call me Tessa. And," Tessa took her free hand and touched his arm, "thank you for everything you've done for me, letting me stay with you, not treating me like I'm a nut case when I told you about Azerbaijan, for trusting me and most of all for saving my life several times over the last few days." She patted his arm before removing her touch from him, "Thank you for being nice to me this morning when I was so..." she paused.

"Difficult?" Chase said as he opened the door with a chuckle.

A light laugh floated in ahead of her as she nodded, then took a sip of her coffee only to choke on the liquid as Sam stood before them with her killer looks baring down on them. Her eyes went to Tessa with disdain and then to Chase.

Even in jeans and a loose cotton blouse, Sam was stunningly beautiful. Long black hair fell down her back, straight and shiny. Her skin, a lovely olive, had never seen a blemish or sunburn. The large round eyes were pools of green, maybe hazel. Thick black lashes and a wide, sinuous mouth gave her heart shaped face the look of a goddess. Toned and slim, Sam's body left Tessa wishing she'd not eaten the Little Debbie cake or had sugar in her coffee.

Sam stepped forward and slipped her long fingers into Chase's hand and pulled him forward so that he was nearly touching her generous breasts. "I tried to call you last night, Chase."

"Tired. Went to bed early."

Sam smiled and cut her eyes over to Tessa who seemed to be feeling a little embarrassed by the attention the captain received. "I could have come over and helped you relax."

"Oh, I did that!" Tessa said with a fake smile and patted Sam on the back. "But, gee, thanks!"

Sam jerked away from Tessa's touch. "Ha! And where did you spend the night, Betty Crocker?"

Tessa wrinkled her nose and smiled sarcastically as she walked away. "I spent the night in his bed," in a 'oops, you caught me' voice.

Chase removed Sam's hands and started to laugh loudly from somewhere deep inside. "I think you've met your match, my beautiful Sam!" Walking away, Chase laughed again and in two strides he'd caught up with Tessa. "You really do have a death wish, don't you?"

Tessa looked up at him then over her shoulder at Sam, who glared murderously at her. "I have a feeling terrorists are the least of my worries." She looked back at the captain whose mood had definitely improved. "Are you two...?" Tessa let her question fall incomplete.

"No. Another rule of mine besides no married women is no Enigma women. Makes life too complicated." Chase pulled out a chair with wheels for her to sit down at a table then he did the same. The windowless room seemed small compared to the one used two days ago. The soft purr of air conditioning and the smell of freshly brewed coffee permeated the room.

Tessa smiled again at Sam who had taken a position across the table from her. "Guess I'll have to double trust you now," she said to Chase as her eyes locked with Sam's. Women like Sam knew their power over the human race; whether it is a man or woman. Tessa figured Sam usually got her way with everyone, except for Chase of course. That probably made him all the more desirable.

The steel doors opened again as Vernon, Zoric and Carter strolled in casually, all carrying their own empty coffee mugs. Each poured an amount of hot brew into their cups before finding a seat at the table. While nods of greetings passed between the team, Benjamin Clark entered calm and stoic. His appearance caused a quiet attentiveness to take hold of his team. Sitting down at the head of the oblong table, Benjamin laid a plain file folder before him. He locked his hands into a fist atop the table as another woman entered the room carrying a stack of folders. She quickly began passing them out to the Enigma team, smiling at times when their eyes met hers, except for Sam who ignored her completely.

"Tessa, this is my assistant, Ms. Coleman." Benjamin's voice, matter-of-fact, did not indicate whether she might be another team member. The two exchanged nods and a quick smile, before the assistant exited as quickly as she'd appeared. "It appears," Benjamin spoke calmly as he opened his file folder which signaled everyone else to do likewise, "that Essid has been a very busy terrorist over these last few years." Ben looked at Tessa with his eagle sharp eyes and smiled patiently. "Tessa correctly identified the mosque in Azerbaijan."

For some unknown reason, Tessa felt a surge of pride. Zoric, sitting across from her, gave her a wink with his bloodshot eyes. "It seems there was indeed a woman involved. Again," Benjamin raised a hand Tessa's way, "our unwilling team member was correct about Essid's motive for terror."

Sam narrowed her eyes at Tessa in contempt before swiveling her chair toward Benjamin Clark. With a slight straightening of her body, Ben's focus temporarily left Tessa and fell on Dr. Samantha Cordova who met his eyes boldly, as if reminding him not to be so stupid as to forget her presence.

Benjamin casually placed a pair of black glasses on his nose, adjusting his head slightly to bring things into focus. Frowning at Sam, he tore his eyes away to look back at the file. Sam irritated him on a regular basis, what with her sexy mind games she practiced on his people. The only one that appeared to be immune to her charms was Chase Hunter, and he wasn't one hundred percent sure about him. Perhaps Chase felt confidence in knowing that he could have the beautiful Samantha Cordova whenever and however he chose. Ben noticed, on occasion, their eyes meeting with a kind of smoldering effect. Nothing beyond those glances indicated anything romantic might jeopardize the work at Enigma.

Turning a couple of pages of information, Ben spoke so matter-of-factly that he could've been reading a stock market report. "Essid married a Chechen girl he'd met in Azerbaijan while he traveled throughout the region. He took her home to Libya where his wealthy and political family resided. In 1995 she returned to Chechnya to visit her family before the birth of their first child."

"Wasn't that about the time the Russians came in with guns blazing?" asked Chase as he lifted his eyes from the information before him.

"Correct. In February of 1995 the Russian forces eventually took the capital. Essid's wife was raped by some drunken Russians days later. Both she and the unborn child died, along with her entire family. Essid possesses a deep hatred for the Russians. Anything he can do to cause Russia to forfeit their attempt at making themselves look like humanitarians…"

Carter interjected with concern. "By Russia providing so much material to make isotopes for the medical community at large and the U.S.'s inability to provide the much needed protection would cause a great deal of friction between the two nations. The Russians could withhold the materials until another facility is built on foreign soil making another isotope shortage for several years. Thousands would be at risk."

Chase picked up a pencil and began rolling it between his fingers angrily. "Facilities that make medical and research isotopes don't require the same kind of security as, say, military and utilities type plants. Homeland Security knows that these instillations are sitting ducks for terrorists groups."

Tessa felt sick to her stomach at the possibilities. "Why would terrorists want isotopes?"

Carter took a deep breath and closed his folder. "Besides ruining the medical communities here and throughout the world's chance to diagnose deadly cancers and heart disease, they would have access to weapons grade uranium."

"Dear God!" Tessa breathed incredulously.

"The U.S. alone uses isotopes some 55,000 times a day for noninvasive scans." Carter stood slowly and moved toward the coffee pot behind him. "Even if they never make a bomb, Essid can hold the world hostage by this."

Tessa frowned at her lack of comprehension. "I don't understand."

Chase ran his calloused hand across his face. He rolled his shoulders to remove a kink as if he'd been sleeping the wrong way. "Essid tried to take out the reactor at Oak Ridge and Los Alamos where we're able to produce medical isotopes. Fifteen months ago there was a problem at the facility in Canada where a third of all isotopes are produced. They went off line until this past May. The shelf life of isotopes range from twenty four hours to six months. It didn't take long for there to be a six month waiting period for valuable isotopes in order to complete treatment of sick patients. Because they never came, in some instances, doctors were forced to do exploratory surgeries and just guess at possible solutions to treatment."

"I had no idea," Tessa said despondently. "Why am I just now hearing about this? I'm a news junkie, I read all the news magazines and yet I knew none of this."

"Because, Betty Crocker," Sam snipped, "people are more interested in how some drug induced celebrity is doing in rehab than the real life drama that is playing out every single day in this country. The news media downplays the characters that would harm us and the dedicated soldiers and civilians who are trying to make a difference."

Tessa met Sam's hard stare head on. "I'm not one of those shallow people, Sam."

Sam rolled her eyes flippantly but kept further remarks to herself after noticing Chase glare at her angrily. What was it with him and this insignificant housewife? This *keep the innocent civilian safe* crap was beginning rub her the wrong way. "There's another problem," Sam said tearing her eyes away from Chase to look at her boss.

"Sam?" Benjamin Clark arched one eyebrow in anticipation.

"According to this intel," Sam tapped her folder, "someone has been buying and stockpiling all the Molybedenum-99. It's very possible that Essid's primary goal is to corner this unusual market and be a powerhouse, the likes that OPEC has never seen."

Vernon let out a whistle. "Screw the Russians, the Americans and make a few bucks on the side. Gotta hand it to him, he's one smart..." his eyes went to Tessa Scott before dropping one of his colorful nouns, "terrorist."

Benjamin nodded to Sam. "Thank you, Sam. As always your insight is refreshing."

Sam leaned back in her chair and smiled over at Tessa as if waiting for her contribution to the situation. "Any questions?" she said narrowing her large round eyes at Tessa in contempt.

Meeting Sam's eyes with bewilderment, Tessa didn't dare ask anything that would continue to show her ignorance of national security, terrorists, isotopes and the world of Enigma in general. No wonder they called this organization Enigma; no one was who they seemed, scenarios were riddled with mystery and complexity, and there always seemed to be more questions than answers.

"As a matter of fact I do. Where are Mr. Crawley and Dr. Haskin's boys? Have they been found?" Tessa took note of a sudden chill in the room. Something wasn't right. "What's wrong?"

"Essid still has Dr. Crawley, Tessa. We are moving in on that even as we speak. As for Dr. Haskin's boys, we've located them and have sent a team to Tahoe to extract them and will send them to the same safe house as their parents." Ben's forced smile was followed by his casual rise from his chair. "Now, Tessa, if you don't mind, I'd appreciate it if you'd wait outside with Ms. Coleman while we go over a few items that doesn't concern you."

"Of course," Tessa said as she stood up, coffee cup in hand. Carter circled the table and refilled the cup. She thanked him, still in a little awe that here stood the famous astronaut she'd admired for so long. His charming personality, good looks and incredible brain power, had the ability to make Tessa feel a little tongue tied. As hard as she fought the reaction, a warm blush began to spread across her neck and up her face. Carter took note and smiled wolfishly at her before opening the door for her retreat.

"Didn't know hot housewives lived in Grass Valley," Carter chuckled as he poured the last of the coffee in Chase's cup. "And where did she spend the night, oh honorable captain?"

"With him," Sam said tartly as she folded her arms across her chest.

"Really?" Carter slapped Chase on the shoulder. "And how was that stuff?" Carter nudged Vernon as he returned to his own chair.

The captain leveled a dangerous look at Carter Johnson, the daredevil and Don Juan. Frowning he let his eyes cut to Sam who smiled teasingly. "That 'stuff' as you call it is married. You'd best remember that. Wouldn't want another incident to tarnish that super hero reputation of yours."

Carter slapped his hand over his heart. "Oh, that hurt, Chase. Not my fault I'm popular with the ladies."

Zoric had remained quiet, carefully watching his friend Chase, from the time he'd sat down at the table until now when he appeared to be uneasy at the teasing. Normally, Chase ignored Carter's jabs, but today Chase's tone could be perceived as a feeling of guilt. "She stayed with you?" Zoric tried not to smile.

Chase turned his head slightly to glance briefly at Zoric. "Yes. She stayed with me, everyone!" Hearing Ben clear his throat, Chase switched his focus to his boss who looked at him with disapproving eagle eyes. "I slept on the couch."

Everyone erupted into laughter except for Ben who rattled his papers a bit and nodded for everyone to settle down. "We have other business to attend. I thought it best if Tessa," he seemed to catch himself, "I mean Mrs. Scott, not be privy to this next bit of information. After all she may still be of some use to us." Ben glanced at Chase with controlled amusement. "If she knew everything I'm afraid she just might escape, go to the press, call the police or heaven forbid," he smiled but for an instant, "injure the captain permanently this time."

Laughter again broke out at Chase's expense. This time he smiled in spite of himself. You had to know when to lighten up. "I thought you were above this kind of harassment, Ben."

Ben raised his head and appeared to look down his nose at the entire group. Clearing his throat of a possible laugh, which no one had ever heard, Ben waved a hand, signaling an end to the joking. "I have my moments Chase. Now," Ben reopened his folder, "unlike Mrs. Scott's folder you have a few extra pages. It concerns Mr. Scott and the children. However impossible it sounds, the Haskin boys are indeed in the area where the Scotts are vacationing. They were spotted this morning hiking near the Ponderosa Ranch."

"So what are we waiting for?" Zoric said as he began cleaning his fingernails with a dangerous looking knife he'd pulled from his dark pants.

"There's an FBI team on the way. Helicopter experienced some problems and had to return to Sacramento twenty minutes ago." Ben leaned back in his chair.

"Didn't you say we had someone in place to assist if necessary?" Zoric said returning his knife to his pocket.

Ben took a second to survey his team calmly before speaking. "True. We've had the Scott family under surveillance since their arrival. It seemed prudent after the botched intrusion at the Scott house in Grass Valley. When the pieces started to fall into place it appeared our eyes on the ground needed to keep it close and personal."

Captain Chase Hunter stiffened with a gut feeling he was about to hear something to make his job harder. "Just who did you send, Ben? I assured Mrs. Scott her family was safe."

Ben reached into his folder and pulled out two pictures and shoved them out into the middle of the table. He hadn't expected Sam to inhale so quickly or Chase to drop such a look of disdain on him.

"Are you insane?" Sam questioned as she grabbed the picture, gave it a glance then passed it over to Zoric who motioned to have a look. "Honey Lynch is a psychotic killer and should never be around kids! For God's sake, Ben, what were you thinking?" Sam stood and placed her hands on her hips. "I can't believe you'd use her. She can't be trusted! How do we know she isn't playing us? It wouldn't be the first time." She reached for the second picture. "Who's he?"

Captain Chase Hunter growled a response. "His name is Mansur. He's Essid's brother. God help us."

## Chapter 17

Robert Scott felt that terror grow in the pit of his stomach like a cancer eating him alive. His eyes narrowed as he shaded them against the morning sun all the while scanning the horizon for his sons. Gently he lowered Heather to the ground. He swallowed so hard one of the Missouri parents asked if there was something wrong. Although he tried to sound nonchalant, Robert's heart beat rapidly as he explained that his boys had disappeared. Leaving Heather in the capable hands of the Missouri mom, several of the visitors volunteered to help him which he gladly accepted. Even the singing cowboy mounted his horse and joined in the search. Each chose a different area to begin and several were given walkie talkies the cook carried on his chuck wagon for emergencies. They all had cell phones and quickly took Robert's number. The cook, Bill, said he'd ring the dinner bell for everyone to return if the boys were located or came wandering into camp.

Robert quickly reached the tree line, pushing through until the forest opened up into another meadow. Stopping to catch his breath, he could hear the other visitors calling out the boys' names in the distance. He now was living a nightmare that could very well destroy his life. In his heart he prayed so hard for his boys to be safe that he nearly missed seeing two small figures wave at him from some one hundred yards away. With his pounding heart in his throat he could do nothing but wave back at his sons in large circular motions until he saw something black raise up behind them.

"Dear, God! No!" he choked seeing the black bear sniff the air. Two small bears tried to stand with their mother. "Boys! Don't move!"

Robert pointed behind them and they turned to see the large bear nearby. Instinctively, the boys began to back away, holding to each other like a life line. Later, Robert thought he had heard Daniel cry out, but couldn't be sure as the mother bear let out a growl that made his skin crawl. The boys panicked and began to run toward their father who screamed for them to stop. Sean Patrick tripped and fell, causing his little brother to fall over his sprawled body. The bear began running toward them, swinging her head and crunching sticks, and leaves beneath her feet.

Robert felt frozen in time, his legs made of logs that would not move fast enough to reach his boys. Just then he heard a sharp, ear piercing whistle that caused the bear to stop and sniff the air. The boys scrambled up and darted toward their father. Robert rushed toward them even as he witnessed Honey Lynch appear some twenty five yards from the bears. Honey whistled again, and then began yelling at the bear all the while lifting her rifle and taking deadly aim at the mother. The first shot staggered the mother but the second brought her down just as Robert scooped his boys up into his arms. A sob escaped his throat but the boys never noticed as they buried their heads and tears in their father's shoulders.

As he hugged his boys Robert watched Honey turn the rifle toward him and smile cynically. In that instant, he saw a dangerous woman toying with his sanity, wondering if the next time she pulled the trigger it would be at him. Suddenly, she slightly turned her rifle toward the rise of the hill where two hikers moved leisurely along a path on the ridge. She reloaded slowly, methodically. Robert thought he saw her straightened her shoulders just before she pulled the trigger twice. His mouth opened in astonishment as the two hikers fell. When he turned his eyes back to where Honey stood, Robert saw that she had vanished.

Setting the boys on the ground, they quickly grabbed their father's hands and pulled him forward toward the breakfast crowd. When they broke through the trees a cheer went up from the rest of the visitors followed by a loud ring of the chuck wagon bell. Everyone talked excitedly as the three rejoined them. The boys quickly told how their father had saved them from a bear. Robert quietly mentioned to the singing cowboy about a woman ranger named Honey, shooting the animal in the nick of time. The cowboy didn't know anyone by that name but wasn't that lucky for them? He also mentioned about the hikers which concerned him even more.

"Maybe it was those convicts you were talkin' 'bout!" the cook broke in. "I'll be sure to call it in to make sure. Now you folks don't worry any." He patted the air with his stubby hands. "There won't be any bears at the old west town of Virginia City where we're takin' ya now! Now wasn't that excitin'?"

Robert thought he could do without that kind of excitement and just wanted to get back to the cabin. But the terrorized boys appeared to have gotten their second wind and couldn't wait to see the gunfight coming up on Main Street in about two hours.

\* \* \*

Ms. Coleman took out pictures of her college age kids to show Tessa, since she asked about her family. She found Tessa an easy target to chat with about her life. No one at Enigma seemed all that interested. Why should they? After all, thanks to the librarian, Claudia, her life was an open book. Part of the job, she told herself. Nothing too personal around that bunch of *killer brains,* as she liked to call them. Deep down Ms. Coleman wondered if any of them had enough common sense between them to come in out of the rain.

"That's right, Tessa. Dr. Cordova, or Sam," she said rolling her eyes in contempt, "teaches advanced economics here at the university."

"You're part of the university?" Tessa asked in bewilderment.

"Oh my, yes! They all have second jobs. We don't just go around saving the day all the time." With that she gave a little giggle that made Tessa smile as she pulled up a chair alongside the glass topped desk.

"And the others? I mean if it's okay for you to tell me."

Ms. Coleman clicked her tongue. "Seems to me you're in it up to your eyeballs, sweetie. You can go online anytime and see what they teach."

Tessa's eyes widened. "They're all teachers?"

"PHds!" she giggled again. "That means piled higher and deeper, you know." She laughed at her little joke and Tessa joined in for the benefit of milking her for more information. "Dr. Zoric teaches art. Looks the part don't you think?" She shivered. "That one scares the life out of me, what with those bloodshot eyes, greasy long hair and switchblade he's always flicking out."

Tessa continued her plastic smile. "And the others?"

"That astronaut teaches astrophysics or something like that. Way over my head." Again she rolled her eyes upward with a breathy giggle. "Vernon manages the computer systems around here. Trust me, that's a huge job. I believe last semester he taught a class called Government Conspiracies: Truth or Dare." She leaned in closer to Tessa. "Those Pentagon types drop by sometimes and they usually get in a shouting match. He's loose cannon if you ask me."

"What about Captain Hunter?" Tessa ask casually. He was the one that really interested her.

Ms. Coleman smiled wickedly and winked. "Now isn't he a peach! Always says 'hello, Ms. Coleman, how are you today, is that a new hairdo, makes you look so young. If I were a few years younger I'd set my cap for that one," she laughed. "He's solid."

"Does he teach here too?" Tessa said off handedly.

"Sure. Renaissance literature and the romance languages. Dr. Hunter is a popular professor; always has time for his students." Another giggle. "The women in his department are pretty fond of him too. Seems to me he has a new lady friend every couple of months. Never lasts very long."

*Good to know,* thought Tessa trying to imagine the warrior teaching literature and escorting a lady to dinner. "And Benjamin Clark?"

At this Ms. Coleman sobered. "He heads Enigma. That's enough." She pushed her chair back suddenly and stood. "I need some refreshment. Anything?"

"Water?"

"No problem." Ms. Coleman disappeared into another room, leaving Tessa alone at the desk.

Tessa started to stand when she accidently caught her sleeve on a folder, pulling it to the floor. The contents spilled out and she bent down quickly to pick it up, not wanting Ms. Coleman to think she'd been rummaging through her things. When she came across a memo that said, *leave out of T. Scott's folder,* her curiosity got the best of her.

Ms. Coleman returned to see Tessa sitting quietly at her desk. "Here you are, Tessa."

"Thank you, Ms. Coleman."

"Oh please, call me Glenda."

"You know I drank so much coffee that I really need to use the ladies room, Glenda." She stood and made a movement that made her knees knock together. "It's that time of the month too. Is there anything…"

Ms. Coleman smiled in understanding and pointed to the door. "Just outside there to your left. You'll find everything you need in there. Need some change?"

Tessa backed toward the door. "No thanks. I put some in my pocket before Chase locked my purse in the car." Tessa pulled out a flat wallet from her pocket about the size of a coin purse and held it up in the air. "Thank you, Glenda." Tessa smiled sweetly and casually opened the door.

\* \* \*

The gunfight turned out to be very entertaining for the Scott family. Although still shaken by the events of the morning, Robert too, enjoyed the activities at the Ponderosa Ranch and town. The boys easily ate a Hoss burger, but Robert had to finish Heather's. After that he longed for a nap. Souvenirs, horseback riding and warm summer sun eventually wore the children down. All three were asleep before they ever left the park. Knowing that he shouldn't talk on his cell phone with the children in the car, Robert pulled over at a scenic overlook to try and reach Tessa one more time. He just didn't understand why she wasn't picking up. By the sound of her voice two nights ago, Robert had thought she'd forgiven him and Tessa would soon be joining them. How was he going to tell her about the bears? He shuttered to think what might have happened if Honey had not come along.

That created a longer list of questions. Why hadn't Honey joined them in the park? Who were those men she shot? What if Honey really wasn't a ranger? Strange no one knew her. Someone that looked like Honey Lynch would certainly leave an impression on a man. Yet, the two cowboys didn't know her. He'd heard sirens soon after they left. Was it possible the police were involved?

Closing his phone, he pulled back onto the highway. Another twenty minutes and he turned into the gravel road that led to the cabin. His heart leaped into his throat when he saw a Nevada Parks Department truck in the driveway. Honey Lynch stood outside the driver's side with her hands stuffed into her tight jeans. She was out of the uniform that she'd been wearing that morning. Her red, scoop neck tee shirt didn't leave much to the imagination. It appeared she hadn't bothered to put on a bra as well.

"Hi!" she called with a wave, peering into the car. Seeing the sleeping children she smiled over at Robert with hooded eyes suggesting something, he wasn't sure what. "Wore them out did you?"

Robert didn't answer her as he slipped the keys into his pocket and reached over to unlock Sean Patrick's seatbelt. Honey opened the door and ruffled the boy's hair until he opened his eyes, clouded with sleep. "Hi, Sean Patrick! Did you have an exciting day?" Honey asked as he nodded and took her hand to pull him out. She opened the back door and unfastened Daniel's seatbelt, noticing that Robert had gently lifted his little girl up into his arms, where she quickly snuggled her curly head into his neck.

At that moment in time, when the boys joined their father, putting arms around him as they walked toward the house, Honey felt a pain of regret. She looked around her at the beauty that engulfed this place before her eyes went to Robert who had all but ignored her for his children. She heard sweet whispers to his little girl and instructions for the boys to assist in opening the door. Torn by two masters, she thought regretfully; good and evil. Sometimes it was difficult to distinguish between the two which made her job easier. But this family, innocent of any wrong doing, teetered on the threshold of destruction without a clue to their precarious position or what lie ahead for them.

Honey waited only a few minutes before the boys returned with fishing poles and ran to the lake. Robert carefully closed the screen door so Heather would finish out her nap. He walked toward her, shoulders pulled back, jaw set and anger in his eyes. The boys called something to him and Robert waved.

"Looks like they're not traumatized by the bears," Honey said with a smile as she too waved to the boys. "Guess I have some explaining to do."

Robert eyed her with caution and put his hands on his hips. "What were you doing there? I mean, thank God, you were, but why were you there?"

Honey narrowed her eyes against the afternoon sun as she pulled a pair of sunglasses off the dash of her truck. "I'm working undercover for the FBI, Robert," she lied. Why was it people were so trusting of those magic letters, FBI? He dropped his hands to his side and tried to meet her eyes, now covered with dark mirrored glasses.

"You don't work for the forest department?" Robert's reasoning power shifted into overload.

"Yes and no. I work a lot of places, this being one of them. The FBI wanted those two men I shot today." She saw him cringe then look toward his boys. "They were dangerous men. They had escaped from a facility in Las Vegas five days ago. I've been tracking them."

"Are they dead?" Robert asked drily, not sure if he wanted the answer.

Honey smiled, revealing a pretty smile, except for a small chip on one of her lower teeth. "No. It was a tranquilizer gun, Robert. The bears are long gone and the FBI got their men."

"I didn't stick around because I had to secure the scene. Didn't want all your breakfast buddies discovering their lives were in danger. The California and Nevada Parks Department frowns on that. Tourism means money up here. If people think they're not safe they won't be spending those must coveted dollars up at Tahoe. They'll go someplace else and I'd get transferred to Alaska or some other god forsaken place," she laughed leaning back against the truck. "I hear about threats and I make sure they don't happen."

Robert sighed as if a huge weight had been lifted off his shoulders. He extended his hand to Honey and pulled her into a friendly embrace. "Thank you, Honey, for saving my boys' lives. I can never thank you enough." Just then the screen door slammed and Heather stood on the steps rubbing her eyes. Robert quickly ran to her and scooped her up in his arms.

"I can think of several ways you could thank me, Robert Scott," Honey whispered to herself as he walked back to where she stood. He was a good looking man, strong and lean. Honey tickled Heather's barefoot as Robert joined her at the truck. *What did a girl have to do to get a little attention*, she wondered as the sun bounced off Robert's wedding ring.

\* \* \*

Glenda Coleman noticed a red light flash on her phone. She rose slowly, smoothing her skirt and fussing with her hair. Opening the door to Benjamin's conference room, the efficient secretary poked her head inside. "Yes, Director?"

"Would you ask Mrs. Scott to rejoin us, Ms. Coleman?"

The secretary looked over her shoulder with a little concern. "She went to the ladies room about fifteen minutes ago. I'm afraid she might be sick."

The entire group jumped to their feet, startling Ms. Coleman. She looked confused as Sam darted past her and out the double doors toward the ladies room. "What is it?" Ms. Coleman ask, suddenly troubled by the commotion. "Should I call the doctor?" Ms. Coleman said backing up as the team began to spill into her office.

Vernon clicked something on her computer and turned the screen around for everyone to see. "Betty Crocker has left the building!" he smirked at Chase Hunter. "See that?" He said pointing to Tessa moving toward an ATM structure outside the building. "Where did she get the card?"

Chase slammed his fist down on the desk. "She must have gotten it out of her purse last night when I was in the shower. I took her phone and thought that would be enough."

Zoric put his bony hand on the shoulder of the much taller Chase Hunter. "I'd suggest taking her into the shower with you next time, my friend." Zoric's humor could not be disguised in his raspy voice.

Benjamin Clark glared at Chase with narrowed eyes. "Once again we seem to have underestimated our Grass Valley housewife. What would have made her bolt? I thought she was on board with us."

Ms. Coleman noticed a file folder on her desk that had been repositioned. "This," she said lifting up the file of information. "I went to get her some water. She must have gone through it. She knows about her family," she said with irritation, knowing that this was her fault. "Director Clark, I'm sorry. I trusted her."

Ben sighed. "She's good at that, Ms. Coleman." His eyes watched the security loop on the computer screen. Tessa removed roughly three hundred dollars from her account, punched in another account number, and took another three hundred from savings, the daily maximum. Hailing a yellow cab, Tessa took one look behind her and disappeared into the backseat, and into congested morning traffic. "Vernon," Ben said with an eerie calm.

"On it! The cab is stuck in traffic just four blocks from here." Vernon loved having access to street cameras, traffic monitoring devices and information the general public had no idea was available. It was a one man peep show for him. "Better hurry, Chase. Police are on the scene to get traffic moving after a little fender bender."

"Oh no!" Ms. Coleman started lifting other files on her desk and pulled out a couple of drawers.

"Ms. Coleman?" Ben asked impatiently.

"My Enigma phone! It's gone." Her eyes went to Ben. "Will she be able to use it?"

Chase shook his head in disbelief. "That would be like putting the launch codes for thermal nuclear war in her hands." He motioned to Vernon. "Do what you can. Maybe we can track her with it. She'll probably try and call her husband."

Sam returned after trying to make her way downstairs to follow Tessa. It didn't take her long to realize the woman was gone. "When this is all over I want to wring that little Wal-Mart housewife's neck."

Chase started out the door with Zoric. "You're going to have to wait in line!"

## *Chapter 18*

By the time Chase and Zoric reached the yellow cab, someone else rode in the backseat. The driver in a thick Indian accent waved his hands in alarm, saying the crying lady jumped out after paying him twenty dollars for a ten dollar fare. He motioned the direction in which she'd gone and begged to leave.

Vernon broke in on Chase's earpiece: "See a car rental nearby, Chase? Got a hit that our little Grass Valley commando paid cash for a blue Chevy Equinox; no destination or return date listed, but plans to keep it at least a week. Clerk added a note that the woman appeared upset."

"If that vehicle has *On Star* get them the stats and shut her down!" The two Enigma men were already in the Hummer, zigzagging through traffic toward the Interstate 80 on-ramp.

"Me again, dude." It was Vernon. "Yeah. Refused the On Star option. Guess she thought it might be a problem." Vernon chuckled and continued. "Don't worry. I have enough info to hack into On Star and get her stopped. It's going to take me about twenty minutes. She's a piece of work. Are you sure she doesn't work for us? Wait a minute." There was a pause. "Headed east about five miles from Auburn on Interstate 80 and she's breakin' the speed limit. Want me to call the highway patrol?"

"Negative. I want to take care of this myself!" Chase stormed.

Tessa finally regained some composure and realized her driving could draw unwanted attention to her location. Her thoughts raced at supersonic speed, jumping from one image to another. A blaring horn jolted Tessa to swerve back into her lane and concentrate on the road. All this time she'd believed her family vacationed in a safe location, unaware of the sinister world of terrorists, isotopes and a secret government agency called Enigma. Yet she discovered by accident that two unsavory characters were actually watching her family. Why would they do that? Why would they not want her to know? Could Enigma think she possessed more information than she actual had? Perhaps they planned to use her family as leverage for her cooperation in something illegal against her country. Maybe they weren't with the government at all but some private vigilante organization that took the law into their own hands.

Taking deep breaths she turned up the air conditioner so it blew full force into her face. Checking the rear view mirror for a tail (Tessa couldn't believe she was even thinking such a thing could happen to her), she started to relax just a little. Knowing full well it would only be a matter of time before Vernon found her on some of his futuristic spy toys, Tessa tried to make a plan. She'd have to find a secure line that Enigma couldn't stop her from calling Robert and warn him to leave Tahoe. The bio sheet stated some unsettling characteristics: dangerous, sociopath tendencies, assassin, known IRA soldier and chameleon extraordinaire. Pretty, younger than herself, Tessa remembered the picture of Honey, pale brownish blonde hair that had been pushed behind her ears. A cool narrow smile spread across thin lips and a kind of deadened pain filled her eyes. Freckles across her nose gave the woman a kind of youthful wholesomeness. There was no way of telling how long ago the photo had been taken.

It was the second photo that had confused Tessa the most. The man named Mansur, looked to be of Middle-Eastern descent. Why would someone like that be watching her family? Before she could read anything of value, Tessa had heard Glenda Coleman returning with their drinks. She wasn't going to sit by and let the lies continue to mount up. Just when she'd started to trust Captain Hunter, even like him a little, she realized everything that had occurred was shaded in half truths. Maybe Enigma was a government sponsored assassination agency that the CIA didn't even know about. *You've got too much imagination, Tess,* Robert always said.

Startled by the ringing of the stolen Enigma phone, Tessa lifted it to see a picture of the captain frowning. It was a live feed.

"Tessa! I know you're upset," he started firmly.

"You lied to me, Chase!" she screamed at the phone. "You lied about my family being safe!"

"Tessa, you need to find a place to pull over. Tell me where you are and I'll come get you. Let me explain." His voice, calm and reasonable irritated Tessa.

"Go to hell!" Tessa threw the phone against the passenger door, bouncing it back to the cup holder.

\* \* \*

Zoric couldn't help but grin as he turned his eyes away from his friend. "Pretty strong language from an innocent, don't you think?" He knew this woman both fascinated and confused Chase Hunter. That was a first. He was a man used to being admired, respected and even sought after by beautiful women. Even Sam, a prize in her own right, could not resist making herself available to the elusive captain of the Enigma team. Yet, Chase never let anyone get too close, especially a woman. Zoric understood that. Women made men weak, forcing them to see their own shortcomings and vulnerability.

Maybe if he hadn't loved his wife and daughters so much he wouldn't have morphed into such a monster he reasoned. Their love had made him whole. When that had vanished in the length of time that it took to bomb the playground where his daughters played, a hideous demon of revenge crushed the joy of living from his life. He'd done many unconscionable things since that time. If it hadn't been for Chase Hunter, he'd been hanged, shot and butchered by now. Their warped bond of friendship forced Zoric to put his life back together. Although far from trusting, his willingness to think about the future carried him forward. Love could leave a hole the size of a bomb induced crater in you if things went wrong. Zoric still longed to feel his wife's loving arms wrap around him and the laughter of his little girls. They were the only good memory he had left.

Zoric eyed his friend briefly. He knew the murder of Chase's parents and the tragic death of his sister kept others at arm's length. Don't get too close. Nothing is forever. 911 proved to Chase once and for all that he should keep his feelings in check. Afghanistan had also taken a toll on his friend. Zoric had not been allowed to go, but Chase would share that life when he'd had too much to drink. It had been a long time since he'd heard his friend laugh. Yet in the last few days he'd heard Chase burst into light hearted laughter with Tessa Scott. Maybe the simple fact that she was clueless about the terror around her made Chase feel normal. Of course a man could get lost in those blue eyes. Chase had been protective of her, warning Zoric not to be so forward. She'd shown uncommon bravery for a civilian in Knoxville. How she'd stood up for them, saved the pregnant woman's life and protected one of the Chase's men had been nothing less than a miracle. Now as he turned his eyes back on Chase he watched the soldier's jaw clench over and over. The veins of his hands bulged as he gripped the stirring wheel.

"You are worried." His thick east European accent said matter-of-factly. "I think this woman is smart and will be careful. She has a lot to live for, my friend. You should've told her the truth—about everything."

Chase cut his dangerous dark eyes quickly to his friend then back to the road. "I'm going to wring her neck when I catch her!" he growled through gritted teeth.

Zoric shrugged. "I think you shouldn't let this woman get to you. After all, she is just a woman."

Chase accelerated around an eighteen wheeler. "Just a woman!" he stormed. "She's a menace. Let's just put her in charge of Homeland Security! She'll scare the hell out of any terrorist outfit thinking about another attack. Then within six months our troubles will be over! Let's hope the Israelis don't make her an offer she can't refuse. And I'm not letting her get to me!" he said forcefully.

The blinking light indicated low fuel. Taking the second exit to Auburn, Tessa passed two gas stations near the highway in case Chase was following her. She turned the phone off, hadn't opted for the *On Star* and hadn't made any obvious moves they would expect. But then again, everything Enigma set out to do was to over compensate for the unexpected. She wondered if her picture was now displayed at Enigma with an overlay of red crosshairs with the words *Know Your Enemy.*

The quaint town of Auburn, filled with cozy shops and cottage like restaurants, bustled with Friday tourists from Sacramento. Tessa found an out of the way gas station and pulled in slowly, making sure no one had followed her. As always she turned off the car and slipped the key in her pocket. Several times when Sean Patrick was an infant she'd locked the key in the car and had developed the habit of not stepping out of the vehicle until the window was rolled down enough to reach in and unlock the door. *Paranoid,* Robert teased. Of course, Robert didn't travel with children or understand the amount of trouble they could get into. Tessa smiled. *I bet by now he knows,* she thought cynically. She longed to hold them in her arms one more time before Enigma found her and locked her up.

Tessa kept watch over the area with a keen eye, expecting Chase's Hummer to materialize any second. When it didn't she tried to reassure herself that there was no way they could track her. Her mind switched gears when something caught her eye moving across the street into a large parking lot. A slow moving vehicle, a late model Volvo, drove around the lot several times before parking in the back row, furthest from the street. Tessa didn't think it odd that they backed into the spot since she always tried to do the same thing to avoid having to look over the heads of children and flying McDonald straws. It made it so easy when you needed to leave.

At least four spots up front were open and yet the Volvo parked in the back. Two men exited from the backseat and looked around as if waiting for something. Tessa leaned down and looked across her front seat so as not to be seen. Someone still inside the car popped the trunk. The man farthest from her reached into the backseat and pulled an old man out onto wobbly legs. The other thug, as Tessa started to call him, lifted the trunk lid and helped shove the man inside. The old guy hadn't put up a fight.

When the truck slammed shut two other men casually exited the car. One appeared to be in charge for the other three didn't move until he walked forward toward the Chinese restaurant on the side street. The leader then turned his face in Tessa's direction before slipping on his sunglasses like a movie star in disguise. There was no mistaking that the man in the sunglasses was the same man in the photo at Enigma. Essid. Where was Enigma when you needed them?

"It's Tessa, Chase. She's calling you." Zoric gave the picture before him his yellow smile as he clicked to respond. "Tessa, are you safe?" Zoric tried to sound sincere and concerned; both difficult emotions for him.

"Zoric?"

"Yes, Tessa." Just then another picture of a license plate of a black Volvo appeared on the phone screen. She must be right on top of the vehicle to get such a picture.

"Essid is here!" she said in an excited whisper. "I saw them put Mr. Crawley in the trunk!"

Chase grabbed the phone away from his partner. "Listen to me, Tessa. You need to get away from that car and find a safe place. I'll come get you, then take care of Mr. Crawley. Do you understand?"

"I was across the street from the Exxon station in Auburn. Essid and his thugs went into the China Garden restaurant about ten minutes ago. I'm going to help Mr. Crawley. He'll die in the trunk. It's an oven in there!"

"No! Tessa, these people are dangerous. If they catch you…"

"No time, Chase. Hurry. My blue Equinox is parked next to theirs. It'll be easy to get him inside that way. He looked pretty frail."

"Don't disconnect, Tessa!" And then she was gone. "Dear God in heaven," Chase yelled as he hit the stirring wheel with his fist. "She's going to get herself killed!" He slowed seeing an accident ahead. Traffic began to back up as flashing lights appeared on the scene. "I guess we won't be getting any help from the locals," Chase said as he spied the exit ramp just out of reach.

The highway blocked any forward momentum. Not wasting another minute, Chase pulled off onto the shoulder of the road, down a ditch and up onto an outer road. Tires squealed at his sudden exhilaration toward the small town where he feared all hell was about to break loose. Would Tessa heed his warning or do what she usually did, seize the moment? With no understanding concerning the magnitude of her impetuous behavior, Tessa had so far been able to survive the last few days' events unscathed. Either she had incredible luck or those angels she mentioned, were looking after her. Would it hurt if he prayed they continued to chart her course?

Why had this woman been the victim of such random terror events, plunging her into his life? He wondered if this was God's way of retaliating for his open disregard for religion and faith. His parents certainly had crammed that way of life down his throat right up until the time they were killed by the Chinese soldiers. His faith regenerated from the love of his little sister who never faltered in her faithfulness to God. Then he'd found her dead in her apartment, overdosed on heroine. The police said she'd been experimenting like a lot other college kids. But Chase knew she'd been murdered by a man she'd been seeing. The evidence said otherwise and the case closed as did the remaining scrap of faith he carried precariously in his heart. Fast forward to three days ago and Tessa Scott opens her front door, pretty as a soap commercial, the smell of baked bread earlier in the morning wafting through the house, pictures of family on the wall, and a view of the garden he couldn't get out of his head. The surreal feeling of coming home stunned him so suddenly that he had nearly forgotten the reason he'd rang the doorbell. The reluctant cloak of courage Tessa displayed over these past few days earned Chase's admiration. Tessa, unaware of the profound effect her tenacity had on Chase, forced him to acknowledge for the first time in years that there really might be good in the world. That good was no other than Tessa Scott. And now he was afraid of losing her.

\* \* \*

Having parked in the sun, the trunk's temperature moved toward 140 degrees. Mr. Crawley heard someone outside speaking to him. What did it matter? Those men were monsters and this is where he would die, robbing them of his assistance to further their terror. Were they taunting him?

"Mr. Crawley! It's me! Tessa!" She tried the doors of the car and found them locked so the hope of popping the trunk faded quickly. "I'm going to get you out. Can you hear me?"

Mr. Crawley couldn't believe his ears. "Mrs. Scott?" His voice, weak from exhaustion and thirst, could barely be heard.

Tessa instructed Mr. Crawley to look for a cable beneath some carpeting. Nothing. "Okay, look behind a panel of sheet metal and pull the cable." A click followed and Tessa lifted the lid to see a withered and bruised old man she hardly recognized. Mr. Crawley had always looked fit and clean whenever she'd seen him. Here lie a dirty, scared human who looked more like a homeless person who had roamed the streets for months. Struggling to get him out of the trunk, perspiration began to form on her back and arms. She'd left her car running so the air conditioner would cool off her passenger. As she helped him slide into the front seat she handed the old man a bottle of cool water. "Drink slowly, Mr. Crawley."

"How...how..." he swallowed the water, "did you find me?"

A shadow slowly fell across her body. "Yes, indeed, Mrs. Scott," came a calm and calculating voice. "How did you find us?"

Tessa turned slowly to see Essid standing a few feet from her with his arms crossed in front of him.

## Chapter 19

The president of the United States, Buck Austin, stared out the windows of the oval office pondering his upcoming meeting with his Home Land Security Secretary. The secret organization, Enigma, which he'd conceived as the CIA Director would be the topic of conversation. Enigma was a source of pride for him. There were things the CIA could no longer accomplish thanks to the former President Chavez, the first Mexican American president. A liberal of monumental proportions, the former president began making rigid rules for the secret organization after a wealthy website entrepreneur released stolen documents, emails and text messages from the State Department and the Pentagon. Ten corporations began to meet secretly with the director to form Enigma, fully funded by their billions of dollars in order to make the country a safer place to live. Having secured legal documents preventing sponsors from interfering with the work that occurred under the Enigma title the president felt confident its director would operate freely.

He knew that greed motivated the initial interest and backing of Enigma, not national security. Geopolitical conflicts around the world stunted business growth. But the president soon proved to them that a safer America was good for business. The organization would fall under the protection of Homeland Security. Only the director of that cabinet post and the president would know the full extent of their reach and capabilities. The CIA, NSA, and FBI knew of Enigma, but continued to dance around the truth of its purpose, only knowing that their own work benefited from the secretive, sometimes questionable means in which Enigma operated.

Even before Buck Austin took office, Enigma began to set up shop in universities all over the country. Here the brightest and most talented people were recruited and trained, all the while working toward a more educated populace. Nothing suspicious about intellects wanting to attend a university. The coming and goings of political and military personnel trying to better themselves would appear to be nothing out of the ordinary. Benign activities failed to draw attention from the liberal media. Now located at over twenty universities throughout the country, Enigma had become the watchdog of Homeland Security. Even though most of the employees of these institutions continued to be uninformed of their proximity to the everyday job of protecting the county, they worked and complained as you might find in any other place of employment. The authenticity of wanting a raise, more time off, lower tuition, and more help, provided a deceptive cloak that added a layer of protection needed by Enigma.

The commander-in-chief reflected on his predecessor. In spite of the fact that Chavez had been a one term president enough damage had been done to national security, military preparedness and contacts abroad, that now, Buck Austin, began pushing all his agencies to make up for four years of complacent head-in-the-sand politics. His no nonsense attitude toward terrorism was perceived as a little over the top, but that's why the American people had chosen him. They loved that western sheriff mentality he brought from Texas to Washington D.C. Although the press presented the president as rude and arrogant, the American public felt like for once, someone was on their side. It was often said he had the manners of Harry Truman, the imagination of Ronald Reagan, the savvy of George Herbert Bush and the patience of General Patton. No one totally liked him, but everyone respected him. When his staff began looking ahead to the next election and tried to tone down his rhetoric President Austin made it perfectly clear he'd not jeopardize the country's future by worrying about the next caucus in Iowa.

Every Enigma section had a director, but they all answered to Benjamin Clark. The president didn't like many people in politics, especially congress, but he admired Benjamin Clark and trusted him completely. He didn't care that the prime minister of Israel was Ben's half-brother. In his opinion it was more of an asset rather than a conflict of interest.

Tobias Stewart, the Homeland Security Secretary, entered the president's office and extended his hand. "Mr. President."

"Sit down, Tobias, and tell me what Ben and his team are up to. I've read the brief on Lion's Breath. Got that Essid character under lock and key yet?"

"Getting close, Mr. President." Tobias waited until the president was seated before he found a place on the tightly upholstered fabric of the couch. "Mrs. Scott spotted him just minutes ago."

The president smiled with a nod. "How is it that her name keeps popping up? Does she work for us?"

Tobias returned the smile. "Not yet, Mr. President."

\* \* \*

Essid undressed Tessa with his eyes as he placed designer sunglasses on his nose and pushed them up with one finger. "So we finally meet, Mrs. Scott." Essid touched the back of his head gently remembering how hard she'd slugged Jamaal with a rolling pen, giving Chase Hunter the advantage. "How is it that you know Captain Hunter?" He smiled revealing straight teeth that had been whitened. As he spoke one of his thugs pushed Tessa aside and pulled Mr. Crawley from the car. To steady him, Tessa tried to slip an arm around his waist. He made a feeble effort to stand on his own, removing her hand in defiance. "I'll ask you one more time..." Essid now spoke through gritted teeth.

"He showed up at my house just before you did." She spoke quickly, hearing the growing irritation in Essid's voice. "I never saw him before."

Essid looked behind him at one of his men and motioned for him to start their car.

"He'll be here any minute!" she blurted a little too quickly. "I sent him a picture of your license plate and car. By now every cop in California is looking for you," Tessa said trying to sound confident as she raised her chin.

Essid chuckled. "Well, thank you very much, Mrs. Scott, for that heads up. I guess our plans have changed then."

Tessa realized she'd given her only edge away through her own fears as Essid's thug retrieved the Enigma phone from her front seat. He turned it on and began searching for something. "I think we'll be taking a few pictures in a bit," he smiled satanically.

"There!" Zoric pointed as several men screeched tires peeling out of the parking lot and onto the street. "Look out!" Just then one of the men stuck his automatic weapon out the window and began spraying Chase's Hummer with bullets. He swerved onto a curb, taking out a UPS mailbox and newspaper case. Having to back up gave Essid and his men time to escape through the streets. "I couldn't tell if she's in there, Chase." Zoric checked his weapon but knew he wouldn't fire as long as Tessa and Mr. Crawley might be in the Equinox. His phone vibrated. "They've got her, Chase!" Zoric said showing him the picture of Tessa and Mr. Crawley bound and gagged in the back of the Equinox.

The blue Equinox raced east out of town. "Vernon, I need your eyes," Chase said forcefully, trying to focus on the problem at hand instead of the outcome possibilities.

Vernon said quickly, knowing Mrs. Scott was on board the runaway vehicle. "I'll have *On Star* locked in to my network in six minutes."

"We might not have six minutes, Vern!" Minutes began turning into miles as both cars raced forward through the countryside. "I see road construction signs, Vern. Looks like a bridge repair."

"Right. There's road construction on your side of the bridge. That should slow them down."

Chase pursued at a reckless speed, trying to get a visual on the Equinox. "I see it!" Zoric leaned forward in his seat. "They're not slowing down!" he continued as they passed a *road work ahead* sign.

The Equinox approached the orange vested men at work too fast. The vehicle swerved then over corrected as it crashed into the left side of the bridge, flipping it over the top like a child's toy. The workers ran to the side, in time to see it crash below. Chase and Zoric braked hard and exited the Hummer and rushed just as the Equinox exploded.

Zoric paled as he pulled out a cross that hung around his neck and kissed it. "Dear God in Heaven," he said incredulously.

\* \* \*

The two Enigma men didn't wait around for the proper rescue workers to arrive on the scene. Both knew there wouldn't be anything left to find with a full tank of exploded gasoline burning below. Vernon had heard everything and solemnly voiced concern about telling Tessa's family about the accident. Chase did not respond as he glared out the windshield of his Hummer, heading back toward Auburn. Zoric informed Vernon they were going to check out the other vehicles on the parking lot where Tessa sent her last communication. Maybe someone witnessed the kidnapping and could fill in the gaps. As they slowly rounded the corner of the street where Tessa had spotted Essid, the flashing lights of a fire engine, ambulance and police blocked off the parking lot. The two Enigma men parked the Hummer and slowly crossed the street to see if maybe Essid's vehicle had also been torched during the escape. Several officers were gathering spent shells left by the spray of bullets.

He heard an officer questioning someone in the back of the ambulance then a voice he recognized; a soft frightened voice that had been a source of irritation for the last three days. Both he and Zoric froze and looked at each other in shock. Another officer stopped them until both flashed a badge and were motioned on toward the ambulance. Sitting on the step of the rescue vehicle, Tessa nodded when the officer spoke to her as she looked at Mr. Crawley sitting on a gurney behind her. She reached back patting his leg and smiled sweetly before taking a sip of bottled water.

"And you have no idea who these men were?" the officer questioned with a glum face.

"None, officer," Tessa lied like a pro, Chase noticed as he stopped some five feet from her. When her blue eyes glanced his way then locked on him, Chase felt that hammering pain in his chest again. He folded his arms tightly across his muscled chest in mock displeasure as the paramedic applied a bandage to her forehead. A bruise had begun to form over one eye and a small cut on her bottom lip showed traces of dried blood.

"And you say there were three of them?"

Chase noticed Mr. Crawley reach out and put his hand on Tessa's shoulder.

"Yes. Three men. Looked like college age boys."

The officer shook his head in disgust. "Probably had too much to drink on the river and looking for a little thrill with all their fake courage. Booze and guns. Dangerous combination."

"And your name?" another officer readied his pencil.

Her eyes went to Chase. "Melanie. My name is Melanie Glenn. I'm sorry. I have no identification. It was all in the car."

"Thank you, Ms. Glenn. We'll take you to the emergency room if you're ready."

Chase and Zoric stepped forward, flashing their badge. "We'll take it from here, officer."

The officer looked at the badge then at Chase and only briefly at Zoric. "You boys from Sacramento don't usually get up here. What's up?"

"We've been following a few leads on some punks from Sac causing problems up this way. They made the mistake of harassing the governor's daughter."

"No explanation for stupid."

"Got that right," Chase said slapping the officer on the back as he looked at Tessa. "If these two feel up to it, we'd like to take them with us. Sounds like they had a run in with our guys. We'll have someone retrieve the car too. Could be evidence. The governor wants this resolved ASAP. I'll mention you in my report."

The officer pulled his chest back and straightened his shoulders. "Sure. Go 'head. Hope you get your man."

Chase offered his hand to Tessa which she grabbed eagerly and scooted off the step. Zoric assisted Mr. Crawley and together they all walked toward the Hummer. Tessa shook Chase's hand from her elbow and growled: "I want to see my family now! You have an assassin watching over them and she doesn't even work for you! I was such a fool to trust you."

"Your family is safe. If you would have just waited I could have…"

Tessa stopped short as he opened the car door. "Wait for what? Another fabricated story? Another reason I have to stay?"

As Tessa buckled herself into the passenger side of the vehicle, Chase leaned in inches from her face. "I thought you were dead." It was hard to read such a calm voice.

Tessa sniffed and rolled her eyes. "Well if I left it up to you to rescue me I would be!"

## Chapter 20

Benjamin Clark stood staring out his six story office window. The sun beat down on the students walking to and from class among the manicured landscaping and red brick pathways. Although he couldn't hear the outside, Ben knew their voices probably were light and carefree as they chatted about an upcoming test or local coffee house where they could study later in the day. The movement of leaves and branches spoke of a summer breeze; one that was much needed on such a hot day. He laid his hand on his stomach, as if by doing so the ache would vanish. He tried to remember what he'd eaten at lunch that soured his stomach. The movement of fluffy white clouds across a sharp blue sky distracted him long enough for the pain to ebb. Lost in the common, every day movements of the world outside his office, Ben pretended nothing ever changed, people were basically good and students were actually here to improve themselves. He spotted a lost dog meandering along the walkway below, looking for someone to pat him on the head or be offered some kind of snack. Ben watched the dog stop wagging its tail and find a shady spot to lie down.

"Don't give up, buddy," Ben said aloud.

"Sorry?" Vernon closed the door behind him. "I knocked."

Ben shrugged as he sat down in his leather and chrome chair. Pulling himself up to the desk, Ben looked sternly at Vernon. "Yes? What is it, Vern?" He eyed the young computer genius and realized again that even though Vernon Kemp got on his nerves, Captain Hunter had chosen wisely for the Enigma team. Having a loose cannon like Vernon among the masses made his heart skip a beat. At least here Chase could keep all that youthful energy channeled toward the greater good. *He looks like a hippy,* Ben thought with exasperation. Knowing Vernon had often crossed swords with the Pentagon both amused and frustrated Ben. When Vernon infuriated the brass, it was he who had to run interference. Being a military man himself, Ben found Vernon's shoulder length, deep red hair, sloppy clothes and sandals all a little insolent.

Vernon pushed his hair behind his ears. "Essid stole another car off the parking lot while his men lured Chase and Zoric away with Mrs. Scott's Equinox. He then ditched the car not more than a mile from Auburn. We think he then stole another and disappeared off the radar."

"And Mrs. Scott?" Ben scowled up at Vernon.

"A little banged up. Considering what Crawley went through he's not too bad. They're stopping some place to interrogate the old guy. Maybe we'll know how to proceed then."

"And just how is it that Mrs. Scott is still alive?" Benjamin had been raised as a Messianic Jew, practicing a blend of Christianity and Judaism, but wasn't sure how to fit a higher power message into his life. At Enigma you didn't wait for divine intervention.

Vernon shrugged. "I donno. A miracle?" He watched a disapproving frown form on Ben's angular face. Vernon excused himself quickly, breathing a sigh of relief as he closed the door behind him. Benjamin Clark could be one intimidating dude. If it weren't for him the Pentagon goons would have locked him up a long time ago. Aloof and guarded, Ben rarely revealed his feelings other than an occasional outburst of anger. No mystery in how he regarded Vernon; he could no longer count the number of times Chase had run interference on his behalf. Still, Vernon craved a little positive recognition from the head of Enigma.

\* \* \*

Chase wondered repeatedly how all these events kept leading back to Tessa Scott. Everything appeared to be a coincidence at first but after three days the innocent housewife from Grass Valley was over her head in trouble. She'd stared straight ahead after he'd secured her in the Hummer, silent, hands folded tightly and breathing heavier than normal. Was she hiding some important information, or planning another way to get to her family? Either way, Chase now knew better than to trust her. He'd made that mistake for the last time; suckered by blue eyes and that sweet innocent southern drawl she conveniently dropped on him from time to time.

They drove for nearly ten miles north to the small town of Apple Valley. Nestled in the foothills of the Sierra Mountains, the town rested at an elevation of over two thousand feet. Entering the quaint, outdoorsman-like town that tourists found irresistible, Chase spotted several motel chains that catered to travelers, but chose one on the outskirts. He parked in the back after checking in.

Zoric made a quick trip for some sandwiches and drinks while Chase and Tessa gently assisted Mr. Crawley into one of the rooms. Casually, Chase retrieved Tessa's bag she'd secured the first day into the nightmare. There were two other backpacks belonging to the two men which were carelessly dropped on the floor by the door. The room was nondescript, like so many motel chains across the country: two double beds, dresser and TV stand, a digital alarm clock that blinked red numbers next to a black phone on the nightstand. A swivel chair and footstool sat next to a small round table beneath the window covered in dated pin striped curtains. Located at the back was the bathroom, small but efficient. A four cup coffee maker rested on the vanity with a selection of Earl Grey tea and some off brand coffee, both regular and decaffeinated. It could've been a room anywhere in America that travelers stop and rest before continuing on with their holiday.

Tessa realized she would never look at another motel quite the same way for the rest of her life. So far this little respite from Robert and the kids was turning out to be the vacation from hell. She stood in the doorway watching Chase sit Mr. Crawley down in the only chair before removing his San Francisco Giants baseball cap and laying it on the table. He looked over his shoulder at her and motioned to move away from the door with his stern, chocolate eyes. Tessa met his gaze with her own narrowed eyes, pretending to show contempt before coming inside, closing the door behind her with her foot. She needed to make him feel as off centered as she felt.

"Where would I go?" she snapped, knowing the captain thought she'd try and escape again. He hadn't shown one ounce of surprise, relief or outrage when discovering she'd not been taken hostage by Essid. The only moment when she'd known the gravity of her actions was when Chase had pulled over on the bridge then pulled her roughly from the Hummer. He'd forced her to look over the side at the burning wreckage below, remaining silent long enough for the seriousness to sink in to her thick skull. Grabbing her arm, Chase pushed her back toward the car and waited for her to buckle herself in.

"Don't ever do that again!" he growled before slamming the door shut.

Tessa had been shaken to the core. What if those thugs had forced her in the Equinox? What if Essid had made good on his threat to shoot Mr. Crawley if she didn't cooperate? What if he'd taken her to lure Captain Hunter to a secluded spot in order to kill him? After all Chase had done to protect her, she had nearly made it possible for a very evil man to murder him without remorse or hesitation.

Only by focusing on the road ahead and gripping her hands tightly did she keep from breaking down into a sobbing idiot. She hadn't known the mighty Captain Chase Hunter very long, but she already knew he had little patience with weakness, disobeying of orders and compromising a mission. In a matter of a few minutes she'd managed to accomplish all of those things. His menacing dark eyes landed on her like a hammer when he'd seen her talking to the police in Auburn. Maybe he wished she'd been in the Equinox. Now here she was in a remote part of California with Enigma agents, Mr. Crawley and confusion as to why they were holed up in a motel.

Zoric arrived back with food, looking to Tessa with hands shoved in her jeans pockets then to Chase who kept looking out the window in every direction. "Eat something, Tessa," he said with a familiarity that drew her eyes up to meet his. "Mr. Crawley, are you hungry?" Zoric tried to be civil but his raspy, smoker's voice, pale skin and sharp features made it easier for Mr. Crawley to ignore. Short sleeves, revealed tattoos running up both hairless arms. His clothes smelled of cigarette smoke and perspiration. A bulge at the waist under his loose fitting shirt hinted at a weapon.

Mr. Crawley shook his head and looked down at his hands.

"Mr. Crawley, sir, if you don't mind my partner and I need some information." Chase came to stand in front of the old man.

He continued to stare at the floor as if in a trance. The two agents looked at each other impatiently before glancing at Tessa. Having her here changed the procedure.

"Sir, can you tell us…"

"I don't know anything," he mumbled, shaking his head. "Leave me alone!"

Tessa moved toward the agents and pushed them aside. "Go make some coffee," she said looking at Zoric. When he hesitated, she pointed toward the bathroom. "Now, Zoric. And you," she looked at Chase, "warm that sandwich up for me in the microwave—over there." Tessa opened a bottle of water from the table before leaning down to whisper in Mr. Crawley's ear. "It's me. Tessa. You're safe now, Mr. Crawley." She put her hand on the old man's shoulder and gently rubbed it. "Boy that was pretty exciting wasn't it?" Tessa began telling the old man about the last couple of days and how she'd managed to clobber the macho captain standing there with a sour face. Mr. Crawley smiled a little and took the water. "Mmm. Smell that? Zoric is making us some coffee."

"It's hot outside," he said hesitantly.

"Never too hot for a good cup of coffee, right Captain Hunter?" she said looking over at the agent who'd returned with the warm roast beef sandwich. He nodded and forced a smile when the old man looked his way. "Why I've been known to drink coffee when it's 100 degrees outside. Remember last summer when you saw me eating ice cream and drinking coffee?"

Mr. Crawley smiled sheepishly. "You were at Dairy Queen. I said that was ridiculous."

"Yep. You sure did. Then my boys ran right into me spilling coffee all over the floor and my ice cream." She laughed. "Wasn't funny then, of course. I yelled at the kids and you came over to help me wipe up the mess. Remember? I thought I was going to crack and then there you were, reminding the boys to be good and telling Heather she looked like a little princess. I calmed down and you left before I could say 'thank you'."

"Ungrateful!" he teased softly.

"Well you are an old grouch sometimes, Mr. Crawley." Zoric returned with two cups of coffee. "Here, warm your hands." Tessa pulled up the stool and placed the cup in his hands, covering them with her own. The shaking stopped in his wrinkled hands. His light brown eyes looked into hers, searching for answers. "Eat something. Smells so good." She tore the sandwich in half and gave him the larger side. She nibbled one end of her sandwich in spite of not wanting it. Tessa reached out and pushed the other sandwiches toward the agents. "Eat. It'll make you feel better." She nodded toward Mr. Crawley. "Isn't that right, neighbor?" Mr. Crawley began to eat a little faster and soon finished off his coffee. Tessa dabbed her mouth with a scratchy paper napkin, wadded it up and shot it toward the waste basket. When she missed she groaned. "Man! I never miss. I must be off my game." She handed Mr. Crawley a napkin. "Here. You try." He also missed. The two agents tried next, both finding their mark with little effort. Tessa turned back to Mr. Crawley. "Showoffs!" she smiled.

The old man leaned back in his chair now, shoulders pulled back and surveying his surroundings with interest. She'd sent Zoric for a bucket of ice to wrap in a wash cloth for the bruise on Mr. Crawley's face. Tessa pulled her stool closer and laid her hands on his knees and patted gently. "Mr. Crawley, I know you've been through a lot. But these men are trying to stop the man who kidnapped and beat you. The man, who took you, Essid, is trying to hurt a great many people. They need to ask you some questions. Do you think you could talk to them a little while and then maybe we can both take a rest? I'm exhausted. How about you?"

Mr. Crawley laid his free hand on top of hers and leaned close enough where he could place a kiss on her forehead. "You came for me? Why?"

Tessa cupped his brown face in her hands. "Beats me. I guess because you're the closest thing I have to family out here in California. I just couldn't stand the thought of someone hurting you. Who would set me straight about my yard, my kids, and my overgrown garden?"

Tears formed in the corners of his eyes and he sat back in his chair. "What do you want to know, Captain Hunter?" Mr. Crawley said handing him his cup for a refill.

\*\*\*

"She is amazing, my friend," Zoric said hours later when the sun had begun to dip behind the trees with a cool breeze drifting down from the mountains. "That old man was almost comatose when Tessa started working on him." Zoric chuckled and slapped his leg before lighting up a cigarette. "He didn't even know she was playin' him."

Chase leaned against the hood of the Hummer and stretched. "I don't think she was."

Zoric inhaled deeply then exhaled slowly. "No matter. She got him to spill his guts. At least we know where we stand now." The smoke formed a cloud around his head making his weasel eyes narrow as he scratched his thin mustache. "I'm in love with her!" he grinned slapping at Chase's arm.

"Well that could be a death wish," Chase quipped as he watched Tessa through the window helping Mr. Crawley stand. "But you're right. He would have never talked to us." He wondered what it must feel like to have those small hands touch your face, your shoulders… "Going for a walk?" he asked Tessa as she linked her arm in Mr. Crawley's and came through the door.

Tessa patted Mr. Crawley's arm with her free hand. "Yep!" She smiled over at her neighbor. "And while we're at it, he's going to show me how to hotwire one of these cars so we can ditch you guys," Tessa smiled over at the agents revealing clenched teeth.

"Better watch it, Jericho." Chase had personalized the questioning by referring to him by his first name. "She'll get you into a heap of trouble."

Zoric took one more puff off his cigarette before flicking it out into the parking lot. "I'll take some of that trouble," he said meeting Tessa's eyes with interest.

Mr. Crawley pointed an arthritic finger at Zoric and frowned. "You watch your mouth, Mr. Zoric."

Zoric nodded and grinned as they slowly strolled away. "Think he's in love with her too?"

"You're not in love, Zoric," Chase said motioning for him to walk with him. "You're in lust."

Zoric clamped a bony hand on Chase's shoulder. "I wasn't talking about me, my friend."

\* \* \*

Tessa entered the motel room with Chase on her heels. He slung his backpack in the chair after sitting her bag on the table. They had walked to a café at the end of the parking lot, ordered a light supper and continued to stroll around the grounds until the light had become dappled. Mr. Crawley grew tired and wanted to go back to his room. When Zoric announced he'd be watching after the old man through the night, Tessa assumed she'd get a room to herself. Chase bolted the door, closed the curtains, and flipped on the light before turning on the television and air conditioner. He removed his belt that held his holstered weapon, keys and tee shirt, revealing a well-muscled chest. Tessa gasped and laid her hand on her heart.

"What are you doing!" she demanded as she backed toward the door.

Chase felt the cool stream of air from the wall unit as he channel surfed until he found the Giants and Cardinal game. It was the third inning. "I'm going to take a shower. I won't be long and then it's all yours." He turned to leave.

"What!" she stormed. "What do you mean it's all mine? Where is my room, Captain Hunter?" she fumed putting her hands on her hips and scowling.

"This is it."

Tessa pointed at the bed. "But that's a king size bed! Where am I supposed to sleep?" Her voice showed an edge of panic.

Chase reached down and patted the covers. "Right here next to me."

## Chapter 21

Tessa waited until the water started to run in the shower before grabbing her bag and unbolting the door. She took one more glance behind her as she threw open the door and froze. Standing six feet away, leaning against the Hummer, Zoric opened his knife and began cleaning his nails. Looking up casually, he smiled and eyed her without restraint.

"Going someplace?" he asked curiously as his eyes fell on her bag.

Tessa turned on her heels and slammed the door in Zoric's face. She thought she heard a snicker as it closed. The sound of the ballgame annoyed her to the extent that she turned it off. Just as she did, Chase came through the door wrapped in nothing but a towel. "Oh my gosh!" she stuttered as she backed away. Chase reached out and grabbed the remote and turned the game back on and the volume up.

"I'm watching the game! Do you mind?" Chase retreated back into the bathroom.

Tessa covered her mouth to keep from screaming her indignation of the whole situation. All she could think about was the captain in a towel, moisture clinging to his chest and hair. "Oh my gosh! Oh my gosh!" *What was happening? Did Chase really think she was going to share a bed with him?* A nervous laugh escaped her lips as she began to pace. *That would just be the frosting on the cake,* she mused throwing up her hands in frustration. Tessa peeked out the curtains and could see Zoric standing in the shadows. *What a ghoul,* she fumed. The bathroom door opened again and this time Chase came out partially clothed in some kind of sweat pants and a wife beater undershirt.

"Aren't you going to put more clothes on?" Tessa jerked up her chin and pointed to his chest as he flopped on the bed and crossed his legs.

"Nope." Chase's attention was on the game. He'd taken a baseball out of his backpack and tossed it back and forth between his hands.

"I want my own room, please." Tessa tried to sound matter of fact and stood in front of the television.

Chase stopped tossing the ball and let his eyes drink her in. "You'll feel better when you clean up. There are plenty of towels."

"I want my own room. This is inappropriate for me to stay in here with you. I'm a..."

"married woman. I know." He motioned for her to move aside so he could see the game. "This was all they had left. This bed is huge. You'll never know I'm here." When she stiffened and put her hands on her hips Chase knew he was in for an argument. Tessa still had not come to grips with the day's events and probably suffered some kind of post-traumatic stress.

Tessa rolled her eyes incredulously. "How convenient for you," she snarled.

Chase cheered as the Giants scored a run before cocking his head and gazing silently at the scruffy looking Tessa. She seemed to fidget under his gaze. "Convenient? Don't flatter yourself." He couldn't help letting a condescending laugh escape his throat.

"You are an arrogant Neanderthal that..." Chase looked at Tessa with amusement and started to toss his baseball up in the air and catch it, over and over without looking at it. "Ms. Coleman told me all about you!"

"Oh that's right. You did interrogate the dear soul. You should be ashamed of yourself taking advantage of such a sweet lady." Chase scooted to the edge of the bed to make Tessa skitter away from the TV.

"I seriously doubt anyone at Enigma is sweet. She told me you're quite the Don Juan."

He yelled at his team for striking out before turning back to Tessa. "That would be Carter. Not me. You've never cheated on good ole Robert, have you?"

"Of course not! I adore Robert."

"Then why didn't you go to Tahoe with him and the kids?" Chase could tell a lie was about to spill from those tempting lips of hers. "Go on and make something up, Tessa." He laughed again. "You were fighting. He ticked you off and you thought you'd teach him a lesson."

Tessa gasped. "How did you know?" Chase cut his eyes up at her and grinned. Tessa blushed. "You guessed, didn't you? Well, he wanted to try and do the trip on his own so I could..."

Chase stood and faced her, continuing to toss the ball in the air with one hand, then catching it repeatedly. "Another lie. You're nervous now because you've not been in a motel room with a man, besides Robert, of course, in a very long time." He watched her comfort level tank. "I bet the only man you've ever slept with is Robert. Am I right?" he grinned as the ball stopped.

"I-I-I've slept with many men, actually," Tessa said backing away and looking down at the floor.

"Well whata ya know. Robert's a lucky man," he said shaking his head. "I'm number two!"

"Excuse me!"

"You're practically a virgin in this day and time." His face went stern as he tossed the ball on the bed. Chase moved toward Tessa forcing her to awkwardly take backward steps. "I'll have to say I've never met anyone quite like you." He made eye contact with Tessa causing her to stumble against the table then into the door. "I know why you ran, thinking your family was in danger but we never did talk about how you managed to get away from Essid."

Tessa dismissed the idea with a wave of her hand. "I simply told him it wasn't a good idea. He agreed and left." A large hand went up on the door beside her head. "Didn't you talk to Mr. Crawley about this?"

"I wanna hear it from you, Tessa," he said as he brought his other hand up on the other side of her head.

"You are invading my personal space, Captain Hunter. I'm warning you, I've had a self-defense class!"

Chase pressed himself up against Tessa lightly so that she couldn't knee him like she had the last time she'd felt threatened by his close proximity. "We're back to captain again. Tell me, Tessa and I'll stand back."

She shivered and nodded as Chase slowly took two steps back. Her eyes blinked rapidly, remembering her encounter with Essid. She owed it to Captain Hunter to fill in the gaps of the morning.

"I didn't see him come up behind me. Mr. Crawley was in bad shape when I got to him."

"He told me how you got him out of the trunk. Where did you learn to do that?" Chase searched her face as her eyes seem to focus on events that occurred earlier in the day. Events he could not see.

Her eyes met his. "Boy Scouts." A confused look sprang to his eyes. "I'm a den mother for my boys. I taught the survival merit badge." Tessa pushed her hair away from her face. "Well, I actually taught myself first."

Captain Chase Hunter smiled at the simplicity of it all. "I'm somehow not surprised. Go on."

Tessa began telling how one of Essid's thugs yanked Mr. Crawley out of the car, bound his hands and mouth with duct tape then shoved him onto the floorboard of the backseat of Essid's Volvo. When Tessa tried to scream for help, Essid slapped her so hard she spun back against the door and cut her forehead. "One of his men tried to put tape on my mouth. I started to cry," she sniffed back tears as a show of strength. "The next thing I knew he had a gun pointed at my stomach. I…" Tessa swallowed hard as a tear escaped squeezed from the corner of her eye, "I told him you would be there any minute and…" Tessa reached out as if to lay her palm on Chase's chest, "I'm so sorry, Chase! I told him you were coming for me." Tessa shook her head. "I could've gotten you killed too, just because I was trying to save myself!" Tessa pushed past Chase and started to rub her arms as if she were suddenly cold. "He's an evil man."

Chase gently turned Tessa around to face him. "Then what happened?"

Tessa blinked back more tears and swallowed. "When he glanced away, looking to see if you were there, I took out the red pepper spray I had in my pocket."

Chase remembered that Tessa had used it on one of the terrorists in Knoxville, and had taken it from her later. "I thought I took that."

Tessa smiled weakly. "I had another canister in the front zipper section of my purse. I took it out this morning and stuck it in my jean's pocket in case…you know---just in case."

Chase smiled warmly, feeling that surge of respect and something unfamiliar well up inside him. "Please tell me you assaulted him."

"When Essid looked back at me he reached out and grabbed my blouse." Tessa pointed to the front just over her breasts. "He said something in a language I didn't understand. It didn't sound like he was paying me a compliment. So I," she paused.

Chase chuckled. "You didn't!"

Tessa had rammed her knee into Essid's groin, rendering him unable to make good on his threats. When the second thug had caught Essid and pushed him aside to rest against their car, he lunged at Tessa only to be sprayed in the eyes with her pepper spray. He collapsed moaning and cursing into her Equinox, rubbing madly at his face and eyes. Another pair of hands from behind knocked the spray from her grip and managed to duct tape her hands behind her back. They secured her feet by tying them to her hands after pushing her onto the backseat of Essid's car onto her stomach.

"Someone took a picture of you two tied up and sent it to me. We thought you were in the back of the Equinox." Chase realized after he'd found her alive neither he nor Zoric had taken the time to distinguish between the vehicles.

"The phone I stole from Ms. Coleman's desk, I guess. He threw it on the ground and stomped it before throwing it at my head. My mouth was taped, and I couldn't move."

Chase thought she must have turned her cheek to receive the full impact of the phone. The bruise was now visible in a soft shade of blue. "Mr. Crawley says they locked the doors with the windows up and took off."

"I saw the Equinox back out with two of the men, but Essid wasn't with them. They must have been trying to lure you away from him."

Chase nodded, hating he'd fallen for such an amateur's trick. "And then?"

"It was so hot! Mr. Crawley hadn't recovered from being in the trunk. It was even hotter in the car. I scooted as close to the door as possible and started kicking the door, but no one came. I heard gunfire and thought you'd arrived. Just when I thought I'd pass out I heard two women screaming for others to get down. I started kicking again. The next thing I knew the fire department was breaking out the window and pulling us out." Tessa unconsciously rubbed her hands together as if finishing something important. "I, I was so scared!" she confessed rubbing her arms again as if chilled.

"You've been through a lot these last couple of days."

"This was far worse than at the house, nearly going over the cliff or in Knoxville," she said meeting his softened gaze.

Chase grinned boyishly. "Why is that?"

"Because I thought you might not come in time," she said with a helpless shrug. Chase stepped forward and Tessa fell into his arms. He held her so close he could feel her heart beat and the warmth of her cheek on his skin. Without thinking his hand went to the back of her head where he could feel the blond curls twist around his fingers. Chase felt her begin to breath normally and then stiffen as if she became aware of her close proximity to his body. Carefully Tessa pulled away, straightening her shirt, her hair and tear streaked face. "Thanks. Robert always says I'm such a baby."

Chase cringed at her husband's name and took out his phone. He saw that he had a message; read it then deleted. His eyes went back to Tessa. "Tell you what…" he pushed a button on the phone. "Why don't we give ole Robert a call? You can catch up; reassure yourself that someone really is looking after your family." He handed her the phone and went back to the edge of the bed to watch the game.

Tessa had no illusions of privacy. Chase appeared to be intent on the baseball game, tossing his ball in the air and catching it over and over again without so much as looking at it. But Tessa knew the captain would not miss a word.

"Robert!" Tessa clasped the phone like a romantic embrace. "How are you?"

Robert watched the boys cooking marshmallows over the grill with Honey. She bent down and helped Heather shove her marshmallow on a long stick she'd found earlier. Laughter drifted up from the four as they began making s'mores. This scene almost didn't happen, he reminded himself. If it hadn't been for Honey shooting that bear… Robert thanked God again for Honey Lynch.

"Great! Let me just say how much I love and miss you, sweetheart."

Although the volume was low, Tessa knew the speaker phone could be heard over the ballgame. "I miss you too, sweetie. How are the kids? They doin' okay? Do they miss me?"

Robert's warm laugh helped relieve Tessa without him ever knowing it. "The kids are great and yes they miss you."

"Are you guys staying safe?" Tessa just had to ask as her eyes cut to Chase who appeared to be ignoring her.

"Well, actually we had a near miss this morning, babe. Now don't get crazy on me before you hear the whole story."

Robert retold the incident about the Ponderosa breakfast in detail, trying to remain calm, even though talking about it unnerved him more than he'd expected. When Tessa didn't say a word Robert anticipated a meltdown at the other end of the phone line. But instead he heard a calm, rational voice.

"Let me talk to them, Robert."

Robert felt uneasy at Tessa's acceptance of the story. The children were soon chatting away with their mother telling about the Ponderosa and how much they liked their new friend, Honey. Soon they scooted off to finish the s'mores and left the talking to their father.

"You're lucky she was there, Robert," Tessa said carefully. "What's she like?"

"I donno. Young."

"Attractive too, I bet." Tessa already knew she was more than attractive. Usually her husband fell all over himself for a pretty woman, trying to impress them with his wit and charm.

"Yeah, in an outdoorsy kind of way."

"Honey has your s'mores, Dad. Better come eat it!" called Daniel.

Tessa felt a wave of panic knowing a known killer was near her family. "She's there now!" Tessa hadn't meant to sound alarmed. Looking over at Chase, she noticed the ball had stopped flipping into the air.

"We took her out to dinner for saving the day then the kids invited her back for s'mores." Chase cleared his throat. "You know I was thinking about coming back tomorrow to get you."

Tessa smiled and switched the phone to the other ear. "Oh? Why is that?"

"I miss your cold feet," he laughed.

Chase began tossing the ball up a little higher this time.

"And I want to show you how much I love you," he said sincerely. "I'm such a jerk." He paused before going on. "But, this has been amazing,

Tessa. You've done a great job with these kids and I've just let them slip away."

"Can you survive a few more days?" Tessa said hopefully.

"I'm getting the hang of this now! Sure! And I'll keep them away from cougars, bears and convicts."

"Don't forget terrorists and assassins," she said feeling a cold shiver creep up her spine.

## Chapter 22

"Excuse me, kids! I've got to take this call." Honey stepped off the deck and walked further into the yard out of earshot. Darkness had fallen, stars scattered recklessly across the sky with brilliance and the air had cooled to the point of needing a jacket. She let the darkness swallow her so that her observant eyes could follow the Scott family activities without notice. Honey smiled when she'd seen Captain Chase Hunter's picture appear on her phone. She let it ring longer than she needed before answering.

"Ahh, the mighty Captain Hunter. What do I owe the pleasure?"

"Mrs. Scott wants to speak with you. She knows all about you, Honey so don't play games."

Chase would put her on speaker phone. "Only with you, baby." Remembering fondly his preoccupation to detail, she knew he would listen to every word. "Put her on," she said somewhat amused. There could be no doubt Chase intended to manage both women at the same time. She blew him a kiss just as he handed the phone to Tessa Scott.

Honey frowned seeing Robert's wife for the first time. Tessa Scott wasn't what she'd anticipated. Although the day's events had left her exhausted and her eyes were puffy from either allergies or crying, Robert's wife was pretty. Maybe wholesome was a better description, with her shoulder length blonde hair, piercing blue eyes and pale smooth skin. She looked like a cosmetic ad, Honey decided. That could be the reason why her husband hadn't been tempted to stray from the marital nest, what with having an angel-type looking wife.

"Mrs. Scott." It was not a greeting; more of a declaration.

Tessa smiled weakly, trying not to notice that the park ranger guarding her family was more than a little attractive. "Honey?"

Honey's eyes smiled but her mouth remained unmoving. "Yes."

"What you did for my boys today..." Tessa could feel her heart in her throat. "I'm indebted to you. If I can ever return the favor..."

"Tessa," she cut in, "if I may call you that."

"Of course," Tessa said eagerly.

"Let's not pretend here. You're never going to help someone like me."

Tessa looked bewildered. "Why? Because..." Tessa let the words fall.

"Because I'm not exactly one of your typical book club members."

"Well, thank goodness for that," Tessa chuckled noticing a look of disbelief spring to Honey's eyes as she cocked her head sideways. "I've got plenty of those friends, Honey. But thank you for being the hero for my kids. Sounds like they adore you. They're a pretty good judge of character."

Honey watched Chase move up behind Tessa and stare over her shoulder into the phone with critical appraisal. She arched an eyebrow and looked up at the deck where Tessa's family laughed and sang songs. Suddenly a lurch of loneliness washed over her. Honey fought back the sudden feeling of isolation. "Your husband is a pretty good judge of character too," she smiled wickedly.

Tessa had no way of knowing that Chase frowned over her shoulder or that he'd given Honey the 'let's wrap this up' sign. The implied meaning to Honey's words both terrified and angered her. Swallowing a threatening retort, Tessa smiled sweetly. "You're absolutely correct, Honey. That's why I trust you completely. Thanks again."

Handing the phone to Chase, Tessa grabbed her bag and pointed to the bathroom for her turn at the shower. Chase nodded and pointed that he'd be outside talking to Honey. Closing the door behind him he saw Zoric come around the back of the Hummer. Honey waited patiently while Chase found his spot, leaning against the hood of the car.

"Got a message from Ben," he said looking sternly into the phone.

"How is the old stick in the mud?" she said flippantly.

"He's beginning to wonder what side you're on, Honey."

Chase's growl of disapproval irritated Honey. "I'm sure I don't know what you mean."

"He wants to know what the hell you've done with Dr. Haskin's boys!"

Robert watched Honey slink out of the darkness as she shoved her phone in her pants' pocket. She looked upset, or was it anger. He couldn't tell. That cool exterior made Honey hard to read. His Tessa on the other hand read like a book who wore her feelings on her sleeve. Even the way she walked across the floor could alert Robert to a problem. "You okay?" He patted Daniel on the head as he motioned for Sean Patrick to go inside. The kids were so tired they volunteered to go to bed on their own.

Heather wouldn't let her father pick her up, but instead raised her chubby little arms up to Honey. She lifted the little girl up and felt a strange sensation as Heather laid her curly head on Honey's shoulder. Heather's little hand patted Honey's face and then she felt a wet kiss on her cheek. "I'm sleepy."

Honey hugged the little girl and surprised herself by returning the kiss. Robert picked up Daniel who circled his father's neck and mumbled sleepily that he wanted a bedtime story. "Not tonight, buddy. Let's get you dressed for bed. Okay?" Daniel nodded.

After helping Heather with her pajamas, Honey tucked her in beneath a thin quilt. "There! All ready for bed. Your daddy will be in shortly to say goodnight."

Heather gave her a sleepy smile. "I want to be just like you."

Honey stood up tall and looked down at the little girl, and tried to remember such a time of innocence in her own life. "Why is that? You want to be a park ranger?"

Heather closed her eyes and shook her head 'no'. "Cuz you're nice."

That depiction rarely was used in describing Honey Lynch, she realized. Suddenly she felt claustrophobic, a little panicked and a lot guilty. Honey patted Heather's head and returned to wait for Robert by the enclosed fire on the deck. She stacked up their paper plates and threw them in the fire, closed the box of graham crackers and poured some water on the fire.

"Thanks for your help." She barely smiled and made no eye contact as Robert softly closed the screen door. "Your call, is there a problem? You seem a little upset."

Honey dusted some crumbs from her hands and moved toward the steps. "No. Just a guy I know."

"Boyfriend?" Robert asked with some interest.

"Not anymore."

Lights faded in the Scott cabin two hours later as Honey waited in the cover of darkness. Another beautiful night, Honey thought as her eyes searched the heavens splashed with starlight. A gentle breeze initiated her tug on the hood of a sweatshirt she'd slipped on after leaving the Scott family. She could smell the smoldering fire where she'd made chocolate s'mores with the kids a few hours earlier. Their laughter still raced in her head. But nothing haunted Honey more than Heather's words: "I want to be like you cuz you're nice." She smirked at that comparison. Robert appeared to be unaffected by her charms. That definitely was a first. Maybe he really did love that plain-Jane-of-a-wife; why else would he not take the hint? There existed the possibility he just didn't find her attractive. Other happily married men had strayed to her from time to time. They paid dearly for that mistake. No matter. It would soon be over. Honey took out her weapon holstered at her waist. She moved toward the cabin. Orders were orders. Playing both sides against the middle was starting to take a toll on her. Maybe this would be the last time.

\* \* \*

Mansur frowned at the Haskins twins sleeping on the floor. Their gags had been removed but their hands remained bound with flex ties. He'd fixed a simple meal of tomato soup earlier in the evening, pouring it into chipped Fiestaware cups. The boys cautiously drank the liquid, always conscience of what Mansur did next. His bulky form seem to lumber from one simple task to another as night fell around the three room structure that was more of a shack than a cabin. The windows were open to let the night breezes cool the musty smelling room. A camping stove hissed as Mansur brewed some coffee. His thick fingers looked awkward handling the utensils needed to make soup and coffee. His curly hair needed washing and his beard trimmed, but there had been too much to do the last few days to worry about personal hygiene.

Honey had managed to take care of herself, often complaining that Mansur smelled like a pig and why didn't he take more after his brother.

Mansur ignored her, knowing his appearance both irritated and repulsed her sensibilities. It had been the only way to tolerate her overbearing insults and provocative body language. Moody and unpredictable were not qualities he liked in a woman, but confidence and beauty were and Honey Lynch possessed more than her fair share of all those characteristics. He hated and admired her. Longing to strangle her very tan neck and caress it passionately kept Mansur a little off balance. It was better to keep his mouth shut and follow orders than to ponder the possibilities with the volatile assassin.

He lumbered to the window when the sound of gravel crushing beneath tires reached his ears. The headlights of Honey's truck swung in off the road and stopped at the edge of the small porch. Moving away to the stove he stopped long enough to rap on the bedroom door with his knuckles. Jamaal timidly joined him waiting for Honey to enter the cabin. He looked to Mansur for some kind of signal, a message, anything that would let him know everything was okay with the world again. Mansur just shrugged and smirked, knowing Jamaal was terrified of Honey and dreaded this encounter.

"I thought I smelled pig grease," Honey said casually, knowing the reference insulted his Muslim upbringing. She held a blood splattered ranger shirt and hoody in her hand which she tossed on a nearby wooden chair. Her purple camisole, tight and damp, left little to the imagination. Mansur diverted his eyes when Honey started to stretch but Jamaal couldn't tear his eyes away from her breasts that showed through the flimsy garment. When she'd finished, Honey let her hands fall to her hips. Their eyes locked at that moment and Jamaal dropped his head and slithered away to sit at the unsteady table. "Creep!" she fumed as the bedroom door swung open and a self-assured Essid walked into the room. His clothing, jeans and a red polo shirt made him look more like a golf pro than a Libyan terrorist. He devoured Honey with his eyes, letting them linger on his favorite parts. Frozen in his gaze, Honey waited for the light skinned Libyan to speak.

Essid spied the blood splattered clothing on the chair then extended his hand. Honey removed her weapon from its holster and handed to him. Sniffing carefully, Essid caught the scent of gunpowder. Smiling, he checked the chamber and decided four rounds had been fired. He walked to the stone fireplace and laid the gun on the mantle before turning to face the still frozen Honey. Opening his arms he continued to smile at his enchanting assassin.

"I have missed you," he said nodding to her.

Without a moment's hesitation Honey ran to Essid and jumped into his arms, circling his hips with her legs. She found his mouth, kissing him passionately. As he began to pull away, Honey sunk her teeth gently into his bottom lip and pulled as her own smile spread across her face. "Send them away," she moaned into his ear as her feet touched the floor. "Now!"

Essid motioned toward the door with his eyes making Mansur and Jamaal quickly leave. He looked at the boys curled up on the floor and knew with the drugs he'd given them they would not hear anything from the bedroom.

\* \* \*

"Still no answer," Tessa sighed as she handed Chase the phone he'd dialed for her. "They must not be getting a signal. I wonder what they're doing." Tessa verbalized her thoughts out loud. Chase continued to drive silently, keeping an eye on his rear view mirror. She turned to look at the two men in the backseat; Mr. Crawley who looked much better today, and Zoric who also kept a cautious eye on the surroundings. When Zoric shifted his eyes suddenly to meet Tessa's, he narrowed them and smiled, almost impishly like he knew a secret. Her sudden turn to face the front drew a small chuckle from the backseat. *He thinks I slept with Chase!* The truth of the matter, she actually had slept with Chase Hunter. Tessa started pulling her hair up into a ponytail as memories of the night before came flooding back.

Exiting the bathroom, Tessa had found Chase propped on the bed again grumbling about how the Cardinals had beaten his team. "Well they are the first place team in their division," Tessa smirked with a shrug. "And they've beaten the Giants the last three times at home. What'd you expect? They choked, just like always."

Chase pushed a button on the remote to turn the television off. "You're a baseball fan?"

"Only if it involves the Cardinals. My dad took me to a few games when we visited my Aunt Marie in St. Louis."

Chase boldly eyed her standing there in front of him, dressed in a pair of cut off pajamas and a long sleeve tee shirt that wasn't really meant to be slept in. She'd made sure all the important parts were covered and started to fidget under his appreciative gaze. Her lazy blonde curls damp from the shower and her face scrubbed clean, gave her a youthful appearance. The scent of soap clung to the air as the remaining steam escaped the bathroom.

"I'm tired. Can we go to bed now?" As soon as the words had spilled from her mouth, a blush bloomed on her face. "I mean..." the stutter forced her to move to the other side of the bed.

Chase reached over as if to turn out the light. "I thought you'd never ask," he grinned mischievously, knowing that Tessa Scott was so mortified that she'd probably stutter the rest of her life.

"No! I meant..."

Chase paused before darkening the room. "Relax, Tessa." Again that smile: "I know what you meant. Which side do you want?"

"Side? Side!" she said nervously. "You don't honestly think I'm going to sleep in the same bed with you?"

He jumped off the bed and went to the closet, pulling out another blanket and pillow before throwing it at Tessa. "Suit yourself. I paid for the room so I'm sleeping on the bed," he said off handedly as he flopped back onto the bed.

The lights went out. "Will you be reimbursed?"

"Probably," came a yawn response.

"Then as a taxpayer, I also paid for the room." No comment. "Fine!" Tessa pulled up the faded wingback chair and wiggled into place, propping her feet on the bed.

Two hours passed and Tessa still couldn't fall asleep. She tried to curl to the side, scrunch down, take her legs down and lean back, but nothing worked. Chase hadn't moved after conquering the bed and a soft snore started soon after. But around midnight, Chase began to toss and turn, and then seemed to be agitated, mumbling something that Tessa didn't really care to understand. Obviously a man like the captain would have nightmares from time to time. *Serves him right,* she thought without sympathy.

Quietly she tip toed into the bathroom to get a drink when she heard Chase start to speak. He called out a woman's name. Christina. Tessa stood in the doorway of the bathroom and watched Chase become more restless, rolling from side to side, yelling for Christina to be careful, Christina watch out, Christina don't do it, until his voice grew louder and more troubled.

Tessa gingerly came to the side of the bed where Chase had rolled. Even in the ribbons of light that came through the cracked curtain, Tessa could see that perspiration had formed on Chase's forehead.

When the words "My God! No!" came out in a near scream, Tessa reached over and gently touched Chase on his shoulder.

"Captain Hunter?" she whispered. "Captain Hunter," she repeated as her hand firmly shook his shoulder. "You're having a…"

In a split second Chase grabbed Tessa, throwing her on her back, next to him. Before she could scream, Chase was on top on her with one large hand wrapped around her throat, murder in his wild brown eyes. She tried to buck him off, knowing he might still be asleep. When she landed a fist on his face, Chase blinked, releasing his grip.

"Chase!" she cried. "It's me! Tessa! You're having a bad dream."

His breath was ragged and his heart beat so fast it felt like it might jump out of his chest. The fog began to clear and Chase realized Tessa lie beneath him, terrorized. Slowly he withdrew his rough hand from her milky white throat and slid it up to her face, stroking it tenderly. He could feel her body trembling and her gasping breath as he removed himself to sit on the edge of the bed.

Tessa quickly jumped from her position and ran to the door, cowering like a wounded animal. She watched the captain take deep breaths as he closed his eyes and outstretched his arms on his knees like a Buddha in meditation. In a few seconds he appeared to be at peace. He stared into the darkness toward the window where only a sliver of light pierced the room. Tessa was well aware when his focus turned to her. Although silence hung like thunderclouds before a storm, Tessa timidly moved toward the bathroom to get a cup of water and a wet washcloth.

Returning to Chase's side she held out the cup of water to him. It seemed like an eternity before he looked up at her and took the cup. Tessa was startled at the broken look in those eyes. Up until this moment in time, Captain Chase Hunter had been the epitome of strength and bravery. Now here sat a man haunted by ghosts and some crushing deed that visited his dreams, robbing him of sleep. Tessa remembered how Chase had cooled her hands when she'd saved a soldier's life then watched him kill a terrorist in front of her. Carefully she laid her hand on Chase's and brought it up so that it could be wrapped in the cool wet cloth she'd brought from the bathroom.

"This will make you feel better, Chase," she whispered nervously, not knowing how he would react to her touch. He seemed limp beneath her touch as he turned his eyes to her and began searching her face.

"I'm." He stopped and swallowed, then laid his other hand on Tessa's. "I'm so sorry. I haven't had dreams like that in a long time."

Chase's voice was so low that Tessa found herself leaning in to hear him. "You said 'Christina'. Your wife?"

Chase took in a deep breath and removed the washcloth from her hands. He ran it over his face and ears. "Sister. Died some years ago." He knew he owed her more of an explanation. "The coroner said it was a drug overdose, but I know it was murder."

Hesitantly Tessa rested her hand on his forearm. "That's awful. I can only imagine the pain you've had to endure. Chase, I'm sorry," she whispered tenderly.

Chase turned his head and found himself inches from her face. Openly he admired Tessa's delicate bone structure and smooth skin. "You remind me of her. She was head strong too." Chase smiled weakly. "She also had a strong faith, like you seem to. Talked about angels being among us, giving people second chances and charging in without a thought to her own safety." Chase watched Tessa smile and felt her fingers squeeze his arm. "I should have been there to protect her. But I wasn't. Some big brother I turned out to be."

Tessa withdrew her hand. "We always see what we should've done in 20/20 vision, Chase."

"Today when I thought you were in that car that crashed, I felt I'd let your family down, let you down. That probably triggered all this night terror." He stood and grabbed the blanket and pillow from Tessa's chair. "I'll sleep on the floor." She started to protest. "I just got back from a six month stint in Afghanistan. I slept on the ground most of the time. And," Chase stopped and looked down at the still shaken Tessa, "thanks for the rescue."

Tessa crawled up onto the bed and pulled the covers after her. "Thanks for not strangling me," she said flippantly. Tessa thought she heard a short breathy laugh, then silence.

It had taken Tessa longer than Chase expected for her to fall into a deep rim sleep. When he glanced at the digital clock Chase realized it was already after 2 a.m. He stood and quietly moved to the air conditioner unit, turning it up on high. Tessa sprawled in the middle of the bed on her side, facing away from Chase as he slipped quietly beneath the sheet. He waited patiently as the room temperature fell below sixty degrees. Goosebumps formed on his exposed arm as he lay on his side, looking at the relaxed body of Tessa Scott. The leg she had rested on top of the sheet now went under it. Pulling the blanket up onto their shoulders, he felt her move restlessly and scrunch her body up into a fetal position. Chase waited, watching, what he knew would eventually bring Tessa to him.

This scenario, in bed with a married woman, went against the grain for Chase Hunter. Something in Tessa Scott reminded him of a life long ago, when his mother made cookies from scratch, his father took time to throw him a baseball and his sister teased him about the village girls liking him. The darkness in his life began to fall when he fled China, leaving his parents behind to be slaughtered by Madame Mao's recruits. The escape across the Tibetan Plateau left him and his sister dangerously ill. Had it not been for the kindness of Buddhists monks risking their own lives to protect them, Chase and Christina would never have returned to start new lives in the states. Less than ten years later his baby sister was dead too. Nothing had prepared Chase for the deep loss he experienced when Christina died. A deep seeded anger swallowed him so savagely that Chase swore he'd take revenge on the man who extinguished the light in his life no matter how long it took.

Upon finishing his training in Delta Force, Chase had been called upon to do things he never thought his conscience would allow. But the darkness in his soul told him it was for the greater good and love of country enabling Chase to live with his sins and trespasses. He'd continued his studies until he'd received a Ph.D. in literature. There had been times when he wondered how his father would react to his choice since Chase had been expected to follow in his footsteps as a surgeon. Upon entering West Point Chase had indeed tried to follow in his father's path, majoring in Chemistry and then training as a medic for the Rangers. It had been his courage under fire, saving lives that forced him onto the radar of Benjamin Clark. With Ben's stern leadership and guidance, Chase began to channel his rage and focus on the big picture rather than his own selfish, vindictive world. Ben helped him take on a new role, doing what he loved; teaching. He also provided the adrenaline rush of lethal force in Enigma he needed to survive.

Tessa inched closer, snuggling into her pillow.

Chase conjured up the imagine of Honey Lynch, comparing her to the innocent creature now less than a foot from him. Honey had been the vessel he'd taken refuge, spilling his rage, fear and torment into whenever the opportunity presented itself. She'd taken his lust, never asking for anything in return. There had been no allusions to what the chameleon did for a living or that her loyalties always went to the highest bidder. Targets were subjected to her lack of conscience which made Honey's expertise in elimination attractive to the most perverse clientele. Her passionate love making skills came without a heart or strings attached. She and Chase worked together on occasion, celebrating when victorious, separating with suspicion when failure prevailed. You could never really be sure of Honey's intentions. Knowing that she watched the Scott family, gave Chase more than a little concern.

Tessa reached out for more covers, but Chase lifted the blanket where she couldn't reach it. His eyes narrowed as a devious smile formed across his lips. Just a little closer, he thought without shame. *I want to know what redemption feels like in the flesh, Tessa Scott.*

Chase waited another few minutes before Tessa rolled over into his chest. Holding his breath, Chase continued to wait; would she be startled awake and scream or continue to sleep, catching the warmth of his body? Cold feet and nose forced Chase to drape his arm across Tessa and draw her tightly into his body. In minutes Tessa relaxed and stretched out along his body, so warm, soft and inviting. Chase felt her breath on his face as her hair fell down around her chin. The smell of soap and shampoo clung heavily to her body. His eyes felt heavy. Sleep often evaded Chase, but not tonight. Having something good in your life made the world appear to be a better place. Tomorrow he would get on with the business of Enigma, but tonight he would pretend that his mirage would last forever.

The sun had risen slowly when Chase began feeling the stirrings of Tessa Scott. She lay in the crook of his arm, her hand flattened on his chest. Her foot rested on his leg and from time to time, Chase felt her snuggle into his shoulder. Carefully, he turned on his side, facing her, so that he could watch the way she slept. Had he ever looked so peaceful? Her movements indicated she was about to awaken and have a major stroke at finding him in her bed. When Tessa's breathing changed and her eyes began to flutter, Chase pretended to be asleep.

Suddenly Tessa's body went ridged and a gasp escaped her lips. He felt her scramble so fast to the other side of the bed that she fell out onto the floor with a loud thump. He stretched his arms out sleepily as if feeling for her only to hear her say. "Oh my gosh!" It was all he could do to keep from bursting into laughter. Through eyes narrowly opened, Chase watched Tessa trip on the blanket left on the floor and stumble into the wall. She grabbed her things and rushed into the bathroom.

## *Chapter 23*

Sandwiched between mountains covered in a thick forest Tessa still could not reach Robert on her phone. She imagined now that they were stopped and at the top of a mountain her phone service would be better. Thoughts of her children skipping pebbles across the glassy blue surface of Lake Tahoe while their musical voices echoed happily in the crisp mountain air drove Tessa to distraction. The weight of missing their sweet faces and loving arms made her heart ache.

The surreal danger she'd plunged into gave every mischievous deed of her children seem like a trip to Disneyland. In the extended moments of silence between her and the two Enigma men, Tessa dwelled on backyard cookouts with her family, Robert's passionate kisses, doing laundry and choir practice at church. Anything mundane whisked her mind away from the last couple of days of terror and the possibility of destruction to that perfect world.

Once more she attempted to call Robert with a sigh. The battery died and her screen went black. Tessa suspected the only reason she'd been given back her phone was its limited range capabilities and battery life. She'd never been very vigilant about charging it until the last possible minute. Robert plugged his in each night in the bathroom before going to bed. *You'll be sorry someday,* he'd warned. He'd even tried to get her to upgrade to a better phone, one with all the fancy apps, email and GPS. But Tessa had resisted, rationalizing that she only needed it for emergencies when on the road. Besides it would cost too much money for all those extras. Robert loved all that techy, savvy, state of the art gadgets and justifying to Tessa had been as simple as saying it helped him at work. That would be the first thing she purchased when this was all over, a phone she'd be able to use on the moon if the situation ever arose. Tessa glanced over at Chase and Zoric, heads together in conference. And with Enigma, maybe they'd already used a phone like that on the moon. Tessa slipped the dead phone into her jean pocket and sat down on a small boulder next to Mr. Crawley.

"I say we try and escape," Mr. Crawley teased as he bumped Tessa's shoulder with his.

Tessa sighed. "I've already tried that. They're like some kind of mysterious ghosts that always know where you are."

"Thus the name Enigma." Mr. Crawley patted her knee gently. "I think we're in good hands. They seem to value what we have to say."

Tessa grimaced. "Sweet trick, if you ask me. Those two," she nodded toward Zoric and Chase, "are…" Tessa stopped, not wanting to verbalize her anger, but even more, not wanting to hint at the respect and admiration she felt toward them, especially Captain Chase Hunter.

Pulling down the pair of sunglasses she'd pushed on top of her head, Tessa covered her eyes to enable herself to stare secretly at the larger than life captain. Even in jeans and a tan camouflaged tee shirt, the captain's muscled strength was evident. The edge of a tattoo at the bottom of his short sleeve hinted at something Asian. Tessa hadn't noticed it at the motel because she'd worked so hard not to look too closely at his body, afraid Chase would get the wrong idea at her appreciative glances. Dark black hair, straight until the very ends, where it curled slightly had been cut recently, but not short enough Tessa guessed by the way he kept running a hand through it and frowning. Perspiration gleamed around his neckline where he occasionally took his shirt and wiped it clean. Besides the scar over his eye she noticed a longer one just below the tattoo; another indication he wasn't exactly a choir boy. Chase's skin and the color of his eyes suggested there may be Native American or Polynesian heritage in his blood. Although Captain Chase Hunter would never be considered handsome by Hollywood standards, his rugged looks, and tall self-assured body, conjured up images of Tessa's favorite characters from the Victoria Holt books she read in high school. She remembered how breathless she'd felt when reading the novels of the rich dark lord with questionable motives and realized Chase Hunter affected her much the same way. That dangerous glare he so easily dropped on her sent shivers up her spine. Tessa both feared and admired that trait. The imperturbable leader in times of desperation mixed with the impeccable manners of a gentleman sent Tessa's senses crashing into uncharted waters. *I'm a happily married woman, for crying out loud,* she scolded herself. *I'm acting like a silly school girl with her first crush!*

Then there was Chase's partner, Nicholas Zoric, the vampire, Tessa had wrongly judged. His bloodshot eyes and long oily hair of an undetermined shade of brown or black had given Tessa pause when they'd first met. Zoric had been aggressive in his improper advances toward Tessa, curtailed only by Chase's looks of reprimand. Tessa realized his brutal treatment of her in the Enigma cell on that first day was second nature. The Serbian probably lacked a conscience when it came to those who terrorized others. But his kindness to Jericho Crawley and his soft voice when addressing her became a disarming charm. Zoric had shown valor in Knoxville, quick on his feet and responsive to what needed to be done, almost before anyone else knew what to do. And through it all, Zoric remained light hearted, even flirting with her and professing his intentions of a relationship between them. Strangely it had created a calming effect on Tessa, concentrating on Zoric's advances rather than the dire situation surrounding them.

The cloud of cigarette smoke that swirled around his head added to the distasteful impression Tessa had formed about the five foot ten inch man who looked to be in his late forties. Although thin, Zoric was wiry and quick on his feet. She half expected him to hiss, revealing blood drenched fangs when he smiled, but exposed a missing tooth near the corner of his mouth instead. Zoric's fingertips were yellow with tobacco stains, and an unsuccessful attempt at whitening his teeth had given them a strange shade of pale gray. A long narrow nose that looked too big for his bony face made his close set eyes of light brown appear sinister and condescending when he leveled a gaze at you. The lazy, unconcerned stance Zoric used impressed the onlooker of no particular threat, but Tessa knew differently, having observed Zoric for several days now. He killed when necessary and remorse never disquieted his actions.

Zoric glanced over at Tessa hiding behind the sunglasses. He'd felt her eyes upon them, a gift from his gypsy mother, which came in handy working with shadowy characters and less than trustworthy governments. "Think she suspects?" he said turning back to the map laid before them on the hood. When Chase wiped his sleeve across his forehead and frowned without a word, Zoric continued, "If you tell her about Honey…"

"I don't like any of this," Chase said folding the map. "When I get my hands on Honey Lynch I'm going to kill her in the slowest possible way," he growled. "We should've gotten Robert and the kids out two days ago."

Zoric lit a cigarette and puffed several times. "Too late now," he said despondently. "What's done is done."

\* \* \*

The convoy of three trucks carrying heavy shipping containers rolled through Sacramento without incident, even in rush hour traffic. The decision to transfer the containers of Molybdenum-99 by trucks instead of train had been a last minute adjustment. There were too many miles of empty stretches of land that a train traveled. Intel revealed an attack was imminent, hijacking the isotope material for purposes not yet known. Enigma and Homeland Security realized the possibility of capturing the Molybdenum-99 would extinguish more than a third of the medical isotopes needed worldwide. The risk of using the material to further a nuclear weapon seemed minimal now that Enigma knew the revenge Essid sought originated from his own twisted sense of justice. With control over materials that potentially could save thousands of people every day, Essid had created another type of terrorist bomb. Canada, Belgium, France, the Netherlands and South Africa had been put on alert for terrorist activity which could potential destroy medical isotopes in production and especially shipping.

France, slow to respond given their on again, off again relationship with the United States, grudgingly increased security at their plant. Their relationship with Libya had flourished in recent years and they saw no need to be concerned about an attempt on their isotope transfers. Unfortunately, the French were also in bed with the Russians; giving aid, oil refineries and weapons for their own self-promotion. Enigma knew it would only be a matter of time before Essid's people took advantage of their complacent snub toward the United States. Belgium and the Netherlands quickly took steps to halt transfers of medical isotopes until assurances could be given that supplies would successfully reach market. South Africa, like Canada, had been forced to shut down their aging reactors due to heavy water leaks. Canada had been out of commission for more than a year. Both countries quickly saw the need to establish a tighter security presence.

The trucks hauling the life-saving Molybdenum-99 lumbered up an unnamed mountain outside of Auburn toward Apple Valley where Captain Hunter planned to rendezvous with the rest of his team doing escort duty. No extra protection followed. Special containers had been loaded onto the train resembling the Molybdenum ones to make it appear "business as usual". Unwanted attention to flashing lights and armed men were deemed unnecessary since Enigma people traveled in the truck.

The sun climbed higher in the sky as afternoon heat bore down on the dusty service road that led into Global Navigation. Breezes did little to cool the perspiration clinging to the captain and the two reluctant civilians who sat in a shady patch just beyond the Hummer. With a computer, Enigma phone and aerial surveillance equipment, Chase and Zoric were able to monitor the progress of the trucks. Watching their progress grew mind-numbing for the two men even though they alternated in twenty minute shifts. The trucks were only forty five minutes away, coming into a heavily forested area. This would be a narrow, winding stretch of highway that forced the graceless semis to navigate carefully.

Tessa stood and stretched as she crossed to Zoric who focused on the computer. Chase had disappeared into the forest when relieved by Zoric. Looking at the time on the computer, Tessa realized he'd been gone far longer than a twenty minute shift.

"Need me to take over? Tell me what I should be watching for and you can get over there in the shade. I felt a breeze earlier." Her voice sounded like a whisper in the vastness of the forest. Zoric turned his haunted eyes to her for only a second and smiled before looking back at the screen. "Don't trust me?" she quizzed.

Zoric continued to smile at the screen. "This is not your job, Tessa Scott. But I would like very much for you to wait here with me to break the, how you say it? Monotonous?" He felt her shuffle nervously at the suggestion. "It is you who does not trust. Why are you afraid of me? Is it because of my looks?" His eyes never left the screen until he felt a timid hand on his forearm.

"I'm sorry. You seem to like capitalizing on your dark aura," Tessa withdrew her hand and stepped up closer to get a look at the computer. "You did come on a little strong our first few encounters."

Zoric lit a cigarette and exhaled the first puff of smoke as he turned squinted eyes to observe the reluctant housewife of Grass Valley. "Control by intimidation."

"That seems to be workin' for you, Zoric." Her light chuckle seemed to float. "And how did you come to work for Enigma? You're an artist not a gun toting, black ops kind of guy."

Zoric's smile faded suddenly. "That's where you're wrong, Tessa Scott. I am the devil incarnate. I have done many terrible things in the last twenty years."

"Then it's a good thing God forgives us I guess," she said off handedly. Zoric frowned.

"God? Where was God when my wife and daughters were blown to pieces at the hands of the Bosnians?"

"Dear Lord! Zoric, how horrible!" Again she touched his arm. "I'm so sorry. I can't imagine losing all that I hold dear." Suddenly Zoric grabbed her hand in a vice-like grip. Tessa instinctively tried to pull away without success. She looked up into his bloodshot eyes to see a warning.

"Anyone who plays with the devil gets burned, Tessa Scott. You'd best remember that," he said, seeing flames of fear leap to her beautiful blue eyes. He smiled crookedly and tried to pat some comfort into her shoulder with his other hand. "Chase and I will protect you." Cocking his head slightly Zoric searched her face with unabashed admiration. "When this is over I think we should sit and talk over coffee. What you say, Tessa Scott?" He watched the anxiousness ebb away from Tessa's posture. "This way I make Chase Hunter crazy. Hmm?"

Tessa failed to understand why the captain would disapprove of a causal cup of coffee with a friend you'd been to hell and back with, but the thought of getting even with the mighty Captain Chase Hunter was just too tempting. "Then count me in!" They shared a low laugh as Chase emerged from the woodland trail.

Tessa strolled back to the shade where Mr. Crawley napped peacefully. Avoiding eye contact with the captain had taken great restraint. Every time her mind wandered to him the scene of being wrapped in those muscled arms against his naked chest flashed before her eyes. A tremble of embarrassment and something else, she wasn't sure what, rippled across her body like a mild earthquake. The feeling of contempt mixed with admiration kept Tessa off balance. Would this nightmare never end?

"What was that all about," Chase asked as he came alongside Zoric. "Looks like you two are getting chummy."

"We made a date." Zoric grinned sheepishly down at the computer screen. Chase's deep silence drew Zoric's sideways glance. "I think she likes me. You, not so much."

"Married," Chase said bluntly.

"Don't care," Zoric chuckled. "The woman is so trusting and gullible I could not resist."

A deep, disgusted sigh escaped Chase. "You're going to hell. You know that, right?"

"Yes." Zoric's laugh was contagious as he slapped his friend on the back.

"You also know I'm not going to let you do that, right?" Chase landed a friendly fist on Zoric's arm.

"It's just coffee, my friend. Coffee. Nothing more."

"When we're done here we disappear from her life."

Zoric then turned his evil eyes on Chase like loaded pistols. "And let her pick up the pieces alone? No. We both have been there and I will not abandon this woman. She does not deserve any of this. Her family…" Zoric let the words drop as a beep came from the computer.

"What the hell is that?" Chase said looking closer at the screen?

"Fire!" screamed Tessa as she ran out of the woods and stood aghast at the trailhead. "Look! On the ridge!"

All eyes went to the ridge above them where a curtain of smoke bellowed over the tongues of flame marching steadily toward them. With each wisp of wind the fire advanced to spots where moments before had been a refuge from the afternoon heat.

\* \* \*

Carter tapped his ear piece. "You get that Sam? Vernon?" Just when he thought things couldn't get worse, they crashed and burned. Literally. He motioned for the driver to stop as he pulled out a map from his vest pocket with one hand while running the other over his closely cropped blond hair. It had been sheared so close that Carter ran his hand through again to assure himself there really was more than just skin. His pale eyes narrowed as his focus out the windshield searched for signs of smoke. Unfolding the map matter-of-factly did not cause the driver to question his guard. He remained silent as Carter ran an index finger along numbered red and blue lines that indicated roads, trails and topography.

The passenger door swung open and Sam looked up at her partner who swung his feet out onto the step, then hopped down in front of her, so close he could feel her breath. The smell of spearmint reached his nostrils as he watched her spit her gum out at his feet. She didn't step back in retreat, rather put her hands on her hips and snarled at the cocky ex-astronaut. "You did that on purpose," she said suddenly shoving Carter back with her fist that had more force than most men possessed.

"I love it when you get physical, Sam." Carter chuckled when Vernon joined them wearing a sour look. His eyes fell on Sam then the astronaut. "There's my favorite techy," Carter said offhandedly as he opened the crinkled map up again. He noted the redness in Vernon's face, the rushed breathing, and the *if looks could kill* expression he leveled at him before continuing. *Poor, jealous sap,* Carter grinned. Vernon just didn't realize Sam was way out of his league. If a handsome, dare devil astronaut couldn't win her over then Vernon just didn't have a snowball's chance in hell. Besides, Sam only had eyes for their captain, not that Chase paid much attention to Sam's obvious availability tactics. Sometimes he seriously worried about that guy. A babe like Sam loving all over you could make a man change his tom cattin' ways. Then he smothered a grin; not even Sam could do that, Carter thought logically. He loved women too much to restrict himself in matters of the heart.

"We're here," he pointed to the map, holding it awkwardly with one hand until Sam lifted one side. "Chase says the fire is moving fast. We'll never make it through there in time. Even if we could, Chase thinks it's too big of a risk. So if we go on this old mining road here," Carter pointed to another spot on the map, "it comes in less than a mile from the Global Navigation facility. We'll rendezvous with Chase and his people then head north here." After tapping the spot, Carter folded the map and stuffed it back into his vest pocket. "This will all be over within less than an hour if we can get through the pass."

Vernon searched his hand held electronic device quickly and nodded. "Roads are in good shape. Global had them widened and resurfaced with a chip and seal mix just a month ago in case of emergencies."

"How far sighted of them," Sam quipped. She sniffed the air. "Smoke. How soon will Chase be here?" Sam glanced at her Rolex and then to the darkening skies. "I don't like this."

Vernon continued to look at his hand held computer. "The aerial link shows that fire has jumped the ridge. I think the captain is trapped, Carter," Vernon said with all the calm he could muster. "If they're not on their way..." He left the sentence unfinished.

Carter looked up the road as if Chase Hunter and Zoric would appear in that monstrous black Hummer. He never understood why someone like Chase didn't get a fast and furious sports car like his. Chicks dug that kind of crap, not that Chase really cared what his lady friends preferred. Those brainy types he attracted seemed contented to just breathe the same air as Dr. Chase Hunter. All those old books, Jazz music and candle light dinners in Old Town just prolonged the inevitable; a roll in the hay. Carter found a couple of beers; a jukebox and flattery got a guy from point A to point B in record time. Of course he stayed away from all those brainy, high brows. He'd tried that at Houston and the Kennedy Space Center. NASA's combined IQ if turned into rocket fuel could have easily gotten man to Mars and back in record time. The women, although more enjoyable to work with and easier to respect, tended to over analyze a weekend at Coco Beach. That Russian astronaut certainly didn't understand the concept of sharing and nearly killed him on the International Space Station. All hell broke loose when the American female astronaut sent a revealing photograph of herself with the words *bring your rocket to my space*. Unfortunately Natasha had been floating by at the time he opened the picture. That had been the beginning of the end of his career at NASA.

Carter and Chase met only a few years after that episode during a Buck Austin campaign event for president. A gunman managed to out maneuver the Secret Service. Chase, having been invited by Benjamin Clark to the event, hoped meeting the future president of the United States would help the Delta Force captain understand the idea of Enigma. Just after

Buck Austin finished his speech to a roaring crowd of enthusiastic voters, he moved from the stage to shake hands with his fans on the ground. Chase stood in the first row with Ben noticing that the ex-astronaut, Carter Johnson, also enjoyed the admiration of the crowd. From the corner of his eye he saw a short, chubby man with glasses pull out something dark from under his shirt. As the gun came up, Chase leaped on the future president, taking the bullet through his arm. Without thought to his own safety, Carter lunged at the shooter, who began screaming some socialistic mumbo gumbo. Knocking his stocky body to the ground, Carter began pounding the shooter's face with doubled fists. Secret Service, embarrassed by their lapse in security, tackled all three men, knocking Carter unconscious, and giving Chase a swift kick to the side and a goose egg size knot on the back of his head. Both protectors ended up in the same hospital room and became fast friends in spite of their personality differences. Chase admired the astronaut's carefree attitude and reckless disregard for danger. He would have made a good Special Forces man. Carter respected the former Delta Force captain for no other reason except he deserved it. He was a man's man. No nonsense. Honest. Fearless.

"Look!" Vernon pointed toward the road. "It's Zoric. He looks hurt!"

The three rushed toward their comrade who awkwardly carried someone else over his shoulder. Even though the old man had not been over weight, the effect of smoke in his lungs, a downhill trek and trying to out run a forest fire, had winded Zoric. Blood trickled down the side of his face from a wound on the side of his forehead. When Carter gently removed the old man from his care, Zoric felt his knees buckle only to be pulled back up by the capable hands of Sam and Vernon.

"Where the hell are Chase and Tessa?" Carter yelled, hearing the fire marching toward them.

"We were cut off! He's still up there."

Sam stiffened. "Dear Lord in Heaven!"

"We were ambushed. I tried to push Crawley inside the Hummer to escape but they shot out the tires so we took cover in the rocks. They managed to separate us long enough for the fire to make it impossible for us to regroup. Last I saw Chase they were headed deeper into the forest. I forced the old man to his feet when the shooting stopped, figuring whoever ambushed us needed to get in front of the fire." Zoric nodded toward

Jericho Crawley. "He just couldn't make it with the wheezing and coughing." He wiped the blood from the bullet graze on the edge of his black tee shirt, and then examined it as if surprised to see the evidence of the near miss.

Carter carried the old man like a baby until they reached the trucks where he sat him down on wobbly legs. He felt Jericho Crawley pat his arm as he leaned against the truck. "Thank you."

"We're leaving now!" Carter motioned for the rest to return to the truck they were to be guarding.

"What about Chase?" Sam demanded. "We can't just leave him up there."

"If we don't get this Moly 99 to Global a lot of people are going to die. Now, Sam! Chase will find a way. He always does!" Opening the door of his truck, he stepped up to find his driver gone. "What the hell?" Carter looked down at his crew and was stunned to see all three drivers holding them at gunpoint.

"Guess you didn't count on this, did ya, Mr. Hotshot Fly Boy." The other drivers grinned smugly as the one in charge ran his gun up and down Sam's back suggestively.

Carter sighed. "That's really not a good idea, buddy."

## Chapter 24

Gunfire exploded around Chase's team as the forest fire began its steady death march toward them. Seconds earlier Jericho Crawley meandered to the Hummer, stretching his legs and arms from sitting too long in the shade. Removing a bottle of water from the Styrofoam cooler, he turned a watchful eye towards him. His concern at smelling smoke alerted Tessa first. She rubbed the old man's back gently and reassured him that two years ago forest fires could be smelled sixty miles away. She whispered that she'd just take a quick look while everyone put supplies back in the Hummer so preparations could be finalized to meet Carter and the convoy of trucks.

Just as she screamed a warning, gunfire erupted causing everyone to scramble for cover. Tessa crouched down and covered her head while desperately looking for someplace to hide. Later she would realize a bullet pinged off a tree above her head making her scream again. She felt like being trapped in a carnival shooting gallery where you would take a shot and something would ping then send the duck in the opposite direction. The image of her family floating gently in a rented canoe on Lake Tahoe swam up into her consciousness just as something heavy slammed her to the ground. Large hands pushed her head down as arms covered her back and neck. Tessa could still hear bullets hitting boulders and the gravel as their sting slammed against her arms and legs. Barely able to catch her breath, Tessa heard Zoric call out to them, with a deafening response from Chase that made no sense; something about go without them. In that instant of confusion Tessa felt Chase's warm breath on her ear, his left hand in her tangled hair, and the pungent stench of the world burning all around them. Alarmingly the sound of ricocheting bullets had been replaced with the crackle of fire.

"Get up! We're leaving!" Chase seemed to defy gravity as he sprang to his feet jerking Tessa up roughly by the back of her shirt. Flames of fire licked up the sides of trees and danced recklessly at the tops of evergreens only to bend as if to hand their destruction to other life forms around them. He nudged her firmly toward the fire. "We're cut off, Tess! Down the trail is our only choice!"

How a body could freeze amongst the inferno confused Chase momentarily as he watched Tessa look in awe at the burning Hummer. She appeared unaware of the death trap creeping toward them for its final assault. Snatching her hand, Chase felt pieces of twigs and gravel embedded in her palm with the wet trickle of blood mingling with his own. Just as Tessa turned her wide eyes of terror up at him, Chase yanked on her arm to get her moving after him. "Move!"

The smoke swirled around them like some twisted death dance. Flecks of fire rained down so quickly that their progress became a zigzag of jerky movements to avoid being burned by the tentacles of flashing flame and dead tree limbs. Tessa's eyes watered so heavily that the lightly applied mascara began leaving black trails of fear down her cheeks. Her lungs burned as she began coughing and staggering after the captain. He pulled her after him at a dead run. She had not expected the intense sound of burning debris, dried underbrush and tree bark, to be so deafening. Tessa found it confusing and disorienting as she clung with both hands to Chase Hunter's outstretched arm. If she slowed, he jerked. If she stumbled, he paused a split second to let her fall into him only to rush forward again, dragging her out of breath body with him. Besides stomping impatiently ahead, Chase failed to exhibit any fear or concern as to where he led them.

Just when Tessa thought she couldn't take another step he stopped shortly and pulled her up beside him. "We can't go any further, Tessa," he yelled above the fire.

Tessa looked around her, alarmed that they'd been boxed in by the raging fire. The heat seemed to scorch their skin as it began to enclose them in a ring of hell. "Dear Lord!" she cried as Chase pulled her forward.

It was then she realized they teetered on the edge of a cliff. Below roared a river created by a waterfall still full of late spring rains from mid-May. The opposite side of the ravine smoldered with burnt underbrush and pine needles. Fire had already devoured its beauty and had moved on to the ripe hillside where they stood.

"What do we do?" Tessa yelled above the fire. She hadn't realized her hands clutched Chase's forearms in some desperate plea for rescue.

"Jump!"

Tessa pulled away, choking on her fear of heights. Shaking her head obstinately, Tessa pointed at the water below. "I can't! I won't! There's gotta be another way!"

Chase reached out and grabbed her roughly by the arm and jerked her forward. "You've got two choices. Jump or I'll have my way with you here and now like I should've done in the middle of the night. I've got nothing to lose," he grinned sardonically as he narrowed his eyes. "I'll burn now or burn in hell. Makes no difference to me."

Horrified at the dilemma, Tessa opened her mouth to protest when Chase jerked her into his arms and squeezed so hard, she felt faint. Struggling wasn't an option as he stepped off the cliff and began to drop into the churning waters below. Something like a scream escaped from deep inside her. She felt Chase release her seconds before water swallowed her, knocking the breath from her seared lungs. Feeling the flow of liquid into her throat caused Tessa to fight at the invisible hand of death until a cloud of eternal darkness began its final hold on her soul.

Chase fought his way to the top of the turbulent pool and looked around for Tessa. Diving back under the water, he saw her stop fighting and grow limp with surrender. Grabbing her around the waist he swam upwards and then to shore where he dragged her limp body out and began CPR. When she began to spit and cough up water he rolled her over not caring that he had straddled her body with his legs. Gently, Chase pushed the matted blond curls away from her face along with the soot and smeared mascara. Realization slowly swam up into her eyes that Captain Chase Hunter had only been scaring her into a decision she couldn't make alone.

Tessa coughed one more time and wiped the spit and water from her mouth as she smiled weakly up at her protector. "I was going to choose having your way with me!"

Chase laughed. "Next time I feel like bursting into flame I'll remember that," he said standing up and pulling Tessa up into his arms where he steadied her wobbly legs.

She weakly pushed at his chest, not liking the way he made her feel so safe and something else she couldn't identify. "Lost your chance, big guy!" Tessa staggered a bit as she pushed her hair back and tied it up into a knot. "But," she smiled in spite of herself, "thanks. I'll try and save you some day."

Chase started down the burnt trail. "We've got to get to Global. Can you do it?"

Tessa squared her shoulders. "Do I have a choice?" she said trying awkwardly to keep up with Chase's already long strides. For every one step he took Tessa scrambled to take two, sometimes three. "Freakin' robot!" she muttered under her breath. When Chase turned and frowned back at her as if he also possessed some supersonic hearing capability, Tessa decided to keep her thoughts to herself.

She kept a vigilant eye on the ridge above them knowing that the sweep of fire could very well cut off their escape further up the trail. The pungent smell of smoke clung to her body as she tried to spit the taste of ashes from her mouth. Sweat mingled with the remaining river water evaporating from her torn blouse and jeans. The trail meandered upward for what seemed an eternity. Tessa felt like they'd been walking far longer than was true. The squish of wet tennis shoes managed to make her steps awkward and unsure as she followed after the captain like a lost puppy.

Resentment returned to her consciousness, knowing that once again, she depended on a man to save the day. All her life men stepped in to protect their little Tessa; her father, brothers, her husband and now the mighty Captain Chase Hunter. A part of her just wanted to be given a semiautomatic and turned loose. Maybe she could be the next Tomb Raider or female Jason Bourne. Scenarios played rapidly in her head when something large and hard loomed in front of her. "Oh!" Tessa found herself stumbling backwards until her feet flew out from under her.

"What are you doing?" Chase asked with his arms folded across his chest. He had turned back to see Tessa falling behind, staring into oblivion, barely putting one foot in front of the other. He waited patiently, not an easy task for him, so she could catch up only to have her plow into him with a glazed look in her eyes. Hearing a grunt from her parched lips, he watched her sprawl backwards onto her bottom.

Tessa quickly masked her embarrassment by a cynical retort. "Trying to figure a way to get us out of this mess.

She began a clumsy attempt at trying to stand only to slip and land on her butt harder than the first time. The uncontrolled laugh of the captain and his large frame moving to assist clumsy attempt at standing halted before reaching out to touch her.

Chase understood the hands off gesture and folded his arms across his chest again, forcing patience upon himself. "And how will you save the day, Mrs. Tessa Scott, because up until now you've been a great deal of trouble."

Tessa took a deep breath as she shoved at his chest. "Trouble! Trouble!" Throwing her hands up in the air, she elbowed her way past him and headed up the trail. "You don't know what trouble is, buster! When we get done here my husband, the lawyer, thank you very much, is going to fry your high and mighty attitude in court!" Chase had easily caught up and remained quiet. "I've been attached to a bomb..."

"It wasn't a bomb," he added.

Tessa waved him off. "I thought it was a bomb! Shut up!"

"Sorry. Continue."

"Kidnapped! Dragged half way across the country and back, delivered a baby, shot at, forced the indignity of sharing a motel room with you..."

"Now that hurt," Chase said drily as he laid a hand over his heart.

"A cheap motel room at that!" she snorted. "I've been hog tied, left for dead..."

"With all due respect, if you had only listened..."

Tessa held up a hand to silence the captain, "nearly burned alive, and pushed off a cliff..."

"I gave you a choice," he said with an amused shrug.

"Nearly drowned and now forced on a death march through an eerie scorched land that leads to nowhere! I'm tired, I stink..."

"I noticed," he smiled.

Tessa halted suddenly as she reached down and picked up several rocks. Hurling them at the captain gave her much pleasure when one hit him in the leg. Only a minute flinch of Chase's eye indicated it smarted. His wide, disarming grin forced Tessa to reach for another rock only to be overpowered by Chase's unexpected grip on her wrist. He squeezed the wrist so tightly that the rock dropped aimlessly to the ground.

"Feel better?" he said in a condescending voice.

"Don't patronize me, you over grown Neanderthal. I want to go home. I want to see my family."

A tidal wave of regret washed over Chase, knowing that he kept the truth of Robert and the kids hidden from her. He couldn't risk Tessa being paralyzed with the stark reality of getting involved with all things connected to national security. In the end the price of her sacrifice would be greater than the gratitude of the thousands she helped save. Tempted fate never revealed a happy ending and Tessa plummeted toward a revelation she'd have to live with the rest of her life. *If only you'd gone to Tahoe with Robert,* he thought regretfully. *I can't save you from what's ahead.*

Jerking her hand free, Tessa rubbed the wrist furiously to start the circulation of blood again. That strange contemptible look of danger Chase so often exhibited dropped on her. In the last week she'd watched him pummel a man on her kitchen floor, unload his weapon into a dead man, or so he claimed, shoot with deadly aim in a fire fight at one of the most secure laboratories in the country, and save her life on several occasions. He showed no fear. Paranoia crept into the back of her mind. When this all came to a conclusion, what then? Realizing that she knew too much about all their secret shenanigans at Enigma, buried inside a California university, would she become a victim? The phrase 'silence is golden' began to take on new meaning as Chase nodded up the path, expecting her to follow blindly.

"What's going on, Chase? Who shot at us? Where's Zoric and Mr. Crawley? Shouldn't we be seeing the cavalry swoop in by now?" Already she found herself panting. "Join a gym" kept popping up on her to do list.

Chase continued steadily up a steep part of the trail, reaching back occasionally to pull Tessa forward so he didn't have to wait for her to navigate the pit falls of the eroded trail created by spring rains. "Donno." His tone, matter-of-fact, failed to end Tessa's stream of endless questions. *How much further? Can we stop a minute? How do you know Honey Lynch? Does Carter still work for NASA? How did you come to work for Enigma? How did Enigma originate? How do you know Essid?* Blah. Blah. Blah. Chase stopped listening until he realized Tessa no longer trailed behind him. He turned to see her propped against a boulder, hands on her knees, trying to suck in more oxygen.

Patiently he waited for her to lean back against the boulder. Even now, disheveled, ripped clothes, smudged face and stinking of river water and burned wood, Tessa looked like an angel to him. That pain tapped at his chest again just as he diverted his eyes to survey the surroundings. Out of shape and exhausted, Tessa remained a trooper when it came to pressing on in the face of adversity. He saw resolve in her eyes but her body screamed 'enough'.

"Let's rest," he said standing so still all sounds became magnified.

"Are you…" she began hesitantly.

Chase turned his dark brown eyes like lasers toward, Tessa causing her to swallow with a gulp. "More questions. I would've thought you'd run out by now!" he snapped.

"It's not like you've answered any of them," she said softly, hoping to disarm him like she did Robert. The frown and angry step toward her confirmed once more that this man was nothing like her Robert.

"One question. Then no more!"

"Are you going to kill me when this is all over," she said so casually that Chase hesitated to answer.

The realization that this woman thought him a cold hearted monster caused that tap of pain in his chest again. Got to see the doctor, he thought with disgust. He'd left his weapon at the Hummer and it most likely looked like a piece of melted plastic by now. He'd just removed his gun from the holster moments before to make sure it was loaded and ready. Laying it on the front seat he'd turned to go to the back of the Hummer for extra magazines. When bullets began flying Chase's first instinct was to protect Tessa. By the time the bullets stopped, retrieving the weapon was out of the question.

His hand slid to his belt, where the soft, damp sheath holding his knife, easily pulled free with the tug of his fingers. Holding it up in front of him, Chase walked quickly to Tessa. The sound of shock escaped her mouth as she started to edge off the boulder and down the path only to feel Chase's hard grip on her elbow that jerked her to a stop. The raw fear looming in her eyes softened his anger enough to openly search her face with confusion. Why Tessa Scott? Why me? The thought of losing her in this fight because of his obstinate attitude and ego sobered him. The tremble in her arm as he pulled against the resistance Tessa exhibited, encouraged him that just maybe she'd be able to take care of herself if he were captured or killed. Squeezing her wrist so hard that the palm of her hand popped open, Chase laid the knife gently within her hold.

Quickly removing the sheath from his belt, Chase unzipped her pants only to feel her squirm away. "Look if I wanted you, which I don't, I could've easily taken care of that last night. Now stand still. I'm trying to hide this inside your pants in case we're taken. They'll tear me apart looking for weapons, but not you." Tessa nodded in surrender as Chase unbuttoned the last barrier before slipping his hands inside her jeans.

The steady movement of his hands caused Tessa to divert her eyes up through the trees at first but ultimately curiosity forced her to watch his face. The skillful way Chase looped the sheath to lie next to her skin sent shivers up her spine. A fleeting thought of regret at not taking advantage of the two for one sale at Victoria Secrets managed to cloud her confidence when she remembered the panties Chase slid his hand against were the St. Patrick's Day special from Wal-Mart. Nothing said sexy like a bunch of smiling leprechauns holding shamrocks. *Dear God, let me live until I can go to the next lingerie sale!*

"There!" Chase carefully, almost slowly, zipped up Tessa's jeans and buttoned them before she had time to protest. "In the event we're captured, hopefully the luck of the Irish will be with you," he grinned. Embarrassment edged up into her face giving Tessa a healthy rosy color. "Robert's a lucky man," he said in his best Irish brogue.

Tessa smoothed her ragged blouse over the edge of her waist. "Very funny. One more Irish comment…" Tessa pushed at Chase's close proximity to no avail. His warm laugh caught her so off guard that she couldn't complete the empty threat.

"You seem to forget pretty quickly that I'm the good guy," Chase said realizing his nearness unnerved her. "We're in this together and no, I'm not going to kill you when this is all over. However you'll not be able to access anything that has gone on with this mission."

"So, are you going to put on dark glasses and flash me with some Pentagon pen that erases my memory?" Tessa said flippantly.

"Something like that," he said as he turned away.

"What? Seriously? You can do that?"

His warm laughter spilled unexpectedly out again. "Someone watches too many movies." He started back up the trail. "Come on. We're not that far now." He suddenly stopped and turned to face her as she tried to catch up. "Tessa, you've got to trust me from here on out. I need one hundred percent from you no matter what I say or do."

"I don't understand."

"I know. If all hell breaks loose, I need to know I can count on you. Things are not always what they seem. You've got to believe in me. No more doubting, escape attempts, complaining or trying to out maneuver me. Got it?"

Tessa nodded as she licked her dry lips nervously. "I owe you that. I'm," Tessa pulled back her shoulders, "I'm sorry I accused you of…"

"Forget it. We get through this and I'll get you some big girl panties," he laughed as he heard Tessa's exasperated snort.

The day faded quickly in the mountains as did the thought of escape in Tessa's mind. This man really meant her no harm. It just was unnerving being so close to a real American hero. Captain Chase Hunter would remain unknown to millions for his efforts. His team carried on the work without them, hopefully safe at Global, waiting for help to arrive without incident so the mission could be put to rest once and for all. Essid would be captured and dealt a blow of justice. Her family, vacationing at Tahoe, would never know how close to disaster the country had come and the roll she played in saving it. A pride began swelling inside her. Finally her life made a difference. Nothing would ever be the same for her.

## Chapter 25

Benjamin Clark could smell the smoke of the burning fires around Auburn and the nearby foothills even before he saw the flames devouring hundred year old trees. From the helicopter he could see firefighters scrambling to cut its march short as smaller fires were lit and debris pulled away from the hungry monster that Essid created to insure no outside interference compromised his recovery of the isotopes. The Scope and Discovery department notified Ben of the fire just as Technical Support confirmed authorities suspected an arsonist. Thoughts of both teams being separated or pinned by Essid's death trap only mildly concerned him. Both Chase and Carter thrived on the impossible. When both teams failed to call in, Ben knew the plan had been jeopardized.

Aerial photos revealed empty roads except for one burning Hummer. Ben back tracked the information on the trucking company. Although the company checked out, the drivers all had one thing in common: money problems. One sold his soul to the gambling gods of Vegas; another one faced a barracuda of a divorce lawyer. Only one week remained before the bank foreclosed on his house. The third had a sick kid waiting for a kidney transplant with no insurance. Three desperate men with the need for quick money tended to resemble a flask of nitroglycerin. How many others on Essid's payroll bowed down to the god of money? In the current economy the potential prospects for a little extra work began to mount. It no longer involved Essid and a few of his radical lackeys. Americans bent on vengeance against government intervention in their lives, paramilitary groups, and religious nuts of all denominations could be a significant pool of support for Essid's operation.

His people needed a miracle to salvage this mission. That's when he'd called the Secretary of Homeland Security. Looking down now at the destruction, he observed another helicopter, an Erickson 64S Aircrane, assisting with loads of water releasing from its on board tanks, to reign down on the hungry flames below. Ben turned his eyes forward to focus on what lay ahead. Although the ultimate goal was to secure the isotopes, he knew the only thing he really cared about was getting his Enigma people out alive.

\* \* \*

Carter evaluated their situation as the labored squeal of brakes on the eighteen wheeler jerked to a halt. The three truckers didn't have the good sense to tie them up before ordering them into the back of the first truck. His driver, who appeared to be in possession of the worst attitude and foulest mouth, made the mistake of touching Sam seductively with his gun. He smiled remembering how in a blink she'd not only removed his weapon but jammed it in his open mouth as he hit the ground with a kick upside his head. Sam always amazed him with her incredible beauty and brilliant mind. But when she exploded into action he loved to just stand back, dreaming of what it must feel like to be tangled up with all that energy and power wrapped around him.

Carter had chuckled watching the trucker crab crawl backwards away from Sam as she removed the gun from his mouth. The short trucker stepped forward and pointed his weapon at Sam's head. "Put it down." The nervousness in his voice caused Sam to slowly turn her eyes on him. He stumbled back waving his weapon under her fierce gaze. "I'll shoot them right here and now. Pretty boy will be the first."

Carter looked over at Zoric. "Did he call me pretty boy?"

Zoric crossed his arms and rubbed the blood trailing into his eye with his shoulder. "I think he did. You are pretty, Carter."

"Thanks, Zoric," he said happily. "Sorry, trucker buddy. I'm not available. I just don't roll like that. Do you even know who I am?" The truckers' eyes darted to each other in bewilderment. Carter threw up his hands in exasperation. "Carter Johnson? Astronaut? Surely that rings a bell." Carter looked over at Zoric with a smile.

"NASA keep that locator chip in your chest so they know where you are at any given moment?" Zoric spoke quietly as if the thought just occurred to him.

Carter scrunched up his face as if to protest too much. "No. No. Of course not." But when he cut his eyes to the lead trucker, he recognized the seeds of doubt had been successfully planted.

"Shut up! Just shut up! Al," he said looking to the man on the ground, "are you okay?"

Sam dropped the nine millimeter and refocused on the man on the ground.

"Al, you okay?" He repeated nervously.

The wounded pride smeared on Al's face transformed into rage as he awkwardly stood then stampeded toward Sam. He looked over to make sure his two partners held their weapons ready just before he landed a doubled fist against Sam's cheek. Carter grabbed her as she fell backwards, clearly dazed by the blow.

Vernon lunged forward to retaliate only to have a rifle jammed into his gut and shoved backwards. "Pretty safe in hitting a woman," Vernon snarled.

"I didn't sign up to hurt anybody," the third trucker complained. "Much less hitting a woman. What are you thinking, Al?"

That insignificant moment of concern revealed a possible ally for Carter and his people. He smiled at the third man. "Guess you don't know what this is really about then do you-what's your name?"

"Joe. What'a ya mean?"

Al stepped back and motioned with his head to move the prisoners to the back of the truck as he picked up his semi-automatic from the ground. "He's just tryin' to get in your head, that's all. Put'em in the back of the truck so we can get goin'. That fire is comin' fast. If we want to get paid we better get movin'." Al unconsciously touched the side of his head where Sam landed the toe of her brown leather boot. It still smarted. His backside hurt from hitting the ground and he was pretty sure his wrist needed medical attention after trying to break his fall.

The team quickly assessed the three truckers as amateurs; no gags to keep them from communicating, no restraints (thinking all you needed were guns to keep control), and no idea what they were doing. Carter bet the truckers would get careless now that they'd managed to hold them at gun point without getting their butts kicked. He felt the sloppy looking trucker, Joe, could be nudged into helping them with this new layer of concern. His nervousness originated not from assisting a terrorist, but hitting a woman. Al apparently was the brains so that certainly made their chances much better. The last trucker, a follower, looked confused and more than a little intimidated by Sam.

The screech of rusty bolts being slid back and the squeaky sound of metal doors slowly opening brought the Enigma team to attention as light began to filter into the truck. Instinct drove their hands to shade their eyes as guns waved, motioning them forward. Slowly, as if gauging the appropriate action needed, the Enigma team joined their captors on the ground.

The smell of smoke still permeated the late afternoon air. Ash floated down from a gray sky as Carter squinted his visual survey of their surroundings. Global Navigation appeared to have acquired some new security forces that looked a little rag tag at best. Counting ten armed men, Carter knew there were probably a few more inside along with Essid's devoted "anything for the reward of virgins after death," crowd. These freelancers were not much concern. They were in it for the money; probably lost their jobs, discontent tax evaders or just out for a cheap thrill. But Essid's people were fanatics that suffered from a blurred sense of justice. They had nothing to lose and everything to gain, or at least the promise of virgins seemed like a reasonable prize.

Carter grinned and agreed that even he might jihad for such a prize, if he actually believed all that inflammatory nonsense. He'd settle for a long hot bath with Chase's little Grass Valley housewife if she was of such a mind. After all, he thought he'd picked up on a more than casual interest when she'd started trying to talk NASA shop with him. He admitted to himself that her rapid questions and comments were a little on the naïve side but so deliciously adorable. Obviously, Tessa Scott belonged to the Carter Johnson fan club. Wonder what the mighty Captain Hunter would do about that?

His eyes fell on Sam. Her cheek, already deeply bruised, painted her disabled and fragile. If that had been true, he would have gladly torn that trucker apart. Why try to ruin such a piece of art? But Carter knew that having the truckers think Sam was out of commission only gave them an edge. When their eyes locked, she sent him a message not to worry.

Carter felt a nudge of a gun barrel in his back. "Move!" It was the trucker with the attitude, the one that liked slapping women around. "Don't use any of that macho crap and try to escape. I'll put a bullet in your little red haired freak."

"Take it easy, Al. They just look like a bunch of nerdy scientists to me." Joe pulled up his pants with one hand as he rolled his neck to relieve the tension.

"Does she look like a nerd to you? Probably some kind of ninja or somethin'." Al slowed when Sam turned her eyes on him and touched her cheek. A sense of foreboding swept over him. "You guys move'em along while I go find who's in charge." His short legs moved quicker than usual under the narrowed gaze of the woman.

The second trucker moved off to the side, aiming his gun at Zoric who assisted the old man. Safety first. Let Joe protect the other three, he reasoned.

"Looks like your buddies left us to you," Carter said stopping to bend down and tie his hiking boots. "Who hired you guys anyway?"

"Shut up."

"I'm thinking you're in way over your head."

"Yeah? How ya figure?"

Carter stretched. Vernon and Sam moved forward giving Carter room. "You didn't like your boss hitting Sam. If you were like them you wouldn't have spoken up for her."

"Move it." Joe nodded forward and Carter took small steps.

"He get you into this?"

"Maybe. What do you care? You're only here to make a little extra money just like me."

Carter turned slowly so as not to threaten. "Not true. I'm here to prevent these guys from stealing life-saving isotopes."

"What the hell is an isotope? Never mind. You're just tryin' to con me. I wouldn't do nothin' to hurt no one," he snapped. "I just need some money for my kid. This guy offered us two thousand dollars apiece to protect the load and take you out. Said you guys wanted to steal it and sell it on the open market to terrorists. I've been helpin' Homeland Security lately. They'll vouch for me," he said puffing out his chest. "You call my buddy Chase. He'll tell ya."

Carter stopped and grinned. "Well, hell's bells! You're the trucker that ran those crazy guys off the road in the van the other day!"

"Yep!" The obvious pride in his voice faltered when he looked closely at the five captives. "Who are you guys?"

"Joe, I think you and I are going to become best friends."

\* \* \*

Kneeling down behind some boulders, Chase and Tessa watched as the Enigma team moved toward Global Navigation, prodded forward by armed men. Several of the guards got in the trucks and drove them around the back of the building while the others meandered after them. Their posture revealed confidence of their take down. The crackle of radios communicating drifted in the air but the chatter was too distant to understand. The guards didn't bother to keep a constant watch around them which was a tipoff that they were amateurs. Soldiers wouldn't have let their guard down.

The smell of smoke, sweat and dried pine needles swirled around Chase and Tessa as they sat down to catch their breath. Tessa's labored breathing told Chase he'd pushed her too hard. She wasn't up for this kind of grueling march or confrontation, yet for the last hour no complaints escaped her parched lips. When he'd ask her if she needed a break, the response came as a nod forward. Sweat dripped down her face as the sound of heavy breathing followed him without question. Finally he realized her attitude adjustment concerning his trustworthiness compelled Tessa to become something more than a hindrance. Resting her head back against the rock, she drank in as much air as possible while rubbing her drawn up legs. With her body, so close to Chase, he sensed her heartbeat through the pale skin of her arm that lay casually against his. Reaching over with his other hand he moved the wayward blond curl hanging down across one eye. This time Tessa did not push him away, but smiled and squeezed his forearm.

"I'm a mess, I know. I bet Sam still looks fresh as a daisy."

"Probably." Chase grinned boyishly. "Of course, she didn't run through a forest fire, jump off a cliff and hike for hours. I think you're entitled."

Tessa nodded, smiling at Chase. In spite of herself, she liked him, even though he manipulated her at every turn. His bullying came from needing her to do what was required. Chase Hunter was a remarkable man in Tessa's mind although she wasn't quite ready to forgive him of all the entanglements of danger he'd managed to drag her into these past few days. He'd kept her from Robert and the children and in her place put a dangerous, back-to-nature beauty that apparently impressed her family. After this whole mess ended she would drive straight to Tahoe to show a little appreciation.

She realized in that moment that the mess she'd tried so hard to escape had managed to rejuvenate her life. Everything around her appeared sharper, more beautiful. Although dangerous, the people at Enigma were intoxicating and fascinating. Intrigue fueled her heartbeat. Nothing would ever be the same Tessa realized as she tilted her head and looked up at Chase's profile. In a rugged sort of way, he was handsome. It was hard to imagine him teaching literature and playing the violin. Perhaps that paradox created a cocoon of safety for what he really might be on the inside. But here, hidden by white boulders, breathing air that tasted like smoke, Captain Chase Hunter looked like the guy you wanted in a tough situation. She tried to imagine Robert doing this macho, G.I. Joe, crazy hero stuff she'd experienced with Chase. The quiet laughter that escaped her mouth caused Chase's forehead to wrinkle in bewilderment.

"Sorry," she whispered innocently. "I was just trying to imagine Robert doing something like this." Another broad smile.

"And?"

"Robert would be slapping subpoenas down so fast your head would spend. I imagine search warrants would fall in there somewhere after contacting an old fraternity buddy who's a judge somewhere. Next he'd be calling news channels and a private investigator."

Chase smiled too. "That's not really how it works in the world I live in."

Tessa pushed her hair back behind her ears. "Yeah. Well, I won't mind going back to the basics when this is all over. But," Tessa paused and bit her lower lip which seemed to force his eyes to her mouth, "if I should get killed or…"

Chase laid a large hand on her knee and squeezed. "I won't let that happen."

It felt so natural just to cover his hand with hers. "Okay," she smiled. "So what's the plan, captain? I've caught my breath. Ready when you are."

"We wait until the sun starts to set. That shouldn't be long up here. The sun will drop like a rock behind these mountains. I'm betting by now Carter has overpowered the guards with his bullshit and Sam has rearranged somebody's face," he patted her knee, not wanting to remove his hand. Tessa still rested her hand on his and he wasn't ready for that to change. "Zoric is either taking care of Jericho or is torturing some deserving soul into hell."

"Geeze! Is he really that violent?"

"Second thoughts on your coffee date with him?" Chase's face was near enough to taste those lips that moved so easily when she spoke to him now. Trust created a dangerous situation he knew he couldn't afford to compromise.

Tessa removed her hand from his and stared ahead so she could stop drowning in those dark chocolate eyes. "He said you'd not approve so I said I'd do it." When Chase moved his hand to his own drawn up knees she continued. "Why wouldn't you want us to have coffee? Is there something I should know?"

He sighed as he ran his hand over the top of his head. "When we're done here, really done, you go back to being a Grass Valley housewife and Zoric goes back to being—Zoric. You'll never see us again, be able to find us, or find any trace that we were ever in your life. Zoric likes you. You remind him of his family. You aren't like us. Sometimes I think we're not all that much different that the men who are stealing the isotopes. We couldn't do what we do if…" he stopped, not wanting to tarnish the good karma growing between them. He felt her blue eyes on him, waiting for an explanation. "None of us are choir boys, Tessa. Nightmares stalk all of us, not just me."

She nodded in acceptance. "I kind of figured that one out on my own." Her elbow jabbed Chase good naturedly in the side. "So tell me what you want me to do so I can get back to my boring, meaningless life in the suburbs."

Again a jab of pain stabbed his heart. He rolled to his knees and rose up to look over the boulder at Global Navigation. "How are you at acting?"

"I'm a woman. I've had lots of practice," she said proudly.

Chase looked down into her upturned face and smiled with admiration. "I just might buy you a cup of coffee myself, Tessa Scott."

"Captain, when this is done, really done, you'll never see me again or be able to contact me. It will be as if I never existed." Her stoic voice mocked him. "Besides, that soldier I saved in Knoxville is ahead of Zoric. So I'm not sure I could fit you in."

"Good to know you're making friends."

## *Chapter 26*

When the expansive glass doors swooshed open at Global Navigation, the Enigma captives quickly assessed their situation. Carter's quick observation that only two armed guards carried weapons which had seen better days realized how nervously they paced across the sparkling floors. The reflections of the guards appeared to bounce up from the polished floor resembling glass. The black guard uniform, worn by the one with a sparse mustache and rolled up shirt sleeves didn't really impress Carter that he was dealing with a spit and polish outfit. A rag tag bunch with mismatched uniforms would not be guarding a facility holding enriched uranium or the lifesaving Molybdenum 99 for isotope development.

The half wall of dark granite topped with a chrome counter, minus a pretty and efficient receptionist, revealed five computer screens constructed of some kind of clear translucent material that seemed to levitate over the shiny surface. Carter surmised the real security people manned those computers during a regular work day. Their absence meant hostages, maybe even causalities.

The lobby, a three story atrium, revealed balconies with steel guard rails that looked like they should be on the bow of a ship. A fusion of blue and green tiles rose up to the third floor next to the walls of glass that normally matched the California sky when it wasn't blanketed with hazy smoke. A spiral staircase on either side of the lobby leading to the upper levels looked more like a piece of art than a functional means to ascend to the mezzanine level. Elevators were probably tucked neatly down the corridor opening up in the center of the building. There were no people milling about, no idle conversations coming from the teal blue sofas and chairs scattered about the lobby. The quiet spoke volumes.

"Do those guys look like security guards you'd have in a place like this, Joe?" Carter whispered out of the corner of his mouth.

"Hey! Carl, takin' these two to the john. Can you take Amazon woman?" Joe said suffering the angry glare of Sam. He looked at the guards. "John?" No response. "Where's the toilet?"

Nothing.

"They don't speak English, Joe." Carter tried to speak without his lips moving.

"Geeze, Louise. Serious fellas, huh?" Carl frowned as he motioned for Sam to join Zoric and Jericho who had begun to limp and move slowly. "You," he waved the gun at Sam. "Help the man in black with the old guy. No funny stuff."

Joe pointed to his crotch with one hand while keeping a firm grip on his weapon with the other. "Toilet!" he yelled at the guards. This time they understood and pointed down the corridor and to the left. "I'll be right back. Al should be here any minute."

As Joe shoved his two hostages into the women's restroom he lowered his Tactical M40 rifle. and shook his head. "Sorry." He let Carter take his weapon as Vernon cracked the door to see if Carl would follow. "I had no idea!" He moved away from them and pulled up his sagging jeans again. "I would never have thrown in with terrorists. You gotta believe me. I'd never double cross Homeland."

Carter checked the rifle and found it fully loaded. He wondered how a truck driver came into possession of a Marine Corp weapon system. Making a mental note to pursue that line of questioning later, he realized the poor guy still experienced a Homeland Security high from helping out Chase earlier in the week. Joe probably never considered the possibility Essid was a terrorist.

"We don't exactly work for Homeland Security, Joe, but we're on the same ball team."

"I don't understand. Chase said…"

Vernon closed the door. "Clear. Chase is our team leader. Hopefully, he made it through the fire with," Vernon paused trying to remember the name she'd been assigned, "Melanie."

"That little scrawny woman who mouthed me?"

Vernon and Carter looked at each other and grinned. "Yeah. If you think Sam out there is trouble you should be around Chase's partner for a few hours."

"He was pretty rough on her when I saw them."

Vernon took another peek out the door. "That's the only way to handle her. You know how 007 has a license to kill?"

Joe nodded as his mouth began to hang open beneath heavy cheeseburger jaws.

Carter slapped him on the shoulder. "She makes Bond look like a boy scout. Good thing you didn't cross her."

Joe released air from his lungs as if he'd been carrying it around for a while and shook his head in disbelief. "Man!"

"They're getting on the elevator," Vernon turned to look at his partner. He pulled open a janitor closet door, then reached for a mop while eyeing the contents. "Well, well, well. Looks like we have all the ingredients we need to call in a HAZMAT team."

"What's that? Look, fellas, I donno what you're planning but I don't want to get into any more trouble." Joe bobbed his head and hands at the same time. "I gotta kid to take care of. If something happens to me he dies, cuz I ain't got no insurance to pay the bills."

"Then I guess we better wrap this up nice and pretty so when Chase arrives we can get you back home." Carter joined Vernon at the janitor closet and smiled. "Hmm. I just love janitorial supplies." Looking over his shoulder at the suddenly nervous trucker Carter tried to reassure him. "Here." He tossed a bottle of glass cleaner to Joe. "We're going to freshen up the men's restroom next door. Then you're going to go get our two armed," Carter looked up at the ceiling as if pondering some revelation from God, "hmm, armed 'death to America' friends carrying those ridiculous guns." He took the bottle of bleach from Vernon's hand. "Better get to work. We don't have long before they come looking for us."

As they entered the men's restroom Joe looked at the glass cleaner. "How is all this stuff going help us?"

"Spray every faucet, sink and mirror. Then spray more over the paper towel dispenser and up into the towels if you can. Most glass cleaners contain ammonia, or at least that one does. The fumes can irritate the skin, eyes and even the respiratory system. Prolonged exposure can even cause death. Great stuff."

"Holy cow!" Joe said as he began spraying the surfaces.

Vernon began pouring the toilet bowl cleaner in and around the toilets. "And this stuff by any other name is hydrochloric acid which will definitely affect their breathing."

Carter filled some paper cups with bleach and sat them around the restroom where the terrorists would be sure to kick them over once they tried to wash their faces only to get more ammonia on them. If the other chemicals didn't get them maybe pulmonary edema would set in to assist. A cough escaped Vernon and Joe. The fumes were already filling the small space. "Let's get out of here!"

Joe took back his rifle, leaving Vernon and Carter in the women's restroom. He ran to the hall corridor and whistled drawing the two gunmen's attention. He waved to them desperately to come help him, talking loud and pointing at the restroom. The scowl on their faces revealed they believed Joe was unable to manage the prisoners. They stormed into the men's restroom and lowered their weapons as if to make a point. In that instant someone tapped them on the shoulder. When the two jerked around, Vernon and Carter sprayed them in the eyes with the glass cleaner. With a scream they dropped their guns and started rubbing their eyes.

The restroom door slammed shut and Joe slid a mop through the handles of both restrooms to provide a lock. "Why not just do this in the first place?" Joe said watching the two Enigma men checking the newly acquired weapons. He could hear the men inside moaning, running water, crying and stumbling around the room. Finally one of them rammed up against the door, moving the make shift lock.

"That's why. In a minute they'll not be able to breathe enough to break out. Since we can't lock the door we needed them incapacitated enough to not break through."

Joe smiled. "You fellas are smart!"

"Your tax dollars at work, Joe," Carter said with a wink as they moved down to the corridor. "Vernon, get to work on those computers. Shut this place down and make sure Essid can't see a thing that's going on."

Vernon nodded and slipped out into the lobby. He could see guards outside watching something coming out of the woods. Whatever that distraction might be it gave him time to locate the main frame in the building. Another glance at one of the monitors, he saw a woman staggering out of the trees onto the road toward Global Navigation. Although her clothes were ripped and that wholesome L.L.Bean look had faded, there was no doubt that Tessa Scott would soon be joining them. "What are you up to?" he mumbled as his fingers flew across the keyboard. His eyes alternated between his monitor and the image of Tessa approaching the guards at the gate. "And where the hell is the captain?"

\* \* \*

Ben knew that the approach of a helicopter normally could be heard for miles. Fortunately the latest technology provided the military with a stealth helicopter now used by Special Forces. After Homeland Security Secretary Tobias Stewart pulled the necessary strings, one became available. As he neared Global Navigation in the smoky haze of sunset, Ben felt his heartbeat begin to increase and adrenaline surge through his veins. His hand lifted to his bullet proof vest then fell to his sidearm. A sigh escaped his chest thinking that this fight should not have gotten to this point. All the contingencies in the world to ward off a terrorist attack could not match the incredible stupidity of one reckless cabinet member trying to get his sexual jollies with a man he'd just met. Hopefully the president did shoot him at point blank range and had the Secret Service bury him in the rose garden.

"You have a coded message coming in, Director Clark. Check your phone." The co-pilot looked around his seat at Ben through a shaded visor attached to his $25,000 helmet. "Be there in twenty if we can see to land, sir."

\* \* \*

Ben nodded as he retrieved his Enigma phone from inside his vest. Frowning at the screen, he once again realized how complicated the world had become. He remembered the rotary phone his mother had growing up and wished things could be that simple again. It was Vernon. A wave of relief washed over him. After reading the text, Ben quickly erased the message before one corner of his mouth turned up slightly in a show of satisfaction.

\* \* \*

Limping really wasn't that much of a stretch for Tessa since she could barely put one foot in front of the other. Every bone and muscle in her body seemed to be screaming to stop and go to the local spa for a massage and makeover. Glancing down at her hands, she noticed several of her manicured nails were chipped or torn. Scratches, now covered in dried blood, itched along her arms. The blond hair had dried into cascades of curls that circled her slightly oval face and fell to her shoulders. Before leaving the woods Tessa had unfastened two of her buttons and tied the bottom of her shirt into a knot where her midriff showed smooth white skin. Her ripped jeans, tight from drying onto her body, didn't leave a lot to the imagination. The scent of sweat on her body horrified her almost as much as the metal gates swinging open and two guards pointing their weapons at her. She staggered, then groaned before lifting a hand toward them for help. Several colorful, unladylike words formed in her mind when they remained rooted to their position.

Tessa tried stumbling to a fall. Nothing. Looking up at them from the ground, she noticed both men fixed gazes down her shirt. Pulling herself up for one last time she approached with all the false courage she could muster and fell against the smaller man. The bigger one slung his weapon as he muttered something to his partner. He put his arm around her waist to remove her embrace long enough for the small one to also reposition his weapon. Both spoke rapidly, in some kind of confused state, nodding toward the entrance to Global Navigation. Neither seemed concerned that their personal hygiene could repel a female goat.

Knowing her movements could get her into serious trouble she let her hand dangle down against the big guy's crotch as she started to collapse. With unreasonable energy she pushed him away, taking a step and falling into the face of the little guy who appeared stunned at her proximity. She let her lips rest against his cheek as her hands went around his hips in a helpless movement of surrender. "Please," she whispered. "I need water."

In seconds they had lifted her arms over their shoulders as they dragged her gently toward the Global Navigation building. The big guy circled her upper back where his fingers could spread out against her breast. The other did the same on her buttocks. Captain Chase Hunter was going to owe her big time for this. She hoped he wasn't wasting time watching the little helpless act being offered up for him to sneak inside.

When the doors of Global Navigation opened into the massive lobby the sweet, cool air of modern convenience flooded over her so quickly she could barely contain the feeling of relief. When they neared the plush, teal couches, Tessa sensed something else the two men had in store for her. She squirmed free, stumbling to the half wall where she hoped unrealistically to find a letter opener, flame thrower or grenade that might haphazardly have been left lying innocently to hurl at the men. After all, isn't that how things worked in the movies? The knowledge that she hadn't anticipated how this scenario would actually conclude sent waves of revulsion through her body.

"Water!" she croaked, making a drinking sign. "Water!"

Words of contempt passed between them. But in the end when she seemed to roll onto her chest looking over the counter, the two liked the exposure of her back and the roundness of her bottom enough to fetch a cup next to the water cooler some ten feet away. Tessa froze as she looked over into the eyes of Vernon Kemp smiling up at her. When Vernon had seen that they were bringing Tessa into the lobby he ducked down out of sight. He handed up a bottle of glass cleaner as he nodded toward her captors and pointed to his eyes.

They shouted at her from behind. Slowly, she turned around to face them, startled to see that the big one had laid his rifle down and had begun to unbutton his pants. Swallowing hard, Tessa knew she had to do something unexpected to throw them off guard. Although her knees were shaking and bile threatened to choke her common sense, Tessa forced a smile and with one hand finished unbuttoning her shirt. Both men looked at each other in surprise and began to snigger like young boys at their first peep show. She'd left the small bottle of cleaner lying behind her back on the counter. Placing her right hand behind her, Tessa felt the grip before closing her hand around the trigger. She pointed to the big guy with one finger and motioned him to come to her, before spreading her blouse open so her lacy bra was fully exposed.

"Come here," she teased licking her lips seductively, "so I can..." But before she could say another word, he had rushed her, burying his hands in her hair and yanking her to his mouth. When she began to fight, the big guy reared back to slap her only to be blinded by a spray of ammonia cleaner. When a swift knee to the crotch doubled him over, he managed to knock the cleaner from her grip. Tessa locked her hands into a fist, knuckles facing up before bringing it down so hard on the back of his neck that he crashed to the floor. Looking at her locked hands in wonder, Tessa found herself frozen with awe at what she'd managed to do. That little three day self-defense class Robert forced her to take just paid off—again. The sudden agonized groan jarred the small man into action as he bent down to pick up the dropped weapon.

"Down!" she heard Vernon yell. As she fell to the floor and Vernon jumped up to send a shot into the small gunman. The bullet hit his shoulder, sending him awkwardly to a sitting position. Dazed for only a second, he scrambled to reach for his dropped weapon. With all her strength, Tessa rolled to her knees, grabbing the bottle of ammonia cleaner and sprayed him long and hard, collapsing him backwards into a screeching fit. The rifle somehow made it into Vernon's capable hands just as he knocked both men unconscious by directing a blow to the head with the butt of his gun.

"Mrs. Scott!" Vernon smiled slinging his new weapon. "Sorry about the shot. I aimed for his head. Need a little more practice on the firing range, I guess." His voice sounded matter-or-fact. Carefully, he placed the other AK-47 on her shoulder. "Did I mention you're my hero?"

Tessa looked from Vernon to the bottle of ammonia to the unconscious men on the floor. She'd never been someone's hero before.

Looking at Tessa's open blouse, Vernon blushed enough that she quickly fixed the problem. "Help me get these guys behind the counter. Want to hurt them some more before I tie them up?" He watched her eyes widened. "That was a pretty big risk you took. If anything happened to you Chase would have my hide."

"Chase!" she stammered looking out the door.

Vernon began dragging the big guy and welcomed Tessa's assistance when she grabbed the other hand. "He's in. Came in through the back. Saw him on the monitor. All security is down except where I want." After securing both men and shoving them into a large cabinet, Vernon rubbed his hands together as if dusting them off. "Can you use that rifle?"

Tessa shook her head 'no'. "I went paintballing once. Is it the same?"

Timidly, Vernon stepped closer and demonstrated with his gun. "Kinda. Robert take you?"

She shook her head. "Girls night out actually."

"Don't tell Carter. He'll try to meet your lady friends."

"They're all married with kids."

"He won't care. Now let me show you a few things just in case."

The *just in case* scenario, delivered another punch to Tessa's nervous system as she contemplated the possibility of dying before telling her family how much she loved them. The constant question of *why me* kept returning to her brain when time allowed her to take a deep breath. She didn't realize her breathing had escalated until Vernon timidly touched her shoulder, drawing her eyes up to examine his freckled face.

"You're doing great, Mrs. Scott."

Tessa reached up and patted his hand. "Call me Tessa. Mrs. Scott makes me feel like an old lady."

Before Vernon could stop himself, he said: "A hot old lady." Their eyes met suddenly as Vernon awkwardly pulled his hand away from her shoulder. "Sorry. That didn't come out right."

Tessa grinned. "You just made my year, Vernon. I'm going to remember those words for a very long time. Thanks." She couldn't help but notice Vernon square his shoulders a little more as he pulled his chin up confidently, knowing that his comment would be remembered by the fairer sex.

"We better get moving." Vernon nodded toward the corridor. "Let's kick some butt!" he grinned as if doing so would reassure his charge.

Taking a deep breath, Tessa nodded and slung her weapon on her bruised shoulder, trying not to show the pain that shot up her neck.

\* \* \*

Essid paced angrily as he slapped one of the Global Navigation people on the back of the head. His voice had lost that unnerving coolness. "What do you mean the computer is locked? Fix it!"

"I'm trying," he stuttered nervously. "Someone has gotten into the main frame and locked me out."

Essid stopped his pacing and stared at the twenty men and women sitting at the conference table under the watchful eyes of Mansur and Honey Lynch. Half of them were Russian, the visitors that were to celebrate the joint venture with the Americans in creating the lifesaving isotopes. The others, scientists and board members of Global Navigation, perspired nervously as they appeared to wait for some rescue operation to begin. At first knowing that Global's security people and lobby secretary now remained in a similar state of control at another location, crushed any thought of resistance. After hearing someone had managed to lock down the computer the hostages appeared to cling to some ridiculous ray of hope of rescue. He could see it in their sideway glances to each other.

The Haskin boys sat near the frosted windows. Exhaustion and fear had taught them to remain quiet. Their eyes diverted when he looked their way. A smile spread across his face, knowing they now had experienced enough traumas to render them useless to American society. Their plans to make the world a better place probably would never materialize thanks to the fear swallowing them. Years of American style therapy definitely loomed in their future provided they were alive at the end of the day. He noticed a wet spot on the young one's shorts last night after he and Honey had their fun in front of them. He had wanted to complete their love making there but Honey insisted on the bedroom. It wasn't like her to be modest. Killing the Scott family made her a little crazy he guessed. Hopefully she wasn't developing a conscious. That trait could get an assassin killed. What a waste that would be.

Essid stepped up behind the bald man at the computer, noticing that he flinched and tucked his head to avoid another slap. "Well?" He sucked in his breath and let it slowly escape to regain calm. When the middle aged man slightly lifted his hands in helplessness, it was all Essid could do from knocking him out of the black swivel chair. Fortunately for him, the frosted door swung open and two of the truckers entered with three of the Enigma team.

His heart thumped with pleasure, seeing Nicholas Zoric, the old Jericho Crawley and an extremely beautiful woman with a bruise on her cheek. "Where are the other two?" he said distracted by Sam's lovely figure that he eyed openly. As he reached out to touch her cheek, Sam turned away and snarled. Essid laughed good-naturedly. "Spirit! Honey, did you see that? She is like you."

Sam spit on the floor. "I'm nothing like her."

Honey grinned sardonically and slid her bottom off the glass conference table, approaching Sam nonchalantly. "You kill, just like me." Her Irish accent came through all of a sudden. "No difference. You think because your government sanctions the lives you take you are better?"

"I kill only to protect the lives of others." Sam leaned toward Honey, nearly touching Honey's nose with hers. "You are one psychotic bitch," she growled through her teeth. In that instant Honey landed a fist on the bruised cheek, staggering Sam back into the door. Sam resisted touching her jaw, but opened her mouth as if to stretch it back into place.

"I see you ladies have met before," Essid grinned. "Perhaps I can watch the two of you fight to the death when this is over." He slapped his hands together. "Yes! I would very much enjoy that! Mansur, my brother, will watch with me," he said throwing out his arm toward Mansur holding an AK-47 pointed at the hostages. "I think my brother does not like you, Honey," he said turning his eyes back to the computer man who desperately worked to save the day before looking back at to the truckers. "Do not keep me waiting! Where are the other two; the one they call Carter and the red headed kid?"

The truckers met eyes before stammering a reply. "I came ahead to find you. Carl and Joe took the prisoners."

Essid stepped toward them suddenly and pushed his face into theirs. "So where are they now?"

"Joe took them to the john." Carl tried to sound confident.

Essid threw up his hands in frustration. "Idiots! You better hope that is all they did." He saw Zoric grin like the devil he portrayed before guiding Mr. Crawley to a seat. "You! Why do you smile?"

Zoric reached for Sam and pulled her to his side. She did not resist. "You're screwed. Leaving Carter and 'that kid', as you called him, with your brainless trucker was the beginning of the end for you and your little fiasco." Putting Essid on edge made escape easier.

Essid frowned and grabbed his radio to contact the four guards below. A soft crackle then a jovial voice came across the airways. "Joe here! On my way up. Sorry about the wait. Had to knock some heads to get them movin'."

Essid clicked off and let his narrowed eyes move to the other truckers. He pulled out a nine millimeter from inside his black vest. The truckers took a step back as sounds of shock came from his hostages. "I hate incompetence."

"Hold on there," Al said lifting his hand up level with the barrel of the gun as if doing so would magically protect him from a bullet. "Joe said they're on their way up."

"Your stupid trucker friend is not capable of controlling special agents of the United States government, especially if they're working under," Essid looked over at Zoric and Sam, "Captain Hunter. Am I right, Honey?" She took a step back, knowing what would inevitably take place. The room exploded with screams, chairs being shoved back and a few sobs of terror when Essid pulled the trigger, blowing a hole in Al's chest. Carl, the other trucker caught his buddy in his arms by accident before slinging him aside to try and escape the room. Another blast rattled the room as he too, fell victim to Essid's twisted sense of reprimand. Two guards standing outside the door kicked the door open, ready to defend their leader if need be. Their dark eyes went from the bloody corpses on the floor to Essid lowering his weapon to his side. He nodded at the dead impatiently for their speedy removable as he turned his attention back to the bald man at the computer, who now hunkered down by his chair. With only one lifted eyebrow, Essid forced his hostage back to work at the terminal.

"I'm sorry you had to see that," he said looking painfully sad at those coming out from under the table. "Good help is hard to find in this country. In Libya there are many who will work all day for practically nothing, without complaint, I might add." He sighed as the second dead body quickly disappeared out the door. The sound of dragging and display of blood annoyed him. "Honey, get someone to clean this up." He watched her move stealthy out the door only to return moments later with a bucket and mop.

She walked over to Sam, throwing the mop at her. "Give me a reason to blow your face off. Clean it up," she growled through a clenched teeth smile.

Zoric put his bony hand on Sam's forearm. "Easy." He felt the tension in Sam's arm relax slightly.

Essid narrowed his eyes at Sam as she began to remove the signs of death. "Be sure to keep your gun on her," he advised to Mansur with an amused look. He placed both his hands on the shoulders of the computer man just as the screen revealed a view of the lobby. "Empty!" he snapped. "Where are my men?" he yelled in frustration.

Zoric grinned. "Dead or incapacitated would be my guess."

Essid whirled around violently. "And your captain? Where is he?"

"Last time I saw him he was headed into the fire you started. Probably didn't make it." Zoric continued to grin devilishly. "But then again..." He let his words fall sarcastically.

Essid addressed one of the guards who Zoric recognized immediately. "Jamaal, take the two guards outside and look for them! You," he said pointing at one of his hired guns from the trucking company who appeared to know his way around a group of armed thugs. He had barely flinched when Essid shot the two drivers. "Check to see if your people have finished unloading the trucks."

Jamaal, recognizing Zoric from several days before understood he'd been played, made to look like a fool in front the woman with the face of an angel. He slinked closer to make direct eye contact with the Serbian. When Zoric eyed him recklessly with a smirk and a devilish laugh, Jamaal started to ram his weapon into the hostage only to have Mansur cut him off with his large body.

"Do as you're told. If you screw this up too, I'll let this worthless piece of Serbian trash eat you alive." Mansur growled impatiently.

A nod of acceptance forced a speedy exit.

Essid suddenly felt the need to pace with his hands clasped behind his back, fidgeting his fingers. He stopped next to several Russians, older and heavier than himself. He faked a punch at the middle aged scientist. The scientist dodged so quickly, he fell out of his chair.

A grey haired Russian slammed his fist down on the table. "Why are you doing this? This material will save the lives of thousands, even many Libyans. It can be of no use to you. Time is of the essence. The life of this material is critical to production. I beg you. Let these people do their jobs."

Essid frowned and kneeled down next to the Russian. "There's no one to do the job," he smiled. "Most of the people were sent home when the fire started. The party was canceled and the caterer sent back to Sacramento before anyone in this room knew there was a problem. Besides," he said standing up and stretching. "This whole place is going to blow sky high soon. So you see I am merciful. Creating a few isotopes will be the least of your problems. I've left plenty of signs that the Russians are behind the attack. Did I say 'Russians'? I meant Chechens." He chuckled as a confused look came over the older man's face. "Mother Russia has imported her problems to the United States, or at least that is how it will be perceived. The president will be forced to invade your land and take care of these terrorists." He slapped his hands together so loudly that everyone jumped at the table. "Like Afghanistan, I think. You couldn't take care of them either as I remember. How do you feel about a little shock and awe in your country?"

Zoric stepped forward. "You would have us go to war because of your dead woman!"

Essid snapped his head around, focusing on the dark looks of his enemy. He smiled with condescension. "You are a Serbian. I remember you with Captain Hunter. I heard about your family." A slight glint of surprise flickered in Zoric's bloodshot eyes then disappeared. "Oh yes, I have sources too." He looked over at the sour look on Honey's face. He extended his arm toward her so that she could slip it around her shoulders. "I know all that you found were pieces of those sweet little girls."

"Shut up," Zoric spat. "I don't need you to tell me about my family."

The bald computer man cleared his throat to draw Essid's attention. He was there instantly. "Yes?"

"We're back on line, but only limited. I can only open up the cameras in the lobby, the loading dock, and this hall. The others have been so scrambled I think they may have been destroyed for good."

"What's that?" Essid said pointing at the screen. But he already knew.

# Chapter 27

Learning to become invisible became second nature if you were a member of a Special Forces team living in the mountains of Afghanistan. Something like pebbles slipping could jerk a combat soldier to attention in a heartbeat. A shift in wind direction could help or kill you. It paid to absorb details of your surroundings. He learned to observe without moving anything but his hooded eyes. Chase often found himself pausing even before pulling out into traffic on the rather docile streets of Sacramento. He could sleep standing up and eat just about anything. Blending in became second nature for a number of years before he returned to the states.

Assimilation into civil society where everyone knows your business and expects to participate in your life posed problems for the captain when returning from the war. Sometimes he had gone for days without saying a word due to the isolation of his outpost. Even his men rarely uttered a word, fearing that doing so might give the enemy a heads up advantage. Then there were times when he lived amongst a village, becoming one of them by adopting their customs and habits. A few tribal leaders thought of him as a brother giving him respect and further training to survive a common enemy, the Taliban. Sometimes a nod or the sharing of a cup of tea spoke more than a litany of promises and threats. After returning home, Chase often craved that solitude he experienced with his tribal family. He let Enigma fill in the holes of loneliness left by war and tragedy. Now someone else had fallen into his life that made him feel anxious. A new war began to stir deep inside him. What weapons did a soldier use against emotions he'd never felt before?

He had watched anxiously as Tessa approached the guards at the gate. Second thoughts nearly caused him to run after her, knowing Essid's men would be less than respectful. Focusing on the big picture kept his feet rooted out of sight. She put on quite a show, maybe too much of one. Even from where he hid, Chase could see that the guards assisted her inappropriately with their dirty hands. A sense of urgency drove him forward when she distracted them. He'd have to go in through the loading dock and make his way back to Tessa before any harm came to her. If America was producing women like Tessa Scott across the cities and countryside the world just might become a safer place to live. Although scared out of her wits most of the week, she never ceased to amaze him with her tenacity and ability to switch gears when the situation demanded change.

A brilliant sunset began to form through the layers of smoke and ash drifting across the sky. Nothing like pollution to bring out a little beauty in nature he thought fleetingly as he pushed himself up against the corner of the building where the loading dock housed three eighteen wheeler trucks. Only one guard with a rifle stood watching the other men completing the transfer of Molybdenum 99 barrels to the cavernous storage facility. Other weapons leaned against the concrete wall. Some appeared to be AK-47s and didn't look to be in the best of shape; more than a little dirty and banged up. He made a mental note to avoid those. After taking another quick glance Chase leaned on the exterior wall some three or four feet from the men offloading the small barrels. Chatter, an occasional laugh muffled by some solemn circumstance they probably didn't grasp, lifted like the translucent smoke filtering the fading light of a red sky.

The last yellow container passed through the double doors as Chase eased his body from the corner of the building and carefully lifted one of the automatic rifles propped precariously against the wall.

Stepping back, he quickly checked to see if the weapon was loaded. It was. He heard their heavy, clumsy steps of indifference echo off the corrugated metal that lined the ceiling of the loading dock. His thoughts raced to Tessa. Too much time had passed.

As in times of battle, things either sped up or went into slow motion mode. He preferred fast. The smell of gunpowder filled his nostrils even before the first round left the chamber. The rat-a-tat-tat of a killing machine silenced any second guesses, knowing Tessa faced terrible danger alone. With an aggressive lunge, Chase appeared before the unsuspecting soldiers of terrorism, pulling the trigger to spray rapid death into their chests. The five unarmed men fell with surprised chokes of pain. Blood pooled so quickly that Chase never noticed the splatter of body tissue dripping from the concrete wall. He stormed quickly, seeing that the sixth man with a gun stood frozen behind a John Deere bobcat. Feeling the rifle jam, Chase swung the rifle around to use as a club. The surprise confrontation gave Chase the split second he needed to rush him. Just as the sixth man stepped out and lowered his weapon, Chase yelled like a banshee, swinging the butt of his rifle against the man's weapon as it began to discharge. Startled the man dropped his gun and staggered backwards only to have Chase jump him with his full weight, slamming him to the ground. Chase felt the air gush from the man's lungs just before he rammed a fist into his Adam's apple. The death gurgle began as Chase bounded to his feet then secured two more working AKs before entering the storage area.

Quickly moving through the holding area, he unconsciously swept the space for other men with lethal force before slipping through double doors that led into several rooms. Finally he found a way into a long corridor. Hearing whispers and feet trying to make quiet forced Chase into a small lobby off the main corridor where a fountain bubbled peacefully. Surrounded by tropical plants and deep blue cushioned stools he guessed it was a place to catch up on emails or read a book. A place like Global Navigation probably tucked several more of these respite areas along the corridor to offer a Zen-like feeling to their employees. But for Chase he plastered his back against the granite wall, pulling his weapon tight to his chest. Chase readied to take out the next person who dared interfere with his rescue of Tessa.

When he knew they were but a breath away he swung out with his rifle leveled, only to see Vernon and Tessa collide into each other trying to escape what they thought might be one of Essid's men. Lowering his weapon, he watched Tessa stop cringing and spring toward him. It seemed like the most natural thing in the world to extend his right arm and pull her body into his. He felt her arms wrap around him and squeeze. She looked up at him with a conquering smile.

"You're safe! I worried." Tessa realized she'd thrown herself at her hero and shyly took a step back. "The isotopes materials?" she asked hurriedly.

"Safe for now." His large frame twisted to survey his surroundings. It was too quiet, too empty. "The others?"

Vernon nodded upstairs. "Carter took your buddy Joe the truck driver…"

"Truck driver?" he interrupted bewildered.

Vernon explained briefly. "The others went to the fifth floor on the elevator."

"Just short of the top," Chase said, pulling Tessa into the secluded area where he'd hid moments before. Vernon followed. They both knew that out in the open meant danger. He looked down at Tessa, who followed his every move, as if he might suddenly vanish.

"Those men at the gate—did they hurt you?" Chase felt a catch in his throat asking such a question. Of course they hurt her; they were animals with no respect for human life.

Vernon felt confident enough standing next to Tessa after her glowing words to put his arm around her shoulder. They stood like soldiers posing for pictures in Kandahar. "My girl took them out with a bottle of glass cleaner."

Her eyes darted to Captain Hunter in hopes of praise, "that 'a girl", or even a proud smile. What she got was a frown and one arched eyebrow of disapproval. "That was stupid! What if you'd missed?" he said matter-of-factly.

"I didn't."

"What if Vernon hadn't been there?"

"But he was."

"Dumb luck!" he snapped.

"I prefer to think I had an angel watching over me. Besides it's not like you rushed in to save me," Tessa argued. Why was the captain ruining her moment? She'd assisted in taking out two men who meant harm to her country. Wasn't that a good thing?

"The men on the loading dock?" Vernon asked carefully, as he slipped his arm back to his side after he noticed Chase's eyes fell on it like a hammer.

"Down," was all he needed to say.

Vernon nodded in acknowledgment. The captain could sometimes petrify the team with his stealth ability to take out an enemy. Vernon had seen him do it on several occasions and would not soon forget it. The most frightening part came when Chase carried on as if nothing abnormal had occurred. Maybe when you live in Afghanistan for several years something gets twisted inside you. He'd once saw him down two paramilitary types in Montana then drive back to town for a cheeseburger and fries. After that, Director Benjamin Clark forced him into therapy. Chase agreed to the weekly sessions so he could remain in command of his team. The therapist often complained Chase provided very little help in the process and even played a few mind games of his own on the doctor. The rest of the team found it hilarious. The director did not.

"Give me that rifle," Chase ordered as he reached for Tessa's weapon. Reluctantly, she pulled it from her shoulder with a flinch when the strap dragged across her bruised shoulder. As he took the gun, Chase also pulled her blouse over to see her shoulder. She retreated against Vernon as she tried to shove his hand away in embarrassment.

"Excuse me!" she fumed only to cringe when he touched her gently on the spot she'd been babying. He slowly withdrew his hand.

He leveled a hard gaze at Vernon. "Did they do that?"

Before Vernon could speak Tessa pulled her blouse closed. "No! You did when you knocked me down…"

Vernon bristled. "You knocked her down!" He ordinarily wouldn't consider standing up to a man a half foot taller than him and a good hundred pounds heavier, but hitting a woman like Tessa Scott was reprehensible.

Chase rolled his eyes in impatience. "Yes! I did, Vernon so she wouldn't get her head shot off! Now if you're finished playing Lancelot I'd like to wrap this mission up so I can take her to Grass Valley and never lay eyes on her again!" Surprisingly when he cut his eyes to Tessa she looked irritated.

It was confusing to see Vernon, normally shy around women, not only slip an arm around Tessa, but ready to defend her honor against someone who could clearly pulverize him. She'd had such a gentle effect on Jericho that he couldn't stop talking about his involvement in this whole mess. Even Zoric, normally sadistically creepy around the fairer sex, curbed his appetite so not to unnerve Tessa. Chase noticed him running his fingers through his oily hair to try and tame it just before approaching her. She corrupted the predictability of what Chase knew worked. Even he felt compelled to be over protective. When this emergency concluded he'd gladly drop her off at her pretty Victorian house and breathe a sigh of relief. If she heard about Robert and the kids, all hell would break loose and her cooperation would end. There would be no fixing those feelings she'd harbor against him for lying.

The elevator softly dinged. Instinctively both men pushed themselves up against the cool granite walls, tense with the adrenaline pumping through their veins. Tessa, sandwiched between Chase and the hard surface of the cold wall, could feel the beat of his heart. It was strong and steady. Inhaling the scent of his body, a mixture of sweat and soot, his large hands came up on each side of her head somehow bestowing a sense of safety. Although her body seemed immobile against the weight pressed against her, Tessa could look up into the rugged profile of the man who'd taken her on the trip of her life for the last few days. His jaw flexed only slightly, the dark eyes narrowed as if intensifying the ability to hear what he could not see. The rise and fall of his muscled chest changed little at the prospect of yet another dangerous encounter.

Even though the unknown emptied off the elevator, Tessa believed her new friends would prevail. Unknowingly, she lifted her hands to his sides, drawing his face back to hers. His dark, troubled eyes searched her face and the creases on his forehead appeared to soften. One of his hands went to the back of her head then slid down to her shoulder like a gentle giant might do; afraid she would destruct at the slightest pressure.

"Stay here," he mouthed inches from her lips.

She nodded as her hands went back to her side. What she really thought was something like *no problem there!* The act of her hard swallow of terror sounded like a cherry bomb in her ears as the pressure of Chase's body removed from hers suddenly. Watching him and Vernon swing out into the open corridor, she heard surprised voices in a language she didn't recognize followed by the rapid fire of automatic weapons.

Covering her ears she pushed back into a corner but could still see the two Enigma men firing, hunched slightly as if trying to find the target. Fleeting questions went through her mind: why weren't the shell casings that flew into the air making any sound when they hit the floor, why did the smell of gunpowder actually smell tantalizing? Would she ever be able to get these moments out of her head to live a normal life again? Did Enigma have some kind of potion to erase her memories into the initiation of Terrorism 101?

The whole action of taking out the ones from the elevator took less than thirty seconds, although it seemed much longer. Not realizing her body still cringed with hands covering her ears, she watched Chase take several long strides toward her as Vernon disappeared toward whoever they'd encountered.

"It's done," he said stopping inches from her. He realized in such a small area the sounds of battle could be deafening, echoing off walls while the smell of death and gunpowder poured over you like a tsunami. "One of them was Jamaal, the one you put the tracking device on in jail."

Tessa managed a nod as she watched Chase sling his weapon back to his shoulder and then reached out to remove her hands from her ears. Her knees felt wobbly as she tried to push away from the wall only to feel Chase's arms go around her for support. "I'm fine," she stammered, yet gripped the sides of his shirt with her hands. "I'm fine," she repeated trying to push ever so cautiously a step back, feeling Chase's capable hands still continuing to firmly hold her securely. "Are they..." She couldn't finish the sentence.

"Yes. It was them or us." Suddenly aware that Tessa was trembling, he felt goose bumps on her naked flesh that touched his arms. Pulling back he rubbed his hands up and down her arms briskly and spoke quietly. "We've got to keep moving, Tessa. I can find a hiding place for you..."

"No!" she snapped in alarm. "Don't leave me behind. Please. I'll stay out of your way and not make trouble." Without realizing it she had begun digging her chipped nails into his arms.

He patted her cheek. "Good. Just remember if push comes to shove you've got that knife." His hand went to her stomach, below the waistband of her jeans. "Think you can use it?"

She shrugged as a weak smile played around the edges of her mouth. "Only if I have to save your life." That brought a wide smile to his lips. "I'm getting pretty tired of all this one way hero stuff!"

Before he could comment Vernon backed up into view. "Better come here, boss." Then he disappeared again.

Chase returned to the hall instantly to join Vernon. Two of the men from the elevator were of Middle Eastern decent, young and clothed in western style clothing. Except for being covered in blood, they looked like almost any college age student you'd find on a university campus in the United States. Their hair clipped short, clean shaven faces and expensive tennis shoes made them blend in much better than the guards at the gate or what you'd stereotype a terrorist to look like.

The third man, Jamaal, was a different story; he could be the poster child for *Know Your Neighborhood Terrorist*. Grimy hair, black and curly, unshaven and mismatched clothes that screamed Salvation Army Outlet, gave Jamaal the appearance of a terrorist who just couldn't transition into American chic. His breathing, shallow and labored sounded like a death rattle. Blood soaked his shirt to the extent the true color no longer existed. Perspiration dripped down his face into his eyes as he blinked lethargically.

Chase kneeled to one knee before taking Jamaal's pulse on his neck. "You're a dead man you worthless piece of crap." He displayed all the sensitivity of an angry porcupine. "Where is Essid?"

"Go to hell," he coughed. Then he began to stare anxiously at something past Chase. "The angels come for me," he whispered.

Chase and Vernon turned to see Tessa staring with horrified eyes at the blood splattered on the floors and walls. Her hand covered a gag reflex when tears began to tumble out of her eyes. Slowly her hands came together at chest level, locking the fingers into a sign of prayer. Her lips began to move silently and rapidly as her eyes lifted up then closed in communication with God.

"I don't see an angel." Chase stood and motioned for Vernon to nudge Tessa into action.

Hearing Vernon's "pisst!" Tessa opened her eyes and shifted them to Chase where he moved his head slightly, indicating she was to move to his side. Nervously she approached, appalled at the amount of blood that poured from the man who created the scenario which inevitably dragged her to this place in time. He lifted a hand toward her.

"She comes for me. I will be in paradise."

"You're hallucinating, Jamaal. No angel here. Vernon," Chase said twisting his body to look at his partner, "do you see anything?"

Vernon stepped closer. "Nope. No such thing as angels. Just me and the captain, Jamaal."

"Tell me where Essid is, Jamaal and I'll help you out with the pain." Chase's voice grew gruff as he nodded down at the dying man then over at Tessa.

"I'm going with the angel," he continued.

Chase stepped in front of Tessa so Jamaal couldn't see her clearly. A look of panic leaped to his eyes. "Where's Essid?"

Tessa stepped around Chase and kneeled down next to the terrorist. She took his hand in hers, feeling his fingers close around her own. It felt limp, cold and clammy all at the same time. Clearly in Jamaal's current state he didn't recognize her from a few days ago. Tessa probably wouldn't recognize her own reflection, she reasoned, if a mirror could be found. "Help the men and then we'll go. Your friend is not a believer of Allah, only in himself. Paradise will be denied to him."

"Now, Jamaal!" Chase shouted. "Or so help me I'll rub a piece of bacon on my next bullet and put it right between your eyes."

The viciousness of the captain's words drew an angry glare from Tessa. "It's almost time. Do this last good thing for me." Uncertainty flooded over her as she felt him gently tug her hand. Lowering her ear to Jamaal's lips he spoke then took his last breath. She felt the strong hand of Chase on her arm as he pulled her to a standing position. No one ever died in her hands before. Tears pooled but stayed in her eyes. "Fifth floor. Go left. Last office on the right. Hostages are all there too. Maybe more of his men. I'm not sure."

Vernon's eyes widened as he looked over at Chase staring down into the face of his Grass Valley housewife. "Trash can is over there," he said pointing in another alcove off the main corridor. In an instant both men could hear her heaving into the can. The running of water from a cooler seemed to quiet the nausea in their saving angel.

"Should we check on her?" Vernon asked as he pulled one of the bodies into the first alcove they'd used as a hiding spot. The only response he received from Chase was a disgruntled look. Something like this didn't usually rattle the captain. Having a civilian along, an innocent as he liked to refer to them, must be giving him a conscious. In spite of the carnage around them, Vernon couldn't help but find the situation amusing that the mighty Captain Hunter was at a loss around this woman.

Tessa reappeared and diverted her eyes as the other two bodies disappeared into the alcove. Crossing her arms and looking up at the high ceiling did nothing to erase the smell and sight of blood smeared on the floor and walls. Bullet casings rolled after Vernon as he dragged another body past her, bumping into other casings. Tessa wondered if she should pick them up or push them to the side or try to hide them. Did evidence make a difference in a situation like this or did the government just send in sweepers to extinguish any trail of guilt? She hadn't expected the smell. Her stomach rolled as her hands slid to her midriff. Even though everything had transpired in less than ten minutes, Tessa felt as if hours had beaten her down with fatigue. She realized breakfast had been a long time ago. When her eyes fell on the blood trail the two men stepped in on their way out of the enclave, Tessa ran back into the nook for the trash can. How could she be thinking of food at a time like this? Not even heaves came this time. More water on her face helped until she heard another male voice. Frozen with fear, Tessa once again pushed herself into a corner of the alcove, unnoticed and hidden.

"Looks like you guys have been busy." The voice, deep and coarse, sounded like a two pack a day smoker. Vernon and Chase slowly turned around, raising their arms and noticing the stairwell door silently closing. They still wore their automatic rifles around their shoulders and chests but knew that the bruiser standing before them would mow them down without the slightest regret.

"Friends of yours?" Chase asked calmly.

The man outweighed Chase by fifty pounds and stood some six inches taller. Lean and deadly, he was dressed in camo and a bullet proof vest. His shiny combat boots and good grooming quickly told Chase their newest troublemaker had been a military man.

"Friends? Hell no. Don't even like Rabs," he grinned. "They were getting on my nerves. Essid will probably give you a reprieve if you killed that little skinny ass guy named Jamaal."

"Why are you in this?"

"Didn't have anything else to do. Business is slow since the economic downturn." He faked a smile revealing crooked teeth. "Money was good. I have expenses." The thug eyed them wearily. "I guess you're thinking I can't search one of you without getting attacked by the other." The Enigma men remained quiet. "I thought maybe I'd just shoot one of you first before trying that unless you have a better idea."

"Vernon," Chase raised his chin toward the new man on scene without removing the steely stare down going on between them. Vernon took a step forward, removing the automatic rifle.

"Easy, Red," the gunman said moving the end of his Israeli Tavor Tar 21 weapon to aim at the younger man's chest. Carefully Vernon laid the rifle on the floor and moved forward locking his hands behind his head. The huge man caught him roughly and spun him around. The search took only seconds as his hands ran over the younger of the two. "Now lie down, spread eagle on the floor." He carefully stepped forward and kicked Vernon's weapon aside.

Vernon locked eyes with Chase, wanting some kind of signal to rebel, but the only message by way of a hooded blink was to do as told. As he lay down he raised his head enough to look down the floor to a shiny metallic light sconce that rose from the floor to about five feet. They lined the hall artfully, probably giving off a transcendental kind of light at night. But the one he now focused on reflected the space of the alcove where Tessa had gone to be sick. He could see a blur which he knew belonged to her. He willed her to stay out of harm's way knowing full well she probably would be trying to concoct a rescue that just might get them all killed.

Tessa could see Vernon lying on the floor thanks to the metallic sconce. She could also see the back of the captain and the other man no more than four feet from him. Sucking in her breath and what was left of her courage; Tessa straightened her shoulders and took a step toward the corridor.

## Chapter 28

Knowing Captain Hunter had compromised his plan merely by showing up gave the Libyan pause. Essid usually possessed a deep calm that others considered unnerving. Standing perfectly still, weight shifted evenly between legs that had been spaced about two feet apart, the only part of him that moved was his dark eyes. As they slid around the room rapidly, attuned to every sigh, shift in a chair, or whisper between colleagues, those eyes now began to show concern. Underneath the thick lashes that women found attractive were dark circles as if he'd not been sleeping. His head bowed just enough to make him look up through eyebrows that met over the top of his nose. The menacing glare finally forced one scientist to ask for her inhaler to ease her ability to breathe.

Without looking at one of his men, Essid snapped his fingers and pointed to the woman that had her hand on her chest. They had relieved her of it shortly after the takeover. The inhaler, tossed gently to the wheezing woman would seem like a normal gesture on any other day. In minutes the woman relaxed as she quickly tried to wipe a tear from the corner of her eye.

"Let them go," Zoric said coldly unaware his friend had arrived. "The kids too," he said nodding at the Haskin boys. "They've done nothing to you. The woman is not well. Release her as a sign of good faith."

Essid turned to Zoric stoically then burst into laughter. "Release to whom? No one knows we're here but your little ragtag bunch. I doubt you shared that with authorities." He laughed again as he moved toward

Honey. She snatched the mop away from Sam. Essid slipped an arm around Honey from the back, kissing her on the neck while never taking his eyes from the Serbian. "I am hoping your captain appears before I blow this place up."

"What about us?" It was one of the Russians.

Essid looked over at the overweight Russian with a full head of gray hair. His face, pocked by acne as a teenager, was flushed and splotchy. "You will die. Here." He spread his hand out to the Enigma group. "With them." He looked at Mansur, his half-brother. "Tie their hands behind their backs. We may need to move fast. I want them to be taken to the blast center so there will be nothing left to find." Essid smiled as he clapped his hands together. "Now if some of you would like to return to Libya with me and assist in the current programs of great scientific study I will spare your life," he said with a shrug. "If not, my men will use the women as they wish before I detonate the bombs. The men will be castrated before we leave." His tease created a smirk as he looked at their horrified faces.

Jericho Crawley stood and moved toward the women to comfort them with a gentle pat on the shoulder. "Don't listen to him," Zoric warned. "He's a terrorist that wants to put so much fear into you that your brains stop working as they should." Zoric could feel Mansur pull his hands behind his back and apply the white flex tie.

"He's right!" Sam said as Mansur jerked her hands roughly behind her. She could feel his foul breath on her neck. She tried to twist away only to be jerked back against his shirt, damp from perspiration. "They're cowards!" She nodded toward Honey. "They'll sell their souls to the devil for a buck." Just then Honey took the mop with both hands and swung it at Sam's midriff. She pushed back against Mansur then sidestepped so that he took the brunt of the blow on his hip. He grabbed the end of the mop with his puffed up sausage fingers and jerked it from Honey. "Thank you, Mansur." Sam said over her shoulder with a dazzling smile. "I see your manners surpass your illegitimate brother's."

She felt him shove her aside and rush toward Honey who had already begun to back up nervously. Mansur was a stocky man, barrel chested and unattractive on every level. But the strength shown in his doubled fists and sudden stride indicated he wasn't a man to be treated lightly. Honey stumbled as Mansur grabbed her blouse at chest level, jerking her forward to level his fist in her face. Essid gently laid his hand on his brother's arm and frowned.

"Enough."

The three women at the table began to cry uncontrollably at the altercation, knowing their fate was in the hands of a madman. They reached for Jericho as he slipped an arm around the frailest with the inhaler. Essid turned to them. "Shut up or I'll give you to my men right now!" he growled impatiently.

Sam and Zoric saw that the hostages were putting their captor on edge. They glanced at each other and blinked knowingly.

"You're pretty tough with women, aren't you Essid. That your Libyan upbringing or the Muslim?" Zoric snarled.

Essid tried not to be baited. "Nice try, Serbian. Considering how many Bosnians you raped and murdered I would think you'd feel at ease with us." He motioned for Mansur and two other guards to tie the hostages to their chairs. "I've changed my mind. They are too much trouble. Bind the feet of the men and just the hands of the women." He tilted his head and smiled at the woman with the inhaler. "I'm sure that my men won't want to waste time cutting the women loose." This brought on another round of frightened sobs causing Essid to chuckle like a child.

One of the women, older and American, tried to resist only to receive a hard slap across the side of her head knocking her from the leather and chrome chair that flipped over on top of her. The guard jerked her up by her frosted hair, slamming her body against the table. After forcing her hands behind her and securing them, he took pleasure in rubbing his body up against her. Jericho stepped toward the man and pushed only to suffer a punch to his gut, collapsing him to the floor.

"Hmmm," Essid said as if examining a news brief. "Who knew the old man had it in him. By the way Mr. Crawley, where is that pretty little neighbor of yours? I nearly forgot about her." He watched the old man crawl on all fours toward Zoric. Lifted up by one arm, the same abusive guard hauled him to his feet before shoving him into a chair. Essid's eyes went to Honey. "Ah that's right. She's with Captain America." He thought he detected something in the assassin's eyes although the glazed expression never changed. "Mr. Crawley, what do you think? Is she still alive? Can I expect yet another untimely interference from your rescuer?"

"Go to hell," Jericho choked as he tried to straighten his oversized Grateful Dead tee shirt Zoric had loaned him earlier that day at the motel. "You're not fit to even breathe the same air as her."

Essid grinned. "Someone has a crush. Perhaps you can watch my men have their fun if she shows up." He watched him fidget. "Better yet, maybe you can watch me. I rather like an audience. Right boys?" He directed his comments to the Haskin brothers sitting silently restrained in the corner of the room on the floor. He chuckled happily as their eyes shifted nervously away from him. Suddenly he picked up a glass water pitcher and hurled it across the room at Zoric and Sam who dodged the impact. He turned to the computer person. "My men, where are they? Do you have a visual?" He nodded and rolled his chair to the side to let Essid come in close to the computer. It helped being out of striking distance of Essid's angry fists as well.

He watched his men leave the elevator unconcerned and looking up at the high ceiling like they'd never been inside a modern building before today. Essid felt his frustration swell knowing his men were poorly trained and unprepared. Just then he saw the backs of two other men step out and begin shooting. In seconds his people were down. He watched as the Grass Valley housewife moved to the side of Jamaal and lowered her blonde head to his mouth. Then he died holding to the infidel's hand. Essid felt Honey at his side watching curiously. The bodies were dragged away as the housewife disappeared for the second time into an alcove.

"Where is Trevor? He went with them." Honey asked, confused.

The next images were of Chase and Vernon raising their hands, slowly turning to face the camera. Another figure stepped into view revealing the back of the man called Trevor, one of Essid's American hires. He had to admit the Americans knew how to train their people. He obviously had refused to follow Jamaal into the elevator knowing that he couldn't control what would be on the floor when the doors opened. Essid watched Vernon lay down on the floor after scooting his weapon to the side. "Just shoot the captain before he has time to form a plan, you idiot!" Essid said as his arms doubled across his chest. Then he watched in surprise as Tessa Scott innocently stepped out into the corridor to create more havoc. Unconsciously, both leaned in closer to the screen to watch the unexpected.

\* \* \*

Hearing footsteps coming down the stairs, Carter and Joe ducked into the third floor. Waiting for the steps to pass, Carter then stole a glance out the door window to see a huge military type carrying an impressive weapon. He wasn't Libyan so he surmised the man was another gun for hire. Unfortunately, there seem to be more and more of those since the wars in the Middle East kept bringing men and women home to unemployment. Possessing marketable skills forced some into the protection business or like this guy, the biggest bang for your buck.

"See what you can find in these labs, Joe."

"Like what?" he whispered as he body pushed up against the wall making him look like a cartoon character with an exaggerated belly. "More glass cleaner?"

"No. First aid kit, cord, candy bars, anything we might use if we find hostages. They've got my people too. Hard telling what's become of them."

"I don't think Al would hurt them, Carter."

Carter looked from the window to his new trucker friend with callous indifference. "Your buddies are most likely dead, Joe. Better be prepared for that."

"What! Why?"

"When you didn't go upstairs with me and Vern, Essid would have come unglued. He's not exactly a forgiving man with Americans."

"Man!" he said shaking his head in fear. "And your friends?"

Carter shrugged. "The old man is tough but he's had a rough few days. They've beat and starved him then left him to die in a parked car. If Tess, I mean Melanie hadn't come along he wouldn't have made it."

"And the others?"

"They can take care of themselves, but for how long I'm not sure. We need to get them back. Now go see what you can find and I'll make sure our storm trooper doesn't return unexpectedly."

He watched Joe push off with enthusiasm only to lumber away like a beach ball with legs as he tried to pull up his sagging jeans. The door to the lab had a clear window so between looking into the stairwell and over at Joe, Carter tried to formulate his next move. Cracking the door he heard the faint distant sound of rapid gunfire echoing up the stairwell. "Vernon," he gritted through his teeth. The guilt of leaving such a mild mannered kid to face a military grade gunman blinded him momentarily with rage.

He liked Vernon. Even though he was nearly twenty years younger than himself, he found Vernon both wise and brilliant beyond his years. After all, he'd out smarted the Pentagon and Langley's' spooks on numerous occasions just for fun. Director Clark constantly threatened to tar and feather him if Chase didn't get him under control. But when you wanted a genius to stop the world in its tracks, just put Vernon Kemp in front of a computer and let him do his magic. His unassuming personality and shyness around women gave him a more human persona. With his long shaggy red hair and surfer attire, he looked more like a beach bum than the artificial intelligence officer at Enigma.

Carter was a dare devil but when Vernon took him snowboarding at Squaw Valley he realized the kid had nerves of steel and a total lack of the respect for gravity. Carter spent most of the day on his butt until he decided to play it safe and ski. Vernon didn't seem to notice the terror in Carter's eyes the first time he did a double flip and offered to show him how to do one.

If anything happened to that kid someone was going to pay.

"Carter! I found this stuff," Joe said pushing the door of the lab open with his elbow so he wouldn't drop his treasure. He moved up beside Carter. "First aid kit. One Snickers. And," he fished in his pockets after sitting the items on the floor, "these!"

Carter looked down at the two black cell phones in Joe's pudgy hand. "Joe, I could kiss you!"

Joe took a step back. "Hey, I never figured you for a…"

Carter took the phones after he handed the gun to him. "It's refreshing to know that there is at least one person who isn't aware of my womanizing ways."

"Oh. You was kiddin'." He said simply. "Hmm. You and that tall woman you were with ever…" he let his sentence fall, embarrassed he'd even ask.

Carter tapped on the smart phone and smiled over at Joe. "Ever chance we get. She's pretty freakin' awesome, Joe. There are times when I think I've died and" Carter cocked his head slightly as a voice answered on the other end of the phone. "Director? Carter. We're in, but we have a problem."

\* \* \*

*The captain is going to be angry with me again,* Tessa reasoned as she tried to talk herself out of trying to help the Enigma men. What could she do that could possibly make a difference against a man with a gun? One wrong move they might be killed; not something she wanted on her conscious. But then again if she didn't do something they'd probably be shot anyway. Where could Carter be? Was he close enough to have heard the explosion of gunfire? Should she wait? Should she hide? Her stomach growled so loud she grabbed it in fear that the new threat would hear. In the end she decided being safe would mean being sorry. *Dear God, just one more time. Please,* she prayed.

"Sweetie," Tessa said stepping out in the open as she rubbed her eye. "My contact lenses slipped. Can you help me?"

In that split second everything seemed to unfold in slow motion, or she would remember it later like that. The big man with the gun shifted his eyes to her and his gun slightly lowered her way. In that split second Chase leaped toward the man, knocking the barrel of the weapon up so that when he pulled the trigger bullets sprayed upwards. Vernon rolled toward his downed rifle, secured it easily and pushed to his feet, where he quickly put himself in front of Tessa for her protection.

Chase could feel the powerful muscles of the gunman swing around and hit him in the side with the butt of the gun. Momentarily his ability to breathe escaped his body when a jolt of white hot pain threatened to down him. But in that split second he saw the man flinch with a satisfaction of victory.

Lunging forward with all the strength he had left, sent the gunman up against the wall with a grunt of surprise. Although Chase's body, tired from escaping a fire, jumping off a cliff and a strenuous hike, demanded a reprieve, he forced his fists into the gut of his attacker. The gun fell, leaving the giant of a man with two free hands to fight back, which he did with a furiousness that nearly overwhelmed Chase. The blows to his jaw and chest propelled him backwards. With each blow he felt as if darkness would soon overtake him. Then he turned his head slightly to see Tessa step out from behind Vernon, horrified at the beating. Remembering the time she'd out foxed him, Chase reached for the vest of the attacker and jerked him forward enough to ram his knee into his groin. With a sudden growl of agonizing pain the big man stepped back half bent, covering his privates. Chase doubled his fists and slammed them down on his neck sending him sprawling face down on the floor before giving him a swift kick to the ribs. Falling on the man's back, Chase finished the man off by twisting his neck so fast he barely heard the snap of death. Staggering to his feet he turned toward Vernon and Tessa and tried to take a step.

Tessa ran to him and managed to slip under his arm to support him around the waist just as he staggered. Vernon slung his weapon to his shoulder and did the same. "Chase!" was all she managed to say. Blood trickled down from his nose and his cheek had already begun to swell. "You need to sit down. Let me get some water for those cuts," she said as if mothering one of her kids. "What were you thinking fighting somebody so much bigger than you?" she scolded as she eased him down on a blue cushioned stool in the alcove where she had waited. She tore off the ripped hem of her blouse before running it under the spout of the water fountain. As Tessa touched his cheek with the coolness he flinched and grabbed her hand.

"What would you have had me do?" he said taking the wet scrap of cloth from her trembling hands and wiping his nose.

"Shoot him," Tessa said flatly as she put her hands on her hips.

Chase looked up at her in surprise as a chuckle came from Vernon. His one eye that hadn't begun to swell shut shifted to Vernon. "Good idea. Why didn't you shoot him, partner?"

Vernon's eyebrows went up along with his shrug. "Didn't have a clear shot. Besides, I thought you could take him."

"Thanks." He frowned as he let Tessa take the cloth and rewet it. "And you!"

Tessa handed him the cloth. "Don't start. I know I took an awful chance, but he didn't know I was here so I thought…"

"Did you call me sweetie?" he interrupted.

Vernon nodded. "She did."

"Maybe. I don't remember really," she lied. "Besides," she assisted Chase as he tried to stand.

"You are a dangerous woman, Tessa Scott!" he said shaking his head and trying to stand tall to make sure he towered over her enough to make her stop fussing over him. "You're not very good at taking orders are you?"

"What orders?"

He looked at Vernon. "This is why I'm not married."

"Oh I thought it was because…" Vernon stopped when his boss leveled a dangerous look his way. "Never mind."

"Do we need to tie that guy up or something? I would hate for him to get a second wind," Tessa said pointing out into the corridor.

"I don't think that's going to happen." Chase said through clenched teeth. He watched the reality of his kill dawn in Tessa's wide blue eyes as his hand went to his side to examine the spot on his left side where he'd been punched. He raised his shirt to have a closer look when Tessa suddenly put her hand on the bruise. Sucking in his breath at her cold touch forced him to take a step back. "Woman, your hands are like ice!"

Tessa slapped his hand aside and touched him again. "Stop being a baby. I know they are that's why I'm touching you. You'll feel better in a minute." She managed to put both her hands on the ugly bruise with an awkward unsteadiness. Feeling Chase's right arm circle her waist, she managed to gently keep her hands still enough until his heat swallowed her healing touch. Looking up into Chase's face, she found him watching her like an angry lion.

Her daughter's favorite Disney movie was *Beauty and the Beast*. The scene where Belle doctors the Beast's wounds raced to mind and she couldn't help smiling inwardly knowing the Beast was eventually tamed.

"Better?" She slowly removed her hands as she gently lowered his tee shirt over the area. He nodded, but didn't immediately release his hold on her body. "I, I…" she battered her eyes nervously at him, "should get something for those cuts." Timidly, Tessa touched his face and felt him pull away.

"I'm fine. Let's move," he said firmly. "Gotta get the hostages to safety. Any idea where Carter got to," he said turning his eyes on Vernon who had taken a position of watching the corridor for further action.

"Find a female hostage and Carter will be there making sure he's the hero."

"Makes sense. Let's go."

\* \* \*

Straightening up to his full five foot ten inches, Essid looked at Honey still glued to the computer screen. His silence, flaring nostrils and twitching index fingers at his side drew Honey's attention back to him. Essid began to pace like a caged beast.

"We're in trouble, Essid," Honey whispered forcefully. "Chances are the men on the loading dock are dead too. That leaves Mansur, me and the two goons eyeing the women over there like they're a piece of meat. Ever since you said they could have them their attention has been on that, not what we're trying to do here!" Honey stepped so close Essid could feel her breath on his lips. "We've got time to get out. Let's cut our losses and leave while we can," she insisted.

"No!" he snapped as he walked away and began to pace. "Not without destroying this place!"

Zoric sniffed with disgust. "Fine! Blow it to hell, but let these innocent people go. Have some humanity."

Essid stormed up to the Serbian and grabbed him by the throat. "Humanity! When has your country ever shown my people humanity? Was in in Iraq or Afghanistan? How about in Libya when we begged for you to intervene with Kaddafi? And them," he said pointing at the Russians. "They killed my wife merely because she was from Chechnya."

"These Russians had nothing to do with that," Zoric choked feeling Essid's fingers tighten on his windpipe. "They want to make the world a better place."

Sam tried to push Essid with her body to force his release of Zoric. He did so with a back hand slap to her face, knocking her down only to be jerked back up by the hair. He pulled her head back with one hand and slid the other down one breast. "American women try to be like their men." Shoving her into Zoric he smiled. "I will have this one for myself."

Honey angrily stepped in front of Sam. "You are no better than them if you take her!" She shoved on his chest putting distance between him and Sam. "I hate you!" she screamed.

Essid jerked her in his arms and held tightly as she tried to squirm away. "Jealousy becomes you. And all along I thought you were void of any feelings at all," he teased with a condescending tone. He felt her relax within his hold. "Now that's better. Get these two ready to move. We'll take them to the area where the Molybdenum is being stored. I want nothing to be left of them when this place goes."

Honey nodded as her breathing began to return to normal. She turned and slammed Sam up against the wall as she landed a blow to her stomach. "I regret we will not fight to the death," she said listening to Sam gasp for breath.

"Let me loose. Let's do it." Her voice gasped with pain.

Essid held up his hand in impatience. "As attractive as that sounds to me I do not have the time. Mansur, you take them down. I cannot depend on Honey," he said with a smirk, "to not try and kill the beautiful one before time is up. Go!"

Mansur nodded and gave Zoric a shove toward the door. Sam followed obediently as she gave Jericho a fleeting look of regret. He smiled weakly and mouthed he was okay. The two Libyan guards spoke loudly as if disappointed when Sam disappeared through the door. Essid frowned at them so sternly that they soon hushed.

The two military guards reached out and patted Sam on the butt as she passed only to be assaulted by a borage of adjectives and nouns from her pretty mouth. Her onslaught only managed to bring masculine laughter and a volley of insults. She attempted to spit at them but missed.

"Elevator!" Mansur commanded and shoved them in roughly when the door opened. He lowered his weapon to push the first floor button. As he turned to look at his prisoners he saw they had removed their plastic cuffs and held them loosely in front of them. "I was afraid I'd made them too tight," he said with relief. "We can't go to the lobby. Essid will be watching." He touched each floor button. "Let's get off before then."

Sam took the Glock he'd hidden under his shirt in his waistband. "I'm going to strangle Honey Lynch," she warned as Zoric took his knife from Mansur who'd been able to hide it in his boot.

The elevator doors opened slowly to the third floor, soft jazz playing in the background as if it were any other day. Both he and Sam put their hands behind their backs to appear contained as Mansur took a defensive stance.

Waiting with AK-47s aimed at chest level were Carter and the trucker named Joe.

"I was just about to come rescue you," Carter quipped as he lowered his weapon.

Sam snarled as she stepped off the elevator. "We got tired of waiting on you. Figured you'd lost your nerve."

Carter grinned and looked sheepishly over at the trucker. "She gets like this when we're apart for very long."

Sam whirled around and crossly snapped: "What!"

Joe took a step back and nodded respectfully to the beautiful Samantha Cordova. "You kids will be together again before you know it.Sam looked from Joe to Carter with an arched, angry eyebrow. "What's he talking about?"

"You two have a thing. I get it. Carter shared with me how you two…"

Sam shoved Carter so fiercely up against the glass wall it rattled. "A thing! I would rather lay with a pig before I had a 'thing' with him." She shifted her sharp eyes to Joe. "Better yet I'd take you before him!"

Joe lifted his hands in protest. "Wait a minute now. I'm a married man!"

Sam rolled her eyes. "Oh shut up!"

Carter continued his grinning as he straightened and leaned in to whisper in Joe's ear. "I told you she was crazy about me."

Joe shook his head as the team began moving down the hall. "That kind of crazy can get you killed." He began listening to Sam plan all the things she planned to do to Honey Lynch with a little concern. "Why does she hate that Honey person so much?" he said in a low voice.

Zoric heard him and volunteered the information. "Honey killed her cat a few years ago."

Joe looked even more concerned. "She's going to do all that to her over a cat?"

Carter smiled watching the backside of Sam. "The cat was a Bengal Tiger."

## Chapter 29

The air conditioning failed along with other electrical services on timers throughout Global Navigation when Vernon Kemp tinkered with the sophisticated computer systems. They promised to have the ability to sense people working at any hour, any floor, in any office or lab by merely recognizing body heat. Climate would automatically adjust to that area insuring the population of Global Navigation felt no discomfort which might interfere with their work. Wanting to be the poster child for environmental consciousness and responsibility, the buildings had been created with all the latest high efficiency mechanisms known to man in the creation of the plant and operational offices and labs. Unfortunately, when Vernon blocked several climatic sensors and fed in a *"Global Warming"* virus he created, the buildings gradually began to warm. Eventually the rooms would become so warm the computers would sense hot spots releasing the overhead sprinkler systems. They would abruptly stop, sending the air conditioning controls into overload, dropping the temperature down in the fifties. After several hours the process would begin again.

Honey frowned at Mansur when he reentered the room, wiping sweat from his face with the shoulder of his faded shirt. She didn't know how brothers could be so different; one docile and easily manipulated, the other an out of control narcissistic maniac who demanded loyalty from everyone. If she were a better person, maybe her feelings toward Mansur would be more sympathetic, more understanding of the shadow he was forced to stand in next to his brother. The fact remained she just didn't like him. His body odor offended her. His eating habits disgusted her and his broken English grated against her nerves. His long bouts of silence since she'd known him made her uneasy, as if he might be keeping notes on her movements. Then there were those sidelong glances of interest he'd used, exploring her body like fingers of twisted behavior. She shivered even though when she looked at the thermostat on the wall it read ninety degrees.

"Ugh!" She stormed over to the bald computer hostage. "Why is it so hot? I turned the thermostat down twice!"

"There's a systems failure. I can't fix it from here," he said rapidly as if by doing so he'd not suffer her rage.

Honey looked around the room at the hostages. Perspiration glistened on their faces and wet spots appeared under their arm pits. Some of the men still wore their suit coats, but a few had wisely removed theirs shortly after the takeover. The woman with asthma struggled with every breath. The smell of fear filled the room and a hint of urine released from someone too afraid to ask for a restroom break now made close quarters even more unbearable. She glanced at the Haskin brothers, sitting quietly on the floor under the windows, watching her every move. Their legs were outstretched but her hard glare made them pull them up.

"Where did you take them?" Honey demanded of Mansur. "We watched for you on the computer."

Mansur ignored her question by turning to his brother. "The men on the loading dock are alive and waiting. I turned the prisoners over to them." His eyes went to the hostages at the table then the two Libyans standing guard. "They were enjoying themselves when I left," he smiled.

"And the containers?" Essid ask anxiously.

"Secured." Mansur took a step near his brother. Essid was the youngest son of his father. Spoiled and given every advantage, Essid had always taunted his sisters while growing up in Libya. Mansur, the oldest, had been a part of the spoiling until he saw Essid as a teen brutalize one of his sisters and eventually caused her death. She had been a sweet, pretty girl of fifteen when Essid caught her talking to one of his friends. He accused her of a sexual relationship with a man. Although she denied, begged and pleaded, their father threw up his hands in disgust as Essid took her into the desert and left her. Mansur, upon hearing of the incident, went after them, only to find her stoned and ripped apart by wild dogs. "When will we set the charges, brother?"

"It is done. The American military guards outside are experts and knew how to," he paused trying to think of something funny, "get the biggest bang for my buck!" Essid burst out laughing then fanned his left hand in the air as if batting away a fly. The laughing stopped as did the expression on his face. "Did you tell the others to watch for the American captain?"

Mansur nodded humbly. "Of course."

Essid embraced his brother for a moment then released him. "You are my only friend, Mansur. I love you!" he proclaimed warmly.

"And I you, my brother."

"The heat in here feels like our desert, does it not!" he smiled.

Mansur took a step back from his brother and patted his shoulder. "Soon we will return."

"Indeed! With victory and pride running in our veins. Americans are such fools. All this time they trust those of us that walk among them."

Honey sighed in boredom. "Blah. Blah. Blah. Let's go. I'm tired of waiting. Someone is bound to start poking around soon!"

Essid smiled over at her. "It is a good thing you are not an American, Honey."

Honey shifted her weight to one hip and ran her tongue across her lips. "It's a good thing you're good between the sheets or I would have killed you a long time ago."

Essid laughed happily. "We are a perfect pair, Honey Lynch."

\* \* \*

There were two exits, one at the end of each corridor on every floor. Stairs led all the way to the roof for the maintenance people to periodically make needed adjustments to any environmental systems. A narrow catwalk between building AA and BB stretched across the fifteen foot expanse. It existed only for those people traveling between sites to eliminate wasted time completing necessary repairs. Some Global Navigation analysts suggested productivity increased by twenty three percent in that one department alone. The Wall Street Business Journal wrote that with such time saving ideas, leaving more money for research and development set a precedent for any large corporation trying to manage their bottom line.

Due to the expansive roof surface, the helicopter pad had been located there. The second building known only as BB, contained the plant which actually produced the life-saving isotopes. Located at the far end of the building, an elevator hidden among a garden of flowers and a gurgling fountain waited for VIPs that arrived by way of helicopter. Guests, clients and Global Navigation big wigs would take the elevator down to a lobby similar to the one in building AA where Essid's men had taken up positions earlier.

Director Benjamin Clark directed the pilot to make use of the helicopter pad as light faded across the foothills of the Sierras. He already knew the schematics of Global Navigation downloaded to his Enigma phone before he even left Sacramento. The ex-Special Forces, all friends of Chase, on board with Ben, carried the plans in their head, memorized before takeoff. Their rescue mission involved retrieving the scientists and Russian representatives before Essid could harm them. Hostages in other areas would be reached as time permitted. Buildings could be replaced but Russian delegates offering natural resources to reduce the suffering of thousands could not. Ben cringed at the thought of just one death. The American scientists were some of the best in the world. They'd been recruited from Los Alamos, Oakridge, NASA, Missouri University of Science and Technology and MIT. Those were the only ones he knew of without more research. Truthfully, Ben didn't care where they came from. He just didn't want them dead.

Scientists were easy pickings and terrorists had begun their systematic hunt for them on a global scale in recent months. Rather than kidnap them to use their brain power, several Ph.D.'s in molecular energy research had recently disappeared in Germany, only to be found several days later with severed heads outside a remote mountain lodge. The media had been fed a ridiculous story about depression and some kind of gay relationship since both men were single. However, when the female petroleum engineer from Canada disappeared with her family while sailing off the coast of Newfoundland a month ago, counter intelligence agencies across the globe began to take notice of the potential problem. Their boat had been found adrift when she'd not returned to her station in the North Sea two weeks later. It was thought best not to alarm the world's brain bank just yet. In the meantime, governments across the globe committed themselves to keeping an eye on facilities and terrorist groups bent on sending the world back to the Stone Age.

Now that he knew Carter was in place, life appeared to be a little less worrisome. Just as the silent helicopter landed a call came from Captain Hunter, who had secured a phone from the dead hired gun. The captain, Vernon and Mrs. Scott were on their way to the third floor to rendezvous with Carter. After inquiring about Mrs. Scott's welfare, he insisted the captain get her out of harm's way immediately. He didn't want any dead civilians on top of the prospect of losing scientists and a Russian delegation. His thoughts flashed to Mrs. Scott's family so suddenly that he placed his hand over his eyes to remove the image. His brow wrinkled in distaste and irritation, knowing their situation had not been a priority. That had proved to be a mistake. Hopefully the Haskin boys would survive this chain of events.

\* \* \*

Captain Hunter felt Sam hug his neck when he came through the third floor door. She whispered something that made him smile wickedly and nod ever so slightly as if agreeing to something privately held only between the two of them. His eyes went to Trucker Joe next and extended his hand.

"We meet again," he said whole heartedly. He felt Tessa and Vernon slip in behind him. "You remember…"

"I remember her." Joe raised his double chin at her a little cautiously. "Sorry I was rude to you the other day, Melanie."

"Melanie?" she said bewildered. Why did that name keep coming up and sticking to her? "How…"

"Oh! Carter here told me you were one of the top agents." He patted Carter on the back not noticing the ex-astronaut squeezed his eyes shut while wrinkling his nose as a little boy might do trying to sneak into his mother's cookie jar without being caught.

"I see," Tessa said shifting her eyes to the former astronaut whose career she'd followed for as long as she could remember. All the stories of womanizing, goof off stunts and lack of discipline that the press loved to write about had never been embraced by her loyalty. Although amused by

Carter's exaggerated sense of humor, Tessa now realized perhaps her ardent defense of his brilliance and competence wasn't the only thing that led to his dismissal at NASA. "Yes, well apology accepted."

"I am relieved to see you!" Zoric came up alongside of Tessa and nearly reached out to touch her, then seemed to think better of it as his eyes mockingly went to the captain. "I see Chase took good care of you."

"He nearly drowned me."

"Ah!" Zoric displayed a yellow grin. "But you are alive."

Tessa took a step closer to him and whispered. "Mr. Crawley?"

He shook his head. "Not good. He needs a hospital. They separated us. He is a brave man."

Dread gripped her heart, knowing her old neighbor might not fare as well as she had in the end. All the complaining and moaning about covenants of the gated community, the gruff hellos, the constant questions, all sounded endearing to her now. Remembering how he'd collected newspaper articles and pictures of the children playing sports made her long to pat his arm and promise to bake him a batch of her chocolate chip cookies.

Vernon didn't wait to be introduced but disappeared into an office to check the status of his Global Warming virus on one of the computers. He returned within minutes. "I've opened a heat sensor scan of the fifth floor to be sure where everyone is located. It'll boot in two minutes. Had to make sure the other systems remained asleep until we get up there. Secured fifth level door, boss so…" Vernon's eyes shifted from Tessa to Chase.

The look passing between the two men was not lost.

Captain Hunter nodded an acceptance and reached for Tessa, pulling her aside. "This is where we part ways for a bit, Tessa."

"Why? I need to go with you, to help Mr. Crawley."

Sam came up next to Chase, shifting her weapon to the other shoulder as she looked down at the blond housewife who'd been the beginning of this mission. "There's nothing you can do. You'll get us killed," she snapped. Sam sniffed as she jerked her head up in contempt and eyed Tessa harshly. "The captain can't be worried about you when he goes in for those hostages. None of us can."

Her blue eyes lifted to Chase and softened even though he glared sternly at her. "Do I stay here?" The tide of resistance ebbed from her voice as she meekly clasped her hands over her elbows as her arms folded across her midriff.

"No. Vernon sealed the fifth floor door so even if they see you, and I can't imagine they can since they are spread pretty thin now, they won't be able to reach you. Go all the way to the sixth floor. Once there enter the corridor. You'll see another exit at the end on your left that indicates another staircase to the roof. Get up there as fast as you can. The director will be waiting with some of my men."

Again that little girl nod that said *I'm terrified, but I'll do it for you*. Chase reached out and put his hand on her shoulder. "It's just about over."

A weak smile played at the corners of her mouth as she placed her hand on the door knob and turned. "Good luck!"

The door slowly closed against Chase's hip as he stood and watched her quietly steal up the concrete stairs toward safety. When she reached the sixth floor she leaned over far enough where he could see her. A short wave of victory with one hand signaled she'd arrived. Chase backed into the room as Vernon returned to the computer terminal. He sighed looking up at the ceiling and counting how many seconds it would take for her to enter the sixth floor and make her way up to the roof. Glancing down at his watch he felt Sam's disapproving eyes on him.

"I know. This is why having civilians around isn't a good idea." He looked over at the trucker who'd managed to find a candy bar and was making quick haste of it. A tiny bit of chocolate clung to his bottom lip, making Chase remember the Baby Hughie cartoon character he'd watched as a kid when stuck in some embassy with his grandfather's secretary or assistant. They had always seemed to locate a VHS of cartoons to keep him from exploring.

Vernon jerked the door open and skidded into the room with alarm. "Boss!"

The captain frowned, expecting bad news as he stepped toward the computer whiz. "What is it, Vern?" All eyes turned on him. He could tell Vernon's breath came quickly and his face had flushed.

"The fifth floor has twenty hostages like Jamaal said. Two other heat sources are outside one of the doors."

"Okay," Chase said slowly not liking the 'but' which was about to come.

"There are five more heat sources that are walking around on the sixth floor, all of them carrying weapons. The director and your men are still on the roof."

"Tessa!" Chase said opening the door to the stairwell.

## Chapter 30

Stepping through the door on mouse feet, Tessa put her hand back to make sure the door closed softly. She'd turned her head as it touched her fingers and was startled to feel a hand grip the top of her shirt, jerking her around to face the piercing eyes of Honey Lynch. The strength in such dainty arms surprised Tessa. The pale, smooth skin was damp with perspiration but clear and lovely like pictures of Irish girls featured in travel brochures. Her hair, tawny, almost blonde had been pushed behind small ears. It was the rage in her eyes, the flaring nostrils and the clenched teeth that told Tessa the Honey Lynch she'd spoken to on the phone the night before was more dangerous than the captain had led her to believe.

Helpless to resist, Tessa felt her body jerk up against Honey's breasts with a force she thought possible only in a man. Honey weighed probably twenty five, thirty pounds less than her, but the grip holding her felt like something the captain might be capable of. Tessa tried to say something but Honey shook her before a word could come out. In an instant she found her body slammed up against the cool granite tiled wall, her head making immediate contact. The pain ripped through the back of her head so sharply she thought her consciousness would fade, only to find Honey in her face breathing like a devil.

"What the hell are you doing here?" Honey growled angrily. "Where is Hunter?" When Tessa didn't answer with trembling lips, Honey grabbed her again by the middle of her shirt and slung her across the hall. She slid to a stop after crashing into a door with a painful yelp. Awkwardly Tessa tried to stand as she faced Honey. Her hand went to her bruised shoulder as if touching it would ease the pain. It didn't. Tessa began to cower as Honey stormed toward her. Realizing too late that the Irish assassin meant her harm Tessa tried to avoid the butt of the rifle swinging at her temple, only to feel its blunt force make contact. Just before darkness swam up to overtake her another pair of legs appeared. The last thing she heard was a voice with a strange, foreign accent she recognized from an Auburn parking lot where he'd left her to die. "I see Captain Hunter's housewife has come to complicate my life once again."

\* \* \*

The air stale and stagnate in the stairwell hit Chase as he pressed himself up against the concrete wall. Every muscle in his body hurt as he stole a glance through the window of the steel door on the sixth floor. Adrenaline surged through his body, numbing the pain to a bearable level. He'd watched as a Libyan lifted Tessa up to sling her over his shoulder like a sack of flour. Essid motioned for him to take her down the hall as he turned and said something to Honey, who didn't look happy. Chase knew that look. He'd suffered her tantrums when things weren't going as planned. Several times, when they'd worked together with Delta Force, he'd had to physically restrain her to keep her from killing someone and blowing the mission. That look collapsed her usual pretty face into a contorted mask of murderous rage. She walked behind Essid, looking back over her shoulder in paranoia. Chase counted to sixty, knowing wherever they had taken Tessa; she'd be there by now.

He carefully turned the metal handle on the door, wondering momentarily how the stairwell could be so hot and the metal still cool. A quick glance in, then back out, then back in revealed an empty corridor. He heard voices two doors down on the opposite side. They would be alert, knowing he would not have let Tessa go too far without him. Speed was of the essence if he was going to save her. This had not been part of his plan.

Making his way through the door and down the hall came in quick order as he pressed himself up against the wall next to the door. Something caught in his peripheral vision as he jerked his head around only to see Honey Lynch step out of an alcove with her rifle leveled at his gut.

The door opened and Essid stepped out nonchalantly. "I'll take that," he said removing Chase's rifle he'd taken off one of the men on the loading dock. In his haste to reach Tessa, he'd complicated the situation by underestimating Essid.

He straightened to his full height as Honey approached him like a tiger ready to devour her next meal. "You're a fool, Captain Hunter!" she eyed him from head to toe, then back up to his face.

"Experience proved that to me years ago where you're concerned," he said with a nod and a smirk. "I'd forgotten, though, how you like to slither around like the poisonous snake you've become." He then turned his eyes on Essid who glared with nervousness. "This isn't going exactly how you planned is it, Essid? Once again you and your fanatical jihadist misfits have failed to take into consideration the American spirit."

Essid shrugged. "Perhaps. It will be hard for you and whoever you're working for now to underestimate the power of the C4 wired to go off with just one call," he smiled, holding up a phone.

"This place is bomb proof, you idiot." It wasn't but Chase figured it would put a doubt to fester in Essid's disturbed pattern of thinking.

"Hmm." He smiled without a hint of believing Chase. Essid's goons came out and forced the Enigma agent into the room before someone landed a blow to the back over his kidney.

With a howl of pain, Chase went down on his knees to face Tessa, crumbled on the floor with the gash over her right eyebrow reopened and bleeding. Noting the rise and fall of her chest, he realized she was alive. Before he could move toward her he felt a kick to his shoulder, sprawling him onto his face. He was ready when goon number one came at him again, grabbing his foot, twisting it until it snapped. A scream of pain filled the room as he let loose a stream of curses in his language. He pulled himself away, and then used a metal chair to pull himself up. Although broken, the wounded man was able to hobble to where he'd leaned his rifle. He picked it up and started toward Chase.

Honey easily knocked it out of his hand. "Sit down before he breaks your idiot neck!" she snapped. "You're no match for him. He's wasted dozens of men better than you." Her eyes turned to Mansur who kneeled down and poured water over Tessa's face. She began to moan as she pushed herself up into a sitting position. When her eyes focused on the man kneeling before her, Tessa reached out as if a life line had been thrown to her before realizing Captain Chase Hunter had been injured. Sweat poured from his brow mixed with blood.

"Chase?" she whispered in desperation, aware of his concern. His look of encouragement through a deep fog of pain touched her more than she thought possible.

Another goon jerked Chase up forcing a painful groan from his lips. He was slammed into the edge of the table. His weight flipped it onto its side. "You better kill me now you worthless Libyan dog, cause when I get done here I'm going to throw your body into a pig pen and watch them send you straight to hell. No paradise for you," he promised menacingly. "Those virgins will have nothing to do with a man whose laid with the pigs," he grinned revealing clenched teeth.

Essid stepped forward and watched Tessa Scott stand awkwardly with help from his brother. His eyes went from her to Chase as he rubbed his chin with his index finger. "So this is the woman who pretended to steal my first bomb," he said approaching her slowly as he watched Chase try to straighten. Even now, beaten and exhausted, the infamous Captain Chase Hunter was trying to be the hero.

"Please," Tessa said, seeing that Chase might try and help her again. She watched Essid give goon number two a nod who rushed Chase and slammed his fist into his gut. Saliva poured from Chase's mouth just as the goon landed a punch on his lip, cracking it open. Blood gushed out suddenly. Tessa cried out as she tried to lunge for him only to be pulled back by Mansur. "Don't. What do you want? Please stop hitting him!" she begged.

"Where are the others?"

"No!" Chase muttered dropping his head forward, but still possessed the strength to lift his eyes, demanding her obedience.

Essid nodded at goon number two again who landed another gut punch.

Tessa screamed. "Stop! They're on the third floor! They're coming for the hostages."

Essid smiled. "Who are they?"

Tessa knew Essid believed Sam and Zoric to be indisposed with his men on the loading dock. "Carter, the computer man and some trucker."

Essid pointed a nine millimeter at Chase. "What else, Mrs. Scott? Captain Hunter's life depends on it."

Tessa gasped and spoke hurriedly. "There's a helicopter and the captain's men on the roof. I was on my way there."

Essid lowered the gun and winked knowingly. "That's much better. Thank you. I guess my plans have changed yet again thanks to you. We had planned to leave that way and cross to the other building before making my call for the final explosion." He sighed dramatically as he waved his weapon in the air. "These people are not your friends, you know, Mrs. Scott." He watched her frightened face freeze as he looked to Chase. "The man you're trying to save did nothing to save your family when he could have."

Tessa choked. "What about my family?" She looked from Chase to Honey. "Where are they?"

Essid looked over his shoulder at Honey standing awkwardly as if someone had just jammed spikes into her feet. "Do you want to tell her or should I?"

"Tell me what?" Tessa's eyes locked dangerously on Honey. "You told me you'd keep them safe!"

Essid looked around at Honey incredulously. "You talked to her?" he asked bewildered. "Have you been talking to this infidel while sleeping with me?" he roared.

Honey did not bat an eye when she narrowed her gaze at Tessa. "I killed your precious little family last night while they were sleeping." She watched as all the air seemed to be sucked from Tessa's body. It reminded Honey of the video she'd once seen of a nuclear blast. All the wind forces the trees to bend to the ground, the buildings explode and a fiery glow devastates the world. Tessa's scratched hand went to her throat silencing a scream. "To think they trusted me. One more day and I would've had your handsome husband in my pants."

With empowered rage, Tessa charged her, only to be yanked back into Mansur's burley arms. A damn of uncontrollable tears gushed from her eyes as sobs racked her body pressed against Mansur's chest. Screams of torment bounced around the room as Mansur struggled to keep her confined.

Chase cocked his head at Tessa hoping to be able to see her with his good eye, not yet swollen with violence. He knew what was coming. Confession. Betrayal.

With one step toward Honey, Essid slapped her so hard she stumbled back in surprise. "You filthy whore! Are you sleeping with him too?" he roared.

Chase spit blood on the floor trying to draw attention back to him. "Do you think I'd lay with someone who took to the likes of you? From what I hear," he smirked, although his mouth looked crooked, "you're pretty short on satisfaction," again the smirk, "and I do mean short."

Before Honey could dodge, another blow struck her upside the head, knocking her to a sprawled position. Her weapon clattered noisily to the floor as she hurriedly tried to scramble to her feet only to be kicked down again by Essid. "Tie her up!" he said to the Libyan that could still walk. Drag her over there," he pointed to a spot on the floor. Goon number one awkwardly tied a dirty handkerchief tightly around Honey's mouth. Jerking it tighter, Honey struggled only to be kicked in the buttocks.

"Although I would love to see how this plays out," Essid motioned for Chase's hands to be tied behind his back before being shoved into a chair with wheels that nearly toppled with the sudden slamming of his weight. A gag immediately was shoved into his mouth. "I think Mansur and I need to make our way out of here before I incinerate this place." He stepped toward Tessa and yanked her from Mansur, shoving her back so she stood in front of Honey. The sobs had been replaced with sniffs as she looked with pure hatred down at Honey Lynch.

Honey struggled against her bonds as she looked up at Tessa with wide eyes. Stealing a look at Chase she tried to say something only to see that he too was trying to communicate with Tessa, not her. Essid stood over her and frowned. "I had hopes for you, Irish trash. Isn't that what the beautiful Sam called you?" He turned to the two Libyan goons as he walked toward the door. He handed them a small pistol he took from inside his vest pocket. "Mrs. Scott?" Tessa turned like a robot to glare at her tormenter. "When I leave, this man will give you a gun. It has one shot. Use it however you choose," he smiled. "Decisions. Decisions. Will it be Honey who actually killed your family or," he looked at Chase who desperately tried to get Tessa's attention as he shook his head 'no'. "Or will it be Captain Hunter who had it in his power to alert authorities and stop her?" Essid watched as Tessa shifted her eyes back and forth between his two captives as she wiped snot, tears and blood from her grief contorted face. "It can only be one." He motioned for Mansur to leave ahead of him before looking back at his men and whispering. "When she is done kill the other one."

"And the woman," his man said looking over at Tessa.

Essid shrugged. "Whatever you please. Just be quick about it if you want to get out of here alive." He nodded and closed the door behind Essid.

With outstretched hand, the Libyan moved to Tessa's side and handed her the loaded weapon.

* * *

The evening at Lake Tahoe once again remained cool and crisp. Tourists meandered slowly from shop to shop, café to café. Music began to drift over the lake as a black SUV passed through the traffic of Incline Village. Darkness fell quickly up here and the Scott family couldn't make out the lodge they'd been ushered to at Squaw Valley once again. Robert looked at the bulky driver before turning his head to look in the backseat at his three kids fighting sleep in the hopes of just one more swim in the pool before bedtime. He'd been awakened the night before by pounding on the door. FBI agents, in full military style outfits, startled him by their aggressive behavior. They quickly told him a female forest ranger had tipped them off as to their location.

"You mean Honey," he said bewildered. "I don't understand."

"Honey works for us, Mr. Scott. She's been tracking a mob boss out of Vegas who killed three people last week in the desert. An eye witness came forth but by then he'd skipped. This cabin you're renting actually belongs to his ex-wife, who by the way disappeared last year. We think he's nearby. Honey spotted him in town after she left you. Get your kids. We're taking you some place safe while we finish this. Sorry for the inconvenience. We'll do right by you."

Robert had tried to reach Tessa but only got an answering machine. When he and the children were settled in the luxurious resort accommodations, he noticed a message from her. Her voice seemed a little too calm. Tessa's confidence in Robert gave him assurance she wouldn't try and look for them in the middle of the night. "Sounds exciting, babe. Talk to you soon. Kiss the kids for me. I'm having a good time too." He had no way of knowing it wasn't really Tessa's voice only a reproduction of what Tessa sounded like.

He'd frowned at the message. Had she lost her mind? Why wasn't she demanding they come home? Was that even her voice? Maybe he didn't sound concerned enough when he'd left the message. But then again he really had tried to make light of the situation. Secretly he had wanted her to inform him in so many words she was either coming up to take over or he should get his butt home where her babies would be safe. It never happened so he continued the vacation without her at Squaw Valley.

Squaw Valley had been the site of the 1960 Olympics. There were fun places to have your picture taken if you wanted to pretend you were receiving a gold medal. The scenery took your breath away anywhere you looked. He and the children had taken the tram up the mountain, went ice skating, swam, and explored every shop and café before their FBI driver had offered to take them into town for a little shopping. Sean Patrick couldn't get enough of the big guy and asked him a million questions. All were answered with patience and respect as they ate dinner by the lake that night. Robert had a few questions of his own but the driver always seem to evade a direct answer.

*Government bullies,* he thought silently. *No telling who really owned that cabin.* The thought occurred to him that maybe the president needed it to go over some peace accord in the Middle East. That would make this guy Secret Service, not FBI. He didn't really care at this point. Tessa would be proud of his sudden spark of imagination. The kids thought he was a superhero and the government would pick up the tab for everything. Tessa wouldn't need to know the money saved on this little trip would now enable him to buy that golf club he'd been wanting but couldn't afford. No cooking, picking up after the kids or spending money; this was turning out to be a relaxing vacation after all. He just needed to make sure he looked a little ruffled with exhaustion so Tessa would fuss over him upon returning home.

A slight pain of guilt once again surfaced as he thought of the way he had been treating her of late. He left everything for her to do: kids, yard, pay bills, make sure repairs were done, cook, clean, and of course the nonstop laundry saga. Some days he worked twelve and thirteen hours at the law firm. He just didn't feel like doing much when he got home. Tessa worked so hard at making their lives perfect. He'd forgotten how wonderful and beautiful she could be. The children adored her, the church depended on her and former parents of students often dropped by the house to just say hello. She always had time for a down and out friend or make a batch of cookies for that cranky old fart next door who complained about everything. He'd never understood why Tessa put up with him. Robert smiled at the children. Sighing, he admitted to himself that he knew why Tessa did all those things. She did them because she loved them. That woman was his angel. This important lesson she'd thrown at him was a gift. When he saw Tessa in a few days nothing was going to stop him from showing her how proud he was of her.

Removing the small box from his pocket, Robert lifted the lid. The necklace he'd purchased was a sterling silver cross with a cubic zirconia diamond in the center. He and the kids had picked it out at the jewelry store next to the restaurant at Squaw Valley. Heather made the final decision deeming it "pretty enough for Mommy". The boys caved, having picked out a turquoise bear to celebrate their brave encounter. But when Robert suggested they might not want to bring that up around their mother, they gave way to Heather's choice. Tessa would love it. She would insist on wearing it immediately, promising the kids to never take it off then would lovingly kiss him for being so thoughtful and sensitive.

His heart missed her. That forest ranger certainly made an impact on him. She'd flirted, laughed and wasn't so subtle about her availability. Had it all been a trick to distract them from her real purpose? His thoughts began comparing Honey and Tessa. Some kind of mental checklist appeared, as only a lawyer likes to do, comparing and arguing the merits of both women. In the end, Tessa's attributes surpassed Honey's with a considerable lead. Closing his eyes he could almost feel her soft, unblemished skin between his fingers. How had he been so lucky to marry such a woman? He unbuckled his seatbelt as the SUV came to a stop outside their fancy resort cabin. As the beefy driver helped the boys out of the backseat, Robert gathered Heather up in his arms, noticing her curly hair felt just like Tessa's. He walked up the steps as the driver opened the door and flipped on the lights. He hoped his wife had not worked too hard while they were gone. A smile played around the corners of his lips. Probably took long baths and naps every day, he mused. That would be okay too. She deserved it.

\* \* \*

"Carter?" Vernon said as he watched Zoric and Sam check their weapons. "They just beat the hell out of the captain and Honey is incapacitated." Vernon had located which room Essid had taken Tessa and the captain by using his heat sensors. Finding the computer access to the room had been child's play for him. They could actually watch the movement of each person in the room.

Carter frowned at seeing his friend beaten, bound and gagged. "We can't worry about them now. We've got to get those people off the fifth floor before Essid melts this place down."

"What about them?" Joe said pointing to the computer.

Zoric pushed passed him toward the door. "They're on their own for now."

"Essid and Mansur are taking the elevator to the lobby." Vernon informed them as he grabbed his rifle. "The stairwell is clear."

Sending Joe to the sixth floor stairwell door had been a last second decision. Setting a five minute lock time on the door would prevent the last two Libyans from surprising them. Chances were they'd panic and use the elevator. By the time they had the hostages to the door, locks would be released. Elevators were to power down at the same time. Escape would have to be through the roof.

"Let's move, people!" Carter ordered. "If Mansur can't handle his brother, we're all going to be front row center to a Libyan bar-b-que."

## Chapter 31

The heat forced sweat mixed with blood into Tessa's eyes as she tried to wipe her head and nose on her shoulder. Her hand shook nervously as she lifted the gun to aim at Honey. She wasn't sure if it was aimed at her chest or her head; it didn't really matter. Tears threatened to blind her already foggy vision as she pictured her children trusting this woman who pretended to care for them. The handsome face of Robert, smiling, teasing her about playing all day with the children instead of paying the bills tugged warmly at her heart strings. All the picnics, Christmases, and vacations at the lake would be held only in pictures if this terrible information were true. How could she exist without them? Why would God let this happen? But then again why did any tragedy in the world occur?

Men like Essid created chaos and disaster for their own glory. It had nothing to do with Islam or being American. It had to do with being evil. They destroyed anything that threatened their narrow world view and kept decent people terrified to stand up and resist. Tessa had to admit her resistance evaporated when Honey blurted out she'd killed her perfect family. Revenge blinded her now. She'd become just like them.

Reason pushed into the back of her mind as her eyes cut to Chase shaking his head vehemently and trying to speak through the gag. "I trusted you!" she screamed at him one last time before turning her back to him. Then walking behind Honey she kneeled down and shoved the gun in the back of her neck with one hand.

Honey stiffened, feeling the weapon push against her brain stem. Unlike Chase, she did not try to talk. It was as if she'd accepted her fate and waited patiently for Tessa to pull the trigger. Her eyes went to the amused Libyans as she felt Tessa's free hand jerk her head back by the hair. As she released her grip, she felt Tessa's breath on her ear. "What you did..." Tessa choked. "Why would you do such a thing?" Honey felt Tessa's hand slide down her back and to her plastic cuffs. "I wish I could kill you for every life you took from me!" Tessa growled. "I hope you burn in hell, Honey Lynch." Tessa stood up next to the woman she'd trusted with her children, her gun held loosely in her hand. "Are you," Tessa swallowed knowing what was going to happen next. Would she be sorry later? This too didn't matter. "Are you ready?" she asked again. Honey looked up at her with resolve in her eyes, hearing Chase trying desperately to free himself to save the assassin. Honey nodded slowly and turned her eyes back to the Libyans.

Tessa took a half step back as Honey swung her arms around with lightning speed. She aimed the knife Tessa had taken from her jeans, hurling it into the chest of the closest Libyan. Before Tessa realized it, Honey had sprung to her feet and slapped the gun from her hand and turned it on the second man, firing before he could even lift his weapon. Stunned by her speed, Tessa turned to Chase, pulling the gag from his mouth. He stared at her with his good eye in disbelief.

"Here!" Honey removed the knife from the chest of the Libyan, wiping the blood carelessly on the leg of her faded jeans before tossing it to Tessa. She stole a look out the door. "Cut him loose. Hurry. We don't have much time!"

Tessa cut the cuffs and helped Chase stand. He appeared to shake off the pain as Honey tossed him a rifle. "Here come the hostages, Chase. We better hurry them along."

When Honey slipped out into the hall the first bald computer hostage saw her and quickly turned to run. Zoric and Sam cut him off and shoved him around. "She's with us. Now get movin'," Zoric snipped. "Now!"

When the last of the hostages came through the door, Carter appeared and ran to Chase with concern. "You look like hell, buddy. Who's your friend?" he said looking at Honey Lynch.

Chase smirked. "Seriously, Carter? You're looking to score at a time like this?"

"Haste makes waste," he said as they followed the last hostage up the ladder to the roof. "Are you two…" implying a romantic connection.

"No!" Chase said as he reached the roof. His hand still clung to Tessa's as he hobbled after the team. He watched Director Clark wave them across the narrow catwalk in what little light remained and then over to the helicopter. The helicopter once full lifted off to take their precious cargo to a safe place before returning for the rest of the team. They were gambling that Essid had not planned to bomb his only escape route. The team left behind felt confident in waiting until the helicopter returned for them. In the meantime they would try and locate Essid and Mansur, taking the appropriate measures when needed.

"Let's go!" Chase said starting out over the catwalk as he tugged on Tessa's hand only to find her resisting with her heels dug in. "What's wrong? Come on this place is going to blow!"

"I'm" Tessa looked over the edge of the six story building. "I'm afraid of heights. I can't."

Chase jerked her arm violently. "Get over there now or so help me I'll give you something to really be afraid of, Tessa Scott!"

He felt her backing away as her eyes returned to the space separating the two buildings. The solar lights began glowing as twilight turned to dark. It was hard to understand how a catwalk made of metal could present such terror. Granted there was only a half inch tube railing with protection slacks every three feet, but unless there was an earthquake the chances of a person falling was almost nonexistent. The thought of a bomb going off underneath them presented a bigger nightmare in his mind than walking across a noisy bridge you could see through to the ground level. But then again danger, risks and impossible situations followed him wherever he went. He tended to measure the danger by how many lives were lost or how many of his bones got broke. So far this hadn't been so bad. The last few days must be spinning out of control for someone like Tessa Scott. He looked around to see the helicopter returning for them. The other team members motioned for him to hurry who were safely on the roof of the other building. Chase grabbed her around the waist, squeezing her so hard he winched with pain.

"I got you, Tess." He brought his face so close their noses touched. She reached up and laid her hand on his wounded cheek. The fate of her family still clouded her judgment, yet she was compelled to put her life in the captain's hands once more. Their eyes locked in some unknown resolve as she nodded acceptance of yet another trial.

The sound of metal rattled beneath their feet as they awkwardly stumbled across the grated catwalk. It wasn't wide enough for two to walk side by side so Chase walked sideways pulling her gently along, one step at a time. "Almost there, Tess! Don't look down!" he yelled as she seemed to freeze, eyes turning downward in horror. He once again felt her try to step back just as something pinged off the railing, stinging his thigh. Looking down he saw Essid aiming a rifle at him. The Enigma teammates raised their weapons and started firing unsuccessfully at the target. Essid had stepped back into the shadow of the BB building so he couldn't be seen, except by Tessa and Chase.

"Faster!" he yelled at Tessa as he pulled her behind him to use his body as a shield. Another shot bounced off the grate between their feet causing Tessa to hop suddenly and lose her footing. A scream split the air. Chase felt Tessa slipping away from him as her body slid between the widely spaced slats. He caught her by her collar with one hand, feeling the fabric start to rip away, as the other went instinctively under her arm. He jerked her upward with what strength he had left. Chase's weapon clattered to the ground below all the while, struggling to hold on to Tessa. Stealing a glance downward, Chase could barely make out the bulk figure of Mansur running to Essid's side. He knocked the gun from his brother's hand just as he pulled the trigger. Shots sprayed precariously close.

Zoric made quick haste, jumping down to assist Chase with Tessa who still dangled from the catwalk. Awkwardly, Zoric kneeled down and reached out to grab Tessa under the other arm. Carter rushed in behind the two men hoping to get a shot at Essid. Once Tessa regained her footing on the bridge, Zoric put his arm around her to force her forward movement. The space, now crowded with four people gave Tessa a feeling of safety. She extended her hand back towards Chase, afraid they were leaving him to fend for himself. "I'm coming! Go!" he yelled as Carter now used his body to protect Chase as he hobbled behind him.

Before Chase and Carter could reach the other side Essid reached the gun his brother had knocked from him. He first lifted it at the catwalk, but seemed to think better of it and turned it on his brother Mansur. Essid watched his brother stumble backwards, falling carelessly to the ground. Frightened, Mansur began to crab crawl back away from Essid in fear as his brother sprayed insults and damnation at him. Mansur's eyes bulged as a clap, echoing across the air, stopped Essid. Feeling something penetrate his upper back then exit his lower abdomen, he looked down to see a red spot forming with dangerous speed. He slowly turned and looked up at Carter, who'd taken the shot. Carter's weapon, still poised and ready, did not waver with the possibility of needing to take a skill shot. Essid could now see Chase standing next to his team mate. Essid imagined the captain smirking in victory.

Everyone had abandoned him: Mansur, Honey, his men, and his cause. Why had Allah let this happen? He had to admit in that split second that he had never really believed in his faith. It had been a cause of convenience for his hate. He continued to look up as his hand reached in his pants pocket for his phone. At lease he could make the call by pushing just one button, any button, on his programed cell. He felt the button press under his index finger and smiled.

Nothing rumbled. No sound of shattering glass. No cracks and groans of concrete as it began to fall in on itself. He pushed the button again. And again. Blood began to ooze from his mouth as he crumbled to the ground. Mansur crawled to his side and gathered him in his arms.

"Once you came out here, the man they call Vernon," Mansur looked up to see Vernon looking over the edge of Building BB holding a laptop, "was able to jam any signal you tried to send. The building will not fall, my brother. Your hatred has destroyed you. The lion's breath came near without you ever noticing." Essid continued to watch the men above as they disappeared onto the roof of the second building. He grabbed his brother's arm as the last breath left his body. Mansur carefully laid his brother's body down on the ground and closed his eyes with his hand. "I am glad you are dead." He stood painfully, feeling the punches his younger brother had inflicted on his aging body. There was no doubt in his mind that it would have been only a matter of time before Essid turned his killer ways on him. That fear had been taken care of by the Americans. His life could now be his own once more.

Ben patted Tessa on the back as Chase and Carter joined them at the helicopter. Zoric and Sam were stowing the weapons as Vernon slipped inside. "I think she's got a dislocated shoulder, Chase. The faster we can put it back the easier the pain will be."

Chase could see that Tessa's left shoulder jutted forward slightly. He reached out and gently laid his hand on her forearm. "Tessa, remember I told you about my parents being medical missionaries?" She smiled weakly and nodded. "I used to help all the time with their medical practice. I even served at a medic in the army for a while. I can fix this. It's gonna hurt like hell but not so much later." Taking a step toward him Tessa wrinkled her nose, knowing this was going to be painful. Chase quickly grabbed her arm and twisted it, bent her elbow then flipped it out. She gritted her teeth so not to scream. "I'm sorry, babe," he said realizing he'd failed. Motioning for Carter to stand behind her he nodded at Tessa. "Keep her still, will ya?" Chase told her this time it would work, although he wasn't so sure. But the shoulder did pop back into place as Tessa jerked her head up in pain, but held her scream tightly in her chest. "Better?" Chase said bending down to look into her blue eyes squinted in pain. She nodded quickly with a hint of a smile on her lips as Chase watched her eyes roll back in her head. Her knees buckled and her dead weight collapsed in unconsciousness. Chase tried to stop her body from hitting the ground but was too weak.

Carter caught her lifting her body up into his capable arms. He moved toward the open doors of the helicopter. "I got this, buddy." He handed her off to Zoric who gently laid her down in an open space in the middle between the seats.

Chase climbed in like an old man. He couldn't even drag himself into a seat, so he sat down by Tessa as the others quickly found their place. In moments the helicopter lifted up and out over the dark forest. Small fires still burned, but it seemed the worse was over. Chase closed his eyes. His body ached and he thought he might sleep for a week. He felt Sam's hand on his shoulder but didn't acknowledge her comforting touch. She finally withdrew it. The movement of the helicopter hurt his wounds, but knowing the series of events which nearly spiraled out of control and was now concluded, gave him some comfort.

He felt Tessa's head turn and rest against his leg. Without thinking he laid his hand on her hair, feeling the blond curls push between his fingers like silky threads. Touching the gash over her eye, blood once again seeped out. Someone handed him an antiseptic patch and some gauze. Applying the bandage caused her to flinch, but her eyes remained closed. It wasn't until her once soft hand, now scratched and scarred for life, reached up and laid her fingers on his that he realized Tessa Scott would survive this ordeal. For the remainder of the trip, Chase kept his hand entwined with Tessa's, knowing their lives would soon separate and travel different paths.

After arriving back at headquarters in Sacramento, most of the Enigma personnel had retired for the day. It was late, and all danger had been averted, at least for this particular day in time. The Enigma team walked slowly through the underground parking garage, silently holding in their sense of accomplishment. After passing through several levels of security, the team admitted themselves to the medical floor to be patched up and checked over. Honey resisted at first but after a cross word from Benjamin Clark, she decided to let the doctors tend to her cuts.

The diffused overhead lighting and soft beeping of lifesaving equipment began slowing down everyone's adrenaline. Food, drinks and pain killers began to work its magic on their bodies. Tessa found a metal chair with a padded seat in the hall and sat down carefully, as if by doing so the sore muscles would stop their throbbing. The doctor had been extremely gentle with the exam. Suggesting a sling for a few days, he assured her the shoulder would heal and only a tiny scar would remain after the stitches disappeared from her face. The Enigma psychiatrist, Dr. Wu, dropped by to see her and gave her his card. He wanted to see her in a couple of weeks as a follow up to her ordeal. Tessa assured him she would not need him. With a knowing smile, he moved on saying he'd see her soon.

She bowed her head to stare at the floor while resting her hands on her knees. Counting each breath, then each heartbeat, reassured her that she was still alive. Something inside her wanted to move to a couch or at least an armchair with a pillow for her back, but that would involve standing up and moving again. It wasn't until she saw two boots stop in front of her feet that she realized she wasn't alone. It took effort, but Tessa managed to slowly look up at the larger than life Captain Chase Hunter. He looked down at her with interest and concern. She couldn't tell what his expression was because his eye and cheek, swollen and bruised, gave nothing away as to his mood. She blinked quickly, expecting some kind of reprimand about being such a baby when it came to heights. He said nothing as he continued to stare at her. Finally, he awkwardly got down on one knee and laid his large hands on top of hers. He then revealed a smile, as he squeezed her fingers.

"Those pain killers are going to make you feel like a million bucks in a few minutes."

Tessa tried to smile, although her face hurt when she did. "Good," she whispered, feeling the warmth of his hands spread through her fingers. It felt good. She was cold. The air conditioner must have been turned down to sixty, she reasoned. No other words came as they searched each other's face, trying to find the person they met just a few days earlier.

Chase extended his hand and snapped his fingers. Tessa noticed for the first time a man in camouflage army fatigues approach suddenly and handed Chase a phone. How did a person know what the captain wanted when he snapped those demanding fingers? Would she ever have that power? It took a second, but Chase connected with someone who he gave simple directions.

"I need that live video now." Tessa didn't move as Chase turned the Enigma phone around and held it up eye level.

Tessa could see her boys rubbing their eyes and leaning on their father as he patted their heads. He held Heather who slept on his shoulder, hugging him like there was no tomorrow. Disappearing into a bedroom he soon returned and took the boys into the kitchen to make them a snack. Light laughter floated toward her as the realization that her family remained safe reached her heart. When her eyes left the screen to look at Chase he turned off the phone, handing it back to the soldier who'd produced it. "I told you they would be okay." His voice, although hoarse, was low and comforting. "Why did you cut Honey free? How did you know she was helping us?"

Tessa tried to remember cutting the ties loose so Honey could save them. She wrinkled her forehead in pain as she shrugged. "I donno." She tried to lift her arm on the side where her shoulder had been dislocated. It was too sore to lift. Chase noticed the movement and reached up to move the curl that had fallen across her forehead and into her eye. "You said things would not be as it seemed before I left you in the woods. Remember?"

Chase didn't. He couldn't possibly have known things would have gone so wrong once they were inside.

"Mansur told me when he grabbed me from attacking Honey that my family lived. I remembered then what you said." She swallowed as she felt

Chase's hand trail down her arm and rest again on her fingers. Taking a deep breath, Tessa grinned. "That night at the motel she sounded so sincere. I-I believed her."

"You are the bravest woman I know," he praised as his hands tightened around hers.

In that moment when he pushed himself up, Tessa came up with him into his arms that closed around her tightly. She felt his lips on the side of her head and the warmth of his back beneath her hands. "I will never forget you, Captain Hunter."

Sam rolled her sleeve back down as she looked through the glass wall at Chase pulling Tessa up into his arms. Something about Tessa had won her respect, not that she would need to tell her. Tomorrow her competition would return to life in Grass Valley.

Honey Lynch tucked her shirt into her pants as she cocked her head at Sam standing next to her. Her back was to the glass and couldn't see Sam's interest.

"So, Sam. You and Chase ever…" Honey asked sarcastically.

"No," she quipped. She nodded to the glass so that Honey turned around and stared with displeasure at the woman she'd saved hours earlier. "When you and Chase were together did he ever look at you like that?" Honey frowned and moved toward the door. Sam chuckled as she cooed. "I'll take that as a 'no'."

The sounds of morning tickled Tessa's dreams until she realized the bed she slept in was not her own. Stiffness prohibited her from rolling to her back as she opened her eyes to survey the surroundings. The room looked like a college dorm, small, sparsely furnished with a tiled floor that someone had thrown down a short piled rug to give it a little warmth. Bed springs creaked with the slightest movement. Although the mattress wouldn't win any awards, it was comfortable enough. The blanket around her shoulders smelled clean. A small window let the east sun flood into the room while the soft breathing of the air conditioner made Tessa pull the blanket tighter around her body. What was it with these people and cold rooms?

Four feet across from her rested another bed against the wall. Someone moved in it as a white sheet slipped away from the face of Samantha Cordova. Tessa reluctantly admitted that this woman even looked stunning first thing in the morning. She experienced extreme annoyance at that realization. Carefully Tessa swung her bare feet onto the cool floor, looking down at the same dirty clothes she'd been wearing for two days. Her mouth felt like a camel had been trampling around in it and body odor made her nose wrinkle in distaste. Her eyes went to Sam who stirred. Tessa guessed the woman probably smelled like a flower and managed to not so much as get a snag on her designer jeans. She wouldn't be surprised if under that sheet was some kind of a futuristic weapon as well.

"What are you looking at?" Sam asked crossly without opening her eyes.

"Sorry. I didn't mean to wake you, Sam." She watched as Sam stretched lazily then sat up in much the same manner as Tessa.

With limited communication, Sam led Tessa to the showers and provided her with clean clothes and other essentials to make her feel like a human being again. Following after Sam like a dutiful puppy, Tessa realized she was starving when they entered the cafeteria. The other team members were already eating a hardy breakfast of bacon, eggs, hash browns and toast. Chase had even added a stack of pancakes with maple syrup. They were all talking at the same time about a new car for Chase, Carter's latest female conquest, and Vernon's latest conspiracy theory. Zoric watched them in amusement as he patted an empty seat next to him for Tessa. She sat down with her French toast and bacon as Sam scooted in tightly next to Chase. Even though he had a mouth full of pancake, he managed a special smile for Sam who reached over and removed a dot of maple syrup from the corner of his mouth that she quickly sucked off her finger.

Tessa sat quietly, captivated by these people who had filled her life in the last week. Nothing indicated lives had been lost or that the United States had suffered a terrorist attack. There was no talk of the dead, isotopes or Essid. All was right in the world for what anyone outside this building knew. How would she ever be able to go on knowing that evil men bent on harming her way of life existed in her own land? As she shoved the last piece of drippy French toast into her mouth, the answer came to her. She could go on because men and women like these at Enigma stood ready to do whatever it took to protect this country.

Chase had not directly spoken to her since last night. He'd handed her off to Sam around midnight. They were all sleeping in house so they could get the early morning briefing out of the way. The medical staff wanted to keep them close in case of problems and the resident shrink wanted to observe them in case any peculiar problems surfaced. Now those dark eyes landed on Tessa as if seeing her for the first time. He nodded casually but didn't inquire as to how she was faring this morning.

Being summoned to Director Benjamin Clark's office put everyone in a quieter mood. Breakfast trays returned the group headed up to the office where several hours of debriefing would commence. Having everything out in the open sobered the team. Causalities reported and counted, damage assessment discussed, problems of security to be addressed, brought home to Tessa the reality of how close to death she had been. She gripped the arms of the wooden chair where she sat, feeling the overwhelming disregard Enigma felt for their personal safety. Her eyes darted to each one. The sense of being among incredible valor seemed to be lost on everyone in the room but her.

The cafeteria hosted lunch for them, but it wasn't more than pizza and salad. They ate in a conference room where once again, small talk over rode national security. Tessa found Ms. Coleman and apologized for her bad behavior on their first meeting. She waved it off, saying it certainly was refreshing to see Samantha Cordova have a melt down over someone other than herself. The doctors all had another crack at them including Dr. Wu.

Night had fallen driving Tessa once more to her cramped quarters for a much needed rest. Other than a pain pill she didn't require a sleep aid. Her body fell limp into the mattress that had seen better days.

The following day followed a similar pattern with quiet voices in rooms where reports were entered on computers and follow ups with foreign states were briefed. Chase, never very far from her, sat hunched over satellite images on his computer. Once he strolled past her and laid a hand on her good shoulder with a slight squeeze. When Tessa lifted her eyes to his he almost smiled before walking away. Then the call came to return to Benjamin Clark's office to pick up where they'd left off the day before. Tessa could see that sunset purpled the sky outside Ben's window.

"Do you have any questions, Tessa?" the director inquired matter of fact.

"Where is Honey?" Tessa had wondered about her since she'd awakened earlier in the day.

"Gone," was the only answer given her. Before Tessa could speak again, he brought his hands together palm to palm as if going to pray. "Mr. Crawley was taken to the hospital for a few days. The FBI wants to have a conversation with him."

"Good luck with that," she mumbled loud enough for Zoric to hear and chuckle. "Mansur?"

Chase rubbed the stubble on his jaw. "On his way back to Libya. He can do us more good there than here. He's a good man."

The phone buzzed on Ben's desk and he lifted it up to his ear casually. As he listened his brow furrowed and his eyebrows met over his hawk like nose. Clicking off, he returned the phone to its cradle and looked at Chase, then Tessa.

"It would seem that your husband and children gave our man the slip when he went to get some carryout." Tessa froze. "He's on his way back to Grass Valley."

The entire team stood and turned to Tessa. "I don't know how to thank you. I'm not sure if I can say goodbye. You have given me," they waited uneasily, "you've given me a headache, a scratched face and enough nightmares to last a life time," she laughed. They seemed to be relieved at her teasing and one by one embraced or shook her hand.

Sam did neither and chose to glare judgingly at her. "Good job, Betty Crocker."

"Thanks, Sam!" Tessa beamed with the crumb of appreciation. "Maybe we can go shopping some time or go out to lunch."

Sam rolled her eyes impatiently as she brushed past her. "Don't be ridiculous."

Tessa covered her mouth so she wouldn't laugh out loud and draw angry attention to herself from the Enigma diva. She looked at Ben and Chase happily. "I think she likes me!"

The director tossed Chase his keys. "Since your Hummer was lost in the fire take my car. Zoric better tag along. Mrs. Scott tends to get my people in trouble. Maybe if there are two of you I can count on you returning in a timely fashion. Good luck to you, Mrs. Scott. And thanks for everything you did." The director's minivan had surprised Tessa. Somehow she thought, given his personality, he might drive a tank to work. There were hints of a woman in his life and a small child, a girl, Tessa thought. It smelled of spilled cappuccino and McDonald's fries. A couple of Cheerios clung to the corner of the front floor mat. A tube of lipstick rolled around in the cup holder and coins worth no more than a dollar slid loudly as Chase whipped the van into the gated subdivision Tessa called home. He pulled in Mr. Crawley's drive and quickly joined Zoric and Tessa as they exited the blue minivan.

Touching his ear, Chase took Tessa by the arm with his free hand noting that Zoric had already slipped his arm through her other arm. They guided her across the lawn to the porch, then front door. "They're twenty minutes out. Highway patrol helped us out by pulling them over for a bit. Then the inspection guys on the state line decided to examine every suitcase and package in the car."

Tessa knew Robert's patience could be measured in inches so he probably would be in a bad mood by the time he arrived. "When he sees the mess inside the house he'll probably ask for a divorce," she mused as Chase swung the door open to her home she'd left in shambles.

Claudia, the librarian, stood alone in the foyer that ran between the dining room and living room. She pushed her glasses up on her nose and smiled shyly as she hugged her computer tablet up to her chest. "Surprise," she said clearing her throat.

Gasping at the rooms before her, Tessa thought she'd just walked into a model home by Pottery Barn. Furniture, sleek and contemporary mixed with her antique pieces that hadn't been damaged by the gunman. Shiny wood floors, freshly painted walls and new light fixtures completed the look. Her heart pounded as Claudia handed her the Pottery Barn catalog she'd been saving for ideas. Tessa then remembered Chase handing it to Claudia the day they'd returned to look for a bomb.

"I hope it meets with your satisfaction, Mrs. Scott." Claudia handed Tessa a black folder of information concerning the decorating choices, location of services used and a certificate "This certificate proclaims you won a $70,000 make over contest as advertised in your favorite magazine."

"Which one?" Tessa said wide eyed as she went over the room in amazement.

"Pick one. It doesn't matter, Mrs. Scott. What does matter is that your husband believes it. From what I understand that shouldn't be a problem."

Tessa grabbed the black woman in a bear hug and squeezed so hard her glasses tilted on her nose. Once released, Claudia straightened her glasses then her clothes impatiently and walked outside toward Mr. Crawley's driveway. Looking around like Alice in Wonderland, Tessa put her hands over her heart and smiled at Chase then at Zoric who seemed to be pretty proud of themselves.

"Thank you," she said with deep emotion.

Zoric winked at her and leaned in to kiss her cheek. "Coffee. Soon."

She nodded as he left Chase alone with her. "Remember. Robert cannot know about us or what you've been up to. Got it?"

"You want me to lie to my husband, is that it?" she frowned.

"That's exactly what I want you to do." Chase didn't like goodbyes or hollow promises about tomorrow. He just needed to leave and be done with her so he could go talk to the doctor about this recurring pain in his chest, like now. He touched his ear. "They're almost here." He turned to leave when he felt Tessa's hand on his arm.

"Chase" was all she needed to say for him to swing her up in his arms and embrace her tightly. She felt a kiss on her cheek as he released her and darted out the door.

For a few moments Tessa became lost in thought about the surge of warmth she felt for the captain. The sound of car doors slamming, loud boyish voices and a little singing girl, drew Tessa's attention outside. Lazily, Tessa moved through the open front door to see Robert hurrying to her. "I'm sorry! I'm sorry for being a jerk. I promise I'll be a better husband and a father from now on, Tessa."

Tessa stepped into his open arms and laid her face against his chest. Little hands circled her waist as they started talking all at once. Sean Patrick and Daniel broke away first and ran into the house only to return begging their father and little sister to come look at the new house.

"Wow!" was all Robert managed to say. "Guess this is why you haven't been answering your phone." He noticed the cut over her eye, the scratched arms and bruises along her arms and face. "What happened?" he said turning her face gently with his hand.

"I started working with this secret government agency who hunt down terrorists. We got in a bit of a mess. There was a fire, I nearly drowned watched a bunch of Libyans try and steal isotopes and blow up Global Navigation outside of Auburn. That's pretty much it."

"No. Really, Tessa, what happened?" He sounded concerned.

Tessa sighed. She had tried to be honest. "I fell off the ladder when I was painting and cracked my head as well as dislocated my shoulder."

"You're such a clumsy goof, Tessa. Can't leave you alone at all," he smiled kissing her on the lips. "I'm glad to be home."

"Hey, Mom, you should meet our friend Honey!" Daniel blurted out much to Robert's embarrassment.

Sean Patrick elbowed his mother gently. "She was a real hotty."

The two Enigma men sat in their car listening to the family chatter about the new house, their trip and the mysterious Honey. They momentarily stiffened when Tessa began summing up her week with Enigma. They realized she merely wanted to tell the truth, because telling the truth would be impossible to believe.

Zoric frowned. "Did he call her a goof?"

"Give me your gun."

"Why?"

"I'm going to shoot him," Chase said drily.

Claudia turned out the lights in Mr. Crawley's house before joining the Enigma men in the van. Careful not to wrinkle her black skirt, Claudia slipped into the back seat. "What do you think, Captain Hunter?"

Zoric laughed as Chase grinned. "She's perfect."

"I'll start the paper work then."

"Use the name Melanie Glenn."

*  *  *

"Mommy! Mommy!" Heather came running to her mother in the kitchen as she made lemonade for her thirsty bunch after only a few minutes of reconnecting.

"What is it, sweetheart?" Tessa laughed happily as she bent down and lifted her youngest up into her arms.

Heather pointed next door as if her mother could see through walls. "I just saw an angel!"

"You did?" Tessa remembered not taking her daughter seriously a few days ago when she'd seen a falling star. "Where did you see this angel?"

She jabbed a finger toward next door. "Mr. Crawley's! His yard light was on and this big guy was a standin' there big, big. He had big wings."

Heather motioned with her arms to show size of the wings. Tessa smiled knowing the lights under Mr. Crawley's bushes had cast shadowy like wings on one of her friends. "You believe me?"

"I sure do!"

"Can I make a wish on an angel?" Her eyes were wide with anticipation.

Tessa kissed her daughter and carried her to the living room window where she watched a car slowly pull out of Mr. Crawley's drive. "I hope so."

# Chapter 32

## *Epilogue*

The August sun remained hot during the evening stroll through the fairgrounds in Grass Valley. Carnival rides sent squeals of joy over the heads of families enjoying the corn dogs, funnel cakes and fried pickles. Snow cone drips on tee shirts created the style of small children hanging on to the hands of parents and grandparents. The concert started at the far end as a country music star began to belt out his only hit from five years earlier. Ladies wearing their blue ribbons from prized pies or home grown tomatoes chatted loudly with neighbors and friends they usually only saw at this time of year.

Tessa laughed when her husband won a teddy bear for Heather at the ring toss. The boys cheered their dad on then suckered him into riding the Ferris wheel with them one more time. As Heather swung her mom's hand back and forth happily, Tessa noticed a woman staring at her. When Tessa turned her face away and began walking a little faster, the woman quickly rushed to her side, carrying something in her arms.

"Melanie? Is that you?" The excited woman turned the bundle around for Tessa to see the baby girl. "I thought that was you!" Her accent was definitely southern; unusual in this part of the country.

Tessa smiled warily. "Excuse me. I'm not Melanie. But that is sure a sweet baby. How old is she?"

The woman blushed and pulled the baby back to her shoulder. "Two months. I'm sorry. You look just like the woman who helped deliver her in Tennessee. I named my baby after her because she saved my life."

"How wonderful."

"I'm sorry I bothered you. You look so much like her."

"No bother." Tessa watched as the young woman moved away and joined other people at the food stands. Her heart pounded. Perspiration beaded up on her forehead. All the danger and excitement she'd experienced with Enigma washed over her. Had it been two months?

Robert and the boys joined her and Heather with hotdogs and sodas.

Robert eyed her. "Are you alright? You look like you've seen a ghost."

"I did."

Made in the USA
San Bernardino, CA
18 March 2014